It Must Be
True Then

ALSO BY LUCI ADAMS

Not That Kind of Ever After

It Must Be True Then

A NOVEL

Luci Adams

ST. MARTIN'S GRIFFIN
NEW YORK

First published in the United States by St. Martin's Griffin, an imprint of St. Martin's Publishing Group

IT MUST BE TRUE THEN. Copyright © 2024 by Luci Adams. All rights reserved. Printed in the United States of America. For information, address St. Martin's Publishing Group, 120 Broadway, New York, NY 10271.

www.stmartins.com

Designed by Jen Edwards

Library of Congress Cataloging-in-Publication Data

Names: Adams, Luci, author.
Title: It must be true then : a novel / Luci Adams.
Description: First U.S. edition. | New York : St. Martin's Griffin, 2024.
Identifiers: LCCN 2023045835 | ISBN 9781250842220 (trade paperback) | ISBN 9781250842237 (ebook)
Subjects: LCGFT: Novels.
Classification: LCC PR6101.D3633 I8 2024 | DDC 823/.92—dc23/eng/20231004
LC record available at https://lccn.loc.gov/2023045835

Our books may be purchased in bulk for promotional, educational, or business use. Please contact your local bookseller or the Macmillan Corporate and Premium Sales Department at 1-800-221-7945, extension 5442, or by email at MacmillanSpecialMarkets@macmillan.com.

Originally published in the United Kingdom by Little, Brown Book Group

First U.S. Edition: 2024

10 9 8 7 6 5 4 3 2 1

To all the working mums out there.

Statistically speaking, at least one of us must have the perfect balance.

If that mum could get in touch and teach me, that would be very appreciated.

It Must Be True Then

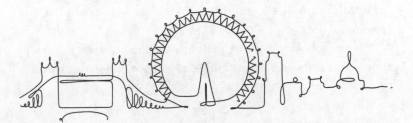

One Year Ago

"You see, it all CAME down to the data in the end," I squeal, nervously. "I realized early ooOOOOOOOOn that there was a statistically significant correlation between the sales of their skin caaAAAaaare products and folic acid—a vitamin typically taken by women in their first . . . first. . . . FIRST trimester of pregnancy and then I GoooOOOOOOOOOOoogled it and it looks like many women experience skin changes when they get pregnant because of . . . of all the hormones and so they tend to also buy . . . OH MY." I take a deep breath. With my new, fully stocked lung capacity I start again, "Buy extra skin care products at the same time and the Partn-AhhhHHHH! The Part*ner* didn't realize that his facewash was so closely linked to the fertility inDDUUUSSStry but after I shared my findings, they were able to leverage this link into their maaAAArketing campaigns and the profits of their Hydration Face Lotion have nearly douUUUUUBLED overnight!"

Without much warning, Jackson looks up from between my legs.

I stop talking instantly, unsure.

His blond hair is styled short. The most mesmerizing ocean eyes you've ever seen. Clean-shaven. Shirt rolled up uncovering the leanest set of abs you could witness. He's literally fresh out of an aftershave ad while I'm—at a push—a nerdier version of the girl next door. Blonde. Squirrel-esque. I'm not sure if my intense frequency of freckles would ever be described as "sexy." More "cute." Hopefully.

But this man isn't "cute." Oh no. He's the sexiest man I've ever seen in real life.

And he's looking right at me with the kind of stare that stops time. His hands grip the outsides of my bare thighs so hard his fingers dig into the skin.

Oh, Jackson.

"Daisy," he says, his voice like warm drizzled honey. Oh my gosh, my name from his lips. I'm not sure if I'll ever get used to it. His voice has the silky-smooth texture of the famous M&S ads: *This is not just **any** man between my legs, this is the sexy-as-hell, highly ambitious, incredibly sultry, six-foot-one demigod that is the Director of Marketing, Jackson Oakley, between my legs.*

He takes a deep breath, and I can't help but take one with him.

"It's alright," he says, and his eyes alone shut down my thought process entirely. "We're not at work."

I bite my lip, trying to stop myself from letting anything else stupid fall out of my mouth. I'm talking too much. Of course, I am—I'm nervous and I always talk too much when I'm nervous. I'm not used to this kind of thing. I've never had the free time to date so I'm not sure what the protocol is. Work has always gotten in the way. But he's looking up at me with those swirling, hypnotizing blues and he's just so cool. And relaxed.

That's what I need to be in his presence. I need to inhabit that vibe. How do I do that?

Well, I don't know how. But I do know how to be quiet at least. So, down I bite. Hard.

"Now," he says to a much quieter room. I can hear my own heartbeat now, hammering away. "We can talk about your meeting, if that's what you want," his hands slide down my smooth legs right to my bare toes, "However," they creep back up them again, higher, and higher. I can feel my whole body react as the electric tips of his fingers tickle right up the insides of my thighs, "I'm thinking there are more pressing matters."

I gasp as his fingers make contact.

I open my mouth to say something—anything—I'm not even sure yet but like a terrible instinct I feel my vocal cords get ready. Except before I can let any words out, Jackson's spare hand touches my lips shut.

Sitting up on his knees now, so his face is in line with mine, he moves his hand around my jaw and gently moves my face forward towards him. He could just about take me anywhere like this. I feel his breath against my lips as he whispers: "Relax, Daisy. Because the only words I want coming out of these lips," his fingers run across them as he whispers, "is *my* name."

He lets go of my chin and I fall back, looking up to his ceiling lights as I feel his hands creep back over my thighs. I close my eyes. Overthinking. As per usual.

Because this is amazing. This is unreal.

But why did I talk about data?

Why did I talk about the campaign?

Why did I—Oh MY.

I seal my lips shut. I do. But before I can help myself I feel them pull open one more time:

"JACKSON!" I cry.

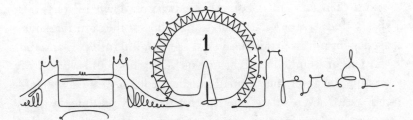

A Year Later

Bailey, the one on the left, the one with "don't fuck with me" eyes and warm coffee-colored hair cut short and sharp to match, looks up from her tablet. Her eyes are piercing. Emerald green. My nerves hit my stomach like a punch in the gut.

I give her a smile, then immediately regret it when I see her raise her right eyebrow. With that one look, I'm not only worried they won't take me seriously, but I'm also panicking that there may still be a little bit of my pre-interview Pret almond croissant stuck between my teeth. I knew I shouldn't have ordered it, but it was so tempting, and I thought a bit of comfort breakfast might bring me luck. Turns out it's only churning in my tummy while I breathe in a way that hopefully hides the unwelcome swirling noises issuing from my gut.

Oh, why didn't I check my teeth for bits on my phone outside? Rookie error. I pull my face into a position that hides my gums, just to be on the safe side.

"You're probably wondering why my CV looks a bit empty," I hear myself say.

Sorry, what? Did I seriously just say that?

Bailey's eyes shoot up to me.

Well, she's definitely wondering about it now.

I take a deep breath. *Come on, Daisy,* I tell myself. *Just breathe.*

"Well, what it really shows is that I'm a very dedicated individual," I say confidently. There we are, I just need to not panic and I'll be fine. "I'm a . . ." oh god, present tense. Slow down, regroup, then speak. "I *was* a senior data analyst, working for the same marketing agency for just over thirteen years. I got an internship as an office assistant at Branded straight out of high school and worked my way up. They were just a small independent PR firm back then—there wasn't even a data department—but they got bought up by Everest—do you know Everest?"

Something about Bailey's unmoving expression makes me think no, she does not know Everest.

"Well, they were one of the largest agencies in the UK—still are in fact—and since the merger, Branded has expanded its offering and is now seen as one of the advertising elites. I founded the Data Department myself actually. I realized that we could harness the insights of our social media posts in order to create better, more profitable campaigns. It was my old flatmate who gave me the inspiration to be honest, she's a math professor over in . . ." I'm looking at their faces. They don't care where my ex-flatmate teaches. Fair enough. "Well, a few online courses later, and what began as a side project became an integral part of the whole business. I specialize in social media insights, but I've been able to deep-dive into sales data too, showing cross-product correlations for clients that have helped them with their marketing."

Bailey seems completely unimpressed and, quite frankly, bored, but at least Cara is smiling at me. I wonder if it's in sympathy more than anything else. Perhaps she senses I'm a bit out of my depth here and is taking pity on me.

She's the smaller one of the two, her hair long and curly but not too dissimilar in color to Bailey's. If they're playing good cop/bad cop, then it's clear which one she is. But perhaps she's *too* good cop. Maybe her purpose is to disarm. I reshuffle my tooth-hiding smile in an effort to regain composure.

"Well, my tenure there should show just how dedicated I can

be. I'm not someone who just quits or walks out at the first sign of trouble. I'm a loyal employee, through the good times and the bad."

Bailey turns back to her tablet and a small silence settles in the room.

After the first minute, I pride myself in riding out the wave. After the second, I feel my nose twitch. I've had enough time to think about what I've just said and realize how it must have sounded. In the third minute I suddenly feel the urgent need to correct myself, but I must stay strong. I must not do something stupid and say something like:

"You're probably wondering why I left then, given I've just told you how loyal I am."

Except I do. I say exactly that. What is WRONG with me?

It captures Bailey's attention again alright. Oh jeez. This interview is not going well and all three of us know it. Plus, I now owe them an answer.

Suddenly my mind peels back. To two weeks ago.

To one of the worst moments in my life.

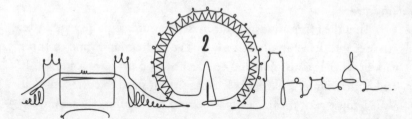

2

"It's bad bitch o'clock," I say, out loud.

Gosh, that's unlike me.

I don't usually say things like that. Only, I'm looking in a mirror, and I don't usually look like this either, so maybe this just *isn't* me anymore.

I switch my Spotify playlist to Lizzo's "About Damn Time" for the third time this morning while my eyes trail up my half-naked body. Black stockings stretch up my legs, topped with lace roses clinging on for dear life to my newly shaved thighs. "Low-rise geo crochet thong-cut" panties wrap around my hips, which is the longest name possible for what is really just a thread of material covering the bare minimum needed to still qualify in the "knickers" category. My top half is only partially concealed by the small slither of fabric included in the "Elodie Corset and underwire brassiere," and tying the whole outfit together (quite literally) is the *piece de la resistance*: the midnight black, FKME string bodysuit with detachable neck collar.

What it really is, is a logistical nightmare. The thing comes with no instruction manual and has more clips and holes than an IKEA shelving unit. But here it is, a geometric headache of strings that wrap around my body, centered by one long string that runs right up my chest and wraps tightly around my neck with the sole purpose of making me look *"Sexy AF."*

I look across to my discarded girl boxers and perfectly regular underwired bra on my duck egg blue bed. That's more me. Both of them are at least a decade old, but although their colors might have faded, they've still held the test of time. No holes means no reason to upgrade. Except, as I've discovered, the upgrade literally is holes. Lingerie these days is apparently the absence of lingerie. Who knew?

"It's bad girl o'clock," I say, and then—getting all flustered—switch off my music and correct myself: "Bad *bitch* o'clock."

Lizzo said it, and she knows. So, come on. Confidence, woman.

Except, when I look at myself in the mirror, I don't see a confident woman staring back at me. I just see me. Playing dress-up.

I think about taking it all off again, and I almost physically have to stop myself. Because maybe this is the new, improved Daisy Peterson.

The Daisy that's going to leave the genuinely "sexy AF" Jackson Oakley absolutely and completely speechless in the ninth-floor boardroom when she strips down and guides his hands to NSFW places with a panoramic view of Soho below.

The one whose left bottom cheek appears to be considerably bigger than her right.

Wait, really? That can't be a thing?

I check the mirror, sashaying left and right. It does, it definitely does.

Oh bollocks. I must have done a strap wrong.

I open the Instagram post I bought it off to cross-check.

When Bae's mum thinks you're the cutesy type, the caption reads, followed by multiple fire and devil emojis.

The post shows a beautiful, flawlessly smooth-skinned woman wearing what I am now. Her ass, of course, in this bodysuit, is out of this world. The dream bottom. The behind of all behinds. Probably photoshopped, but like, who actually knows? Some people might just look like that.

Luckily, the image shows me exactly where I've gone wrong.

With a delicate pop, I unclip the rogue suspender strap and switch it to its rightful side. Bottom evened out again, I take an awkwardly-shallow-based-on-corset-restrictions breath.

I quickly top it with one of the only non-pastel-colored outfits I own: a black pencil skirt I once bought to look uber-professional matched with a sheer white shirt, just clear enough to see the outline of the bodysuit below. Then I stuff a thick jumper and jeans in my backpack for after. Obviously.

I check the time: 6:01 a.m. I'm pushing it now, but I still stall by that mirror. Coat on, headphones in, ready. My long blonde hair, usually styled with zero effort, is pulled up in a tight ponytail for once, showing I mean business. My lips are stained with a new blood-red lipstick, the only shade appropriate for an inappropriate rendezvous. My freckles—well, they're my freckles. There's no hiding them. So, I pick up my keys and hit American Authors on Spotify before I open the door. Because that's the kind of optimism I need to channel right now.

This is going to be the best day of my life.

~

"Have you ever been to the ninth floor?" Jackson asks me, from his sleek monochrome bedroom. It's all sharp corners and up-lighting in here. He likes things clean cut.

I shake my head. Not that he notices. His blue eyes aren't on my face. They're lower, his words tickling my stomach as he imprints small kisses up toward my chest.

I hold my lips together purposefully.

Six months in and I know how Jackson likes it now. He gets straight to the point, always, and I'm exceptionally bad at doing that. Especially with him. You would have thought I'd have mellowed in his presence over time, but I can't help it. I see those eyes and I stare at that sharp, clean-shaved jawline and I turn into a teenager all over again.

Maybe, partly, it's because six months into seeing Jackson isn't really half a year in his company. Jackson Oakley is a busy man. He time blocks, and I don't just mean for work. He time blocks for gym. He times blocks for dinner. He time blocks for pub outings and after-work drinks and vacations. There's not a night we share together that isn't blocked in the diary by his equally efficient, promotion-worthy EA, because if it wasn't there, it wouldn't happen.

I see my initials pop up on his notifications sometimes:

Calendar Invite from Stephanie Chu
7:30 p.m. — Home-DP

DP.
Daisy Peterson that is, before anyone gets any other ideas. Little old me, at his flat, from 7:30 p.m. sharp.

It's sexy. Aspirational, even. I can only focus on one thing at a time, and 90 percent of that time that focus is on work, but Jackson has juggling down to an art form.

But it means that half a year of seeing him is actually distilled down to only twenty-two evenings, and even then, it's efficient: Drink. Small talk. Work talk. Music. Strip. Sex. Takeout. More sex.

Wild sex. Against-the-wall sex. Floor sex. Shower sex. Lying over his kitchen counter surrounded by takeout boxes sex. And I could never in my wildest dreams have imagined I'd have had so many screaming orgasms with a man so undoubtedly sexy as Jackson Oakley. I keep waiting for that moment when he turns around and realizes I'm not worth his time-blocked time. I get terrified that he's going to book over me and my freckles with someone a little less "cartoon bunny rabbit," and a little more "Megan Fox."

So, no, six months in, I'm not over it. I'm still the girl trying to impress, and I get all nervous and mumble and go on tangents and . . . well . . . I don't want to say anything to spoil the moment, not this time. So, I've learned instead to say nothing at all.

"It has a panoramic view of the city up there," he continues, his nose tracing the curves of my body. "You can see for miles in all directions.

The rooms are built for privacy. Early-morning meeting room, no one around to walk in on you. You can fuck to the sunrise." Slowly he runs his tongue up to the base of my throat, nibbling at my ear and I can feel my whole body melt.

"What about it?" he asks.

I open my eyes to see him face-to-face, towering over me. My god this man is beautiful. Completely beautiful. So beautiful, I don't even know how to answer. Because what he's just propositioned is outrageous, right?

Sex? In public?

Worse! Sex at work! What if someone caught us? I've spent years trying to be taken seriously in my career, just imagine what would happen if someone saw us . . .

"I mean," I stutter, unsure how to phrase this. "I'm not sure that . . ." I begin, but with a disappointed little laugh and a shake of the head, he rolls off me.

"I knew you wouldn't," he says, and I feel the atmosphere change instantly.

I physically feel the chill now his body's not over me. I look over to him beside me, but he's not looking at me anymore. Instead, he's reached out to the bedside table to his phone. He switches on his emails, scrolling through for anything new that just came through in the last half hour.

What have I done?

"I mean, maybe . . ." I say quickly, trying to remedy the situation.

"It's fine, I'm not asking you to," he says, and I can see him replying to an email from the corner of my eye. My time-blocked time has somehow merged with work time. "You're too much of a good girl. I knew that."

"I'm not a 'good girl,'" I try weakly.

"Oh, you are," he says, texting away.

"I can be a . . ." Quick—what's the opposite of a good girl? "A . . . bad girl if I want to be," I tell him, trying to sound more confident than I am. Realizing those words alone aren't enough to bring those eyes back my way, I do something a little more drastic.

A little too spontaneously, I grab hold of his phone from his hand

and throw it to the end of the bed, out of reach. Before he even clocks,
I quickly haul my body over him, pinning him down.

"Hey!" he cries, and I can't tell if he's being serious or not but I hold
strong, my legs wrapped around him. I hold down his hands to the bed.
I'm about half his body weight, with zero upper-arm strength, but he
doesn't put up much of a fight. Instead I can see his lips twist into a
smile.

"Whoops," I say, channeling this "bad girl" version of myself, but
I'm bad at it, so I accidentally add: "Sorry."

"Sorry?" he questions. With a wicked grin he breaks his hands free
of my hold and grips onto my waist. I let out a scream as he twists me
back under him, a dangerous gleam in his eyes. His torso is ridiculous.
It's like it's been hand-carved from pure marble.

Here we are then. Back to where we began, his body over mine. Eye
contact, his phone officially discarded. Looks like I've got his attention
again alright. My time block has remained intact.

"You're not sorry," he tells me, smiling wickedly. "But if you ever feel
like making it up to me, you know what to do."

❧

I open my eyes and the vision of Jackson disappears back to the
elevator doors in the Everest offices.

Well, right now I am sorry. Very sorry.

And thankfully, I know how to speak his language.

Quickly I turn to the mirror on the back wall, realizing this is
the best opportunity I have to check myself out.

With my coat slung over my arm, I tuck both of my boobs into
place below the shirt, happy that the smallest outline of the thick
black ribbons underneath can be seen right through. You know, I
have to give myself some credit here. I look good. Very amateur
porn video, but still, worthy of some site somewhere. I'm not just
any old "bad girl" right now. I'm Lizzo's "bad bitch." I mean, I'm
not. But it looks like I am and that's what matters.

Adrenaline is pumping through me so loud I can't even hear my
music anymore, so I take my headphones out of my ears and stuff

them into my handbag with my pass. I check my phone and can see the diary entry pop up on my notifications banner:

Calendar Invite from Stephanie Chu:
6:30 a.m.—Room 9.10—Daisy Peterson Catch-up

I sent him one text last Friday asking for time to explain, and within three minutes of hitting send, his precious time was blocked. How efficient is that?

I try not to be embarrassed at the thought of being fully named. I always did wonder if Stephanie knew who "DP" was, but it makes sense that a meeting in office hours needs to be more explicit.

Regardless, I think it must be a good sign. One that he's willing to listen. One where he'll hear my side and forgive me.

I pull out my phone from my bag. I can't help myself. I've never done anything like this before—I have to say something. So, I open my Instagram messages: our usual communication forum.

Me
I have a surprise for you x

I'm smiling as I hit send, already feeling naughty. Maybe this bad bitch life is for me, after all. I do feel empowered right now.

Before I know it, the doors open again. I turn away from the mirror to the long corridor before me. No turning back now.

I can hear a small murmur of a man's voice coming from Room 9.10, and I feel a twinge of excitement. He must be on the phone, which isn't unusual for Jackson. Should I knock, I think?

No.

That's not confident.

I want that moment where I push open the door, and his phone slides out of his hand he's so in shock. The "I'll call you back" moment from the movies.

So, that's what I do. With one little push the door flies open with gusto. In I step, one black boot before the other, dropping my coat and handbag to the floor beside me with a shot of confidence, the likes of which have never been seen in sensible "good girl" Daisy Peterson before.

And he is shocked. Clearly, visibly shocked.

Only to my absolute horror, it's not Jackson.

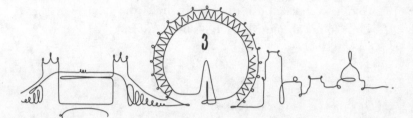

3

I feel a hard cold stone punch the back of my throat and block off my airways, I feel my stomach drop down to the bottom of my black ankle boots, I feel an unfortunate wave of water strike the back of my tear ducts. I fight them back. I can't cry. Not now. Even though it is becoming frighteningly obvious that I have misunderstood my calendar invite, I must not cry.

So, I smile. One of those forced smiles. One of those teethy, professional smiles that I'm sure everyone knows you're faking but you do it anyway because you don't trust your face to do anything else.

"Hi, Daisy," Matthew says, standing up a little awkwardly.

Matthew. Matthew, my line manager. Not Jackson, but Matthew, and he's not the only one.

His tree-trunk thighs accidentally send his wheelie chair flying back toward the window, but he catches it quite swiftly and sits back down. It must be an occupational hazard for a man of his stature. He earned his bulk off the rugby fields of amateur leagues, something you might have guessed by looking at his two-or-three-times-broken nose and his slightly crimped right ear. Years on now, he's seen only as the friendly giant of the office.

He doesn't look friendly right now.

"Thanks for coming in so early," he continues, pointing loosely to the chair at the end of the table.

"No problem," I murmur weakly. Or I think I murmur. I can't hear myself it's so soft. Courage, girl. Sound like you're capable. Sound like this is exactly what you were expecting when you walked through the door.

I place my phone slowly on the table in front of me and sit down in the chair. Instantly I get stabbed by one of the bones of the FKME bodysuit digging into my upper thigh.

Oh GOD, I think to myself, now in full-blown panic mode as the reality of my situation kicks in. I was so shocked not to see Jackson that I didn't even remember how completely inappropriate my outfit is! Oh god, oh god, oh god. Desperately trying not to look desperate, I move my hand up to my chest to subtly pull together the unbuttoned top of my shirt before anyone notices. Matthew, clearly noticing but delicately not looking, turns away to point at the brunette woman beside him.

"This is our head of HR, Gemma," he introduces.

If there is someone that you would probably prefer not to see you in a wildly inappropriate work outfit it's probably someone in HR, right? And the head of HR at that. I try to tuck my chair right in below the table, hoping that my skirt hasn't risen enough to see the lace straps.

"Hi, Daisy," Gemma says, in a hauntingly neutral voice. I swallow, feeling that pebble in my throat expand down my esophagus.

Both their laptops are shut, I notice.

Both of their eyes are on me.

"Look, Daisy, I'm going to get straight to the point," Matthew begins: "We know you've been with us now for coming up to eleven years—"

"Thirteen," I correct.

He looks a little stunned at the interruption. He looks at Gemma, as if cross-checking this fact. She shrugs, as if I'd probably know best. He nods, once at her, once at me, and speaks again: "Thirteen years now. And although we fully appreciate the hard work you've given to us over the years . . ."

Wait, where is this going? I look over at Gemma. Then at Matthew again. My line manager? The head of HR? A wave of fear passes through me. This can't be . . . no, they couldn't . . . can it?

I swallow, as a horrible piece of the puzzle fits into place.

The calendar invite was sent from Stephanie Chu.

Jackson's EA.

Only, Jackson's EA is Noelle now. Because Stephanie did get that promotion she deserved. To work for *the Head of HR*.

Why did I not even think this could be a possibility? Why did I not question this for one second?

I know what happened in that boardroom last Friday. I know why I had to make things up to Jackson. What, did I seriously think that fulfilling his sexual fantasy would just . . . make it all go away?

Why? *Why* did I think that?

Because you're a total idiot, my brain replies unhelpfully.

My phone pings on the table, and naturally my eyes spin down to see it. Before the screen turns dark again I see the Instagram DM notification. The preview shows the whole message, because the whole message isn't long:

Jax_O
I think we should take a break.

Jackson is . . . ending it?

I thought he was about to listen to my side. I thought we were about to reconnect. I thought he was about to spread my legs and take me with a "panoramic view of the city": his words.

I don't even have time to take in what those words mean before Matthew opens his mouth again. My world has already begun to shatter.

". . . I'm sorry to say that today will be your last day with us at Branded."

My heart pounds. My knees weaken. Those tears are making a Take That style comeback. This isn't Jackson's fantasy fulfilled. This isn't a filmic erotic love scene. I'm pretty sure I've just been dumped and fired in the same minute.

This is my worst nightmare.

As if to hammer in the point, he threads both his knuckles together and leans across the table. His kind eyes aren't kind right now. They're hard. They're cold. They're completely unforgiving.

My fake smile falls. My heart stops.

"What happened on Friday might have been out of character, but it was entirely unacceptable. We're terminating your contract, Daisy," he says, his words clear and uncompromising. "Effective immediately."

"So, what did you do after?" Betzy asks.

I wipe the tears from my cheeks.

I've reached the point that I almost can't feel them anymore. They just keep falling whether I want them to or not.

"I just came home," I tell her. "I texted Jackson of course. I asked if we could actually talk. I thought, I don't know. I thought maybe if I could patch it up with him then maybe he'd be able to have a word with Matthew or something. Only I can see he's read the messages, all of them, and still he's said nothing."

I've been torturing myself reading those unanswered messages all afternoon.

"And then I hated myself for even thinking that. Because I told myself that I'd keep a firm line between our relationship and work, and here I was thinking that sleeping with him might be enough to get me special favors. Here I was blurring the lines I set. I became *that* girl. I hate that, Betzy. I really, really hate that."

Betzy sighs. I can hear her breathe through the receiver.

"So, you just . . . went home?" she asks.

"I didn't know what else *to* do. I don't know what people do when they're unemployed. So, I came home, and I cried. And then

I threw my FKME bodysuit out the window and got cold, which made me angrier, because my window never shuts properly and it's March and yet it's absolutely freezing outside which meant it was then absolutely freezing inside too. And then I cried some more, and then I ran downstairs and picked up the bodysuit from the pavement because I don't like littering and then I came upstairs and cried some more. And then, eventually, I called you."

I can hear Betzy breathing on the other end of the phone. I can imagine her mouth opening and shutting, not sure what to even say. I don't blame her. I wouldn't if someone unearthed all of this on me and it's still 8 a.m. her time. I don't know if she's even had her morning coffee yet.

Plus, I have this nasty habit of not being able to stop once I open my mouth. It's what's led me to this point in the first place.

Knowing she'll need a few minutes to digest, but unable to bear the silence that has been haunting me in my flat since I got home over ten hours ago, I start up again.

"Look, I know being fired is not the end of the world," I tell her, sounding strangely reasonable. Probably because I've played out this sentence in my head multiple times all day, hoping one of those times it would feel true. "But the problem is, my whole world *was* my job." Painfully, this time doesn't change my mind either. "And Jackson wasn't just any man. And he was *the* man for me. They don't make men like him, Betz. He was ambitious and strong and . . . generous and . . ."

"He was great in bed. We get it."

"He was. But he was *so* much more than that. I couldn't have written a better man for me!"

"A man that dumps you by text? I teach math for a living and I think even *I* can write better than that."

"He's just busy. And efficient. He time blocks—it doesn't matter. He was everything I wanted and in one strike, in one meeting, I've fucked that up too."

I sit, alone on my little love seat; slowly eating dry Cheerios directly from the box (as they are quite literally the only food I have left in the house) and staring around me. My phone, balanced on my little Freecycle coffee table, tells me the time just turned 5 p.m.

"You know what I think," Betzy says, her tone perfectly pitched somewhere between sympathy and understanding, despite how much information I just pushed on her. I wait with bated breath for her to finish: "Fuck 'em."

I gasp, a bit surprised.

"What?"

"Fuck them all. If they're not willing to hear you out. If they don't know how incredibly lucky they were to have you in the first place and not give you a second chance after thirteen years, then fuck them."

"I couldn't ask for a second chance just because I'm sleeping with Jackson—" I repeat.

"I'm not saying they should give you a second chance because of who you're fucking. I'm saying they should give you a second chance because you're Daisy fucking Peterson and you've given that job everything you have and more."

I feel my eyes fill up all over again. How much liquid can one set of tear ducts create?

"I probably lost them a client, Betz," I whisper, hanging my head low in shame. I shudder at the memory. "A big one."

"And you've personally gained them how many clients over the years? Ten? More?"

I look up to the ceiling in thought. That's true. Of course, it's true. But it's also not the point.

"No," I tell her, "you should have seen it. I completely lost my—"

"Stop making excuses for them, Daisy. Sure, you fucked up. We all fuck up from time to time. Fuck them for not letting you have one fuckup in thirteen years."

The shock of it pierces through me, but I'm not even sure why. I know Betzy. I lived with her for six years before she married her Hinge Alaskan and moved halfway around the world over a year ago.

Anyone else would just sympathize, but maybe I don't actually need sympathy right now. I just need Betzy. This no-nonsense attitude is one of the reasons I love her.

"And fuck Jackson too," she continues. "Fine. He's got a big dick. Sounds great. He can absolutely do one."

"That's not—" I begin weakly.

"Just because you both love your careers does not make you soulmates, Daisy. You can love your career and still be a decent human being. You do, and you are. You can be efficient and still have difficult conversations face-to-face. Not one text over insta-fucking-messenger. I'm glad I never met him. He sounds like a tool."

"You don't understand. They were *his* clients. I doubt he ever wants to see me again after what I did."

"You didn't kill someone. Let's put some things into perspective here."

I wish I could have just an ounce of what she has. She wouldn't have just sat there, letting Matthew take away the thing that matters most in the world, without a fight. She would have stood her ground; she would have turned it all around.

"I just . . . I don't know what to do with myself," I say, and I can hear my voice warble. She must be able to hear it too, as she instantly softens.

"I can't remember one time where you took even a week's holiday. I know you don't want to hear this, but maybe this is a good time to just take a mini career break. You know, to find out what you really want."

She's right of course: I don't want to hear that.

"I don't need to find that out though. I *know* what I want," I argue back to my phone. "I *want* things to go back to before. I want my job and my boyfriend. It's just neither of them wants me."

"I hear you," Betzy's soft, soothing voice floats back. (Is that a faint whiff of an American accent beginning to creep through her Cumbrian roots?) "And this all sucks. It does. But maybe this is life . . . I don't know . . . telling you to take a beat or something."

That catches me off guard. I smile, as if on autopilot. I'm surprised that she's broken through to me so quickly. I've not been able to do so much as shake the tears all day, and here I am six minutes and thirty-nine seconds into a call with her and I can feel my lips twist up.

"Marrying a yoga instructor has really changed you, Betz," I laugh.

"Sorry?" she replies.

"'Life' is telling me something is it? Since when do you speak on behalf of Life?" I say, surprised to find myself laughing. "That's a Patrick-ism for sure!"

"I don't have any Patrick-isms!" she argues back.

"I don't know," I taunt. "The pre-Patrick Betzy would have told me if *I'd* said something like that, that it is statistically impossible for 'Life' to actually 'talk.'"

"Well . . . fine. So, it's not talking," she agrees, laughing along with me, "but it has a funny way of showing these things."

"This isn't *funny*," I remind her, but I can't help but giggle. "This is *sad*."

"That's not what I—"

"And to that point can 'Life' be a bit more specific than that please?" I ask, a full smile across my wet cheeks. "Like *how* would it like me to take a beat? What is this 'something' it's alluding to? Feel free to consult Patrick if you feel your 'connection' with 'Life' isn't strong enough yet."

I hear Betzy chuckle on the other end of the phone, and for just a small second, I can feel something warm inside me. That's the kind of magic that remains in two ex-flatmates despite a 4,278-mile distance between. Despite everything, I smile. I shake my head. Not that she sees. So, I speak: "I wish I had Patrick's outlook on life. I do. But I'm not a 'search for myself' kind of girl, Betzy. I like facts and figures and proof. And unless this Mrs. Life of yours has historic data to prove the benefits of a career break, I really just want my career."

I stand up, stretching out. That little glimmer of happiness in my otherwise crappy day has given me a little burst of energy. I need to move around. I've been sitting in this same seat now for the best part of four hours, waiting for Betzy to wake up and call on her drive to work.

Not that I want to go outside this flat, not with my face looking like this, so Cheerio box in one hand, phone in the other, I do small circles of my little kitchen-cum-living room-cum-dining room.

I live by myself these days. I figured when Betzy moved away, that it was time to fly solo and exchange our spacious two-bed flat-share in a new build in Clapham South for a cramped one bed at the very top of an old Victorian terraced house in Clapham North. It has a bedroom just big enough for a double bed, one miniature side table, and a wardrobe that doesn't fully open it's so squished in (and doesn't fully close either given the amount of clothes piled inside); it has a small skylight lit bathroom that prioritized a half-size bath over sufficient walking space to the sink; and it has this small living space that I pace around in now, back and forth between the small amount of furniture like a pinball ball—chair, love seat, table, chair, table, love seat.

It's small, but it's mine. Just mine.

And on most days, I love that.

Only right now, I really miss Betzy.

I miss lying in bed with her watching endless rom-coms. She was the only one in the whole world who could convince me to close my laptop screen for the night and watch Ryan Gosling take his top off instead. She had this game she used to play: we'd watch it right up until the meet cute and then hit pause. We'd take turns guessing the whole plot of the movie, and then we'd hit *play* and see who was closer.

"Have you ever noticed that there's an inverse correlation between the quality of the filming, and the accuracy of our predictions?" she once told me, using her "professor" voice, as I used to call it. And she was right: a shaky camera and terrible acting meant we were usually on point. Yes, the hotel would be a roaring success once the renovation was complete. Yes, the old man with a beard in the Christmas-themed coffee shop was really Santa. The more glossy and creative films went in directions neither of us had predicated. I'm not sure which ones we preferred though. Both, probably.

She'd also talk the whole way through; tell me how statistically improbable each "chance encounter" was but still swoon at the final kiss. I miss that about her. Like I miss her cooking me meals that aren't from the Sainsbury's ready meal collection. And I miss her telling me that I work too hard, even if I do. Now, when I work too hard, no one even notices.

"So, what do I do?" I ask her, so wishing she was here with me. "Tell me what to do."

She takes a minute, as if formulating the plan.

"First," she tells me, "you mope."

"Mope?"

"Yes. You mope. You mope for two days. Two weeks, tops. Never underestimate the power of a good mope."

"OK, I'll mope," I say. Then I look at the cereal box in my hand, which I have been hugging for the best part of an afternoon. This is what I'm already doing, no? It looks and feels about right.

"You mope," Betzy agrees. "And once you finish moping, you have a long hot bath, rinse off the bad energy—" She must hear my mouth open for she quickly adds, "That's not a Patrick-ism. That's a . . ." She stumbles over her words until concluding, "Fine. Whatever. It's a Patrick-ism but you should still do it. And then you meet up with some friends and get drunk."

"I'll stop you there," I tell her. "There's literally no one I can meet up with."

"That's rubbish!" she says.

"It isn't. I've literally had all day to think about who I can talk to about this. And my conclusion was you, you and you."

"You're sounding like you have no friends," Betzy argues. "Sure, you worked a lot of evenings, but you were always out and about with people too!"

"Yeah," I remind her, "with work people. At work events."

"That isn't . . ." she begins to correct me, but I can hear her struggling to remember a single person I ever hung out with that I didn't work with.

"Everyone I know, I know from work. Past colleagues. Present . . ." I blink, realizing my mistake, ". . . more . . . past colleagues."

I feel the lump in my throat as I say that, bringing me back to the reality of it all. For a second there, the warmth and nostalgia that came with Betzy's Northern twang made me forget how real this whole thing was.

"So, meet up with them!" Betzy tries, her voice so desperately trying to pull me back out of my new lull. I lean against the kitchen counter, needing a minute.

"I can't," I tell her, truthfully. "I can't face them right now. They'll have all heard what happened in that client meeting. Gossip spreads through that office like wildfire." The thought of them crowding around the coffee machine spreading rumors . . . it's too much to bear. "They'll have questions, and I'm not ready to talk to anyone about it yet," I tell her, adding, as if she needed the clarity: "You don't count. Obviously."

"Obviously," she agrees.

I feel myself nibbling away at my bottom lip, trying not to let this lull bring the tears back.

"Plus, they don't know about Jackson and me anyway, so I can't tell them about that part," I continue.

"Are you sure about that?" Betzy sounds skeptical. "People always know. . . ."

I'm about to confirm when I stop myself, as Stephanie Chu— Jackson's old EA—comes to mind.

I know no one else knows, but as for her, I couldn't say. She's the one who scheduled "DP" into Jackson's busy, busy diary. She seemed to forever be avoiding my eye contact in the office, but then again, she was a busy lady herself, and it wasn't like we knew each other. Now I know she only fully named me in HR's diary, I wonder if she *did* know. There must be a hundred DPs. . . .

I don't tell that to Betzy though, as in my thoughtful silence she's already fired back up.

"OK, fine. So, you don't meet up with anyone. You move straight to Stage 3."

"And what's Stage 3?" I ask, trying to push away the horrifying thought that Stephanie might have told someone, and ready to feel upbeat again.

"You research."

"Research? Research what?" I ask.

"*Things*. Things you want to do. Like new hobbies you always wanted to try. Travel maybe."

"Betzy, how many times can I say this: I *want* to work."

Only she's not listening to me. I know that because this is not a new revelation and yet she gasps.

"Oh my god," she says, her voice so completely stuffed with excitement. "Come to Alaska."

I involuntarily let out all the oxygen I have stored, as the thought washes over me.

"I'm not going to Alaska," I say, stunned.

"Why not? You can stay here. I'll show you the sights. You can stay literally forever. Plus, Alaska is one of those places where there is a higher man-to-woman ratio. So, fuck Jackson, find your *actual* soulmate out here!"

And there it is: she's done it again. The smile, that smile that vanished with the reality of my tragedy, has made its way back. Good old Betzy.

"Oh, I've watched enough rom-coms with you to know what happens if I go to Alaska," I laugh, genuinely. "A workaholic gets fired and dumped and runs to a remote part of the world to escape the pain? That's brimming with rom-com potential."

"I don't follow," Betzy says, clearly following.

"I can see it playing out now: There I am, breathing in the Alaskan sea air."

"There's no such thing as the Alaskan sea."

"Trying to get the pain of all that happened out of my system. I trip over accidentally on a jog—"

"There's the 'Arctic Ocean,' did you mean that?"

"By the seafront," I continue, "and get caught midair by a handsome but rugged Alaskan fisherman."

"Since when do you jog?"

"He'll have a beard. And a tattoo of a . . . a fish."

"A fisherman with a fish tattoo?" Betzy questions. "How original."

"We fall in love, probably. At the speed of light too—maybe over a weekend knowing most rom-com timelines."

"It's improbable, but possible. . . ."

"And he teaches me the value of getting out of the office and doing something with my hands. . . ."

"Well, screens aren't as romantic as pottery classes—"

"He'll teach me to fish. And we'll be on a boat. And it will rain. And then I have this huge revelation about how life can be better than churn metrics and regression graphs and we settle down enjoying the simple things in life and have glorious fisher-children and life is good."

There's a pause on the line.

"If that life sounds good," Betzy asks, "then why aren't you already boarding your flight?"

I sigh, thankfully still smiling. I knew I was right to call her.

"It's not my life, Betzy. We'd be married for a week tops before I realize I'd given up everything I actually love for a man with a tattoo of a fish. I *like* my career. I don't want to give it up. And I definitely don't want to give it up because some bearded Alaskan tells me to."

"So, rewrite your story! Maybe you don't learn how great fishing is. But maybe you use your skills in data to . . . I don't know, discover a new breed of fish for him or something and you make the whole town famous and save it from some evil land developer and your fisher-children can pick between your brains or his beard."

That makes me chuckle. More than chuckle. I fall back on my little green love seat, clutching my side.

"I don't even want kids," I laugh.

"You don't know that—" she begins, only half joking this time. We've had this conversation so many times before.

"No, I really don't," I correct her. "If there's one thing my mother taught me it's that women who have ambitions shouldn't have children."

"That's absolutely not—fine," Betzy says, choosing to pick her battles right now. "Then scrap the children. You have your career in data, because Alaska is not the middle of the desert. It still needs data analysts. You breathe the Alaskan sea air. Maybe there's a hot guy with a shark tattoo, maybe not. Either way it sounds good. And most importantly, you get to see me."

I wait for us both to catch our breaths.

"I can't fall in love in Alaska," I say finally, my voice edged in the boring, sad truth.

"Why not?" she argues.

"Because my sister is in the UK."

There's a pause then. Given how quickly we were both talking over one another, the change of pace hits hard. I try to shake it off, but it's impossible. Betzy's voice has, once again, softened, as she asks, so gently you'd think there was a child sleeping in the background:

"Are you even talking to Mia at the moment?"

"No," I shake my head, "not since . . . I can't go into this again. It'll make me cry. And I don't want to cry again. I've only just stopped."

It's a bit late, I've already begun welling up.

"Let it out, Daisy," she says, her voice so soothing it almost breaks me. "It's good to cry sometimes."

I take a deep breath, so filled with emotions I couldn't even tell you which one was strongest. I reach back at that box of Cheerios, feeling my hand scrape the base of the plastic. Finally, when I think I can handle words again, I stutter:

"I'm guessing you're quite close to your office by now."

She only lives a mile or two away from the university and she's been on the phone with me for twenty minutes.

"I've been parked in the car park for like, most of this conversation actually."

"Betz! You should have said!"

"I don't care. I'm here for you as long as you need me. Work can wait."

I take a deep breath. I can't tell you how much that means to me to hear. But I also can't stand the thought that she's late because of me.

"So, first I mope?" I ask her, knowing she can't stay on the phone with me forever.

"First, you mope," she replies.

That's it then.

Time to mope.

But actually, I think, a minute after we say our goodbyes. Before moping, it might be good to go to Sainsbury's, because having eaten the very last Cheerio in this house, I am officially out of food.

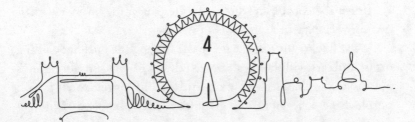

4

"I *have* to have it," I hear a whiny voice in the next aisle say.

It makes me shiver. Something about the whine in the voice is instantly familiar in all the wrong ways. I only went to the clothes aisle of Sainsbury's because I spotted a jumper I liked when I entered and I figured "moping" might include "browsing."

"You don't *have* to have it," the voice of reason replies.

"I do. I do *have* to," the whine continues.

"Why do you have to?"

"Because it says so here, see? Read. It's 'This season's 'Must Have.' So, I *must have* it."

"That's just advertising. It doesn't mean you actually have to have it."

"That's what you say about everything."

"That's because everything is advertising."

I smile at that. I like this mum. She's my kind of mum. I didn't mean to walk around the clothes aisles, but it's not like I'm in a rush to go anywhere, so I keep going, looking through their extensive pastel jumper collection.

"But it brings me *joy*. That Netflix woman Marie Kondo says if it brings me joy I must have it."

"I can guarantee this isn't what she means."

"But—"

"It won't even fit you."

"It will! It does, see?"

I turn the corner, and suddenly the pair come into view, their cart mirroring mine as they walk toward me.

What doesn't surprise me is the age of the little one. She's sitting inside the cart with her head bowed down in concentration. She's not inside the child seat—she's a little too old for that. She's got on purple flowered leggings with giant black UGG boots and a jumper that looks like it's the face of a giant panda. She has her curly hair shoveled on top of her head in a messy bun and held up by a giant yellow scrunchie. I guessed before I saw her that she'd be about seven, and I reckon I'm spot on. She's adorable too. The kind of angelic child pictured in advertisements. As she looks up for a moment I'm instantly caught by her big, mesmerizing green eyes. She looks like the kind of girl very few people say no to.

I try not to let memories instantly fill my mind.

Luckily, I'm too distracted to go too far down memory lane, as the older one does surprise me. I guessed mid-twenties. A young mum type perhaps. I don't even know what exactly I pictured, but in my mind, she definitely wasn't a preteen. She must have only just reached double figures.

So, not the mum? *Sisters,* I tell myself, replaying the conversation in my head all over again and seeing the whole thing in a new light. The older of the two is wearing a more conservative outfit of dark leggings, boots, and a white sweatshirt. She's only just big enough to actually push the cart, her arms stretched wide.

When they're only a meter or two away from me, the little one jumps up to her feet inside the cart, straight into a high fashion pose against the railings of the cart. She swings her arms high in the air, all confidence, before vogue-ing like a true Madonna. Suddenly I realize it's not a giant panda on her top. In fact, she's actually wearing the same plain sweatshirt as her sister. Only on top of it, she's wearing a dark, lacy bra.

The Amora Black 200 Bra to be precise. I know that because

they're level with me now and I can see the hanger in her hand. On a seven-year-old, it looks absurd.

"See, Bailey? It suits me," the little one says. "I must have it."

"You look ridiculous," Bailey replies. She stops pushing, waiting for her sister to sit back down but the little one won't stop using the cart like her own personal photo-shoot location. She swings from side to side, pose after pose. She sees me looking and she smiles. Oh, I see. She's playing for the crowd.

"Emmy Pea says to not let in other people's negativity," she says loudly, very aware that I'm listening. "She says to deflect it and embrace your own values no matter what others say."

"She obviously doesn't realize that your own values are ridiculous."

"DEFLECT!" the little girl screams. It's so shocking I almost let out a little gasp myself. As she does so, the little one karate chops down with a flat hand toward her sister. She misses of course, clearly on purpose. The action is for show, but its impact is lasting. Bailey, or so her sister called her, turns ghostly white, looking around her quickly to check for onlookers. I'm just about to pass them, and given I was watching the whole thing play out anyway, she spots me staring. She catches my eye, if only for a second, before turning back to her sister and leaning in through the bars of the cart.

"SHH!" she whispers loudly. "We're in public."

"You said I look ridiculous," the little girl moans.

"You *do* look ridiculous," Bailey confirms.

"DEFLECT!" the little girl cries out again. I hear someone in another aisle drop something. I'm not surprised, I only saw that one coming because I saw her leg go out in a pretend martial arts kick. Bailey has gone a worrying shade of beet. The younger one screams again. "I AM WORTHY!"

"Worthy of what?" Bailey spits in an embarrassed whisper, her cheeks burning. I'm the only one technically in this aisle with them, but already I can see a few other shoppers peeping their heads around the corner to see what this commotion is. "Sit down and shut up."

"EMMY PEA SAYS TO DROWN OUT THE SOUND OF NEGATIVITY BY SHOUTING OUT ABOUT YOUR SELF WORTH."

And she sure is shouting, alright. She has the vocal range of an opera singer reaching the song's climax. I could not feel more sorry for this Bailey girl. I'm also slightly worried her head might quite literally explode with embarrassment.

"She doesn't mean that literally!" Bailey stage whispers.

"I AM WORTHY," the young girl screams, her arms up in the air.

"Cara, we're in a shop."

"I'M IN A SHOP AND I'M WORTHY."

"That's not what she means!"

"THIS BRINGS ME JOY AND I AM—"

"You're worthy! I hear you! I get it! Now will you be quiet?"

"I've been told by my manager to tell you they're being disruptive. Can you keep them under control?"

I was so wrapped up in watching this drama unfold I barely notice that the Sainsbury's employee is talking to me.

He's a man in his early twenties probably, and by the unsympathetic stare, he doesn't look like the kind of man who has children. I turn back around to the two girls, now slightly behind me. The younger one, Cara from what I've just heard, has sat back down again and has immediately stopped shouting. She's probably realizing that she might be in trouble by the innocent look in her wide eyes, and her tune has changed instantly. She's suddenly looking up to her sister for protection. Almost as an afterthought, she starts trying to undo the bra she's wearing, but as taking off a bra's clips requires a dexterity gained from years of bra removal experience, it's taking her some time.

Bailey's biting down on her lips so hard it looks like they might bleed but she too has changed her stance. No longer is she embarrassed but trying to be strong. Her feet are hip width apart, looking anxious but fierce. She's in full-on defense mode.

Both of them are looking at me, and in a complete wave of confusion, I just stare back at them. To be fair, I am literally the only adult in the same aisle as them. So, I turn back to the employee with my own wide eyes, not too sure what to even say. I feel like I'm being told off at school, when it's not even my fault. I stutter, both the girls staring at me for answers I clearly don't have.

"Sure," I hear my mouth echo.

Sure? As if his request is actually in my remit?

But satisfied, the employee shrugs and walks away, leaving me with two young girls who look just as lost as I am.

"Do you guys have . . . an adult with you?" I try.

I'm already very, very annoyed at myself. This is my problem now, and—like most of my problems—it's something I caused. I can't leave now. Two young girls, apparently solo, in the middle of a London supermarket? No, if something happened, I'd feel terrible.

"Yes. We do," Bailey answers me, her short hair casting shadows across her face under the harsh fluorescent lights. That brings me more relief than I could possibly say. Good. So, I'm not responsible.

Or at least it does for a whole twenty seconds, before the young girl turns the cart around with her sister (now very silent) still inside it and begins walking away. Still, annoyingly, adult-less.

"No, wait," I call out. Bailey ignores me at first, walking into the fruit aisle with such purpose. It's the kind of stride saved only for mic drop moments. Except, I follow them quickly, keeping my voice as hushed as possible in case others are eavesdropping (as I definitely would have). "Where are they?"

From inside the cart, her younger sister twists her head around and back at me, looking through the bars like a nervous caged animal. She's still very much wearing the Amora Black 200. She must have struggled with those pesky hooks at the back. She also looks a bit scared, although I don't think it's because of me. Her sister has snapped into protective mode, and she's in "keep my head down" mode because of it. I absolutely know I can't just let them leave now. So, how do I do it? How do I convince Bailey to trust me?

And then it occurs to me: "Do you want me to get that employee back again? They might be able to help?"

It's true. If I tell the security of the store, then I can walk away from this situation, guilt-free. But that's actually not why I'm saying this. I'm saying this because I recognize this attitude. It's my attitude. From way back when. And I know what would have stopped me.

As I watch Bailey's cart grind to a halt in front of me, I know I'm right. She looks down at her sister (I can see her head curve down to the base of the cart from behind) and then she slowly turns around. She looks me up and down. Assessing me. I do what I can to keep a straight face.

I may not be Mother Nature incarnate or anything, but I'm probably better than a supermarket manager, and that's the internal logic this girl is going through. The manager might call the police. The police might mean trouble. Before she can say anything else, I take out my phone from my pocket and hold it out like an olive branch. Cara twists herself around inside the cart, facing me. She's smiling.

"I can't let you leave here if you don't have an adult," I tell them firmly, proud of myself for being such a perfectly responsible individual.

"We literally live a minute away," Bailey argues.

"At number 32 Dalton Aven—"

"You don't tell strangers where you live!" Bailey spits at her sister. Cara goes quiet instantly, ashamed, her cheeks flushed. I actually know Dalton Avenue. I cycle past it on my way to work. I always wondered who lived down that road, it's a strangely cobblestoned road in the middle of an otherwise paved part of the city. Still, that's irrelevant right now.

"I don't need to know where you live," I tell the older one. "But let me call someone for you." I open the green phone icon and the numbers come up ready. I show it to them. "Whose number might be best?" I ask.

"Dad's?" Cara pipes up, like it's a brilliant-upon-brilliant idea. I nod at her, smiling with the same smile she's shining at me. Only in an instant hers snaps back. Her older sister shoots her a "say nothing" look and suddenly her mouth seals tight shut like a zip-lock bag.

"What's your dad's number?" I ask.

Bailey breathes in deeply. She looks around her, as if searching for literally any other option.

"Bailey, come on," Cara whispers, "I don't want—"

"I got this," Bailey spits back at her sister. Cara tightens her lips again, her nose crinkling up at being told off. But it works at least. I can see Bailey's thought process clearly.

"His number?" I try again, already typing in "07."

"I don't know his number," Bailey says dismissively.

"Do you?" I ask the younger one. She shrugs. Right, so that's not useful.

"Well, is there another number? One you *do* know?" I try.

"What, like, just knowing the whole number? Who knows that?" Bailey asks, confused.

Ah. Yes.

Actually, a very good point. They are a slightly different generation here, and one that doesn't prioritize number memorization. That puts me in a bit of a tricky place though.

"Do you have Instagram?" Bailey asks, before I have time to work through my other options.

"Sorry?"

"In-sta-gram?" she spells out, as if the problem was her pronunciation. "It's a social media outlet where—"

"Yes, I have Instagram," I reply quickly. I'm only slightly amused that, as someone who worked pretty closely with social media datasets for the past decade, I'm being lectured by a ten-year-old in it.

"Then give me your phone. I'll DM."

"Who are you going to—"

"Don't worry about it," Bailey says to her sister, hushing her up. Oh crikey, this really is a different generation. But I hand it over anyway, standing by them so I can just about see that she is doing what she says she's doing. Is it weird that I'm letting young children have free range of my account? I'm suddenly very self-conscious about my posts in case they see them. I hardly ever post. Not really since . . . well, since I first started speaking to Jackson . . . but that's another story.

Bailey barely looks at my profile, she heads straight to the search function on the explore page (which I'm grateful to find is almost exclusively dog-based reels) and then types in some name I can't quite see from my angle.

I don't really know where to look, but Bailey makes it clear that it shouldn't be at her. So, my eyes cast down toward Cara instead.

She's looking up at me curiously, her big green eyes blinking hard. I notice the bra hanger she's still holding.

"Oh! You know why she's headless?" I ask.

Cara looks down at the picture in shock. In fairness I just made it seem like the model's been guillotined or something, when really the picture of the lovely smooth-skinned, flat-stomached woman wearing the bra for the marketing photo on the hanger just stops at her neck. I can see Cara relax when she follows my meaning.

"No, why?" she asks.

"They did various social media tests about the most effective kind of bra advertisement, and every time the headless woman won. Turns out, women don't care to see what the model's face looks like. No head means they can imagine themselves. You should have seen the click-through rate versus the control in the test we ran once! It had a p value of like . . . 0.000002 . . . or something." I laugh.

Cara blinks. I stop laughing. Yes, I reason with my own brain. I doubt she's conquered statistical significance or p factors yet in her math classes.

"It just means that people really preferred the headless models to the ones with faces," I conclude, and then, trying not to sound too work-obsessed, add: "But what do I know, I only use Instagram for dog videos."

"I like dog videos," she agrees, and then—after some consideration—says: "So people don't like eyes?"

"*People* like eyes. But bra buyers don't like eyes."

"Good to know," she says wisely, which is interesting, because I've just tuned in to the fact that I'm talking to a child and I'm not sure why she needs to know about the advertising insights of lingerie. But who knows. Maybe it is "good to know." "You have nice eyes," she tells me.

My cheeks turn a wild rose. She's not even saying it sweetly, she's saying it like it's a fact. I have these boring brown eyes. These forgettable chestnut irises. At least that's how I'd describe them.

"Thank you," I murmur back. And I just know this charm is working on me, completely. The same way it always worked for Mia, my sister. Interrupting both my nostalgia and this moment, Bailey thanklessly passes me back my phone. I can't help but notice the little ballpoint pen drawings all over the backs of her hands. Flowers swirling across one another beautifully. They're very good. Only I don't comment, because catching me looking she shuffles her jumper sleeves over them self-consciously.

"They'll only be a few minutes," she says quickly. "You don't have to wait."

"Oh, I do," I reply quickly, "I really do. And while I'm here, Cara, I might as well teach you the secrets of effective bra removal. . . ."

"BAILEY," a woman cries, "what the HELL were you thinking?"

A rather beautiful woman with braided dark hair and thick eyeliner power walks through Sainsbury's toward the girls and me. I heard her come in, and wondered whether the loud click of heels down every aisle might be her. Her shoes echoed off the cheese-filled fridges, right to my ears.

I'd just assumed I was waiting for a man, given they'd mentioned their dad, but clearly their mum was the Instagram recipient. Cara sighs audibly at her presence. She already looks like she's sulking, preparing for whatever is about to come. Bailey, on the other hand, looks rather proud of herself.

"It was actually my idea," Cara says bravely, clearly trying to own up to her mistakes, but her sister turns back to her quickly.

"Shhh," Bailey hushes. Then looks up at me, probably to see if I'll give her away.

I shrug. I'm not their mother. I don't need to input into this argument.

"Are you actually being serious right now?" the woman hisses. She's furious. Of course she's furious. She's probably scared.

"They're both completely—" I begin, trying to placate the situation, but I get cut short instantly.

"Thank you for your help. I have it from here," she says, cutting me one of those smiles that says "thank you, now fuck off."

Right. I get it. Off I go then.

I whisper a goodbye to the girls, and Cara very sweetly whispers one back, but I can already see Bailey charging up, ready for whatever is coming her way.

I wander off, and a huge amount of me is relieved to no longer have the responsibility, but I'm still curious. So, I leave, yes, but only to the next aisle. Out of sight, but well within hearing range.

"What were you *thinking*?" the mum cries out.

"I asked you if we could go get ice cream. You said yes," Bailey tells her pointedly.

"I thought you meant from the *freezer*."

"There is no ice cream in the freezer."

"Well, I didn't know that!"

"That's not our fault."

"You left the house without my permission!"

"We left the house *with* your permission, actually."

"That's not what I . . . You can't go wandering around by yourself in the middle of London! Oh god, you can't tell your dad about this."

"I won't if you stop going on," Bailey replies.

This argument is going to last some time. I start to get a little chilly in the fridge aisles, so I keep wandering, and after one more aisle, those voices slip away into the white noise of the shop around me.

Shame.

Somehow the madness of the last fifteen minutes had made me forget I was feeling horribly sad. Funny, that.

I don't see them again until I finish up and go to pay. They're standing by the noticeboards at the end of the checkout desks. Bailey's looking forward, defiant. Their mother is distracted, desperately scribbling something on the back of a receipt. Cara's the only one who catches my eyes.

She turns to me and smiles, waving, completely out of the argument so it seems. I wave back at her, watching as her mum pins up her finished scribbling onto the board. I turn away when the cashier tells me the total, and once my contactless pings through I look up again but all three of them are gone.

That should be the end of it, but given what I witnessed, I walk over to where the trio just stood, curious.

The noticeboard at Sainsbury's is mostly filled with local leaflets. Four cleaning services offering similar prices in the local area; a retirement community is selling knitwear for a charity sale pretty soon; a variety of pizza restaurants have snuck their pamphlets into the mix; and this:

PART-TIME NANNY WANTED FOR 2 YOUNG GIRLS, AGED 7 AND 11. HOURS VARIABLE. RATES TO BE DISCUSSED.

A phone number follows.

I laugh, knowingly.

Jesus, whoever ends up taking that job has *got* to be desperate. I put the taupe bag back on my shoulder, and go home for a night of oven cooking my premade vegetable lasagna and . . . I don't know. I haven't had a whole evening with no work to do in years. What do other people do after work when there is no extra work to be done?

Mope. I'm still in mope mode.

It's going to be a long night.

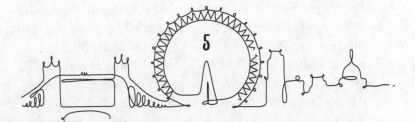

5

"Hi, Chris, how are you?"

"Sorry, who is this?" a man's voice replies. Didn't my phone ID pop up?

"It's Daisy." The phone stays quiet. In fairness even I know a lot of Daisys. "Daisy Peterson? From Branded?"

I stop myself from literally cursing on the phone. I can't say that. Not anymore.

"Daisy!" Chris replies, after a beat of recollection. He sounds surprised, but hopefully not bad surprised. He's a bit muffled on the phone already, noises cut through in the background. It sounds like singing and laughter, or maybe that's screaming and crying? They're weirdly similar from this far away. That's not good. I need him present for this. Engaged.

"How are you?" I ask, trying to keep my voice upbeat.

"I'm actually just finished for the week. I'm at home at the moment with the twins," he says, reasonably. "Is it urgent?"

It is urgent. Very urgent. More screaming (or laughing, hopefully) comes through the receiver. I clearly need to get straight to the point.

"Well, I was just ringing to talk to you about that vacancy you told me about?"

"Vacancy?" He seems genuinely confused. Maybe it's all the distractions he has on his end. I don't have babies, but I can imagine they make it a tad harder to remember things.

"The one you mentioned to me at the PRBS awards?" I remind him, referring of course to the PR and Branded Social awards. My eyes flip over to the small bookcase I own—a pale blue ladder, propped up against the wall of my kitchen—where two awards sit in pride of place. They're both a few years old now, but my team's "Marketing Innovation Award" and the coveted "Rising Star" award watch down on me every day. "You said I should really consider it?"

"Al, don't run with scissors!"

That doesn't sound relevant. I wait for a minute, because even I know a small child probably shouldn't run with scissors. A small scuffle ensues but I'm not sure how long it takes to wrestle with a toddler so I wait politely on the line until I literally can't take it anymore. I need to rescue this pitch before an infant dismantles my chance: "Well, I've considered it and I'd love to dive right in. I can see that you've just started working with the beauty brand Gloria and I had this great idea to—"

"Daisy, that was last summer." I can imagine him rubbing the back of his neck as he tells me this, waving back that thick mop of brown curls. Except more than likely he's just trying to put the scissors back out of reach of his offspring. "You know I'm not sure we have any live roles going at the moment, but I can always let you know if I hear anything?"

"I'm happy to work freelance for a bit actually," I say quickly, trying my best not to sound desperate. Determined, sure. Not desperate. "Help brainstorm some ideas with your campaign managers, that kind of thing."

"Wait, have you left Branded?"

I pick up the Post-it in front of me. I wrote this down, just to make sure it sounded correct. It's all about reframing. A clever turn of phrase can switch a negative to a positive.

"I just think it's time for my expertise to find a new home, and I couldn't think of anywhere better than—"

"Max! Please don't paint on—" I hear his long deep breath. "You know this is a bad time, can I call you back some other time?" The interruption is so quick, that I don't even realize the last part of the sentence is aimed at me.

"Oh right, well, I was hoping to get stuck in and—"

"If I hear anything I'll get in touch for sure. You can always drop off your CV with HR for now—just in case."

I don't want to be one CV of many, that's why I rang Chris. I know what it means to send a CV over; it means getting filtered into an inbox that's literally never read.

"I was hoping to—"

"It's been lovely chatting, Daisy—let's catch up again soon," he says abruptly, and just as a new wave of background noise rises through the receiver, it's gone completely. So is Chris.

I take a beat, looking at my phone as I bite my lip. I reach out to the Branded branded notepad in front of me and pick up my Branded branded ballpoint pen. With a little sigh, I sweep a thin blue line across Chris's name, wiping him out of the running. I look through my list—names of contacts I've built up over the years, each one now with either a strike through or a question mark.

I've actually had a very productive week. Given I decided one night of cereal munching was enough "moping" for me, I spent one day working on my CV. One compiling my list. And then the rest of the week making calls.

But now, a full working week after being fired, I'm still no closer to an employment contract. Sixteen "send CV to HR"s; eight "I'll let you know if I hear anything"s; four "I can't speak right now"s; and twelve voicemails.

I check my phone screen: it's 5 p.m. on a Friday. No one is going to reply to me at 5 p.m. on a Friday. Neither will they on Saturday. Or on Sunday.

"What now?" I whisper to myself.

*   *   *

I switch on a rom-com, but a few seconds later as I pull out my phone, I know I'm not invested. When the main girl bumps into the handsome man in the coffee shop, I hit pause.

"This guy's going to get all mad that she spilled her coffee on him and . . ." I have a little think about everything I know so far: "He's going to turn out to be the landowner that's selling the restaurant where her parents first met to some corporate bad guys. He won't have a choice. Mortgage repayments probably. Something not his fault, so he doesn't come across like a bad guy. She's going to use her culinary skills to make the restaurant Michelin-star worthy. The Landowner gets paid and doesn't sell to the evil corporation and her parents get to relive their nostalgia. Really it means she does all the legwork and he's still going to get a happy ending and all his debts paid off, while she's lowered herself from working a bustling restaurant in central Manhattan to some shitty, small hometown, just to be with some guy. But we're all going to forget that bit because they'll spend the last scene making out in their kitchen with their kids running around and we'll be lulled into thinking this is what she wanted too."

I turn to the empty space beside me on the love seat, wishing Betzy was there. But she's not. So, I hit play and watch what turns out to be an almost accurately guessed movie plot play out while I turn to my phone.

The first four posts are all dogs I follow. One of them rolls over for a slice of puppy carrot cake. Clever boy. Rich and Lucy post some annoying baby photos. Lucky their baby's cute at least. The next is an Instagram ad for . . . I almost laugh out loud: bras. A headless woman in white lace.

I shake off the feeling as I scroll back to the top of the page and hit on Stories instead. A poll from @Grumbles_the_Cockapoo asking "should I boop this snoot? Yes or No." @KingArtyCavalier is running up a coastline. @JackTheJackRussel looks cute dressed in a little bow tie. And automatically, without me even touching the screen, it moves to Marlowe. Marlowe the Brand Exec at Branded who I worked with for four years.

I hold the screen so it freezes in place, looking at the six of them pictured. It's a selfie just outside of Castle—the pub just across the road from the office. He's holding up his pint beside Pauline the account manager, Peter from his team in Brand, Flo and Hattie from creative, and Layla. She's a junior data analyst from data and insights. My team. My old team.

It's the Forest Co. account team. I know it is because I helped Layla pull the insights for them last week.

৵

"You can see the initial drop-off rate of their videos is huge," I tell her as Layla, disinterested, is checking her nail polish for chips. To bring her eyes back to me I point to the graph I created for her, mapped out against the industry benchmark. "Users aren't even making it through the first five seconds before they scroll on."

"What does that mean again?" she asks.

She's a "junior" analyst in the company, sure, but she's also been with Branded for two years. She should probably know the basics. Still, I don't mind as I've actually quite enjoyed this work. It's like going back to my roots. So, without even a hint of "you should probably do your own work rather than touching up your makeup while I do it for you" in my voice, I say:

"It means they need to optimize their opening frame. They need something more compelling, right at the start to draw people in. What's the point of having a kick-ass video if everyone's so put off by the opening that no one is even watching it?"

৵

I wonder if she told the team that I worked on those insights with her. I move the phone closer, looking at their happy smiling faces. In a different world, one where I didn't get fired, I'd have been with them. Probably.

I wonder if they're talking about me. Holding up their drinks under those London pub heaters and talking about how "no one can believe what happened" to Daisy Peterson. "Did she have a breakdown?" "Did you hear what she wore to get fired?" "Good riddance."

I turn off stories, not sure I can handle them. Somehow, *somehow,* I end up on Jackson's profile instead.

Why am I doing this? Why am I torturing myself?

Because it's there. And it's so accessible. And I have no other distractions.

So, I click on our messages.

> **Me**
> I know you'll have heard by now
> Please, meet me. Any time, any place
> I just need to explain x

That was sent minutes before that calendar invite appeared in my diary.

> **Me**
> Thank you x

That was sent seconds after.

> **Me**
> I have a surprise for you x
> **Jax_O**
> I think we should take a break
> **Me**
> **—Missed Call**
> Jackson please pick up
> I don't know what your diary is like this morning but please call me
> I have to speak to you—I can explain everything!

Have you spoken to Matthew?

—Missed Call

I just know if I talked to you, you'd see where I was coming from

Please don't break up with me

—Missed Call

Oh gosh, it all makes me cringe now.

I wrote them all in my panicked state, but now, looking back through them I wish I'd said nothing at all. That's the rule, isn't it? Always wait until after you calm down to hit send. Always. But I thought . . . what did I think?

I thought he might have picked up the phone at least.

Reading back through them, even I wouldn't have picked up the phone to those messages. I sound frantic. Desperate. And the sad little "seen" icon means there's no taking it back now that I've calmed down.

The thing is, I know why Jackson ended it. His clients were everything to him and he put me in that meeting because he trusted me. And in one of our first real tests as a couple, I failed.

Before I know it, I'm scrolling back through our messages, back to before I messed up. Back to before it all. When he first noticed me.

～

Some people just must move in slow motion, I swear, for that's exactly what Jackson Oakley is doing as he's moving through the crowd toward me. The others around him start to move slower too, as if the speed is infectious, a graceful ballet of moving bodies left and right with a balance of bubbles from beer and proseccos swish gracefully across his path. Center stage, Jackson strides straight through them all like a parting sea in his honor. His blond hair is whisked back by the tips of his fingers as his eyes blink wide to reveal those intoxicating aquamarine irises.

He's dressed in a crisp white shirt, sleeves rolled up perfectly, and his top button undone, bidding my eyes linger down. The shirt is tight

enough to see every curve of his muscles, rippling down his arms and back up his chest like a ladder to his jawbone. God, I hope I'm not staring. But I'm three drinks in already, and although my mouth hasn't let me down so far, I can't guarantee my eyes won't.

Dark jeans, black shoes, a balanced six or so foot walking right toward me and I'm captivated.

Wait. What?

He's walking right toward me? Yes, really. Me. I was turned his way, sure, but he's caught my eye and as if in some strange mirage of time and space he's making a beeline. Matthew and Selma's words are a blur in the background as the opening beats to Taylor Swift's "Love Story" start trickling into my mind.

He's heading my way, one size-ten brogue at a time. He's getting closer now, a perfect sly smile whispering on the edge of his lips. Those lips, curved out perfectly above a hard, clean-shaven jaw. A clean-shaven jaw that's walking right toward—

"Jackson!" Matthew calls from just behind me.

Matthew.

He was walking toward Matthew.

Obviously.

I knew they were friends. The two go for runs together on Friday afternoons, which I know because I always notice when Jackson's on our floor. He's a hard man not to notice. He strides with a purpose, his face always immaculate. He is the one smartly dressed person in a building of T-shirts and jeans.

There is also not even a small chance he knows I exist.

"I think Luke's getting served at the moment if you want to try to sneak in an order quick. Avoid the sauna in there," Matthew tells him. Thank goodness we've found a good spot outside, for inside looks like sweat-patch-paradise.

"That's alright, I can handle the heat," Jackson replies, and my word I believe him. He's the only one outside wearing anything with actual sleeves and he looks like he's fresh out of a freezer. "What are you on, Guinness?"

Matthew raises his near-empty glass in understanding.

"Is that wine?"

"Absolutely," Selma replies.

"And what would you like?" Jackson asks.

No one answers though.

That's rude. When Jackson Oakley asks you a question, you should definitely—

"Daisy?"

Oh blimey. It's to me. He's actually asking me.

Wait—Jackson Oakley knows my name?

What world am I in right now? Is this a dream sequence? Has the heat and the joy and the relief of the day actually caused me to collapse on the streets of London, causing this bizarre mirage where Jackson Oakley actually knows me?

At least I'm not silly enough to open my mouth and say something like:

"You know my name?"

Except, sadly, that's exactly what I do.

Why. Why did I do that?

"Of course I do," he replies. "I make it a habit to know the name of all the rising stars in this company."

"Oh, she's one to watch alright," Matthew agrees.

Matthew. Because he's here too, not just me.

"So, what about that drink?" he asks.

His eyes are soft as his head twists, the question lingering and his patience steady.

"Yes, that would be lovely. A gin and tonic please," I think, succinctly and clearly.

"Lovely gin," I hear myself say, my voice in the same trance that my brain comes out of the second I hear those words back at me.

Lovely gin? Did I just . . . Oh gosh. Please, pavement. Devour me.

Jackson smiles, melting every limb on my body. I don't want to even see what shade my cheeks have gone right now. I swear if there wasn't a wall behind me, I would have collapsed already.

"One lovely gin," he answers with a styled-out wink, and I know, looking into those swirling blues, that I never want them to look away. "Coming up."

When I get back home that night, I lie in bed with my phone, not even sure what I'm doing until Instagram is loading up. I just need some reels to watch before I go to sleep. That's all, I tell myself, knowing exactly what I am actually wanting to do.

@Jax_O

I found him three months ago, just after he joined the company and made his first appearance on my floor, and although I never dared hit follow, I've often found myself searching his name. There's nothing new, not tonight, but I scroll through the old ones anyway. Various selfies at marketing events through his career; multiple snaps of him running in various locations; beer-clutching football goers surrounding him in a group shot; a picture of him sunbathing topless from a trip to Mykonos.

Before I know it I've accidentally scrolled through two years' worth of posts, but it isn't hard, because he doesn't post all too much. Still, on every picture of his face, I imagine those lips now moving, telling me "You're a rising star." On that picture of him holding up his brother's adorable new Maine coon kitten, his mouth opens, and he whispers to me: "You're one to watch."

I'm so engrossed in this drunken mirage that I almost miss the little notification on my homepage. I open it, wondering if Mia has tagged me in an otter-based Reel to watch, when my heart skips.

@Jax_O is following you

I blink. And blink again.

As if not believing it, I go back to his profile. The "Follow" button has changed: "Follow back," it now reads. I gasp to my empty room. I think about sprinting in and waking up Betzy, but I know her fiancé

Patrick is with her. Plus, it's 2 a.m. Probably not the most social hour for a wake up.

So, I just sit there, staring at the screen in wonder.

He's following me. He's actually following me.

I think about hitting "Follow back" immediately but I pause. I don't want to seem too keen here. God, no. I need to play this cool. Like him.

Which is when I realize what this means, in reality. Because the thing is, if he thinks "I'm one to watch," it means I need to be worthy of watching.

I need to up my Insta-game.

Stat.

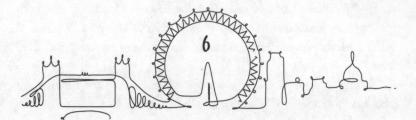

6

After a torturous, long weekend, I'm determined this week will be the one I get to turn it around.

After a week of the same four walls, I realize I also need a change of location. I love my flat. It's the reason I pay so much to be in it. But I've been rejected so many times inside it, that I'm beginning to hate it.

So, when 9 a.m. rolls around on Monday I move my home office to Sallie's Bakery: a little independent café not far away from me. It's quaint, filled with gingham and serves delightful home-made scones.

I go through the list of question marks on my original list one by one, powered perhaps by the sweetness of my jam compote. Scone, jam, cream, then call. The undisputed correct order of those things.

Sadly, even getting out of the flat doesn't stop my mind from wandering. After rejection number three, my Monday motivation seems to be slipping. It's not even 11 a.m. before I mindlessly look at my phone screen rather than my laptop, and somehow, I'm once again zooming in on photo after photo of Jackson.

Why do I do this to myself?

He hasn't even posted since I got fired, so all I'm doing is looking at the same old pictures again and again. I'm about to finally pull myself away when I find myself lingering on one instead.

It's a selfie, nothing special. Just a shot of him outside a fancy London restaurant. It's just I remember where I was that night, even though it was over a year ago.

Because for us, it was the night that changed everything.

~

Mia's wrapped in my favorite pale blue blanket on my green love seat, already opening the large container of Ben and Jerry's Cookie Dough I've just taken out my freezer.

She's beautiful, Mia. She definitely must have got it from our father's side, because there's not an ounce of my mum in her. Helen's freckles and wide deer-in-headlights eyes were exclusively passed down to me while Mia has skin as smooth and as flawless as if she'd bathed in a sea of foundation and emerged like Venus. Only she just wakes up like that. It's literally her face. Untouched.

We both have blonde hair, and yet when we're together mine looks mousy and plain while hers looks like sunshine incarnate. Her lips are large and rouged and her smile is out of this world. And I'm not being biased there. I mean, I am. But it really is.

I never met my dad, or rather I did—apparently—but the last time I saw him I was two and Mia wasn't even born yet so I'm not sure it counts. I've seen pictures though—and annoyingly it's possible to both be a no-show dad and a shitty runaway husband while still being a little bit beautiful.

"Your mother was so blinded by that smile," my Nan used to tell me, disapprovingly. "She was always chasing some pipe dream. And 'that man'" (as she so often referred to him), "was just another one of them."

I sit down beside Mia, handing over a spoon as our legs interlock; it's not actually big enough for two people, but we make it work. With her right leg behind me, and mine under hers, we sit like one giant pretzel as our spoons head for the ice cream in sync.

"Honestly, you're going to love him!" she squeals, and her happiness

is infectious despite the subject matter. I've had a long day, my head has been so close to my laptop screen I'm still blinking away bubbles of white light even now, but when Mia came over my mood lifted instantly. She just has that effect on people.

"I'm sure I will," *I say skeptically.*

She whacks my spoon with hers like a sword in mid-battle.

"Oi. Can you for once start off assuming that someone I'm seeing is nice and let them prove you wrong?"

"So, he's going to prove me wrong, is he?"

"No!" *she cries.* "That's not what I—don't do that Jedi mind trick thing."

"What Jedi mind trick?"

"That thing where you use your . . . your statistical brain to make me admit to things that aren't true!"

"Statistics has nothing to do with persuasion!"

"Ah! So, you admit! You're using persuasion on me?"

I hold my heart like a wounded animal.

"A taste of my own medicine!" *I cry comically, and although I'm not that funny, Mia laughs. It's the warmest, most homely laugh you'll ever hear.*

"Jedi!" *she confirms, victorious.*

Spoon free from Mia's restraint I spy a small chunk of cookie dough emerging from the white wonderland of vanilla ice cream. I go to grab it but using her superior position of "holder of the tub," she yanks it away from me at the last second.

"Madam!" *I cry at her. Quickly I lean in closer, trying to grab the tub back so I can steal my earned chunk of dough when she curves her back farther around the arm of my love seat, pulling it far out of my reach. I don't give up. I unscramble from the pretzel shape and start to climb her, ready to nab it back from her icy grip when I see her eyes glimmer with pure cheek.*

"Don't you dare!" *I gasp, already with the full knowledge of what she's about to do, spurred on by the amount of effort I'm putting in.*

Taking advantage of my pre-shock, she pushes me off her and brings the tub straight to her mouth. Keeping her tongue wide, she sloppily, disgustingly, with no charm in the least, licks the top of the ice cream tub. And not just one lick either. She slimes her tongue over every crevice on the top layer until, satisfied, she then turns the tub to me, collapsed into the other side of the love seat.

"You want some?" she asks, blinking her innocent eyes at me.

"You are so gross," I say dismissively, but I'm (somehow) laughing with her.

I take a deep breath, thinking through my options. Finally, I pretzel my legs back under hers and, like a peace offering, Mia holds the tub back between us. I sit with my spoon ready, waiting for her to peel back the top spit-contaminated layer before I dig back in.

"Whatever," she concludes, delighted with herself.

"OK, then tell me about him."

She smiles ear to ear.

"Well, Freddie's like . . ."

"His name's Freddie?"

"His name's Freddie . . . and he's super intelligent. He knows all this stuff about computers."

"Like he knows how to turn one off and on again? Sounds like a catch," I say sarcastically. I can't help myself.

"Daisy!" she whines, the same whine she's whined since our childhood. Some things never change. "I mean it."

"OK! Go on."

"He's like a proper computer whiz. And you know, he's the only person I've ever met who is completely off the grid."

"What on earth does that mean?"

"Like he has no online presence at all. Did you know that once you post a picture on Instagram, technically they own that picture? He told me that."

I blink a few times.

"Yes," I say, "I do. I work in social media."

"Oh," she says, only slightly dampened. "Well, whatever. I've got rid of my Instagram."

"No, you haven't."

"I have."

"Why?"

"I'm not giving them my data! I don't know what they'll do with it!"

"I know what they'll do with it," I laugh. *"I'm one of those people doing something with it!"*

"You are?" she cries.

"Sort of. I mean, I don't work for them. But I work with their data!"

"So, you're the bad guy?" Mia asks, and by the look of her face she is genuinely confused by this concept.

"It's not bad to use data to form insights," I say. *"I'm not trying to find out what you, Mia Peterson, ate for breakfast this morning and exploit it. But I might be able to find out what brand of cereal 'people in general' are actively telling people they're eating for breakfast this morning. And maybe with that insight and a little research into why that might be, we can help out someone who makes cereal for a living advertise their own stock a little better."*

She bites her bottom lip in thought.

"Oh," she says, thoughtfully.

"Everything I work with is anonymous, Mia. I'm not saying someone out there isn't misusing what's available, so you should always be careful about what you post, but I'm not. We have a code of conduct that we stick to religiously. There isn't an insight we share that isn't hugely anonymized. If you tag a brand in something you post, you should be fully aware that they see it. Mind," I add, shaking my head, *"you have a public profile. So, if I wanted to zoom in to you, Mia Peterson, to see what* you *had for breakfast, I could do that too. But that's your own idiocy for trying to get more followers and not putting up some security settings."*

"Correction: I don't have a public profile. Because I don't have Instagram," she spells out.

The top contaminated layer of ice cream has almost been eaten away, but before I turn back to the tub, I get my phone out of my pocket. I shake my head as the app loads. Then I search for her handle: *@MiaEmilyOfThePetersons.*

"Oh my god," I say, genuinely perplexed.

"See?" she says proudly.

"But why? You love posting on Instagram!"

"They can steal my data!"

I shake my head, tossing my phone between us as I finally get the tub of ice cream back. While I take it from my sister's hands, she reaches for my newly discarded phone. She clicks on Instagram.

"Looks to me like you're missing it," I say wisely.

"It's healthy to go off social media," she says, sounding sad.

"It is," I agree. "Completely." We wait for a minute while she scrolls my feed. "It's also healthy to not eat a whole tub of Ben and Jerry's but we both know this isn't ever seeing the inside of that freezer again," I say, even more wisely. "You pick your battles in this world."

When she opens her mouth, I think she's about to reprimand me. Only she says something else instead. Something shocking.

"Who's Jackson Oakley?"

"What?" I say, panicked. "Jackson? How do you . . . What is . . ." I'm stumbling over words here. "I don't—what do you mean?"

"Woooah," she laughs, looking up at me, realizing what nerve she must have touched. If I'd just played it cool, she'd never have noticed. "So, it's the guy you're seeing then?"

"I'm not seeing him," I say, my cheeks turning a deep crimson. "We just . . . work together."

"You like him though. And wow, he's cute."

I see her fingers scroll in to the screen.

"Don't like his photo!" I cry, worried that her fingers moving too fast might lead to the fatal double tap that would end up in his notifications.

"Calm your horses, I'm not an amateur."

"How do you know about Jackson?"

"He was just after me in your 'recent searches,'" Mia says proudly. She lowers the phone quickly, tapping her spoon out to me like a teacher telling off a naughty pupil. "You might understand the data bit. But I am the expert on the platform."

"You mean the one you're not on anymore? Because this Freddie of yours doesn't like the idea of people like me helping Kellogg's competitors to optimize their posts?"

"Why are you being all judgey before you've even met him?" she snaps back.

"I'm . . ." I begin, but it's no use. *"I am. I'm sorry,"* I admit. *"It's just, he's already convinced you to give up something you actually love. I don't think a man should change you."*

"I don't love Instagram."

"You don't?"

Mia changes the subject instead of answering me. Typical.

"So, this Jackson guy follows you, but you don't follow him? When did he even start following you?"

I wince a little.

"Back in September."

"Has he slid into your DMs?" Mia asks, already tapping my messages.

"Talk about a breach in privacy!" I cry, trying to get it back from her. She moves her hand away, keeping it in her clutches.

"So, what's the deal?" Mia laughs it off, scanning through my personal messages without thought to how I might feel about it. To be fair, there's nothing in there I'm worried about her seeing.

"The deal is . . ." I say, wondering if I'm going to break. For whatever reason, I do: *"He works at Everest. And we've only talked once and for, like, a minute. But then he started following me and . . . nothing since. I've barely seen him in the office."*

"Looks like he's out to dinner tonight," Mia says.

"He's posted?" I say, a little too excitedly. She smiles as she throws me the phone, and—carefully resting the ice cream on the arm of the love seat—I look at the picture. A selfie: him standing outside some fancy restaurant in Soho. He looks good. He always looks good.

"So, I take it you want to see . . . more of this Jackson." She smiles slyly.

"Oh, he'll never want to see someone like me," I reply, accidentally sounding like the new girl at school.

"Why not?"

"Because he's like . . . Jackson Oakley. Like, look at him!"

"He follows you," Mia argues.

"Well, maybe that's, I don't know. To be polite?"

"Don't be naïve," she tuts. "Over one thousand random men followed me before I got rid of my account. You think that's to be polite to me?" She has a point there. "So, what have you posted since?"

I lick my lips. I pick back up the ice cream tub.

"Nothing . . ." I answer back.

"Jesus."

"I don't know what to post! I feel . . . pressure. I can't just post anything anymore. Like he'll judge me for whatever I post."

"Well, no one slips into your DMs from nothing, that's for sure."

I feel the blanket move before I see her untangle herself from me, jumping off the love seat with a delicate little hop.

"What are you doing?" I ask.

"What are we doing," she corrects, holding out her hand for me to stand with her. "We are going to turn Jackson Oakley's head. One story at a time."

I'm not a "brand" person. I've always found content creation quite boring. Only, with Mia, most things aren't boring, and this is no exception.

Before I know it, she's opening up her overnight bag and quick-changing me through her outfits. When we've exhausted those, we deep-dive into the depths of my wardrobe, and she's taking photos from angles I'd never think to take.

"A bit of good lighting, add a strong filter—"

"Oi!" I cry.

"And here!"

Before I know it, she's not just got one story lined up for me, but several. Different outfits making me seem like I'm taking them over multiple days. She even writes up a schedule for me. And copy. She tells me which ones to go on my feed, and which on my stories. My last shot I take is the first one she tells me to post. A selfie, with a face full of makeup that she did for me.

"Soho, I'm coming for you" the caption reads.

"Now?" I question her. "But . . . we're not actually going out, are we?" I ask.

"God, no," she laughs. "But he doesn't know that."

"Won't he work it out when there aren't any pictures of me in the bar later?"

"No," she says, like it's obvious. "You're having too much fun to post from the bar! You can post this," she says, saving a picture of me lying in bed with a smile on my face to my camera roll for later, "in the morning."

"That's silly. Look, both my arms are in that picture. He's going to take one look at that and wonder who's taking the picture."

"Exactly! That's the point! Nothing like a little healthy competition." She smiles. "Now, catch his eye. Hit follow back, then post. In that order. Are you ready?"

I hold the button over the follow back button, unsure. Do I dare?

"And you think this will work?" I ask nervously.

"Seven days," she assures me. "Follow 'Mia's foolproof attention-grabbing' plan for seven days. And I guarantee that boy will be sliding into your DMs like a puppy on a Slip 'N Slide."

She left that night, back to her precious new Freddie, who "I just can't wait to meet," or at least that's what I say to her as genuinely as I can muster.

And I follow her schedule. Because, why not?

I follow it to the exact minute.

Only, I don't last all seven days. Because on the third day, I get a notification. One I can barely believe.

Jax_O
Looking good

There he is in my DMs.
Like a puppy on a Slip 'N Slide.

In a feat of Herculean strength spurred on by the little tinkle of the bell over the door, I put down my phone looking for a real-life distraction because this can't be healthy.

I can't just sit here thinking about Jackson all day. I need something, anything to take my mind off him.

Like the man who just walked in, for example. He looks distraction worthy.

7

He's handsome. Not like Jackson Oakley fresh-out-of-a-TV-commercial handsome. But like, pretty handsome. Normal-guy handsome. No, I'd give him more credit than that. Normal-guy-plus, handsome.

Six foot, probably. Curly dark hair, styled ever so slightly and yet not at all. He's gone for the double denim look with a black jean shirt rolled up at the sleeves. No coat either. I know it's not technically winter but no one seems to have told the cold that spring's begun so I admire his bravery. I on the other hand sit at a table furthest from the door wrapped in three layers of pastel jumpers and still have my puffer jacket on. He's also wearing an overstuffed tool belt and thick boots.

See—that's what I need to take me out of my Jackson stalk-a-thon. A real-life, straight-out, rom-com handyman to walk into my little café.

Betzy comes to mind, and I suppress a surprised little laugh.

So, what would the story be this time?

Not an Alaskan fish tattoo come to rescue me after all, but the rough-around-the-edges English handyman, come to pull me out of my funk and show me . . . what, that Jackson was *too* ambitious for me? That he was *too* driven? That all those things I found so unbelievably sexy in him were actually failings after all?

Maybe this double denim hero will pull me away from my laptop and show me the wonders of carpentry instead. Maybe he'll have a secret stash of furniture he's personally welded (do you weld furniture? I don't know.) and suddenly I'll realize I don't want the 9–5 anymore. He'll teach me the joy and wonder of working for oneself. The complete freedom of having no management above me, telling me what to do. I'll just need him and his handyman babies. Maybe we'll make love slowly to the sound of "Unchained Melody" on a chaise lounge he made with his own hands.

And that all sounds lovely. It sounds like an excellent rom-com. Only it doesn't sound like me.

For one, I quite like having management. Having guidance. I always have. I shouldn't be shamed into hating a bit of structure. And secondly, I don't want babies. Babies slow down careers, and I love my career more than anything. I've just found our third-act breakup before our story's even begun.

No, I cannot fall in love with this handyman, I think.

This is not my rom-com.

Only in my little scenario planning, I somehow forgot to avert my eyes, and having finished his little chat to the woman behind the counter he turns my way. Not to look at me, clearly. But past me, to the back wall where there's a pretty terrible painting of what I'm guessing is supposed to be a duck. It's all shades of brown and green and the creature looks possessed. It's a strange choice for such a quaint place.

So, he's trying, I think, to look at the scary duck. Only I'm in the way so our eyes lock. The man's got lovely eyes too. Striking. A shade of green, which makes me think maybe the shade is more common than I thought. They're a little bit hypnotizing actually.

Gosh, I weirdly wasn't expecting that to go any further than just play out in my head. In a scramble to look normal I knock my notepad sideways, causing my ballpoint pen to fly from the side but I don't have time to correct it before I see him start walking toward me.

The click of his boots against the clean white tiled floor echoes as he draws near, and suddenly I've forgotten the reason that this wasn't my love story. Something about . . . management maybe?

And, quite unexpectedly, like something in a dream sequence, he's on one knee before me.

Wait, what?

His hand reaches toward his pocket.

Is this . . . have I just been knocked out or something because . . . ah, no. He's not going for his pocket. He's going for the floor.

"You dropped your pen," he says, and in a shocking twist, I find he's not the *English* handyman at all.

He's Scottish! That accent is soft, but absolutely unmistakable. I don't know why, but somewhere between him getting down on one knee and him having the most beautiful accent in the world I suddenly feel like I'm having an out-of-body experience. I also am able to reevaluate my handsome plus rating from close up. Is handsome plus an option now? Because he's really quite wonderful.

"I dropped my pen," I repeat to myself in my head, with his soft, Scottish twang. I love how that sounds. How the "e" in pen so delicately sounds like an "I."

No. No, I don't just say it in my head. I actually *say it*. Out loud.

"I drowpped my pin," I repeat. In arguably the world's worst Scottish accent.

"Ah!" he gasps in recognition. "Am faod mi lionn a bhith agam?" he asks.

Is that . . . Gaelic?

"Oh," I say, embarrassed. Oh gosh. "No, I'm not actually Scottish. . . . I'm so sorry," I add. In my own, very British accent. "That's so rude of me."

"You could have fooled me," he says, and it takes me a second to realize he's being utterly and completely sarcastic. There's a thin smile across his lips that looks somehow permanent. So, I laugh with him, hoping to iron out the awkwardness.

"I just . . . wasn't expecting *you* to be Scottish," I add.

"You were expecting me then?" he asks, without missing a beat.

I stutter, not sure how to answer that one. I mean, I know I was playing out a rom-com scenario with him but I wasn't thinking . . . how have I dug this hole for myself?

"Relax," he laughs, with a cheeky grin, and I feel relief flood me instantly. "I'm messing with you. Even I don't speak Gaelic. That's the one phrase I know." Effortlessly, he stands back to full height, his thick knuckles uncurling and dropping the ballpoint pen beside my finished latte. "You're alright. Here's your 'pin.'"

Without so much as a second glance, he keeps moving to the back of the café. It isn't until he's measuring the back wall, already deep in work, that I realize I didn't even say thank you.

I panic at the thought.

"Thank you!" I cry out, in said panic, and he turns around. Those electric green eyes hit me.

He shrugs with a side smile, because screaming "thank you" across a small café an awkward amount of minutes after the thank-worthy incident is obviously quite a strange thing to do.

I turn back to my screen, trying to stare at it. Trying to look like I'm not just playing that over in my mind.

I don't know what's got into me. Maybe I need to stop looking for my rom-com opening scene, as apparently it turns me into a first-class idiot.

I should go back to pining after Jackson and trying to find new management.

That seems healthier, somehow.

Given the catastrophe of the "pin giving" incident, I feel a bit embarrassed to talk to him again, only a few minutes later when I head to the bathroom—I notice he's still by the back wall. He's taken off the duck painting and is wrapping it all up carefully in brown paper, balancing against one of the unused café tables. I don't say a thing as I enter the little bathroom, instead thinking about what I can say when I reemerge just a few seconds later that might salvage the monstrosity of our earlier encounter.

And what I settle on, for whatever reason is: "Using duck tape by any chance? You know . . . duct tape . . . duck . . . It's a . . . you get it."

And then I cringe. Because in the bathroom when I said it to myself, it sounded funny. And he was a funny kind of guy, so I thought maybe it would be on his level. But now I've heard it out loud and it's really, really not.

Still, this nice kind man has forced a smile on his lips in what I can only assume is a kind of sympathy. I appreciate the gesture. And I should walk back to my table and live with this shame, only I don't. I feel the need to make it up to him. To show him I *can* be normal. I'm just not at this moment.

"I'm glad you're taking it down. That duck was giving me the creeps. I'm guessing that's why they're getting rid of it."

"They sold it actually," he says, continuing his work as if my presence was neither here nor there.

"They did?" I laugh. "I can't believe it! The duck looked like a vampire! Who'd want Franken-duck in their living room?"

He smiles, but I've noticed him turn away a little more. And then it dawns on me.

"Wait—you didn't buy it?" I ask, a little warily. "Did you?"

He shakes his head.

"No, I didn't."

"Oh thank God!" I say, relieved. I put a hand on my chest as the breath releases from me. And then he adds:

"I painted it actually."

My face falls. I feel the blood drain from every artery and hide somewhere deep within, not wanting to watch. Leaving me alone in my own mess.

Why? I think desperately. Why did I say anything?

"Oh god, I'm so . . . I didn't mean . . . I mean—what do I know? I'm not a . . . painter or a critic or a . . . I just . . . I thought you were just a handyman!"

"*Just* a handyman?" he questions, looking slightly offended.

"No! Not just a . . . that's not what I . . . I'm so sorry. It was a really good . . . duck. I mean, I knew it was a duck! That's something!"

I need to just leave. There's literally nothing else I can do here to make this any better. And just as I'm about to collect all my things from my table and never step foot in this building again he cracks a smile. And then a laugh.

"Calm down." He laughs again, the lines around his eyes deepening as he chuckles. "I didn't paint it. But the artist is local," he says—nodding to the sign beside it. "Local Artist Spotlight: Duck in Abstract" it reads, "By Bethany Monnington." "So, who knows, they might be here listening in to you calling their baby 'Frankenduck.'"

Ah, yes, I very much doubt this handsome Scottish guy is called Bethany. Thank god.

I look around the café, a little nervously as he has a great point. I've never been so thankful to be surrounded by a room full of mostly men.

"For what it's worth I'm not an abstract duck kind of guy either," he continues, his voice even and light. "We can only thank the world that someone who is, found it. One man's Abstract Duck is another man's da Vinci, or whatever that saying is."

Oh, he's so nice. So nice. And I've once again made myself into a world-class idiot in front of him. Ironically, while trying to show him I'm not.

Anyway, that's enough idiot-ing for one day. Except, before I go, I feel like I can at least right one wrong.

"I didn't mean *just* a handyman either—" I start, but he holds out a hand toward me. Those green eyes are just a little magical. The 5 o'clock stubble across his face relaxes, as his features turn soft.

"You can stop apologizing now. If your British accent didn't give you away, the number of times you say sorry would. We're strangers. Happy, ignorant strangers. To you I am the Scottish handyman who picked up your pen. To me you are the working woman who dropped her pen." Working woman? I can't help but smile at that.

I like the way it sounds. He continues, "No offense was meant, and no offense was taken, so let's just leave it at that and move on."

Let's leave it at that.

Well, that told me. In the politest way of course, but it's probably time to move on, as he said. With a smile, a wave, and a little sigh of relief that at least I can't say anything else stupid to offend this nice stranger, I head back to my "office" for the day.

Back to rejection calls I go.

On Tuesday I decide to try Nonno's instead, a different independent with a very different vibe. Scandi and minimal. It's lovely, but after an hour or two I find myself distracted in a whole different kind of way. For the first time in maybe ever, I find myself staring at the artwork on the walls and actually thinking about it. Pine picture frames, basic line drawings. A bit forgettable. Sums up my whole day really.

It must be the weather that's taken a toll on my mood. No, it's not just the weather. It's the calls themselves too. More "CVs to HR." More names crossed off the list. More "and why did you leave Branded?"

I'm not ready to talk about it. Not yet.

Wednesday's coffee shop is The Peahen. Part bookshop, part coffee shop, which should be inspiring, but I think the other clientele are all budding writers, scribbling away at super-speed around me. I feel like that girl at school who didn't study for her exam, watching everyone around her who did. No art either, just books. Good for some. Not for me.

Thursday, I tried Starbucks, which was, well, exactly as I thought it would be, so on Friday I go back to Sallie's. I couldn't stop thinking about the scone, or at least that's what I told myself. It's not like I want to *see* the handyman again. I'd already placed a pretty terrible impression on him, best not to risk it again. But I still do a little scan of the place as I enter, just in case, and even I'm not sure whether it's relief, or something else entirely, that I feel when I realize he isn't there.

Still, their scone is just as delicious the second time around, and when I nip to the loo, I see what I missed in my earlier search. I find myself lingering by the same table we'd spoken at while he wrapped up the duck. Not in memory, that would be strange. But in awe, actually.

For where Franken-duck used to stand, a new picture now stands.

And this one is a bit more me.

I read the caption: Local Artist Spotlight: *A Golden Customer* by Archie Brown.

I laugh, taking it all in.

Square canvas, and large too, it shows a giant golden retriever with his paws up on a table lined with gingham like a regular customer. It's the exact same shade as the tablecloths around me. I even see the little jar of flowers on the table matches. The poor pup is salivating, its wide eyes looking up to a fresh stack of scones, pastries and delicious-looking tarts, balanced beautifully on his head. I watch him for a while, taking in the details: the water in his hopeful eyes, the small line of drool coming from his mouth in expectation as if at any moment, the whole stack might tumble into his mouth. It looks so realistic, and yet something about the eyes and coloring give it a kind of light, bright cartoony feel.

I love everything about it. Absolutely everything.

But that's the only thing I love about the day, for everything else either feels like a dead end or a waiting game.

Before I know it I've somehow reached a weekend once more; two days where I know my inbox will stay dry.

Urgh.

I'm starting to hate weekends.

8

Back in my flat, I look over to my kitchen from my little love seat I've set up for a weekend's hibernation. Two weeks of unemployment, and you can tell; the telltale breadcrumbs of fourteen empty ready-meal packets from my dinners line the surfaces. I'd take them out, but—I keep arguing—taking out the bins is using time I could be using more efficiently elsewhere. Like finding a new job. Or moping.

Should I call Betzy again? I know she'll make me feel better.

No, not yet. She'll tell me to find something else I want to do instead of work, and I don't want to hear that. She's been texting me. At least once a day, sometimes for long text streams, but I've told her I'm not ready to leave mope mode yet, which is sort of true.

Betzy
I'm glad you're just letting yourself do nothing for a while.
You've been working nonstop; you deserve the break.
Probably a sign that that job burnt you out more than you think.

I'm lying to my best friend about being proactive, which feels backward. I feel guilty for redoing my CV. Writing out cover letter

after cover letter. Ironically, all this rejection is causing me to want
to mope though, so I'm doing everything the wrong way according
to her three-point-two-point plan.

Maybe I should come clean?

When my phone starts ringing, I wonder if it might be her.
Good old Betzy—our psychic bond is still intact.

Only when I look at my phone screen, it isn't Betzy.

Mia—FaceTime

I just stare at it, letting the ringtone blare out.

Oh, I think. So, now you want to talk? Now you're ready?

I can feel the anger bubbling up inside me. I think about answering it. Screaming at her. Telling her this is all her fault because
everything always is.

And our argument, our last argument, comes flooding back to me.

~

*"So?" Mia asks me. I haven't been listening. Instead I've been staring at
the raindrops crashing against the glass, the wind howling against the
weakened hinges of the window. Thinking.*

*It's a Friday night. I found Mia a few hours ago crying her eyes out
on my doorstep. She didn't look even close to the Mia I know. None
of her usual bold bright colors could be seen. Instead she was perfectly
monochrome. Black jeans with a white top and dark biker jacket. I can
still see the black platforms that completed the outfit right next to the
door from where I sit at the kitchen table.*

*I've never seen her dress like this before, but Mia has a nasty habit
of turning into someone else when she's with someone, so once the initial confusion wore off I find I'm not actually surprised. She becomes
the woman of their dreams, often unrecognizable. And so often, this
is where she ends up because of it: on my doorstep, in—for want of a
better phrase—fancy dress. Crying.*

*It's funny, for the men are all so similar. They all look the same.
They all act the same. Most of them are wannabe actors or musicians,*

"just about to make their big break" so their career failures are all the same too. And yet, despite them being an almost carbon copy of the man before, Mia is a brand-new woman with each of them. It's endlessly fascinating to see the likes of such identical humans be so vastly different.

There was the boyfriend she only wore neon for. The one she became a vegan for. There was one man who she wore Doc Martens for, and another, heels. One who she wore no makeup for, and one who she practically wore no clothes for (thank goodness they met and broke up all in the summer months).

The same pattern would play on repeat. There she'd be, at my door, a broken version of a dressed-up Barbie doll in tears. Often, she stayed for the next few days, a week or two in most cases, and over the course of that time my sister would reemerge from whatever costume she'd been wearing. On would go her trademark bold colors. Her vibrant lipstick would return. Her smile with it.

And then she'd head back into the big wide world, where soon she'd meet the next boyfriend, and the process would begin again.

I want to be there for her. I do. And any other night I would have been all ears, and only silent judgment. Only tonight was supposed to be different. Tonight, I was hosting a dinner. And Jackson was supposed to be coming.

Only instead, she was crying on my doorstep. So, after hearing all about her self-sorry tale of why her latest boyfriend left her with dinner, I've begun to lose my concentration.

"Sorry?" I ask, not sure what on earth she's asking.

"Just a hundred or so. It would just really help to—"

"Money? You're asking me for money?" I ask her, coming back firmly into the present.

"Well." She looks like it's an absurd thing for me to question. She shrugs, like it's no big deal at all. "Yeah."

"What about the money I gave you last month?" I ask.

"That went into the flat."

"Weren't you just going to move in with your ex?" I ask, trying to avoid using his name, given I can't remember it.

"Yes."

"Into a flat he owns?"

"Yes," she repeats, and I suddenly don't like her attitude. It's the "we've already covered this, what are you complaining about?" attitude. It's amplifying all through her—in her face, in her voice. She's picked the wrong day to pull that out on me.

"So, ask him to give it back."

"I can't. It's nonrefundable," she spells out. As if I've missed the point.

"How is it nonrefundable? You gave him money to contribute to a flat that he owns, on the premise that you were going to live there, and then he dumped you so you can't live there. He owes you that money."

She stays very still for a minute, leaning against the kitchen counter, screwing up her face in concentration. Who knows what's going through her mind, but clearly not sense given what next comes out of her mouth:

"I'm only asking for a couple hundred here, Daisy! What's your problem?" Her voice has become louder. More unreasonable. Mine follows.

"Only asking for a couple hundred? Can you hear yourself?"

"God, you're just like Nan."

That pierces something in me. I feel the air start to deflate.

"Why are you saying that like Nan was the bad guy?" I ask, furious. "Nan was the one that housed us. That fed us. That paid for everything when we were growing up."

"Don't . . . you know how she treated . . ." If she finishes that sentence, I'm seriously about to scream. Except she doesn't. She pivots. "Nan was great. I know. But she was stingy."

"She wasn't stingy! She was sensible! She brought up two girls she wasn't expecting to look after on a crappy state pension."

"But you're not on a state pension. You're on a good salary so can you stop making this into such a big deal?"

"This is a big deal!"

"It's not like you don't have it!"

I bite down on my knuckles, trying everything to keep my voice from reaching new lofty heights.

"I only have it," I say, as controlled as possible, "because I actually work for a living—"

"Urgh!" Mia cries, "don't go on—"

"I think I have to go on, because you're a grown woman with no idea about how money works!"

"It's just a few hundred—"

"You're turning into Helen!" I scream.

And we both go silent, feeling the weight of those words heavy in the air.

It's not long after that she gets up.

She puts her bag on her shoulder.

And she leaves.

♾

We haven't spoken since then.

And as of today, that was six weeks ago.

So, maybe, maybe I should pick up. But I'm still angry. So unbelievably angry.

Because whether she knows it or not, she's the reason I'm here to begin with. If we'd never got into that fight, none of this would have happened. I'd still be employed, and happy, and Jackson would probably be lifting my legs into the air right now.

Then I realize blaming her for something she doesn't know about serves no purpose. Worse. It would be telling her what happened. Informing her that my life has, in her absence, dwindled down to a pile of fourteen leftover ready-meal boxes and continuous unemployment.

And really, I just want to shout because after fourteen days, I still haven't changed my employment status. I don't think focusing that anger on Mia will do any good for anyone.

So, no, I think, staring at that screen:

Mia—FaceTime

I can't speak to her right now. Not until I have my life back together again. She's never seen me like this, nor would I ever want her to.

So, I drop my phone and physically walk away from it. Except, I don't know where to even physically walk away to. So, I shove my feet into sneakers, and head back to Sainsbury's, to pick up a tub of Ben and Jerry's.

It's week three, and I'm beginning to think I've hit rock bottom. My motivation has been rejected out of me, one "no" at a time, and I'm finding my pace slip.

On Monday and Tuesday I found coffee shops to go to but given that didn't lead to a success story, I decide on Wednesday that I should mix it up a little more and head to a pub instead.

I'm learning pretty quickly that working from a bar is a dangerous choice. Instead of lattes or flat whites, I find myself ordering gins. And the more gin I consume, the less I'm looking for jobs, and the more I'm looking through Instagram.

"Isn't he pretty?" I ask the barman as he pours me another Bombay Sapphire and Tonic. I push the phone in his face, and he winces.

"Very pretty," he says to appease me without looking. He holds the stem of the glass for a moment, clearly wondering whether he should give it to me. But I'm sad. Not drunk. Or at least not *that* drunk. So, finally, he hands it over.

"He's so pretty," I say, staring down at my phone. "And now he's gone. One bad little meeting and my time block has been permanently removed. Bye bye, time block."

I'm talking to myself at this point, as the barman—a buzz cut in his early twenties—is serving the pair of men on the other side of the bar. They're the only other people in this place right now.

I've refound the picture of Jackson holding his brother's kitten. Hot man, baby animal. It's a winning combination. Except I'm not a winner. As the last two and a half weeks have taught me, I'm a complete and utter loser. I look up, but the barman is there no longer. He's on the other side of the bar, setting up probably for post-work drinks given that it's lunchtime and the place is practically empty.

Instead, I catch myself in the long mirror on the back wall of the bar. Sitting here. Laptop open but asleep. Phone out. Tipsy.

"Hey-hey!" I laugh, to myself. "I'm day drinking solo. This is beyond clichéd, right?"

I look around, hoping someone heard me and will laugh along with me, only there is no one. The two men at the other end of the bar are in deep conversation and the barman's busy pouring their drinks. This is seriously a low point in my life.

"Alright, stop worrying. I'm here!" I hear, in a faint Scottish accent.

What is this? My rom-com adventure come to shake me back to life again? For a second, I think I've actually imagined it, only a few seconds later the handyman from Sallie's café ducks under the bar table and reemerges on the server side.

The young guy who served me looks relieved, removing his own apron and chucking it over to the handyman, who fixes it on his waist.

"You're a lifesaver," the barman replies. "I'll be back around three."

"You'll be back *at* three," the handyman tells him sternly. "Otherwise, I'm leaving your bar unattended."

"I'll be back at three!" the young man confirms. "The audition's at two so I may even be back earlier."

"That's what I like to hear," the handyman tells him, giving him a friendly tap on the back as the boy ducks under the bar, and wraps himself in a coat. "You've got this. Smash it."

"Fingers crossed!" the boy replies as he almost physically—probably from nerves I'm guessing—jumps out of the building.

"Are you good for drinks at the moment?" the handyman asks the men at the far side of the bar.

Only he's not a handyman anymore. He's the barman.

The men have just been served of course, so their glasses are full. I'm blinking stupidly as he turns my way, the only other customer he has.

His green eyes soften in recognition, and he frowns in confusion before he smiles, like we're old friends. I'm not sure what my face is doing. I'm a few gins down.

"We meet again," he says fondly.

"So, you're not *just* a handyman after all," I say as he draws close.

"And you're not *just* a working woman," he replies. Only mine sounded more like a joke, and his words . . . they weirdly cut me. I feel my bottom lip quiver. He can clearly see he's said something wrong as the cheeky grin vanishes from his cheeks.

"I only meant that a person isn't just one thing—" he says quickly.

"It's not you," I say quickly. "It's the gin. Probably. And . . . god. I mean, that's the whole reason I'm even here. I'm apparently not a working woman at all."

He moves quick. We don't know each other, so it's not like he's going in for a hug. There's also a long thick wooden bar between us, and a sink I'm guessing. But still he moves closer, centering himself to me behind the bar. He looks on, a little unsure as a stray tear drains from my eye. The gesture weirdly warms me. "I'm so sorry," I say, wiping it away. "Just ignore me."

"You're sorry?" he asks. "You're sorry that I made you cry?" He smiles so warmly I think I might cry more. But I hold it back, as best I can. "I think you need to stop apologizing for things. And last I checked, when you make someone cry, intentionally or not, you're the one who should say sorry. So, I'm sorry."

It takes a few minutes and a few deep breaths but I've somehow managed to pull myself back. I push the gin a little farther away from me. Maybe I do need a little gin break.

"You want to talk about it?" he asks, delicately.

"You mean like in those movies when the sad lonely person at the bar confides in the barman?" I say, cringing.

Only, I still can't talk to Mia about this because we're still not talking.

I can't talk to my old work colleagues about this, because I don't want them talking about me any more than they already are.

And I can't talk to Betzy about this because she thinks I'm still moping in the safety of my own home. Not drunk, alone in a bar.

So actually, weirdly, yes. I would quite like to talk about it. With this beautiful green-eyed stranger.

He leans back against the far wall of the bar as if settling himself in for a long story, and it's a gesture I really appreciate right now. He's ready to listen.

So, I talk.

"I got let go from my job of thirteen years," I tell him, finding those words still feel sticky in my mouth. He nods, saying nothing. Not an ounce of judgment on his face.

"Thirteen years?" he repeats, with some gravitas.

"Thirteen."

His eyes widen as his arms cross before him.

"That's a long time," he says thoughtfully.

I look up at the black screen of my laptop, before shutting it with a gentle thud. I look down at the counter, before my eyes trail back up to him.

"I don't know, you think after thirteen years that you're indispensable. That you're part of the family, you know? And then for that to all end? Just like that . . ." A vision of me walking away from Everest in my FKME body suit springs to mind and my whole body physically clenches at the memory. "It just hurts, is all."

He nods sympathetically, and I feel like somehow a whole weight has been lifted from me. Like that was, I don't know, the real first step.

"So, anyway," I continue. "I need to get a new job. That's what I was trying to do in the café. What I'm trying to do now." I nod at my closed laptop like it's the real enemy. "What I've been failing at miserably these past few weeks."

He winces, as if the pain of the job search is well understood. Maybe it is. I just haven't ever been in this position before. I've always been fully employed.

"It's not a nice place to be," he summarizes.

"Aren't you going to ask me what I did to get fired?" I ask, biting down on my lip anxiously at the thought that I've just preloaded a question. Only, I sort of feel like I could say it. To him. It's not like he knows anyone in that meeting.

"I am not," he replies. "Because that would imply you did something. When that's not always the case."

Wow. Conscientious too. Who is this handsome stranger?

"But I will ask: were you good at it? At your job?"

I think about being modest and avoiding the question, only why should I?

"I was, actually," I say, a little proudly, because I have thirteen years of anecdotes to back me up. I have a glowing annual review. I took pride in what I did, lots of it. And if I can't say that to a stranger, who can I say it to?

"And you liked it?" he asks.

"I loved it."

"Then that truly does suck," he concludes.

"It does," I reply. "And on top of that my boyfriend broke up with me. And my sister and I aren't talking so it's really just been a peachy couple of weeks. . . ."

"That's tough when it all builds like that," he says warmly. And I've said everything that I need to say, only with him being so sweet like that, and with the gin still very much powering through me, it's hard to stop. "I just can't get out of my own head. Wondering if I could have done things differently. Wondering what I'm going to do now. I'm exhausted thinking about it all the time, but I can't stop."

He nods, his fingers tapping against his folded arms. Once he's certain I'm finished, he pulls himself back to full height.

"You're not allergic to anything, are you?" he asks. That's an unexpected question.

"Job hunting?" I try, and he laughs, which—much like his reaction to my duct tape joke—is purely out of politeness.

"Foodwise," he corrects, as if it's somehow a serious question.

"That's a very responsible question," I laugh, a little confused. "No, I'm not."

"I'm a very responsible person, I'll have you know," he laughs with a smirk on his face. "Good," he replies, before grabbing a lemon from the pile behind him. With a little flair, he slices one, quickly and easily, into almost perfect-size chunks.

"Party trick?" I laugh, because I assume he's going to make this into . . . I don't know, the world's hardest cocktail maybe? Only he doesn't. Instead, he hands me the chunk, as is.

"Right," he says. "On the count of three, bite down."

"Don't you need to pour out the tequila first?" I question.

"We're not doing shots. We're doing lemons. Are you ready?"

I look at it, and then him—holding a second lemon slice in his own hands. I feel my mouth instinctively start to salivate.

"Are we really doing this?" I ask.

"Three . . . two . . ."

"OK, we're really doing this." I shrug, just as he says, "One." His mouth clamps down first, mine after but seconds between us and instantly the sharpness curls my tongue. My whole face grimaces. Crikey, that's sharp!

"Ooof." The bartender winces as his face contorts. With a little shake of his head like he's flicking droplets off his curls, he widens his grin once again.

"What is this?" I laugh, washing the sour taste away with a little chaser of gin. It's the only thing I have. "Oh god. Is this a metaphor on 'when life gives you lemons' or something?"

"No," he chuckles, chucking his own lemon into the bin with an accurate throw. He grabs a napkin and shoves it across the table to me for mine, but I ignore him and just add the extra zest to my drink. "But it should be. I think that's better."

"Then what was that?" I wipe the sting from my lips.

He shrugs.

"You said you can't get out of your own head."

"And how did this help?" I giggle. "A five-second stab to my senses?"

"Sometimes five seconds is all you need to reset," he says, his hands up as if swearing in the whole truth. "Look, I'm a barman. I'm not a long-term solution to your problems. But I can be a short-term one. From my experience, you often need both to get you through a hard time."

That's . . . weirdly wise. I wonder instantly what hard time he's gone through. He seems like the kind of guy that laughs at the face of adversity. I can't imagine him having gone through, well, anything sad. Not with his attitude.

"So, I know you have things you need to solve. And I know it can feel lonely dealing with them, and I can't help you with that. But I can distract you, even if it is for one bite. No one can be sad and bite a lemon at the same time. It's physically impossible."

There's something so perfectly warm about him. So touching that he's taken time out of his . . . busy empty-bar-bartending . . . to listen to me. I mean, I joke, but only because I can't wrap my head around how someone can be this nice to me after I've been a horrible concoction of rude, embarrassing, and tragic to him since we met.

"So, what." I wipe my cheeks down, because from laughing, not sadness, I felt a solo droplet weave around my freckled cheeks. "First handyman. Then barman. Now you're a life coach too?"

He shrugs, stretching out.

"I'm whatever the world needs me to be," he replies freely.

"Until three," I laugh, remembering what he said to his colleague.

"Until three," he confirms.

And I would ask him what job he's off to do at three, only at that moment a lunchtime group comes through the door. There's five of them, all chatting away loudly as they approach the bar. Even I know what that means for this conversation.

So, I try and wrap up quickly.

"Thank you," I tell him, pulling my laptop back into my backpack, because I think I'm done with gin too. It's not my favorite lunch beverage—at least not in this quantity. "I think I should probably, I don't know. Lie down for a bit."

He nods.

"You'll find a job, soon enough," he says. "You'll smash it."

That makes me laugh, because isn't that exactly what he said to that other barman when he left for his audition? Just when I was beginning to feel special. Maybe he's just an all-round good guy.

And perhaps it's the way his green eyes crinkle at the edges when he smiles back at me, but it sparks a little memory. The lunchtime guests are all still chatting, none of them leaning forward to get his attention yet, so I have a couple more seconds at least.

"Did you hang up the picture of the dog, by the way?" I ask.

He raises his eye in confusion.

"In Sallie's?" I confirm.

"I did indeed."

"You probably don't need to know this, but I've been thinking about it ever since our talk. That picture, that dog. That's *my* da Vinci," I tell him.

He nods, understanding me completely, which is strange as I didn't expect him to.

"Mine too," he replies softly. And as the first woman waves him down, he turns away from me, ending our second, rather peculiar exchange.

It isn't until I'm back at home, with the alcohol starting to wind out of me that I even realize: He's been the handyman, the barman, and the life coach in the tragedy that is my life.

And I still don't know his name.

Thursday morning and I wake up with a hangover.

I mean, I drank a fair amount, sure, but I actually stopped drinking at like 1 p.m. so it feels a bit unfair that I feel this rough.

Mind, I don't think this is just a "hangover" hangover. I think this is a "nearly end of three weeks of failure" hangover. A long-time-coming one, that just needed the excuse of a gin to show itself.

I think about having a quick shower, trying to shake myself out of this and head out for another day of solid rejections. Only that doesn't sound brilliantly appealing right now. When I walk back from the bathroom in the morning, too tired to even wash my panda eyes free of yesterday's mascara and hit play on the S Club track waiting for me on Spotify, I stop to take note.

"Never give up," S Club tells me.

Never give up. That's what they say. I need to hold my head high and . . .

"I won't give up *tomorrow*," I tell myself, out loud, as if that helps justify this decision.

So, I finally, properly—without a word of a lie this time—decide it's time to do what Betzy thinks I've been doing all this time: It's time to mope.

I never really allowed myself a hangover day, not entirely. I always thought there was something I should be doing, no matter how terrible I felt. I couldn't finish the day without at least one productive thing happening. That would be absurd.

Only today, there is nothing productive to do. Nothing. Except, maybe binge an entire season of *Bridgerton*.

So, I lean into it, wholly and completely, scrunching my blonde hair in a rough bun at the top of my head, wearing the biggest baggiest sweats I own, and wrap myself in my big blue blanket. Hello, sexy dukes and catchy contemporary songs with a violin flair, I think, as I hold my almost-finished box of crunchy nut, hit play, and settle in for the long haul.

By the second episode, during the downtime (and by that, I mean when Regé-Jean Page is not on the screen), I find myself lifting my phone to my eyes once again. The allure of Instagram is too strong for me, even though I know it won't help my mood.

Straightaway I feel a punch to the gut: it looks like Pauline had a client dinner last night. The restaurant looks smart: all red curtains and gold mirrors. She's got an espresso martini in her hands in the classic mirror selfie she took.

I can't help but wonder: what must she think of me?

What must have been said about me in the office?

Would they be surprised if they saw me here, wrapped up in a blanket at 11 a.m. on a working day, watching sexy aristocracy while they're at work after an evening out at client dinners? Or worse—would they not be surprised at all? Would they expect this from me?

"Urgh!" I cry out in frustration, literally out loud, because I know what I'm about to do and I know I can't stop it. I'm thinking of work. And when I think of work I'm thinking of Jackson. So, I hit the explore button, and then the search bar, knowing I'm about to look at Jackson's unchanged page all over again, only instead I stop.

@Tasha_Flore

That's weird. Why is that second in my search list? I never search for people. Jackson aside, I'm not a searcher, I'm a scroller. But right underneath the familiar handle @Jax_O is @Tasha_Flore. I've never even heard of a Tasha before.

I click through, curious, but it makes instant sense. Brown hair, beautiful: it's the woman from Sainsbury's. It's the mother of those two young girls. I look at the screen: looks like the duke still hasn't made an appearance so I start scrolling through absentmindedly.

Looks like she's a wannabe fashion influencer. Picture after picture of her wearing fancy heels and expensive-looking dresses. A few in her underwear: "What to wear, what to wear . . ." the caption reads of her posing in front of her large open wardrobe.

The young one—Cara, I seem to recall—is also a constant feature.

"Twinning" the caption reads, showing both of them with matching-colored sunglasses halfway down the bridge of their noses.

"Stealing my rays" the next one says, with Cara smiling a picture-perfect smile in the foreground of a clearly self-timed picture of Tasha, posing in a yellow dress by a bright yellow door. She must have run in just before the timer ran out and photobombed it. Her face fills up most of the frame.

That makes me laugh. I know that smile: Mia used to use that smile on just about everyone and it always worked. Whatever she wanted, she'd get with that face.

Which makes me think of Mia.

Which makes me sad.

Maybe I *should* call her back. Finally.

Then I do a little stock take of myself: big sweats, mascara still under my eyes probably. No, not just yet. I'll sort my life out first before I sort out her.

But I'm just about done stalking this stranger, so I'm about to scroll away when something stops me. That's interesting. I click on the picture, widening it, but I'm sure.

In the background of one of her pictures is a painting that feels weirdly familiar, despite having never seen it before. Square canvas, a black schnauzer looking proud with a red twig in his mouth. No, not a twig—I see as I zoom in closer—the heel of a shoe. On the floor of the picture, littered around, are a hundred other broken expensive-looking heels.

There's something about the cartoon quality of the dog's eyes and yet the perfect realism around it that makes me think of—oh wow!

"#ArchieBrown capturing my essence to perfection <3" the caption reads. I remember that name—so it is the same artist. How strange that I've never heard of him before and yet now I've seen his work twice in a small space of time. Isn't there a word for that?

Only, maybe it's not that strange. I know Archie Brown is a "local artist" and I'm guessing Tasha is local if she lives on Dalton Avenue.

Curious, I click through on the hashtag—but it's a wasted search. That one post is the only post there is. When I search "Archie Brown" nothing else comes up either. What a shame.

By this time, Regé-Jean is back onscreen, so I chuck the phone on the coffee table beside the various built-up cutlery and crockery I haven't tidied away, and give him the attention his mesmerizing face truly deserves.

It doesn't even go through my mind that in all that search, I forgot all about looking up Jackson.

By the early evening I've once again run out of food—and even if I hadn't, I really fancy pizza. I think a day of feeling sorry for yourself should always end in thick cheese-topped dough. So, I nip over to Sainsbury's.

This is the fourth time I've been in here since my unemployment began, and every time I weirdly find myself listening out in case I can hear the voices of two young girls arguing about . . . well, anything. Of course, I don't. The footfall in this place must be high. The nanny notice is still on the wall though. My eyes glance over to it naturally while I grab myself a basket. No idea why I notice it. It's strange I even looked.

I head straight for the pizza selection, and in a moment of perfect revelation I follow it up by going to the frozen aisle to pick up more ice cream. And it's there that I hear it.

No, not the girls.

My name.

"Daisy?"

Without even turning around, I know who that voice belongs to. Regret suddenly fills me up.

I didn't think to get changed: I was just popping in to get the essentials, so I'm still in my big sweats. My hair is still in a messy bun. My eyes are still mascara-stained from yesterday. I look an absolute mess.

And as I turn around—yes, I was right. It's Layla from work. Layla the junior analyst on my team. Layla the girl who used to ask me question after question: the one I personally guided through her career to date. To her, I was the one who knew it all. And now look at me.

She looks fantastic of course: she always took more pride in her appearance than in her work, and today she stuns in a vibrant red dress.

"I thought it was you," she says, smiling.

I see she's holding a bottle of champagne in her hands. It's a very different picture to the ice cream balanced on my pizza box.

"Layla." I force a smile. "Lovely to see you."

"And you! God—I thought it was you earlier but then I . . ." She stops in her thought process and checks herself. I think she was probably going to say, "I didn't expect you to look like a total disaster, so I didn't recognize you," or something along those lines. I save us both from the embarrassment of her having to complete that sentence.

"Celebrating?" I say, trying to keep the conversation light.

She looks at her hands, then looks a bit bashful.

"Yes, actually," she answers. And that's all she needs to say, because we both clearly don't want to be in this conversation and we can call it quits now, only she continues: "I got a promotion actually."

A bulldozer hits my chest.

But I swallow down the punch, trying to keep my face expressionless.

"Oh," I say, as neutrally as I can. "Congrats."

"Well, it's only because . . . well, after you left there was a senior analyst vacancy and Rachel got that, so I applied for Rachel's vacancy and . . . now I'm an analyst! A junior no longer!" She's laughing, awkwardly, holding up the champagne bottle and waving it around because she clearly doesn't know what else to say.

Oh right. Of course.

So, the company's moved on from me.

It hasn't broken down in my absence. The department isn't pining for me the same way I'm pining for it. It's replaced me. And it's even replaced my replacement. It's moved on. I try to ignore the big knife under my rib cage that digs in deep at the thought.

Rachel should have been promoted years ago, but still, the thought that she took my job feels like a different form of heartbreak. Layla—well, I guess she's been there long enough to get a promotion, whether she's earned it or not.

It's not them though. The fact that anyone took my job is an ouch. A big, bloody ouch. I'm finding it really, really hard to maintain this smile. But somehow, I do.

"Anyway, how are you?" Layla continues, and then remembers how I'm probably doing, and in an effort to maybe seem a little more empathetic than she is, she adds: "After . . . everything?"

After everything.

I wonder how much she knows.

But it does prove something I've feared: they've all definitely talked about me. And there isn't a doubt in my mind that she's going to talk about this tomorrow too.

"Oh, I ran into Daisy at the supermarket yesterday. She looked a MESS. Completely terrible. HOW was she ever employed here? It's embarrassing. Thank god she's gone."

I mean, Layla's slightly nicer than that. But that will be the sentiment for sure. I will be the humiliation of the office. Of the whole, bloody industry. No wonder no one has a job ready for me.

I want to crumble. I want the whole world to swallow me up and never return me. I want to reverse time so I could at least look like I'm not a human mess in front of her.

Spurred on by a whole new wave of trying to look like I've got things together, I flex back out my smile.

"Great, actually!" I reply, my smile thick on my lips. "I've just been researching all afternoon, so I thought I'd get a little comfort break."

"Researching?" she questions.

Why does she question? Just leave it, Layla. Buy your bottle and move on.

"I have a job interview tomorrow," I say quickly.

I don't know why I say it.

I mean, I do. I want her to think I'm worthy of having been her boss for the last six months. I want her to think I haven't completely fallen at the wayside.

"Oh!" she says, breathing out a sigh of relief like that makes all this look better. And maybe it does. "What's the job?"

"A manager role," I lie quickly. "I can't say which company because . . ." Because I don't have one. That's why, but I just laugh, like I've signed some NDA or something. "You know," I reply.

And she is at least the kind of person who hates to be seen to not know something, as she nods earnestly. Like she does know.

"Well, best I head back!" I say finally, pulling myself away. "It was so lovely to see you!"

"And you!" she says, and I know she means it. Because I know she loves a good gossip.

I whisper the F word to myself multiple times on my way out of that shop. I only stop when the woman helping the self-checkouts moves away from me closer to the security man. I try not to read into that.

When I scan my contactless card, I avoid looking around, desperate to not have another encounter with her.

Why did I say that? Probably because I so want it to be true.

I just need one interview.

One, little, interview.

And then I see it. On the noticeboard.

PART-TIME NANNY WANTED

No. I couldn't. I really couldn't.

I'm not a nanny. I'm a data analyst.

Those girls were chaos! Even if I was thinking about it, I couldn't look after *those* girls. They remind me far too much of a time I'd rather forget.

And I'm a data analyst, I remind myself.

And yet, when I'm 100 percent sure that Layla is not looking, I somehow find myself pulling that note off the wall and stuffing it into my oversize sweats pocket.

That was weird.

Weirder still, I think, when a day later I stand outside the idyllic, bright yellow front door, nanny ad in hand, CV in my bag. Looking right into the bewildered eyes of the man who answered the doorbell.

And not just any eyes of any man either.
They're the perfect green bewildered eyes of the handyman.
The barman.
The life coach.
The . . . father?

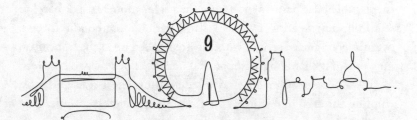

9

"There's no easy way to ask this," he says, as we both stare at each other dumbfounded, "but are you stalking me?"

I blink, unable to speak.

I mean, it's not that out-there a question given I've just turned up at his door. But I've never stalked anyone in my life. I mean, unless you count online. Then I've stalked loads of people. But that doesn't count. That's . . . socially acceptable. I think.

Stalking someone in real life, though, is horrible. It makes me think of Penn Badgly in *You*. And then the thought strikes me.

"I'm not a murderer," I say quickly, to ease him of his worries. Only, as his kind eyes turn into a frown, I realize that's not actually that relaxing a thing to hear.

"That's quite the relief," he replies, probably thinking I'm a murderer now. So, I correct him quickly.

"I'm here for the nanny position?" I say confidently, getting myself back on track.

Because confidence is key.

I may not have done an interview in forever, but I feel prepared for this one. Having spent the night watching *The Sound of Music*, I figure if Julie Andrews can look after seven children in one go, I can handle two.

He leans on the door frame. His knuckles, still clasped around the yellow door, are smeared with paint. Probably from all the handyman-ing he's been doing today. His 5 o'clock shadow is still there, probably a permanent fixture then. He's more relaxed than I've seen him out: wearing a white T-shirt, with a loose hoodie thrown over for good measure, and with his jeans rolled up at the bottom an inch or two it's hard not to notice that he's grounded by two bare feet.

He takes a deep breath and I watch as his chest rises and falls, rippling through his white T-shirt, visible quite clearly under that hoodie. You can literally see every muscle move in turn. It's quite hypnotizing really. A rolling cascade of—

I should probably look up at his face again, staring directly at the chest of my prospective future employer is probably *not* a good thing. Especially given he already thinks I'm a psychopath.

"The nanny position?" he asks, breaking my brain's inappropriate whirring.

"Yes. The nanny position," I confirm.

He looks me up and down slowly.

Oh no. Do I not look the part?

I did Google "21st century nanny," and when that search didn't bring up anything useful other than a few *Mary Poppins* film references, I checked out a few posts from "#nannyswhogram." I wanted to see if there was an unwritten uniform. Turns out, there isn't. Some dress up like they're on a permanent glamorous holiday and others dress like they've just rolled out of bed. So, I went for my usual classic: jeans and a pastel pink jumper.

"Sorry," he says, and he sounds it. He looks sympathetically on with such a kind spark in those round green eyes.

"Have you already hired someone?" I say, a little disappointed.

"No, I think you might have this house confused."

Erm . . . what?

"Is this 32 Dalton Avenue?" I ask in response, stepping back to double-check the number. I already know that it's correct. I did my research, and my research brought me here. To the yellow door of the mews house: 32 Dalton Avenue, Clapham Old Town, London. The same yellow door Tasha was Instagrammed outside.

A little confused myself, I hold out the Sainsbury's note in my hand. He looks at it, almost as if it's the first time he's ever heard of it. And then he flips it over and looks at it again.

Oh gosh, this really is the first time that he's heard of it, isn't it?

"Maybe I should have called first . . ." I say, feeling a rush of blood to my cheeks. His eyes, those kind eyes, have suddenly filled with something. Something just a little bit terrifying.

"Where did you get this?" His voice has changed completely too. No longer the same friendly neighborhood handyman who answered the door. Now he doesn't sound happy at all.

"The Sainsbury's noticeboard?" I say. "I saw your wife—"

"My wife?" His eyes shoot up and I feel the heat rise inside me.

"She put it up a couple weeks ago," I say, dramatically losing the confidence I barely had to begin with.

He says nothing, looking at the note for another minute before shaking his head. I don't know how to salvage this situation, and given that riding out silences is absolutely not my forte, I feel my mouth moving in response: "Bailey was—"

"Bailey? You know my daughter's name?" He looks shocked at that too.

I feel like I just keep putting my foot in it now.

"We met," I say, justifying it. "In Sainsbury's," I add, as if that might help clarify things. But I can see already it doesn't. Another short, stark silence follows. He looks confused, heated, furious maybe? He shakes his head.

"I don't really . . ." he says finally, then remembers to cool his face when he looks at me: "You seem lovely but—"

"Daddy!" We both turn to the voice instinctively.

From behind the man, the long, curly-haired little girl I met just over two weeks ago sprints to her father's side. Cara grips her father's leg like it's the strong mast to a stable ship. It's the most heartwarming thing I've ever seen.

"Can I have a Bakewell tart pleeeeeease?" she says, clearly not registering that I'm somewhere in the background of this picture.

"I already said no!" cries a voice trailing behind her. It's a voice I recognize—and thank goodness, Tasha has appeared. Now we can iron all this out. "Cara, you can't just go to your dad whenever I've—oh! You!" Tasha says, interrupted by her own thoughts.

On seeing someone else at the front door, both new entries to the scene pause. I feel incredibly awkward from having been staring at her husband's muscles now. Maybe she senses this. I don't know, but she looks like the kind of woman who knows these things instinctively. Cara's little face stalls. She clearly wasn't expecting company. Apparently no one was. I definitely shouldn't be here, except, as she draws nearer, that smile shoots back up, like all she needed was a little recharge.

"It's the headless lady!" Cara cries sweetly, although that sounds very odd without context. Before I know it, I have two arms launched around my waist in a strong hug. Oh my gosh! I haven't been hugged by a small child since I was a small child. I don't know how to react, what to do, what to say. I just sort of stand a bit awkwardly, looking up at this man—whose name I somehow still don't know—in complete surprise and hoping he understands how unplanned this is.

He looks just as shocked as I am, clearly lost for words about this whole situation. His daughter is hugging a random person he happened to meet twice, once incredibly drunk, at his door, who's asking about a job he quite obviously didn't realize was a vacancy going.

"Cara! You can't just hug strangers!" Tasha says quickly, joining us all at the door and reaching out for the young girl.

"She's not a stranger!" Cara moans happily, dodging her mother's arms as she continues to hug me: "I know her."

"Do you know her?" Tasha asks me, confused.

"I mean, we've met," I say uselessly. I smile a "I don't know what's happening right now but I'm rolling with it" kind of smile that I hope shows flexibility: a good trait in a new hire. I continue because Tasha probably needs clarification: "When I met you."

"In Sainsbury's?" the man says, the inflexion of his smooth Scottish voice rising into a question. Tasha's perfect face doesn't even flinch. She avoids looking at him directly as she manages to pull Cara off this time, gently moving her back inside and out of my reach. She looks down at the girl, speaking to her like a child maybe half her age. The vowels are elongated, the consonants hard and heavy.

"Cara, meeting someone one time doesn't mean you know them. Sorry," Tasha says, the apology part clearly directed at me although she doesn't look particularly sorry. She looks like I'm an inconvenience she'd like to rid herself of. "Why are you here anyway? Did we leave something?"

"I *do* know her actually," Cara insists grumpily. "She taught me how to remove a bra one-handed before you showed up."

I look up at the two of them like a deer in headlights.

"That's not what it sounds like," I say quickly. But the man doesn't seem to register the first bit. Only the second.

"Before you showed up?" he asks Tasha directly, that fury quickly spreading. He kneels down, drawing his eyes level with Cara. "Cara, who were you with if you weren't with Tasha?"

Cara has just realized that she might be in trouble here. I can see her face fall.

"Bailey . . ." she says weakly.

"Bailey *and* . . ." her father asks hopefully.

"And . . . this woman . . ."

"I was literally just in Sainsbury's . . ." I say quickly, trying to make it sound a little less like I kidnapped them.

As if trying to organize his thoughts, which I imagine are buzzing at super speed right now, he stands back to full height.

"What are you doing here?" Tasha asks quickly, clearly pissed off I've turned up like this.

"She's here about the nanny position," he speaks for me.

"Oh! You're a nanny?" Tasha's whole face does a 360 and erupts into an advertisement-worthy smile. It's like everything falls into place for her, and immediately I'm not the pain she thought I was about to be.

"You're hired!" cries out Cara, jumping on the spot. Her brown ringlets bounce with her in her fit of glee. I can't help but laugh at it, which feels strangely inappropriate in this bizarre set of circumstances I've found myself in, so I stop laughing quickly.

"We have to interview her first," Tasha cuts in quickly to the young girl before returning her gaze up to me. "But what a wonderful coincidence. Come in! Come in!"

"This clearly isn't a good time—" I begin, looking only at him, but Tasha throws back her head in a laugh as if the very idea of that is absurd. She's trying to push through the argument I know is about to happen, and there's a chance she might succeed. This woman is a force.

Before the handsome but clearly angry man has a chance to say otherwise, she ushers me inside and past him. I don't know why my feet move as she beckons me in. Maybe it's because her smile is also mildly terrifying.

Before I know it, the door is closed and I'm on the inside of it.

I try to catch the man's eye, and when those big greens reach mine, I feel everything inside me stop. He blinks, once, hard, then looks back up and past me.

"Tash, I think—" he begins, but Tasha's ignoring him purposefully. She's walking away. I don't know what to do. Follow her? Or hover? I do a strange shuffle-linger that looks more like an awkward shimmy to the left. I immediately regret it.

"Cara, go get your sister," Tasha whispers, and with a delighted smile my way Cara sprints up the staircase at the back of the hallway. She has not noticed anything is wrong with this situation, which actually gives me a little relief.

"Let's talk in the kitchen," Tasha decides, walking past the staircase into the room at the back of the ground floor.

I wait for another second, completely unsure, before I take a step toward her. I don't know what else to do. I probably should have stayed outside, but now I'm inside I can't just stand here in limbo all day.

Except before my foot takes a step, I feel a paint-stained hand touch my arm.

His touch sends goose bumps right up to the back of my neck. He doesn't grab me, or turn me, but the very feel of his fingertips on my forearm halt me instantly. When I turn to look at him, I'm lost back in those eyes.

"Sorry," he says to me, quickly and quietly, "do you mind just . . . waiting here for one minute?"

His voice is soft, forgiving. The good news is that he's back to being the same kind man who I met in the coffee shop. Except now he clearly has an agenda.

I feel my mouth swell without words, so I nod. That's very uncharacteristic of me. I place my feet back together and let him pass me as he, alone, follows Tasha into the kitchen.

"We need to talk," I hear him say far more sternly, and that Scottish accent seems to strengthen as his voice turns.

The door shuts behind him, and the hard wood muffles the words, sure. But not the fight. I can hear that, crystal clear.

There we are then. That's the argument I've been sensing since I knocked come to fruition. I officially started a fight, just by answering an ad. And here I am, listening to a couple getting increasingly louder in the middle of their corridor like a complete goon.

I actually feel sick. I close my eyes a little, letting the wave of nausea pass me, as this brings me flashbacks. Bad flashbacks.

Flashbacks of me sitting on the stairs, hearing the muffled shouts of my mum. Hearing my Nan's usually kind voice cry back at her. Of seeing Mia's face fall beside me, so completely unsure and not knowing what to do to make things better. Of feeling useless.

Why am I still here?

I need to go. They don't want me, clearly, and I don't want to be here.

I turn back to their door—painted yellow on the inside too—which was a little unexpected, only then I realize everything I'm looking at is unexpected.

Unexpected and . . . a little bit wonderful.

I was a little distracted earlier to take in my surroundings, but I can see it all now, and *wow*.

The corridor is long and thin, painted a dark earthy green three quarters up until the paneling ends and then white stretches the ceiling down the top quarter of the wall. That part of the decoration looks incredibly grown-up. Like something straight out of an Instagram renovation account. It's warming and cozy with a perfect country cottage vibe, making this small London mews house feel like a transport straight into the luscious green fields of the beautiful English countryside. Wicker baskets containing shoes and hats and scarves hang from the walls at varying levels, and beside the door a number of owl-designed coat hooks hold winter coats ready for the great outdoors. That in itself is a little bit magical. It's neat but chaotic, charming and inviting. But then, it doesn't just end there.

Above the paneling is where the room comes into its own, for where the white paint begins, so does the jungle. Sketched birds of all sizes and shapes fly overhead across the ceiling, painted chimpanzees lean down from a stenciled branch to steal one of the girls' coats from the owl hook. Several little mice run along the paneling's edge with large blocks of cheese held above their heads and four judgmental bullfrogs watch from above the door, all different stages of mid-ribbit like a little amphibian orchestra. A colorful snake wraps down and around one of the wicker baskets and a lazy panther watches on from where the paneling begins to run up the staircase.

Some are light pencil drawings, some are watercolor masterpieces. There are block paints for some critters and others are etched out in sketchy ballpoint pen. It's jaw-dropping, every creature both a work in progress and magnificently realistic. It's completely—

"Can we help you?" says a voice.

My head whisks round. I remember that face.

Standing halfway down the stairs, just in front of her smiling little sister, is a very sour-faced Bailey. My word, she looks like her father. It's funny, I might not have realized before but now I can't help but see it. Something about her nose, the way her face is shaped like a little oval. Those vibrant green eyes. She's her father's girl through and through.

"We have to interview her," Cara says excitedly from the top of the stairs. She's smiling at me. "That's what Tasha said."

"Oh," I say quickly, reading Bailey's face instantly and knowing she'd like nothing less. "No, that's not what she . . . it's alright. I should go. I was just going."

Because I definitely should go. I shouldn't be here, standing in a (pretty spectacular) corridor of a complete stranger's house waiting to be inevitably told to leave anyway.

"Where's Dad gone?" Cara asks, looking around me into the empty corridor. My eyes turn naturally to the door in the kitchen, and as if on cue, I hear Tasha's voice start screaming. I can't hear the words still, but that sounds explosive.

This is very, very bad. I physically begin shaking as the memories start creeping back.

Except my eyes are open this time as I look over to the girls. I don't think Cara's noticed, but I can see that Bailey has. Her face has half turned to the kitchen door, her face ghostly white. I can see the tremble in her hand. It's identical to my own. I can see the breath as it's caught in her chest: same as me. Then she turns to Cara, her eyes wide and desperate.

I've been there. I've lived this. I know I can just leave, but she can't. Someone's fighting in the house, and she doesn't want her sister to know.

As if something snaps inside me, I feel a strength I never did back when I went through this. I might have been helpless then, but I'm not now. I'm not. I can do something.

"Yes, I need you to interview me!" I say quickly, making sure my voice is louder than the voices behind the door.

Really? Did I actually just say that?

Bailey looks over, at first just confused, and then in complete understanding. There we are: two women in one conspiracy. I can see her release her breath. Cara is absolutely none the wiser.

"Yes, we do," Bailey agrees quickly as her own dad's muffled cry breaks through the door's barrier. She points at the door to my left and she rushes her sister down the stairs. She practically pushes Cara through the open door. And I follow quickly, closing the door behind me at first, before opening it back an inch or two. I don't know these girls. Probably best not to be behind a closed door with them, even if it is in their house. Feels just a little inappropriate.

Still, an open door means those voices still might work their way through, only clearly Bailey's already worked that one out. She's pressing some buttons on an iPad that must have been left in here, and with a little jump I hear music spring up in the background.

Journey fires up with "Don't Stop Believin'" all around us. Now that's cool.

What a clever girl, I think. I used to put on music and get Mia to dance with me. Only Bailey has far better taste than me, I can tell.

Once again, I marvel at the room I'm in. Burnt-orange sofas, a large bookcase at the back filled with old-looking volumes and romantically dark blue walls framed with thin paneling. It's so strange to go from the jungle of the corridor into this: clearly a very adult room but with the flair of something straight out of Grand Designs. No stars are painted onto the ceiling or animals running around in here, but it does have two pictures hanging from the wall.

The first is cute: a dog walking on the top of a hill, a large shadow trailing it. The other, though, is spectacular.

Large. Square canvas. My jaw drops in recognition, although I've never seen this one before.

Two mixed-breed puppies, both dappled with an adorable mix of whites, browns, and tans, and wearing purple party hats. The ever-so-slightly larger of the two has its mouth open, blowing out the candles of a unicorn-themed birthday cake while the other, the smaller, is nibbling away at the icing. Something about the cartoon nature of both their vibrant green eyes, the realism of the surroundings. It must be the same artist.

"You like it?" Cara asks, catching me staring.

"Very much," I reply, stunned. Bailey has sat down already, waiting for us to join.

"They're Scorkies," Cara says proudly.

"Like the Pokémon?"

"That's Squirtle," Bailey corrects, like it was obvious. I forgot Pokémon came back into fashion.

"My daddy painted it," Cara says proudly.

"Your d-dad?" I stutter, completely shocked, and she nods enthusiastically.

So, what, he's a painter too? An actual painter?

I am beyond impressed. Is there nothing this man can't do?

But Bailey doesn't sound impressed. She sounds like she's taking this very, very seriously as she says: "Please take a seat, everyone. The interview is about to begin."

10

Which is exactly how I end up here, sitting on a velvet sofa in an interview that is, unsurprisingly, not going so well.

"You're probably wondering why I left then, given I've just told you how loyal I am," I say.

Why? Why did I just say that?

It makes me know one thing for sure: I need to work on my interview skills. How on earth do you not panic in a real life "job dangling in front of you" moment? I know it's been thirteen years since my last interview, but how did I get hired in the first place?

Before I begin to answer in a way that somehow avoids telling these kids that I dressed up in an entirely inappropriate outfit prior to being promptly let go, Cara raises her hand. That surprises me. It also surprises Bailey. But there she is, looking like a true class know-it-all, her hand high in the air.

"Yes?" I ask.

Cara looks around her, as if double-checking that it was definitely her hand that was being called upon. Satisfied, she lowers it.

"Who are you?" she asks.

Oh gosh. Yes, that's an excellent question. I haven't actually introduced myself.

"Well, I'm Daisy. Daisy Peterson," I say, and after feeling mortified that I hadn't even mentioned that yet, I then feel beautifully proud of myself for answering a question correctly. There, that's a bit better. A question, followed by an answer. No extra waffle.

And up goes Cara's hand again. Thank goodness. This interview will go a lot better if all the questions are like that.

"Yes, Cara?" I say happily, waiting for the next quick win.

"But who *are* you?" Cara asks.

I didn't mean for every question to be *exactly* like that.

I just told her, didn't I?

"I'm Daisy," I reply slowly, my smile wavering on my lips. "Daisy Peterson."

"And who is *that*?" she says again, no hand in the air this time.

Well, that's . . . maybe she means what are my hobbies? Like who am I: what do I like?

"OK," I say, resetting my answer, "well, I'm a hard worker. I don't shy away from a problem, and I have a very strong work ethic."

I scan her face to see if that will suffice, but Cara just cocks her head to the side, wanting more. Bailey blinks at me.

"I'm a big coffee fan," I try, but I feel both of their eyes tear right through me on that one. "Actually, I think what I really like is just hot milk, only I often need the caffeine hit so I combine the two and basically live off constant cappuccinos and lattes. Full disclosure, I can't actually taste the difference between those two. I think it's something to do with the foam but foam, no foam. It doesn't bother me. Hot milk and a shot of coffee is all I need." I'm beginning to waffle again. That much is clear. But that as an answer is still not enough by the looks on their faces. So, I keep going.

Who am I? *Who am I?*

"I'm a black belt in karate?" I try. "I spend a disgusting amount of time watching dog videos on Instagram reels. I like pastel colors and Netflix rom-coms. I tend to buy ready meals as I don't have the time to cook which tend to be filled with so much salt, so then I drink a green juice to make up for the missed nutrients, but they're probably just filled with sugar, and I don't even like them so no one wins that scenario. I do all-nighters if I hear Taylor Swift might release a new song even though some of the time she doesn't so I just end up staying awake listening to *1989* or *Red*. . . . " I'm panicking here.

How has this young girl got me revealing these things? Is she magic?

I stop in my rant, physically holding my mouth shut to stop it from opening again. Bailey raises one eyebrow, as if this is all rather amusing. Cara, on the other hand, leans forward, like a fully trained therapist.

"You have a sad energy emanating from you, Daisy," she says.

Oh holy shit. Did she just use the word "emanating"?

"I'm not sad," I say, with an entirely unconvincing half-smile and a complete loss of conviction. How does this girl see right through me?

"Emmy Pea says to always own up to your true feelings. Only then can you overcome them."

Emmy Pea. Wasn't that the influencer that Cara was talking about in Sainsbury's?

"Well, that's very wise of Emmy Pea but really I'm . . ."

Both of them twist their heads, in uniform, and my heart sinks. It's like staring at two dogs, who know you're going to give in and give them a bit of your bacon but you're all sort of playing the part first. They can literally see right through me.

"OK, maybe I'm a little sad," I admit.

Maybe it's the completely sincere look in Cara's eyes. Maybe it's the wistful color scheme around me. Maybe it's the knowledge that two adults are having an argument in the other room and that brings up things I didn't even realize I'd stored, but something in me breaks. Just a little, but enough. So, when Cara asks, in a voice about a decade older than she is: "And why is that?" I somehow find myself actually answering her.

"I'm just having a really . . ." I realize I'm with two young girls and shouldn't swear right now. "Hard couple of weeks," I say, not sure how else to phrase it.

"Go on." Cara nods wisely. "Let it out."

"I don't . . ."

"Let it out," she repeats strongly.

"Well, I guess . . ." How do I shut the door on this one quickly without giving too much away? "It's just one of those times where you realize . . . something that puts things into perspective a bit, I guess. You know?" Both girls cock their head to the side, and in their silence, I feel my mouth keep moving.

"You don't know," I conclude, trying to rethink how to get around this one: "Well, let's just say . . . I went from apparently being needed, to not being needed at all. And it stings. Quite a bit actually. It's a real, big . . . ouch."

There we are. Clear as mud. But at least it closed down that conversation, I think. Maybe we can talk about my soft skills a little more. Except of course, all I've really done is open the floor up to more questions.

"Is this about a man?" Cara asks, in a voice a full two decades at least above her years.

"Oh no! I didn't mean . . ." I start, but then I stop myself, as the thought clarifies in my mind: "Well, yes, actually. Yes, I guess it *is* about Jackson too. My semipermanent time block suddenly just vanished from his calendar overnight so yes, there's someone else who doesn't need me." I laugh in disbelief at the realization. "In fact, over a year we were together and apparently a text is all I'm going to get too, so evicting me from his life was . . . easy."

"That can't feel nice," Cara sighs.

"So, who else doesn't need you then?" Bailey asks, her tone neutral. Therapist-esque. A little disorientating. "If you weren't talking about a man?"

"Well, my job," I reply, before I realize I have to correct myself. "My *old* job."

"Did you not work hard enough?" she questions, and I feel a surge pass through me in annoyance at such an accusation.

"Oh no! The opposite! I gave Branded everything. I was their go-to girl. I worked hard. I spent hours, *hours* of my own free time analyzing things no one else understood. Late nights. Early mornings. Weekends. And then to go from that, to this? To be dropped at the click of a finger? One little outburst at a pitch meeting after thirteen years of hard service and suddenly I'm 'let go' like I mean absolutely nothing to them."

I sit back on the sofa, my eyes lifted to the ceiling as I recall everything that passed in the last month.

"And don't get me started on my sister," I sigh.

"You have a sister?" Cara asks, as if this is vital information.

I turn my head back to Cara, those big innocent eyes reminding me immediately of Mia at her age. A shiver runs up my spine.

"I have a headache is what I have. A selfish, annoying headache that I just don't have the headspace to deal with right now."

I'm not sure when I started crying, but my cheeks have a flow of salty tears cascading down them now. And I don't just mean a soft, angelic, one wipe of a finger and my face is still flawless tear. A heavy-duty "goodbye freckle-hiding foundation" jet stream that doesn't seem to stop.

Cara throws herself off her armchair and runs to the windowsill behind me, returning with a full pack of tissues, which she hands over. She jumps up beside me as I bring one of the Kleenex wipes to my messy face. Bailey opposite us just sits there silently, watching.

"And now I'm oversharing. I'm oversharing with two . . ." children, I think. Infants almost. "With you two," I correct, instantly embarrassed.

"Emmy Pea says a man that shows disrespect doesn't deserve you. You have to know your worth."

"My worth?" I find myself asking.

"Your worth," Cara repeats wisely, placing a comforting hand on my knee. "Because *you are worthy*."

There's a small pause as I catch my breath. The tissues do their work, but I'm still looking through a film of water. Cara's smiling at me, in a way that makes the whole world make a bit of sense.

"I'm alright, I am. This is just silly."

"Sadness is never silly. That's what Emmy Pea says."

I laugh at that.

Who even is this Emmy person? Seems like she has an answer for everything.

"Maybe that's true. Not silly then. Sorry, I shouldn't have said anything."

"You should *always* say something," she says knowledgeably. "Because you should *always* show the world your authentic self, no matter who that is."

I look at her, blinking those big green eyes at me like she completely understands. I laugh at the idea that a small child is going to give me good advice here.

"I'm not sure you should always show the world your authentic self . . ." I tell her.

"You can't be anyone else but you. So, don't apologize for who you are, embrace it. Show the world your authentic self." At this point I'm wondering if she even knows what the word authentic means.

"Did Emmy Pea say all that too?" I ask.

"She did. The authentic line is her tagline," Bailey adds, her voice completely unamused. Perhaps she was given this advice from her sister once. By the sounds of it, she dismissed it.

I can't believe I've found myself in this mess. Here I am, crying to two preteens and trying to convince them to lock away their feelings while they're telling me to open up emotionally. I really need to reevaluate my life right now.

"Why?" Bailey asks, breaking my thoughtful silence.

I look up at her, sitting on the gray armchair on the other side of the wide coffee table between us.

"Why what?" I ask, rubbing the remaining tears from my eyes.

"Why were you fired? What happened in the meeting?" she says.

Oh god. Oh, please don't ask that question.

Because now all I can do is remember. . . .

❧

"What the actual . . . ?" I whisper. To myself.

Only I'm in a very, very small room. So, everyone can hear me.

"Is something wrong?" the woman in the red suit asks.

I look up from the tablet in front of me.

"No, no . . ." I say instinctively, because that's what you say when you're trying to be polite. And I'm still processing. Still. Processing.

"Well, we actually have you to thank," her colleague, Blue scrunchie, says to me happily. "It was all based on your idea to—"

Something catches in my throat.

"This was my idea?" My voice warbles as it interrupts her. I didn't mean for it to do that. Blue scrunchie smiles at me, all wide-eyed.

"It was your number-one recommendation on our strategy insights you sent: Expand in Online Polling. 'Platforms have increasingly pushed content of profiles that require active participation like Questions or Polls. Let the readers tell you what they want to read and learn from their answers.' And it's worked!"

She's reading out from my insight recommendations almost verbatim. I should know, because that's the most generic one I have. I use it for all my clients, before I even look to see what their social presence looks like.

"I didn't mean . . ." I look down again. There, in all its blue-lit glory, is the latest edition of Finder's Keepers Online; *the fashion magazine looking to expand out its offering from its female-skewing 40+, to those of the newest generations. I look at that photo again on the homepage, every inch of that image before me, and I feel the kind of red-hot anger that I haven't felt in years. I can't explain it, I can just feel it. Right down to my bones.*

But Red suit must not notice my face drain of all color. She must only see what she wants to see.

"You know, when Jackson recommended your team for this job, we were all a little skeptical at first. We don't like the idea of being led by data. We want to flow true to our editorial voice. Only, I can see now how right he was: by using your insights here, the traffic on our page tripled over the last week, and not just passive readership either. Clicks on the site have never been higher as everyone wants to weigh in!"

I shouldn't speak anymore. I should excuse myself and go. I can't be here anymore.

I did this? I think. I *did this?*

I have to leave before I break, because I can feel deep within me the barely mended bits of myself shattering shard by shard.

And I almost do. I push my chair back, ready to stand. But then she starts laughing. "And the figures are in: Ninety-five percent agree! She's an F!"

Her laugh continues. Then Blue scrunchie starts to laugh. Then the third client, the one in the green neckerchief, she starts laughing too. *They're looking. And they're laughing.*

And I'm staring at them with wide eyes, feeling a beast start to roar.

"F meaning . . ."

Blue scrunchie looks at me like not knowing that makes me a fool.

"Well, you know . . ." she says, looking around sheepishly like she can't say the whole word in a business meeting. And yet, they can hint it on a front cover.

"F meaning fuck?" I say, surprising myself by saying it. But I need a bit of clarity here.

"Exactly!" she says, relieved that I said it and not her.

They're all still laughing.

"And you think that's funny?" I ask them seriously. They all continue laughing.

"Well, at least it's better than them wanting to Kill her," Red suit laughs.

They all.

Keep.

Laughing.

And the lava inside me is too much to hold down anymore.

Nope. I can't walk away now. I can't just let that slide.

So, I blow.

"What the fuck are you thinking?" I ask, my whole face contorted in fury.

"Sorry?" the woman in the green neckerchief asks.

"Daisy?" Georgia, sweet Georgia, talented up-and-coming Georgia, sits next to me, her eyes desperately screaming at me to explain myself. But I can't explain myself. I'm angry. I'm furious. I'm angrier and more furious than I have literally ever been. And now I've begun, I just can't stop.

"Printing this shit as your cover story? Do you even know who this is?" I'm not just talking here. I'm shouting.

One of the women must mistake my pause to regain my breath as an actual question and she starts to tell me: "It's the lead singer of Minotaur—"

I ignore her, speaking over her in an ever-increasing volume and tempo.

"Can I seriously believe that this idea was spoken about in your editorial floor and not one of you questioned the underlying ethics?" I look at the women, waiting to see if they might interject. But they don't. They all look at me stunned, like I'm the crazy one.

"Right, OK then, here we go. You, Red suit." I scan down the list of options: "I'd Marry you. I mean, I wouldn't, but given my options . . ." I look at the others. "You, Blue scrunchie. You're a Fuck for sure. And you," I say, cocking my head and scanning the last girl. "Well, that leaves me with Kill for you."

I look around them, all of their faces dropped, staring back at me. Even "Marry" looks completely horrified, and that's the best of the list.

"Oh, I'm sorry. Was that really inappropriate of me to rate you like that to your faces? My bad. Because here I was, thinking that was completely acceptable, given you're asking your readers to rate these women in the exact same way behind their backs."

"That's not—" Red suit begins justifying. "'FMK' is the name of their song!"

"Well, their song sounds shit. It sounds like the kind of song that shouldn't be played, for the same reason this article should never have been run. Because it promotes misogyny. Putting women into 'fuck, kill, or marry' buckets? Is that all we're good for?"

"It's just a game," Red suit continues. "Don't take it so seriously."

"Playing it on a mass scale in a public forum? That's not a game.

That's a form of bullying. How do you think this woman is going to feel that your readers rated her only worthy of a fuck?"

"That's not on us," Blue scrunchie weighs in.

"You printed it!"

"Oh, come on. It's only a bit of fun," she tries again.

"It's not fun for this woman," I say, turning the screen around to their faces.

"She's in the public eye," Red suit says, her smile completely vanished as she refuses to look at the picture in my hand. They're trying to justify this. How are they trying to justify this?

"That doesn't matter! She's still likely to see this and she didn't ask us to rank her!"

"She's not going to read this," Red suit says dismissively.

"You can guarantee that if there's something out there that's horrible about someone, they'll see it. The worse it is, the more likely it is. Bad reviews are always the ones that stick. Horrible tweets are the only ones people remember."

Red suit shuts her lips, unsure. It looks like the laughter's cooled in here. The meeting room feels like the inside of an industrial freezer. I take a deep breath, trying to calm my voice.

"Social media can be a horrible place. And it's the power of brands like yours who should be trying to make it better. Only here you are, fucking it all up by amplifying hate. By turning your magazine—your really good magazine—into a trashy gossip column. Whose shitty idea was this?"

There is a long pause. One which only my heated breaths fill.

"Our CEO's," the woman in the red suit finally replies. I don't think I thought anyone would reply. Now they've said it, I feel the need to continue, but my voice has become softer now, slower. Like a runaway train slowing down on a final incline.

"Well, your CEO is a tool," I say, looking once more at the cover print before me. I take a few breaths, running my hands through my hair as if to wash out the outburst.

And then it hits me. What I've just said. Where I've just said it.

These are Jackson's clients. This is a work environment.

But there's nothing I can do now. Nothing at all.
Oh shit.

❧

"Nothing significant," I say quickly to both girls before me, brushing off the question.

Luckily for me, before my cheeks have the chance to give me away, a sound breaks the silence.

"Tasha, come on. Don't—" a very calm, very level voice calls.

The kitchen door is already open.

We might not be able to see it from where we are, hidden behind the only slightly ajar sitting-room door, but we can hear the clomp of heels as they power down the corridor from there. For one swift moment, we all see Tasha as she walks past the small opening. She doesn't turn her head to see us. Instead, she keeps on flying, opening the front door—

"Tasha, you don't need to—"

And with a little slam it closes behind her.

The echo makes Bailey and I look at one another. Cara doesn't seem to register. A few seconds after, the door to the sitting room is pushed open, and there—standing with a look of unbelievable bewilderment—is Archie.

The way his hair has fallen over his face, it looks like he's just returned from battle. Perhaps he just has. He's some chain mail away from Aragorn swinging open the doors in slow motion.

"Erm, hi," he says, now looking at the bizarre scene before him.

His elder daughter, perched in the armchair with a huge frown across her face. His younger daughter, her hand still holding the box of tissues I've been helping myself to.

And me. Sitting with both of his daughters, in his sitting room. A stranger. A stranger who introduced herself earlier as "not a murderer." Mascara clearly down my cheeks.

This doesn't look good.

Cara smiles, one of those award-winning, big toothy smiles.

"Can we keep her, Daddy?" she asks.

And the shock of it makes me laugh out loud.

Bailey laughs too. With me though. Which, in an ultimately strange set of circumstances, makes this man I barely know start laughing in the doorway as if that's exactly what he needed to hear. Shouldn't he be angry? Shouldn't he kick me out? Tell me I'm being wildly inappropriate and remove me from his life? But no, he's laughing.

Cara looks at all three of us, and a small little frown hits her forehead.

"What did I say?" she asks.

But Archie just puts a hand through his long hair to push it back in place and leans on the doorframe. He smiles at me with a "forgive me" kind of smile that I don't understand, because I clearly need him to forgive me. Not the other way around.

I stand, because I have clearly outstayed my welcome. Only when Archie opens his mouth, he doesn't ask me to leave.

"Do you drink tea?" he asks.

And even though I'm convinced I should go, for whatever reason, I just nod.

11

Archie leans on the edge of his kitchen island, his own tea on the counter beside him cooling down. I can see the peppermint label sticking out and over the edge of the perfectly Nordic handleless coffee mug. The kitchen, so much like the rest of the house, has a complete country cottage feel to it: a baby blue fridge stands by the door to the hallway, wooden countertops are on every surface, white Shaker cupboards line the back wall. On thick wooden shelves I see a cake mixer, pasta in clear jars of different sizes, a variety of different cookie jars. The colors of the backsplash and the far walls range from eggshell grays to the same dark blues found in the living room—although to see the wall behind is quite difficult given the number of paintings. Framed art. Stuck on art. Art drawn directly onto the wall.

It's like every room of this house has a different texture, a different feel. Each one homely and exotic and creative and personal and vibrant and calming all at once. I've never seen a home like it.

I sit on one of the wooden kitchen seats, cupping my mug in both hands. I've never had a handleless mug before. I'm not sure what the protocol is here, but I'm astounded that my hand hasn't burnt off already.

"So, I'm afraid there is no nanny job available," Archie says, his voice jam-packed with a genuine apology that I feel is more than completely misplaced.

"I did gather that, yes," I reply back, a little awkwardly. Except he doesn't look awkward. Not even slightly.

"I'm sorry for wasting your time here."

"To be fair, I just gave a pretty terrible interview in there, so I don't think I deserve the job if there was one going."

Archie laughs, folding his arms before him. That landed a lot better than my duck/duct tape gag of two weeks ago. I dare my own little smile to match.

The calm tone of his voice really helps me see past the bizarre set of circumstances that have landed us here, and that laugh alone helps my shoulders roll back, relaxed.

"Well, Cara likes you. That's something," he tells me.

"I'm sure Cara likes everyone. She's that kind of girl."

"God, no. She hates Tash."

I pull an awkward face, the full teeth-gritting emoji, before I realize that's probably very inappropriate.

"You wouldn't have guessed it looking at Tasha's Instagram," I remember.

"Oh?"

"There are so many photos of her."

"That doesn't mean she likes Tash, that means she likes having her picture taken."

He looks down at the ground, as if deep in thought, but the kind of thought you might meander about in for hours if you didn't have company. When he raises his chin back to my eye level, I see him take a deep breath and replace his soft smile carefully. Still, it proves something to me that I started to get a feeling of soon after I walked in the door.

"I take it she's not their mother?" I ask, although I don't know why. First of all, I have zero rights to any form of clarification here. I came for a job interview, not a life update. Second of all, I don't even know why I'm interested. Or why instead of just thanking him and leaving once I realized the error, I sat down at his lovely kitchen table and accepted a hot mint tea.

I whisper it too, which feels natural given the subject matter, but is probably unnecessary. The girls can't hear me, otherwise I'm sure he would have lowered his own voice earlier. They're upstairs, playing, and we can hear them from where we are below. Their footsteps set the floorboards above us creaking.

Plus, even if they could hear me, they clearly know Tasha's not their mother too.

"Tash is new to the whole 'kids' thing," he sighs. "She's not a natural. And the girls haven't exactly made things easy for her."

I think for a long minute, before my list is long enough to justify it: "*Parent Trap. Cinderella. Ever After.*"

He raises an eyebrow at me.

"What is . . . films with sisters?"

"No," I laugh, then realize, "well, yes, but they're all films where the kids hate their parent's new partners. It's a trope because it's a very real thing. These things take time."

It's his turn to pause now.

"Aren't those new partners like . . . evil? In all three cases?"

I pause, awkwardly.

"You've seen all those movies?"

"I have two girls. And a real love for Drew Barrymore."

"I don't blame you, she's . . . no. Not the point. And . . . maybe they are. But that's also not the point. The point is, it's just something that you work through. In most cases. Maybe not for . . . those three, though."

My words surprise even me, to be honest. I don't know this man nearly enough to share any form of an opinion with him, let alone joke about his problems. I don't know why I instantly became so familiar. A little part of me tenses at the idea that his kind eyes will turn hard. But they don't. They smile at me, like that's exactly what he needed to hear.

"She's the first woman I've ever introduced them to," he shrugs, "I don't know what I was hoping for. A miracle maybe."

"Miracles might take time." I shrug, hoping that might undo any words I said out of turn.

He doesn't seem to be the least bit perturbed though. He sighs, as if taking in my words and digesting them. He holds the bridge of his nose, as if fighting off a migraine before stretching out his neck in a full circle.

"She told me the story," he said, not hiding the pain behind his words. "Finding them in Sainsbury's alone. Finding you. You might have heard. I was furious."

"I think there was some . . . miscommunication there," I try, and I don't even know why I do. He looks up to where the floor-boards creak above them.

"I don't usually shout like that. It's just anything to do with my kids and it's like . . ." He looks around him for inspiration.

"A trigger is pulled?" I try.

"Exactly."

"I get it."

"You have kids?"

"God, no!" I almost laugh, and then realize quite how rude that is. Sheepishly, I swallow my words back. "My sister's my trigger."

He nods in understanding.

"It's family, I guess," and I nod in agreement. "Well, the girls are smart, but it's my job to be smarter and I failed them. I shouldn't have left them with her. I didn't need to. I've been solo now for six years and I've never needed the help. But she offered, and I thought it would be . . . I don't know. A bonding experience or something."

"Maybe she just needs more time with them?" I prompt.

He raises an eyebrow, just like Bailey did moments before. She is certainly her father's daughter.

"That's not happening. In her first few hours of being in charge, the girls leave the house without an adult, and she puts a notice out for a nanny."

A beat falls between us. I gulp.

"Yeah, I see how that looks," I say, unsure.

"Exactly," he replies.

A soft silence whispers through us both.

I don't like silences. I'm about to fill it when finally he shakes his head, one hand reaching out to the back of his neck for support. "I probably shouldn't be telling you about my girl problems."

"I'd say we're even," I say, before I can check myself. "I just accidentally told your girls about my boy problems."

I tense instantly, again, not sure what way that will go. There is no doubt that I too have been vastly inappropriate with his girls here. Maybe not "leaving them to walk solo in London" inappropriate, but still.

"Oh, I'm not surprised about that," Archie says, without even a hint of annoyance. If anything, he seems a little proud as he adds: "Those two can get anyone to confess to just about anything. I should have warned you."

I laugh at that, then sip my mint tea and feel a freshness take over every one of my senses. Archie finally picks up his own drink, walking over and sitting opposite me at the small wooden table.

"I'm so sorry though," he says, keeping my eye contact. "First I waste your time, now I'm oversharing. You're just . . . weirdly easy to talk to," he says, and just like that, he's put into words how I feel. Maybe it's just him though. He seems to have one of those warming personalities, the ones I've only seen on screens. The ones that give you instant comfort in his presence. "Maybe it's the nanny experience or something," he adds.

"Oh," I say, about to correct him, but he keeps going and I feel my mouth slam shut.

"You know when I saw you in that bar," he laughs to himself in memory, "I thought you were crying over some crappy, dime-a-dozen office gig. Finance, I guessed, or something equally boring. I should have known better—thirteen years with one family. I get it now. The bond you must have had with those kids. How hard it must feel when they don't need you anymore. I don't think I would have understood how hard that must be for you before I had the girls, but now . . . god. I can imagine the heartbreak. No wonder you needed a drink or two."

Ah, yes. I see how he was mistaken.

I swallow, hard enough that he notices. Hard enough that he clearly has realized something's amiss.

"You don't actually work in finance, do you?" he asks.

I shake my head.

"Oh thank god," he laughs nervously. "I thought this was going to be just like our encounter at Sallie's but with our roles reversed."

"I'm a data analyst," I say quickly—knowing if I don't say it now, I probably never will. His face drains of color as mine fills with it. Bright red. Cheeks burning in shame.

"I should have seen that coming."

He rubs the back of his neck again, toying with his tea as he leans forward.

"So, you're not a nanny?" He winces, those green, emerald eyes peeling up to me. I swallow.

"I am not," I reply, beyond embarrassed.

"And yet you turned up at my door for a nanny job?" he confirms, cocking his head to the side. I swallow again.

"I did."

He should be absolutely furious by this point. He should be telling me to get out of his home. He let me in on the premise I was someone with, probably, a full police check under my belt, and I'm guessing my little online diploma on SQL proficiency isn't too good a substitute.

I didn't even think about the implications of this.

I didn't even think of the unequivocal trust some jobs have and how I've completely misused that.

"Do I need to ask the question here?" he asks, and somehow, somehow, he's still smiling. I gulp down whatever I'm feeling.

"I'm so sorry. So, so, so sorry. I'm just *really* bad at unemployment. And the day I met your girls, well, they made me forget about it. And I thought, why not? At least interview. It wasn't like

I thought I was a good candidate for it, I mean—look at my CV!"
I fish it out of my bag, pushing it across the table to prove a point.
"I don't know why I thought my analytics experience would help
me here. I just thought—I needed to have one interview. One. And
that sign was still in Sainsbury's, and I kept finding myself staring
at it and thinking about it and finally, well, I'm here." I take a deep,
incredibly regretful breath. "I didn't mean to lie to you," I conclude.

I see his chest rise and fall as he picks up my CV, scanning it
over.

"You never lied," he says, "if anything you came with proof
you had no experience. 'Senior Data Analyst,'" he reads. "Thirteen
years. You didn't lie there either."

He puts my CV on the table, satisfied.

"I should have called first." I wince.

"Maybe," he says. "Was my address just out there? In Sainsbury's?"

Oh gosh. Another thing to own up to.

"No, no. Cara told me. And your yellow door is all over Tasha's
Instagram. I only found her because the girls used my Instagram
to get in touch with her—I didn't just, stalk her out of the blue or
anything. I thought maybe if I called, you might not even interview
me and . . . In hindsight I should have called."

He doesn't correct me, but his face does frown, deep in thought.

"Can I see? Tash's Instagram? I don't have the app."

I've done enough wrong here to do something right. So, I click
on my phone, instinctively heading to Instagram and seconds later
I'm on her profile. I hand it over.

While he starts to scroll, I respectfully look away, instead turning my attention to the artwork on the walls around me. There
are some absolute classics here. There's one of two girls—his girls
probably but they're both facing away, jumping in the air above
an exceedingly large muddy puddle. The whole thing's incredible.
The still moment before you know everyone will be smothered in
muddy raindrops. The hold your breath moment. It brings an instant smile to my lips.

"You're pretty exceptional," I say, then blink with my own wide eyes as I hear my voice echo back in my ears. *Think before you speak, Daisy*, I whisper to myself frantically, but I don't know why I do. If I haven't done it for the last thirty-one years, I don't know why I'd begin now. "At art," I clarify. Because that is what I meant. Mostly. "This place is wild."

Archie leans back in his chair, lifting his eyes from my phone to see what I'm seeing.

"Believe it or not, this place used to be pretty respectable until the girls were born. The first time they used crayon on the wall I was about to paint right over it, before I realized that's just showing their creativity. This is as much my house to decorate as it is theirs." His neck twists back toward the jungle corridor. "Maybe it's become a little out of hand now, but I prefer it that way."

"The whole house is your canvas," I say in awe.

"*Our* canvas," he corrects, pointing at one of the more abstracts in the collection. There's so much to see I didn't even notice the variety of quality around.

"Cara?"

"Bailey actually. Cara doesn't have the patience for painting."

I think about the ballpoint pen flowers I saw on Bailey's hands. That doesn't surprise me.

"I know that it was your painting in Sallie's," I admit.

"It's no Franken-duck, but I try," Archie muses, a coy smile on his lips as he turns his eyes back down to my phone. But I can't help it. I'm not great with silence. So, despite knowing that he's busy, I open my mouth once again.

"So, is that what you are then?" I ask, "An artist?"

He clicks the phone off and I feel a bit bad.

"Do you define everyone by what they do? Or just me?" he asks.

And it's a good question. Because I didn't even notice that's what I was doing.

"I'm sorry, I—"

"I think I'm about to define you by the number of apologies you make," he chuckles.

"I have a lot to apologize for."

"Not to me. Thanks for that," he nods at my phone, still cupped in his large hands. "Can anyone just see those photos?"

"Yeah. It's a public profile," I say. He goes quiet, and it doesn't take a genius to work out why. He must not have realized that pictures of his daughters are on the internet. I assume by the look on his face, it's without permission.

Without saying anymore on the subject, he hands my phone back. I don't want to press. I feel like I've personally got Tasha into a lot of trouble today, and I didn't mean to.

"Are you anti–social media then?" I ask, thinking about Mia's ex. Maybe he's another one who is "off the grid" for a reason.

"I don't know what I think of it. I've got about a dozen odd jobs and two girls. I don't have the time or the inclination to start it."

"Well, socials are really great at growing out businesses like yours."

"They are?" Archie looks skeptical.

"When done well, they are. And I've worked in and around social media for over a decade so I'm not just saying that—see? My CV's right there, to prove it," I laugh as I point to the document that still lies between us. He smiles, barely checking it. Then a thought springs to mind: "I could help you, if you wanted. Get you up and running with some content to see whether it's worth your while. It's literally the least I could do after all the mess I've caused you today."

"You've not caused any mess," he says quickly.

"I beg to differ," I say, thinking about the argument he had in this very kitchen less than an hour ago.

Archie laughs, in a world-weary way.

"You didn't cause mess. You showed me where the mess was. There's a difference."

Oh god. I really hope by that he doesn't mean I've ruined things for him. He seems so wonderful. And kind. The idea that I've hurt him somehow—

"Well, no need to answer me now," I say, trying to turn the conversation back as I take my final sip of tea. "You keep that CV. It has all my contact details on it. If you ever change your mind, you just give me a call on that number. But for now, I think I should leave you to enjoy your evening."

I stand quickly, moving my mug around the island and over to the sink out of politeness. Archie keeps his in his hand as he follows me back out through the jungle corridor right to the yellow door. I notice new details this time: a slightly more basic bird, perched next to a beautifully ornate one; as if a child was imitating the image beside them. A more cartoon fox face hidden by a realistic one. It's heartwarming, really.

As the door opens, I feel the wind's picked up outside. The sun's out though, peeking through the clouds, and, I don't know. I feel, despite having a train wreck of an interview, that I'm in a much better place now than I was before.

Maybe his eyes are magic. Who knows.

As I walk out, I turn to say my goodbyes.

"I'm Daisy, by the way," I add quickly.

"I know," he replies.

"You know?"

"It was on your CV."

Ah, yes. Of course, it was.

"And I'm Archie," he adds.

"I know."

"You know?"

"It was under your work at Sallie's."

So, names finally conquered, there really is nothing left to say. Only, in a classic Daisy Peterson move, I somehow feel the need to speak again.

"Six years of solo parenting," I say, for the words kept lingering in my mind since he said them. "Your girls are . . . unlike any other kids I've met before. You must be pretty great at everything you do."

That was supposed to sound a little less sycophantic than it came out. Luckily it looks like he's not overthinking it the same way I am.

"That's very sweet of you to say, but clearly a terrible lie," he replies dismissively. "I just blew my lid back there in front of them."

"You were fighting because you love them. When there was fighting in my house, it wasn't out of love, I'll tell you that."

Well, that was a bit more revealing than I was hoping it to be. I never expected any talk today to be any deeper than my soft skills, and yet here I am looking at the face of a man who seems genuinely touched by words I genuinely mean.

"I'm sorry about your job, too. You're going to be alright?" he asks, and it seems like a sincere question.

I smile, because I can hear Cara screaming "DEFLECT" upstairs, and it instantly puts a spring in my step. Archie's head flicks round at the noise too, and I see the flicks of blue paint smudged into the back of his right ear. I wonder if that's an occupational hazard.

"You know, your girls have given me some inspiration," I tell him as his head turns back to me, and then before I take up any more of this wonderful man's time, I wave goodbye and start my journey home.

12

When I walk back into my flat, something exciting is fired up inside me. I can feel the energy pulsating from the tips of my fingers, my mind already whirring with fresh possibilities.

"Show the world your authentic self."

It made me think of how Layla saw me in Sainsbury's. That's the image she'll now have of me forever. It's the one she'll have been telling everyone else about this morning. I can picture her so vividly, leaning against those silver coffee machines and whispering in that pervasive nasal tone she has when gossip is truly ripe that I was a grade A mess.

Can one pajama encounter seriously be enough to ruin thirteen years of hard graft? It's been just under a month. Maybe that's enough time to forget how many all-nighters I pulled, toying with correlation graphs to see if any of our clients' products had overlapping audiences.

Thirteen years.

Wasted in one badly timed pizza collection.

Plus, half of the people on my networking list follow me. It's the polite thing to do in an industry centered around social media. How do I stand out as someone they want to make a role for if I'm hidden in the internet shadows?

And lastly, what about Jackson? What if Layla's sighting reached his ears?

Jackson: who has never had a bad hair day in his life. Who wears hangovers the same way most people wear Armani suits. Who makes sickness look like peak fitness, probably. I don't know. Maybe he's too pretty to even get sick.

How did he ever like me? I won the lottery. I had the golden ticket, in my hand, calling my name. And with one little outburst, I just threw it all away.

But something just stirred within me. Something that tells me that I can turn this all around. I know I can.

I need to be noticeable enough not to fall into the anonymous CV piles, and on the Jackson front, I got him sliding into my DMs the first time, who says I can't do it again?

I can't change the past, but I can turn this ship around. I won't have pizza-gate be the last image they all have of me. I'll have an actual image of me be that image. I'll show them I'm living my best life. I mean, I'm not, but that's what I'll show them.

I need a bit of that Cara spirit in me.

So, there we are. My plan.

Show the world my authentic self.

The authentic self I want to show them at least. And in this day and age, there's only one way to do that: Instagram.

The fact it takes me two hours to follow a "quick" thirty-minute makeup tutorial feels a bit like a false start, but it also doesn't kill my vibe. So, I'm not a natural like Mia; I wasn't a natural data analyst either. But I put in the hours, and I taught myself everything I know. If I can do it with SQL, I can do it with contouring.

Finally feeling fresh and photo-ready, I walk from my bathroom to my bedroom. This is where I took most of the photos last time, so it makes sense for this to be my studio today too.

Plus, the rest of my place is a mess right now, and this is the easiest to clean, I reckon. The bed is made. I haven't changed my sheets for a good, long while, but that's not a problem for now. That can be hidden in a blur.

I have four glasses on my side of the bed, on the singular bedside table I own, next to two stacked bowls and a mug. But again—an easy fix. One trip with them all to the kitchen counter and there's a future mess for me to clean, but one that's completely out of shot.

The floor—well, once I've moved the shoes that I pile up in the corners and the clothes from a few days past and the three sets of pajamas that . . . actually, best to avoid showing the floor maybe. I'm sure a good angle will do that. Still, I take away the main offenders and throw them into the corner of the kitchen/living room, where they can stay until the photoshoot is over.

I turn to my ugly old wooden closet.

This ancient Shaker-styled beast was here before I was, and when the previous tenants offered to leave it, I couldn't believe my luck. I had a built-in wardrobe in my flatshare with Betzy, so I didn't already own anything for my clothes. Turns out, closets are expensive, so I thought them offering to leave it was the fates rewarding me for doing such an adult thing like living alone. Only it became pretty apparent why it remained behind.

The old oak relic weighed a ton, didn't fit properly, and smelt like something had rotted inside of it. It took me hours of googling and multiple bottles of air freshener to remedy the situation into a livable condition.

But now, the old, only slightly smelly wardrobe is a staple in my room, and although it cannot open fully because of the bed, nor close completely because of the amount of clothes I own, I have a strange fondness for it.

I clamber up onto my bed to get the best angle of attack, opening the doors as wide as they go (which isn't that wide), and pull out a few items at random. I hold them up to see. Pastel blue jumper. No, not right. I chuck that on the floor and try again. Pastel pink dress. Too cute. I don't want cute. So, that gets thrown. Subtle cream T-shirt. Oh god, this is going to be a long day.

I speed up exponentially, my wardrobe becoming a floor-drobe at lightning speed while still nothing suitable comes to hand. Ordinarily, I'm a rainbow of pastels. Only pastels don't scream "living my best life." They very calmly whisper "living a quite nice life, thank you." So, I reach my arm farther into Narnia, pulling out whatever I can get my hands on.

What helps, of course, is that the whole thing is full to bursting. I just find it so hard to throw things out, so I have over a decade's worth of clothes built up in this mess. I've almost done runs to the charity shop in the past, but it's hard to know where to start—and given I haven't had the time, I've always justified my undoubtedly unjustifiable collection.

With a giant heave (and an awkward shuffle around the half-open doors) I transfer the contents of the beast to my bed. Now I can see it all, I'm sure to find something.

The whole weekend I spend pairing outfits, trying them on in front of the mirror and taking a picture or two, before deciding they're not quite right. Nothing feels profile-worthy. They're not eye-catching enough to stop a scroller, and although the weekend ends with a camera roll stuffed with selfies of various kinds, nothing feels worth posting.

I'm just a forgettable person in a forgettable color palette. That's a sad truth to come to terms with, and with that thought circling my mind, I finally call it quits on Sunday night.

On Monday though, I wake up with fresh determination.

It's the start of a new week here. Yesterday I went from Cara energy to my energy, and I'm not going to let that happen again. I *will* find something that works. I *will* take a killer picture. By the end of the day, I *will* post. Just watch me.

So, my floor-drobe is upturned and re-scattered until, like hidden treasure sparkling at the bottom of a pastel ocean, a dress sparkles through the chaos.

I forgot I owned this. It's not even close to anything else I own. It's a shimmering gold mine of sequins, buried deep in time.

I bought it with my first ever paycheck, ages ago. It was my first "on a whim" purchase. Still to this day, I think and overthink before

I buy things, trying to do some mental calculation of how much I think it's worth per use versus how much I'm going to use it before I hand over my card. But not this one. This one I just bought, that very first payday.

That was over a decade now. I wonder if it even still fits?

I mean, I was in Mia's clothes last time, and none of them fit. I don't need to do it up, I just need to make it look like I've done it up. And having exhausted the rest of my clothes, it's this or it's this. So, it's this.

After about ten minutes of tugging and thrusting and scrambling around my back at the zipper, it's on me. There!

Oh my. I walk up to my full-length mirror and take in my sparkly reflection. I mean, it's tight, for sure it's tight, I can barely breathe, but it's on.

And just like that, a tidal wave of nostalgia hits me. Almost thirteen years ago I wore this dress for the first time. As I sashay left and right, I try to remember how I must have felt. Sure, I'd worked bar jobs since I was sixteen but that was never what I loved doing. And that first day at Branded—wow. It felt like I'd found my calling. The energy was unreal. People walked with purpose, spoke with fire, had money in their pockets that they'd earned, all by themselves. It was everything I wanted and more. It was my dream job. And I had it.

I *had* it.

Oh gosh. Past tense.

Suddenly I can't breathe. This dress is too tight. I need it off me, and I need it off now. Without undoing the zip I try to yank it right over my head, which works at first. Only it stops working right at the point where the bit around my waist gets stuck getting over my quote-unquote "nice handful" breasts (Mia—multiple times through our lives).

Oh, please no. Suddenly my arms are flailing in the air, trapped, and although my pink-boxered bottom is officially exposed to the elements, everything from waist up is tangled in a shimmering nightmare.

Oh hell. What did I do that for?

I try to shuffle it back down to take it off properly, but to my absolute horror, I can't with my arms still stuck above my head. I can't even see what I'm doing—I have a strange, angled view when I bend over looking through the neck hole, but trapped in this human-size glitter slinky I can only look at one thing at a time. I try to squat, thinking perhaps that the action might shift the dress up a little more, but I stumble instantly. My floor-drobe has become my own personal booby trap. It sends my whole body off-kilter until with one gigantic thud, I'm on the floor, face down, defeated.

I lie there for some time, wondering how on earth I can move forward from this. What am I going to do? I shift from side to side, trying to assess if this fall might have helped at all in the removal process, but all it did was wind on me and make it so much harder to sit up again.

"URGH!" I scream in frustration, to no one. Because if someone were here, I wouldn't have been in this predicament to begin with.

God, I miss Betzy. I miss Betzy so, so much.

And Mia. If she were here, if we were speaking, we'd just laugh our way through this.

But solo, this isn't funny. This just hurts, in every way possible.

After a few tense minutes, I lose all the energy I have. I stop, lying there, catching my breath with my arms still very much stuck over my head.

So, there we are then. My final resting place.

I can see the gravestone now: Here lies Daisy. Found with her bum out and trapped in the starry past. Forever alone.

No wonder Jackson ended things with me. He probably saw right through the woman I tried so hard to show him I was. He probably saw this. The real deal. The horror show. And why would he want that in his picture-perfect life?

Just as my fear starts to creep in, I hear my phone ring.

Just what I need. Who might be calling me right now anyway? I look up, and to my surprise, I can actually see the edge of my phone from my dress neck's telescopic view. I shuffle, snakelike, across my

Ikea rug on my floor. This is a good mode of transport, I think, as I push my legs down and scuttle forward ungracefully. I can make this work.

I get close enough to it, and with a feat of core body strength that I wouldn't normally give myself credit for, I lift myself up to an angle where I can briefly see the screen.

Chris, the lit screen says.

Oh my, it's Chris! Chris is calling me! A wave of excitement and shock courses through me in an instant. This must be about a job—maybe there's a vacancy? I have to get this call.

I have to.

Determination rips through me, and with it, my dress. In a She-Hulk move that I will never be able to replicate, I pull my arms down with a small, animalistic scream that heats up my throat in a way that leaves it raw. I hear the dress split before I even feel it, but with a thousand sequins suddenly flying out in all directions, the seams fragment down both sides. I keep going, barely breathing now as I pull what I can and tear the rest until, like a beautiful butterfly emerging from a Zara fashion cocoon circa 2015, I break free of my mold.

The phone stops ringing, if only for a second, and in a state of absolute panic I lurch forward just to see it start ringing again.

"Hello, hello?" I say, breathless, swiping it quickly to answer. I can't immediately hear him, so I back the phone away from me, trying to see the screen, checking I hit answer in time. I feel my bra strap fall down, but that doesn't matter. It's not like he can see me.

And then I realize; they can see me. They can see all of me.

Because I didn't just answer a "call" call. It's a video call. And I'm pretty much naked over here.

Oh, and it's not actually Chris.

13

"Mia?!" I say, completely confused as her big eyes blink up at me.

"Well, hello, Sexy," Mia laughs, taking me all in. "Don't you know how to make a gal feel special."

"I didn't see it was you," I reply back quickly, instantly annoyed. It takes me a while to even pinpoint why exactly, but as the fog of the last few minutes lifts me back into reality and my sister's face is still staring back at me, it hits me.

Because sure, this is not how I'd ordinarily answer the phone, but here she is acting immediately like nothing's happened. Like we didn't have a fight. Like it hasn't been almost two months since we last spoke.

"Give me a minute," I tell her. I put the phone down with the video facing the ceiling on the edge of my bed, reaching out for a blue jumper I find on the floor and throwing it over me while a sigh involuntarily departs my lips.

Before I pick the phone back up so she can see me too, I look back at the clothes piles all around me. Should I hang up? Tell her to call me back another time? Tell her I'm not ready to talk?

No. I've been putting this off for too long now. It's not like I don't have the time. Plus, I hate fighting with Mia. Even when I'm right. So, I take a deep breath, and lift the phone back up to see her.

She looks good. Her hair's been curled, professionally I'd guess by how perfect it is. It looks straight out of an American TV show, the highlights so light and airy they almost make the unnatural look natural. Her makeup is colorful, bright blue eyeliner, vibrant lime-green shadow, tastefully blended in and thick eyelashes to pull it all together. She's wearing a block red jumper and looking just like her normal self again.

"Hi, Mia," I start again, determined not to get angry.

"You didn't know it was me and you answered in your under-wear?" She smiles cheekily. "Kinky, Dais. This part of a new side hustle or something?"

I must not get angry. But if I give an answer to that I will, so I hold my tongue, staring at her face wherever she may be, waiting for her to answer me.

Finally, she gets the hint to move on. She flashes me her pearly whites, blinking like a cartoon character as she quickly says: "Surprise!"

I must not get angry. I must not get angry.

But I can't help it. I'm getting, just a little, angry.

"Oh, so now you're ready to stop fighting?" I ask her in a measured, level tone. My face is completely free from her careless happiness.

"We're fighting?" she asks, her pretty face suddenly frowning.

I feel my blood begin to boil, my ears starting to steam. No, I'm not having this. I'm just not.

"Mia," I begin through gritted teeth, but she's already laughing on the other end of the phone.

"Only joking," she adds quickly with an innocent smile. "I know, I know. Calm down," she says, like that's actually going to work. She continues before I can even get a word in: "I just called to tell you," she takes a deep breath, like she's readying herself for a big, grand gesture. I, for one, can't wait to see what she has in store: "that I forgive you."

That catches me off guard.

In a stunned silence, I walk out of my bedroom. I'm careful to angle the phone in a way that Mount Daisy (my newly named pile of clothes) is entirely hidden from view as I make my journey to my love seat. I sit down, cross-legged in the hope that if I hold myself together physically, I might just hold myself together emotionally too.

I wait, in case she's going to elaborate or expand on this view, except she doesn't. Not even slightly.

"*You* forgive *me*?" I ask her slowly, making sure I understand her correctly. She nods, as if this big misunderstanding has completely resolved itself.

"Exactly. Now, why don't you ask me what I've been up to all this time?"

But I ignore that last bit, because she still hasn't worked out the issue.

"*You* forgive *me*?" I repeat. "Mia, it's *me* that has to forgive *you* here."

She looks genuinely confused. A sweet, highly glamorous doe in headlights.

"What for?" she asks.

"Are you serious?" I cry out. "Take a wild guess!"

She shrugs, making me physically shake in anger. I can't help it now. I'm full on, red-faced, arms-tensed, angry. I'm fuming.

"This game is boring," Mia says dismissively, "just forgive me and let's move on."

"It's not that easy!" I cry.

"It can be," Mia says, coolly and calmly, like none of this matters. "Look, they say when someone is disproportionately angry with you, it probably has nothing to do with you at all."

Oh, come on.

"URGH! MIA! This has EVERYTHING to do with you," I correct.

"Then I'm sorry," Mia says swiftly, smiling like this is the conclusion she was leading to. "Well, I've forgiven you, so you can forgive me, and we can move on. I'm bored of us not speaking."

I don't even know what to say to that. I simply don't have words. So, I say nothing. Not that Mia notices. She's already off on one, moving the conversation on regardless: "Besides," she says, "I'm doing better now, thanks for asking. I'm seeing someone new."

"Oh, are you," I say cynically.

"Don't make any assumptions," Mia says, clearly not understanding my feelings. "You know if you actually met him, you'd really like him."

"I don't need to meet him."

"He's not like the others."

"That's what you said about the others."

"He's not," she insists.

I screw up my face, biting down on my bottom lip.

"Let me guess," I begin, "he's an oh-so-talented musician just launching his career . . ." There's an angry pause on the line, of me being 100 percent correct, and her being 100 percent annoyed about it. "I knew it," I say, once her face confirms it all.

Slowly I watch as her soft face distorts in real time. Finally, she's matched my fury. Finally, I feel like we're on the same level playing field.

"There you are again! You're making assumptions!" she starts shouting, and I feel myself start to smile. "I'm sorry we can't all have handsome businessmen like your man—"

Jackson. She's talking about Jackson, and immediately I feel a swell of tears about to break through. I can't cry about Jackson, not to Mia and definitely not right now. I've only just got the upper hand here, I can't lose it by telling her what's happened to me. But I can feel them about to push through and I don't think I have it in me to stop them. So, I speak as quickly as I dare, stopping my voice from breaking.

"Now is not the time, Mia," I tell her, "I don't forgive you. I'll see you in, say, three more months once he's ended things with you and you're back on my doorstep begging for even more money."

And with that final word, I hit the big red phone and watch my sister's face disappear from sight.

* * *

I'm shaking. Beyond annoyed. In what world does that girl live in where it is her who has to forgive me? Classic Mia. Shifting the blame to someone else. Well, she's to blame for more than she'll ever know.

I mean, sure, if I wasn't unemployed, and if I wasn't broken up with, and if I hadn't just been trapped in a sequin prison, then maybe I wouldn't have been *quite* so angry with her. But like . . . that's not the point.

I need a distraction from my frustration. So, I go on Instagram, hoping to lose my feelings in a stream of strangers' reels, only to remember I still haven't posted anything.

I will not let today be a total failure. I can't. I need something better than a selfie of me in basic pastel day clothes to post.

So, in a feat of determination, I head over to my bedroom, and acting like a human forklift, I shovel a load of clothes from the pile into my arms and rush it out of the bedroom. I chuck it on the floor of the living room, close to the edge of the sofa. I don't have time to do this neatly. So, back and forth I go, grabbing clothes from the bedroom, and dropping them into the living room, until slowly the mountain turns into a molehill turns into a savannah.

Then I make the bed, pulling the edges taut so the sheets looks fresh. I close my now-empty wardrobe doors, brush the crumbs of my toast from the bedside table onto the floor, and run the newest mug on my bedside table back to the kitchen work surfaces. I close the curtains, switch on the lamps, and make sure I have a beautiful cozy "hygge" vibe to the whole room.

Then I redo my makeup—dialing up my eyes—and grab a pastel pink jacket. If a going-out dress isn't going to work for me this time, maybe my smartest work clothes will. On go black jeans and a tight, white, strappy top and I may not look sexy or fun, but my god I look professional.

Then I switch on portrait mode, hit the timer and sprint back far enough to not notice the flaws in my eye makeup (I still need more practice in blending shadow for close-ups). In a last-minute dash before the ten seconds are up, I grab my laptop from my pillow and hold it loosely under my arm. I just have enough time to look away from the camera in a determined power pose before the click sounds and the moment is frozen in time.

I look like I mean business alright. Sure, it's obviously a bedroom in the blurred-out background, but that just makes me look real. This is the exact opposite image of the one Layla saw; I'm clean, focused, and driven. It's not perfect, but right now it's exactly what I need.

Plus, I can't be bothered to do another one. This one will have to do.

"Wish me luck x" I caption. That's mysterious enough. Maybe Layla will think that interview I fabricated was today. And before I can second-guess myself, I post it.

At least I've shown the world a little of my inauthentic authentic self.

Then I walk out of my warm, beautifully tidy room and into my living room. The overhead lights still blare out over the car crash of clothes that now litter every bit of floor space. Knickers cover the coffee table, socks on the sofa. I push whatever is blocking my way aside until I have a corridor free from clothes to walk through, leading me straight to the small bit of sofa I left for myself, item free. I shuffle off my jacket, undo my top pants' button and flop down into it, my phone at hand. The place looks terrible, but I have no energy left in me to do anything about it.

A thought suddenly hits me. I missed a call from Chris back before the whole Mia saga—he must be the voicemail! I click on it, placing it on loudspeaker as the nerves run through me.

"One new message," the automated woman reads. "Message one."

And there is Chris's voice, massaging my ears.

"Hi, Daisy, it's Chris here. I just wanted to let you know that I talked to HR personally, and it looks like we're under a hiring freeze at the moment. So, it doesn't look like we'll have any vacancies in the near future. Just wanted to pass the message on to you. Hope you've found something already and best wishes."

Oh fudgesticks.

Account	Category
@ForestCo	Client
@BlocksAndClocks	Client
@LaVie	Client
@HealthComesFirst	Food
@ChelseaFC	Sports
@HeavensKitchen	Food
. . .	. . .

I sit back, looking at my work, thinking.

I came to the conclusion late last night that posting a random picture of myself in a suit jacket isn't going to change anyone's opinion of me. I'm a planner. I excel at Excel, so if I'm going to turn this ship around and get noticed by anyone, I need to do it my way.

And by "anyone," I more specifically mean Jackson.

So, with a little click I create a pivot table, watching my hard work pay off instantly.

Category	Accounts Count
Client	160
Public Figure	72

Sports	59
Travel	27
Cooking	14
Baking	3
Home Renovation	1

There we have it: his interests summarized.

I sit back, gnawing at the edge of my lips.

This is creepy. I know it's creepy. It's not like I spent hours on it. I didn't go full on and use a web scraper or anything. I just pulled out a few accounts that interested me into a spreadsheet and it turned to . . . this.

I just need some inspiration here. I need to know what posts are most likely to get his attention. That's all I'm doing, I justify to myself.

Plus, really, this wasn't my idea at all.

I would never have thought to check this. Ever.

This was all Mia.

✎

"OK, so what does Jackson actually like?" Mia asked, after an hour of shooting me all around my flat.

I grab a Pringle from the tube she's holding, leaning back against the kitchen counter.

"Work," I say between crunches. "He likes work."

"Work's boring."

"Not everyone finds work—"

"What else?" she interrupts me, rolling her eyes at the lecture I was about to give. She grabs my phone from the counter and unlocks it.

I take a deep breath, helping myself to another Pringle and letting the salt and vinegar flavoring burn deliciously onto my tongue.

"Working out?" I try. "He's always got a gym bag."

"He supports Chelsea," Mia says, clearly ignoring me. I think I knew that. That picture of him outside the stadium he's wearing the blue and white–striped scarf. I'm pretty sure I've also heard him chatting scores with Matthew on one or two occasions.

"*But I'm not big on sports.*" I munch.

"*He likes cooking.*"

"*How do you know that?*" I ask.

He hasn't ever posted about cooking. Mia's ignoring me, scrolling away. Has he posted again, more recently maybe? So, I move away from my edge of the kitchen counter to see what she's up to.

"*What is this list?*" I ask her, frowning. I look through the handles she's moving through. I don't recognize many of them. Actually, I know that one. @EddiePartridge is someone who works at Everest. I don't remember following him though.

"*It's who Jackson follows.*"

"*Mia!*" I cry out, gasping. "*You're looking through who he follows?!*"

"*Of course,*" she says calmly. "*Best way to find out what kinds of things people like.*"

"*That's . . .*" I begin, but I don't know how to articulate it. I step back, not wanting to be associated with this, even if no one can see us inside my flat. "*A breach of privacy!*"

"*It's there for me to see.*"

"*That doesn't mean you should see it!*"

"*Jesus, for someone who claims to know a lot about Instagram you don't know much at all, do you?*" She smiles, before looking back down at the list. "*Everyone does this. Plus, this list is so dull. Boring. Boring,*" she murmurs, flicking through. "*Although a lot of these girls are gorgeous . . .*" she comments, clicking on one of the profiles.

It's a private one. So, she hits the back button and continues scrolling down the list. Annoyed, but just a little intrigued, I lean back over her shoulder. Just to see what she means.

"*A lot of them are people we work with,*" I say, seeing the names I recognize.

"*Better than following random girls, I guess.*" She shrugs. "*But is it like an episode of* Grey's Anatomy *or something in your office? Because all these girls are smoking.*"

"*Some of them are just good filters,*" I say, thoughtlessly, but Mia looks up, her eyes sizzling in delight.

"*Oooo, burn, Dais!*"

"I didn't mean it like that!" I say quickly, but for Mia, that means nothing.

"God, I miss Instagram sometimes," she laughs, clicking on a handle I don't recognize.

"You can always get back on it," I say.

"Freddie would hate that," she sighs.

Ah yes, Freddie. Her latest rock star boyfriend. The "off grid" one. Once again, we have Mia changing who she is just to fit in with a guy. It's so disappointing.

I'm about to start telling her this when I hear her excitement rise.

"Well, this is something. Maybe. This cooking thing's an actual thing. He follows a fair amount of food bloggers."

"How can you tell?" I say, looking back over her shoulder.

"Because their names are terrible puns."

I read them myself

@HealthMatt_ers (Matt Yeoman)

@BroccoliAndBanter (Ben Smithy)

I have to agree.

"So, let's do a few posts from this kitchen," she concludes, putting my phone down and looking around us to the kitchen counter.

"What?" I laugh.

"He likes cooking. Let's show him you cook."

"I don't cook."

"Well, he doesn't know that."

"That's . . ." I stutter, "a bit manipulative, isn't it?"

"No," she corrects pointedly. "It's very manipulative. But we've also just taken about fifteen pictures of you getting ready for things you're not going to. So, what's the difference of taking a few more of meals you're not actually preparing?"

I bite my lip. I don't know. It feels like there is a difference.

And yet this is what I do for a living. I mean, not this personal. Definitely not. I don't stalk users. But I do try and find trends between what users like to show brands how to reach their target audience. . . .

"Isn't it things like this that made you delete Instagram?" I ask her, so unsure where the line is now.

She shrugs, holding the phone out in her hand.
"So, you want to take these? Or what?"

～

Looking through the list, there's not much I can do about the public figures or the clients. Sports?

Well, I'm just not sporty. I guess I could go to the gym, but that would mean getting a gym membership, which I'm clearly not going to use. So, not sports. Travel? Well, I've never really gone traveling before. Plus, it requires a pretty huge dedication to go for one post.

I turn to the next on the list: cooking.

I did it before, I reason. I can do it again.

I do my research, looking through hashtags, watching Reel after Reel. One home-cooked dish catches my attention: "Quick and easy salmon teriyaki," reads the caption. Well, that sounds lovely. So, I watch it, and it's quick alright.

Chunks of salmon, marinated. Then bubbling over the heat. A hand pops in and out of the bird's-eye shot, stirring the concoction and adding herbs and spices. Vegetables chopped, drizzled with oil, and thrown into the oven. Rice is seasoned. Less than thirty seconds of ingredients mixing and simmering later and out comes a delicious-looking dish.

That doesn't look complicated. Not at all.

And the outcome, after what looks like an almost carelessly easy amount of cooking, looks uber professional.

I'm usually someone who buys things I can put straight into the microwave. I own kitchen things, sure, but that's really only because I've lived with Betzy, who loves cooking. When she moved out, her kitchenware didn't make the cut of "items being moved to Alaska" with her, so by proxy I inherited them. Now I own an assortment of pots and pans, an electric whisk, two baking trays, and a cake tin. It may not be a lot, but it's always been far more than I've ever actually needed. The cake tin for example—I think I used it once to catch water from a leaky sink before the landlord could fix it, but that has, to date, been its sole use in my custody.

But Jackson likes cooking reels. He likes cooking bloggers.

It's the kind of thing he would notice.

So, trying not to overthink how creepy this is, that's exactly what I'm going to do. I'm going to cook. And I'm going to tell Instagram all about it.

It takes me rewatching the video four or five times to screen grab all of the ingredients, and once I have them all I head over to my trusty Sainsbury's. By the time I'm back home, I'm so geared up for cooking I jump on the spot like a boxer prefight.

I start easy: I film myself shaking the rice before the camera.

Step 1 complete.

Step 2: "Preheat the oven to 180 degrees."

Done. Simple. A quick film of my hand spinning the dial around. Completed it, mate. On to the next.

Marinate salmon—that only takes a few attempts for the video to look right—and then I need to set the rice in the steamer . . . OK, well, I don't have one of those. But you can boil rice, can't you? I'm sure you can. So, I fill a kettle and run it while I put a saucepan with a small amount of water on the electric burner. Add the hot water, add the rice, and I'm completely delighted with myself at how easy I'm finding all this.

I take a short video of the rice water boiling away from a bird's-eye shot.

It's a bit boring though . . . maybe I should do that seasoning thing I saw in the other video. So, I get the salt shaker out.

As I do it, the top of the container falls off into the water, and salt gushes in like an avalanche.

OK, fine. The rice will be inedible. The camera doesn't know that. So, despite my water now being more salt than rice, I take an extra pinch of salt, fish out the salt lid with a spoon, and do one last video of my hands sprinkling it in.

Yes, that's the one.

Satisfied, I make the dangerous mistake of looking up.

I didn't clean up after shoveling all my clothes in here, so this place is a mess. Oh, how I wish that I could, just like Instagram, click my fingers and have them disappear into the relevant drawers. I both don't have the energy to do anything about the mess, and don't have the ability to just sit in it. It's—

Is that the smell of burning? What is that?

I look around, using my nose as a guide until I trace it back to the oven, probably still preheating to the specified 180 degrees. I open the oven door, trying to work out if I'm right, when a wave of black smoke gushes out of it in all directions.

"WHAT?" I cry, confused as I try and fog the smoke out of my eyes. What did I do?

I shut the door, shock piercing through me.

What do you do when your oven is on fire?

I'm shaking. I'm panicking. But I don't have time to work that out because my eyes look up to the sound of splashing and when I look back at the burner—

Oh gosh, the rice is steaming. All the water seems to have disappeared from the inside of the pan and the grains at the bottom are burning with nothing to soak it. What? I didn't know it could do that? I need to get it off the heat pronto, but I can barely see because of the smoke so I go to grab the handle and move the pan off when—

"AH!" I cry out as the tips of my fingers burn from the heat.

I switch off the burner with my right hand while shaking out the pain in my left. I turn back to the fire in the oven when the smoke and the steam mixing suddenly sets off the fire alarm.

"FIRE!" I cry to no one, in full-on panic mode. "HELP! WHAT DO I DO? FIRE!"

I can't think. I can barely see.

The siren is blasting, my eyes sting from the smoke, my hand is aching, and just to add to the utter chaos that is suddenly surrounding me, my phone starts to ring.

For a split second I want to throw it across the room, entirely overwhelmed, and then I realize: I asked the universe for help, and the universe responded with a phone call. I don't have Betzy here to guide me and I don't know what to do. But maybe someone else knows.

My eyes are stinging in the smoke, but without looking I slide on the call and hit speakerphone.

"QUICK," I cry. "HELP ME! MY OVEN'S ON FIRE! WHAT DO I DO?"

"Is the fire in your flat? Or just the oven?" The voice responds, calmly, strongly, clearly. It's the voice of reason. The voice of sense.

"The oven," I say, almost crying as I wave the smoke out of the way. The siren is still blasting overhead but I can hear them clearly.

"Is the oven off?"

"No!" I gasp.

"Then turn it off."

My hand reaches out to the switches, as I turn them all off. Then I run to the switch on the wall and flick them all off too. I place my phone on the kitchen counter on loudspeaker.

"Is it safe in your flat?" the speakerphone asks me. "Do you need me to call nine-nine-nine?"

"No. I don't know. I don't think so. There's just so much smoke."

"Without opening the door, can you see? Is it fire? Or smoke?"

How is this voice remaining so calm? But it centers me, somehow. I can actually answer in complete sentences. I peer in, through burning eyes.

"Just smoke. A lot of smoke."

"What's in there?"

"Nothing! I haven't put anything in there yet!" I cry over the fire alarm's screech.

"Could there be remnants of something?"

"No, I—" And then I stop. Oh gosh. "I think maybe it's a pizza. I think it's my pizza from a few nights ago. I must have left it in there," I tell the phone.

Because I remember the night Layla saw me. I put the pizza in. I switched it on. I cooked it, and then, exhausted and embarrassed,

I decided I didn't have an appetite. I don't even remember what I did with it, but—I'm guessing—I must have just left it in there. To char.

The panic that has overtaken me lessens slightly at the thought. That's exactly what this is. I'm burning the stupid pizza. This smoke is molten cheese and crusts.

Holy shit. I am an idiot. How did I not remember it was in there? How did I not check before I switched on the oven?

When I'm absolutely sure that nothing's actually on fire, I open the oven door once again. A plume of smoke hits the back of my throat in an instant. Suddenly I start coughing, uncontrollably. The taste of ash stains the back of my tongue.

"Are you alright?" the voice asks, concern evident.

"It's just the smoke," I choke.

"Switch on the extractor fan, if you have one. Do you have a window?"

"I have a window," I say, as I switch the extractor fan's highest setting. Why was this not on already for the burner? I'm such a fool.

"Open that too. Let out the smoke. Waft it with whatever you can find. A towel maybe. Make sure you can breathe. Are you sure you don't need me to call nine-nine-nine?"

"No, I don't think so," I say, trying to swallow whatever moisture I have left in my mouth as I pull the window open as far as it will go.

I can see the dark plumes immediately head for freedom as the cool early April winds gush in in their place. But after the heat, it's refreshing. I grab a towel and start waving it around the flat like a Morris dancer, but already the fire alarm has stopped. The pace of the panic has slowed. My heartbeat with it.

When the chaos has calmed, and the air is breathable once again, I head over to my open oven, already shaking my head in complete humiliation.

There it is. My frozen margherita pizza. Now a circle of pure carbon. When I was filming myself turning the dials, I didn't even think to check inside.

My hand still stings from the burn, so I head over to the faucet,

turning it on to try and get cold water over it. The relief is immediate, my hand smarting under the frozen pipes.

"Are you alright?" my phone speaker says, calmly. Sweetly.

"Yes," I answer automatically, "I'm . . ." but something locks in
my throat.

I look up, trying not to cry, but I'm failing. The shaking takes
over. My body feels full to bursting with adrenaline trying to burst
from my cells. "No," I say truthfully, my voice warbling under the
pressure release.

When the smoke hit, I just panicked. I didn't think sensibly. I
didn't know what to do. I didn't even switch the damn oven off for
Christ's sake. If the phone hadn't rung, I don't even know what I
would have done. Caused an actual fire probably. One that would
have burnt everything I own. That endangered the lives of everyone
in my building. Of next door. Of this street.

But this voice saved me.

"It's alright, let it out," the voice says, so gently I feel every
part of my guard dropping. The floodgates open and tears start free
flowing down my cheeks. And god, it feels good to get it out. A
cathartic release like nothing else.

"Please don't go—" I begin, terrified he's going to leave me.

"I'm not going anywhere," Archie replies, knowingly, "I'm here
when you need me. Let it all out."

"So, turns out, I can't cook," I say, when I can finally breathe a free
breath again. I collapse into my love seat, wrapping myself in a smoke-
smelling blanket. The window is still open to let the fresh air in, but
it's making the whole flat exceedingly chilly in the early April air. I
snuggle up into the corner of the cushions; my phone perched on
the arm of the sofa as I lean my head back, closing my eyes in shame.

"Well, it's good to figure these things out," Archie says in a wise,
deep voice, which actually makes me laugh out loud. He chuckles
along with me, probably to be polite.

"I'm so sorry—" I begin.

"I might start a tally for all the things you apologize for unnecessarily."

I put my hands to my face, wiping them of tears.

"Pizza can be tricky . . ." he reasons, borderline sarcastically which makes me smile.

"Believe it or not, I wasn't cooking pizza. I was attempting a salmon teriyaki."

He makes a long gushing noise.

"Well, that's hardly a meal for beginners."

"It looked easy! It didn't look like the kind of meal I'd burn my flat over. I saw it in this Instagram post and—oh god. I can't believe I almost set my place on fire for a bloody Reel."

"Looks can be deceiving."

"Don't I know it," I say, more to myself, thinking about everything I've been up to for the last few days.

There's a pause on the line. So, I fill it. Obviously.

"I don't know how to thank you enough. Honestly, I don't know what would have happened if you hadn't called," I say, running a hand through my hair. It probably stinks of smoke. Just like this blanket. Just like this sofa, and all of my clothes, which are still scattered throughout this room. It's a smell that stains into fabric. I sigh. "I live by myself, and most of the time that's fine. That's great. And then suddenly you have a panic situation and there's no one around you and you go from a woman living alone to a woman, well, lonely. I needed someone. So, thank you, for being that person."

I wonder if I should be embarrassed about that little revelation. I didn't know it was coming out of me until it already was. Only he takes any worry I have about oversharing and casts it aside as he answers.

"I know the feeling."

His voice is so soft, caring. Thoughtful.

I wonder if he's going to expand, but he doesn't.

"I take it saving my life wasn't the sole purpose of your call?" I ask him.

He goes very quiet for a minute. Too quiet.

"It's alright," he says quickly.

"What was it?"

"It's really fine."

"Honestly, tell me. What is—" And then I realize why he doesn't want to say something. "Do you want my help setting up your Instagram account?"

There's a pause on the line as I sit up.

"Just because I almost burnt down my flat because of Instagram, doesn't mean I can't help you set up yours."

"You don't have to—"

"You just saved my life. Helping you take a few pictures is quite literally the least I can do here."

There's another pause on the line.

"Well, if you have time . . ." he begins, and I laugh. Because that's one of the funniest things I've heard all week.

"Turns out, I have all the time in the world," I sigh. "So, when can I come over?"

Half an hour after the call comes to an end, the buzzer sounds in my flat. I was actually on my way down anyway, to take out the trash. I've been meaning to take it down for a while. I've slowly watched my Tetris balancing skills on top of the trash can grow through the week, but now with the smell of charcoal left in my flat, adding the pizza to the top was the incentive I needed to actually remove it completely.

I figure the buzzer must be for someone else, but I head down anyway only to see a man in a biker's helmet, standing with a brown paper bag in his hand.

"Do you have the code?" he asks.

Code? Is this the start to some sort of espionage movie? My phone pings in my pocket.

As I place the trash bag on the floor by my feet I look past the motorcyclist to his bike, parked on the street just outside. The pack on the back is all too familiar: Deliveroo.

"Oh, I didn't order anything," I say, wondering which of my neighbors it could be for. I take out my phone to call Derrick from downstairs, when I see the new text that's just come through on my phone.

Archie Brown
The code's 51

I blink, twice.

"Fifty-one?" I say, confused, to the man. The man types it into his machine and, satisfied, hands over the bag.

I take out the bin, but I'm still a bit stunned as I walk back up the stairs, all the way to the top where my own flat door is. I place the parcel on perhaps the only bit of free kitchen counter.

I take out my phone again.

I only just saved Archie's number. That one text is our first-ever text exchange.

I reach into the brown paper bag and pull out a box of—I squeal to no one. Wagamama's?

I start texting, immediately.

Me
You bought me salmon teriyaki?!

Archie
I couldn't have you go hungry tonight

I feel another surge well up inside me. A different kind to earlier. A different kind to anything I've ever felt before.

Archie
And before you think I've been stalking you, your
address is literally on your CV

Me
This is the kindest thing anyone has ever done for me

And I mean it. I can't think of a single time anyone has ever done something like this for me before. Ever. I mean, Jackson used to always order me takeout, but . . . not like this. Never like this.

Archie
Nonsense. I'm not being kind to you

It's kind to the fire department
I'm making sure they have the night off tonight

I laugh again at that, feeling all warm inside.

Me

Thank you x

Archie

Anytime x

I'm still grinning from ear to ear as I put down the phone, and for one perfect minute all I can think about is how much better I feel now. He's given me something back that I didn't realize I'd lost. Connection? Kindness? I can't even name what, but I feel so much better.

It looks so good too. Really professional. Nothing like the mess that I would have ended up cooking.

Which is when I think it.

No.

I couldn't.

I really, really couldn't.

Not after everything. Not after almost burning down my flat. Not after burning my hand. After embarrassing myself in front of a near stranger.

But . . . I already have the rest of the video. I have me stirring the rice . . . marinating the salmon . . .

No, I think again. I definitely, definitely shouldn't do this.

Only before I know it I'm lining up my beautiful Deliveroo onto a plate, and filming it from a bird's-eye angle.

When I mash it up together with the other pieces, well . . . it does look fitting. It looks like I cooked it.

Well, I've made the Reel now. I might as well put it out there. Before I can convince myself otherwise, I hit post.

At midnight, when I finally pull myself away from the TV screen, I look back at my phone. As if on autoplay, I click my stories to rewatch them. There we are: a pan and some rice, me shaking the basmati followed swiftly by the most beautiful salmon teriyaki dish I've ever "made." The remains are still in front of me on the slightly cleared coffee table. It was utterly delicious, if I do say so myself.

I take a quick glance through who's watched it as I curl into my soft duck-egg duvet. Who now thinks I'm the next Gordon Ramsey? Fourteen people so far, and all of them from work.

And that's where I see it: @Jax_O has watched your story.

Jackson.

Jackson's actually watched it.

I look again, to make sure my eyes aren't lying to me, but that's it. That's his name, watching the story version of my Reel.

A smile crosses my lips.

"You're back," I whisper to no one, wondering if what I feel now is worth the effort it took.

It has to be, I conclude. It's just hard to remember why right now.

15

Now that I know Jackson's watching my stories, it's time to dial it up. I didn't go through all of that to have me slip through the net. Whatever I do now, it has to be something that catches his eye. It has to be the kind of thing to get Jackson thinking of me, maybe even enough to break this period of silence between us and reach out.

A day later I go back to the list. After cooking was baking. Well, that's not happening. Then home renovation. I look around the flat.

I could really do with some home renovation right now, I think.

I don't know why I've let the place fall to such disarray. It's not like I don't have the time to clean it, more that I don't have the inclination. But everything stinks of smoke still. I still stink of smoke.

What I could really do with is a long hot shower.

Or a bath!

That's it! That's sexy, right? But it's also something people might Instagram in a completely non-sexy way. It's a relaxing activity. It just so happens that it's one you do naked.

It's perfect. To my old colleagues, it shows me living my best life. Maybe it's a reward for smashing an interview? To Jackson, it reminds him of what he's missing.

Because I miss him. I think. Or rather, I miss everything about my life before unemployment.

Setting up a bath is also foolproof. I cannot possibly start a fire by filling a tub with water.

The photos and videos are easy to take too: switch off the main lights, add some candles balanced on the edge, and a large gin and tonic, first for the pictures, then for me generally. A quick selfie (or ten until I get one I like) of me in the mirror with the caption "preparing to unwind . . ."

Then I put my phone face down on the edge of the toilet beside me and I climb into the tub. Oh my word, the water is soft. It must be from the bubble bath, as it feels like silk against my legs. Submerged in the liquid gold (sort of—it's a small bath so my knees are at right angles), I finally lay my head back and breathe.

Actually, this is a really good angle. Quickly grabbing the phone again, I head back to Instagram and, sitting up properly so my legs are straight, I do a little boomerang of my toes wiggling on the water's surface. That's fun.

I switch on music for the background. Just to slow down my thoughts. "Adele," Spotify recommends to me. Yes, yes, that's exactly whose soothing tones will complement this scenario.

I hit back on Instagram all over again, checking to see whether Jackson's seen my last story in the two or so minutes that I haven't looked.

My eyes go through the three names of the people who have already seen it: Ricky, Emma, Dave.

Not Jackson.

Not yet.

Somehow, and I'm still not sure how, but somehow I find myself back on Jackson's profile. I look at his profile picture—a candid shot taken from a wedding a few years ago that he's not updated ever since I've known him—and that natural smile (probably mixed with the very timely rendition of "Someone Like You") brings on a tidal wave of nostalgia I wasn't expecting.

One of his smiles and suddenly I remember all the reasons we worked so well together.

❧

Jackson's palm still drapes over me, his fingers delicately tickling at my bare skin as his naked body curves around mine. I feel the pulse of them ringing through me as we both catch our breaths. Oh my god.

The last few hours have been intense. I'd close my eyes and open them and—oh, I'm against a wall, then nibbling my earlobe would force my eyes shut again in pleasure only to find my hand reach out and grab the faucet of his kitchen sink for support. He made full use of his apartment of course. The armchair in the corner, that became a leaning post. The bathroom—well, about halfway through he added a bit of soap and hot water to the mix for a welcome break, which might have slowed down the pace, but geared up just about everything else. The bed, the more obvious location, was used for the big, grand finale.

Even now, minutes later, I still can hear my cry echo back to me.

And now this; touching, panting, sweaty messes curled up together on his gray king-size bed.

It's late, and it's a moonless night in early autumn, which means despite the floor-to-ceiling river-view window in the bedroom not having its curtains closed, it's still pitch black everywhere. My eyes adjusted a while ago of course. It helps that the only thing I want to see is about ten inches away.

I turn my whole body his way, wrapping myself closer. I still can't believe I'm here, tight in the arms of Jackson Oakley. Never in my wildest dreams did I think I'd be here. I just don't want this moment to end.

"You want something to eat?" he asks.

I laugh at that. The first thing he thinks about after and it's stomach-related. So, he is just a man after all.

"I'm good."

"You sure? I'm starving." He yawns. "I think I'll order something. . . ."

He picks up his phone from the bedside table and heads straight onto Deliveroo.

By the quickness of his decision, this wasn't the first time he's decided to do this. This was a trained response—he wants food, he finds food. He knows where to go to find it. Instantly.

"That's actually a brilliant idea . . ." I say, my mind suddenly on fire.

"What is?" he asks sleepily.

I rummage in the darkness beside the bed to find my underwear, and then do a quick knicker shuffle with my hips to slide them on. I jump out the bed, feeling the soft white carpet beneath my toes.

"Give me one second, otherwise I'll forget," I say quickly.

His shirt is closer than my clothes, so I throw that on, wrapping it loosely around me as I sprint out of the bedroom and back into the living room area. I knew I left my phone around here somewhere and—there it is. Next to my still unfinished drink.

I switch it on, absentmindedly walking over to the kitchen barstools propped up against a small little island.

He finds me in his kitchen moments later. He switches on an under-cabinet light that softly illuminates his steel-gray flat. It brings my eyes up from my phone, and as we find each other I can't stifle my own smile.

Then he turns away, walking toward the kitchen sink (the one I almost fell into hours earlier).

He's completely naked. God, I envy that kind of confidence. I wrap his shirt around me a little tighter now that the light's on, as I lower the phone. He tells Alexa to play, I don't actually know when she even stopped, and some low-fi beats sway out from unseen speakers around.

As he takes out two glasses from a high cabinet, I put my phone down, watching his arm muscles stretch up. Watching the curve of his spine as he reaches and brings it back to counter level. In this dim lighting shadows are doing their part in turning this man before me into a perfect statue. He fills the glasses with water, and turns back to me, sliding one across the kitchen island in a 1950s diner sort of way.

This feels so surreal, like something from a book where the girl is a lot more sophisticated and articulate than I am. The kind of girl Jackson probably adores. So, I shut my mouth, in case I "do a Daisy" and start rambling.

"I went for a Thai platter. Thought you might regret your decision once it arrives," he tells me.

"Do you like to cook?" I ask, thinking about all those cooking bloggers he follows.

"I like people cooking for me," he replies. "I like to watch people cook."

Ah, well, that's probably why he follows them then. But I keep my mouth shut again. I don't want him realizing I can't cook. Not when it's something he probably wants in a partner.

I twist around in the swivel barstool, suddenly feeling like the girl who got everything she ever wanted all at once. I think about saying something like that to him, but I stop myself. I must not ruin this moment.

Jackson downs his pint glass, leaning over.

"Who's your friend then?" he asks casually.

"My friend?" I ask, looking down at my phone. Oh! All he knows is I just ran from his bed to my phone. I guess it's natural to assume I'm trying to tell someone what just happened. "No, no," I say quickly, realizing quite how rude I seem. "No, I . . . I had an idea. For the Stormcloud campaign. They're looking for new app features. They asked us to see if there were any data insights that might lead the development process and I just thought—Deliveroo."

Jackson looks a bit stunned, and suddenly a little embarrassed about the whole thing; I feel my mouth start running away. "Well, not actually Deliveroo. But people want to know where they can get food, wherever they are, whatever the time. Whenever I look into interests associated with travel, food is always in the mix. High up too. So, what about that as a feature? You pick the country, you hit a button saying 'I'm hungry' or something and you can immediately see your options. Any takeouts with their numbers. Any restaurants still open. Day or night, 24/7, wherever you are in the globe. I mean, most of that stuff can be fetched directly from a Google API so it shouldn't be too hard to integrate into some sort of prototype. And I know I'm more the numbers girl than the ideas girl, but I figure I can use data to see if it's possible at least. . . ."

Jackson just stands there, looking at me. Oh gosh, why did I say that? Why did I ruin all of this? I should have just stayed in bed and kept my mouth closed.

"You really don't switch off, do you?" Jackson says, his eyes condensing to a perfect smolder. I feel hot to the touch under their glare.

"No, not really." I shrug. "I'm sorry, it's—"

"It's sexy," he replies, cutting me short.

I don't even know what to say to that. Cutesy, sure, I've been described as cutesy before. Sweet? That one's been fired at me. But sexy? Never before has that word crossed anyone's lips. I look down at my phone, as if remembering a thread I never closed.

"I wasn't planning on telling anyone we're hooking up," I say finally. He stays very still, and I start to worry about what he's thinking. Before I can stop myself, I open my mouth all over again. "I'm not embarrassed or anything!" I exclaim. "But I know how people will see it. They'll think I'm trying to sleep my way up when I work hard for what I get. I've always worked hard."

"I can see that." Jackson nods.

"Well . . . I'd rather . . . people . . . don't know. About this."

Jackson looks down, clearly trying to see how he feels. After what seems like an age, he looks back up.

"If that's what you want," he says finally.

I keep internally pinching myself. I don't really understand what's happened here. How I've managed to get literally everything I want.

Jackson quickly checks his phone before placing it back on the counter.

"Twenty minutes till the food arrives," he says, breaking my over-thinking silence. He puts his phone down and stretches out. As if having a brilliant thought, he walks around the kitchen counter toward me. Naturally I swivel my chair toward him, one arm keeping me steady on the kitchen counter while the other holds his shirt around me. I watch him make his way toward me. He comes in close and I feel every nerve on the back of my neck start to rise. "What can I do in twenty minutes . . ." he says.

I think he's going to lean in for a kiss, but I let out a small scream instead as I feel the barstool holding me whip round, my back to the kitchen island. I start laughing when I've regained my balance. Jackson lets go of the stool, standing there, before me. I try not to let my eyes trail down his body as I feel his hands curve around my legs. Instead I look right at him as my lips peel back into a dreamer's smile.

"I thought you needed energy," I laugh.

"Not for this," he replies, a glimmer in his eye, as slowly, he lowers himself down.

ও

When did I start weeping?

Maybe somewhere between "When We Were Young" and "Rolling in the Deep"?

I finish off my gin and tonic with one swig as I wipe the tears from my eyes, forgetting that with hands soaking wet from the bathwater, all I've really done is spread the moisture around my face. God, I'm bored of crying. Ever since that day I was fired it seems anything can set me off.

The irony is that I did this to show people I'm having the best time when all it's doing is restarting the almost endless waterworks of a girl stripped of all purpose. But I must not show people that.

As if to prove the point I reach out to my phone, drying my hand again on the towel and then go to do another post of my feet. Maybe even my legs this time—is that too much? Or is that the fine balance between "safe to post" and "Jackson, see what you're missing"?

So, I go on Instagram and point the camera as far as I dare go (just below my knee, a Victorian porn angle but a 2020s prude), then hit record. Only my finger, still slightly wet from the bathwater, must slip to the wrong button because the next thing I know it's recording alright, but the camera has flipped over to a selfie mode. The shot I was aiming for was beautifully PG-13, except given that I've sat up for my legs to be straight, my nipples are fully in sight of the camera. This little recording has turned awkwardly X-rated.

At least it's just a recording—one I will promptly delete. No worries there, just an inconvenience.

And that's when I see it.

"Live," it reads.

Oh holy hell. Am I actually live streaming my boobs on Instagram right now?

I gasp at the thought, and in a complete moment of sheer panic, I drop my phone. A satisfying plonk echoes around as my phone submerges into the water's depths, only it's not even slightly satisfying, because it's the sound of my phone malfunctioning just as my boobs hit the internet.

"ARGH!" I scream, because I really bloody need to. I pull my phone out instantly from its unintentional lavender soaking. I see the screen is still lit—no longer with Instagram but of my homepage. Does that mean it's fully out there then? What happens with live videos when you go off the app? Are they recorded for everyone to see?

And before I can do anything else, my phone screen goes black.

I need to sort this out, pronto. So, I jump straight up, bouncing over the side of the bathtub and grabbing my towel as I go. As I throw open the door my leg slams into the toilet, and I howl with pain before I remember that *my boobs are on the internet*. I have days to worry about the bruise on my leg, but every second that passes is another second that my two perky tic tacs are out there for all to see. I have to have some priorities here.

So, I sprint straight to the kitchen, hurtling over piles of clothes on my way like an Olympic athlete until I reach the kitchen. I place my phone into a bowl and make a quick grab for the bag of rice on the counter, somehow forgetting that I opened it to cook as I lift it with gusto into the air.

Suddenly it's raining basmati. Rice goes everywhere. It flies into the air like confetti at a wedding, sticking to my soaking-wet skin like I'm the icing to a cupcake and they're the decorative sprinkles, but I don't have time for this.

"COME ON!" I cry out to myself, more as a blessed release of power than in anger as I pour what's left of the rice into the bowl over my phone.

As the last of the bag empties over my phone, I pause.

It's like the whole world stops and stills, waiting.

"Well, that was unexpected," says a voice inside my kitchen.

I look up, scream, and in an instant, my towel drops.

16

There, standing by my open door while I expose myself like a foolish birth of Venus, is Mia.

My sister.

She kicks the door behind her shut with the back of her heel
and then leans back, thoroughly amused by the look on her face.
She's still wearing her usual big bold colors, I see—a bright yellow
hoodie over tight green jeans. Bright red lipstick frames her face,
in contrast to her minimalist eye makeup. Block colors have always
been her way. It's a Mia trademark.

Only every time she's with a man I tend to watch these colors
fade over time into something else, something unrecognizable. Not
yet though, I think. She's still Mia so far.

Her hair is unbelievably long at the moment, styled with a glorious four-point wave just like a 1950s Hollywood starlet. She smiles
at me, like her presence was completely expected. In fact, in case I
was under any illusion that that wasn't the case, she confirms it with
me by adding: "Calm your horses, it's only me."

"Are you actually kidding me?" I scream. I duck down below
the small kitchen island and make a grab for my towel, messily
throwing it over me to cover anything possible.

"I've seen your tits before," Mia replies nonchalantly, completely relaxed about this situation. I'm about to absolutely blow, I really am—and yet the smallest part of me stops. Because I've just remembered why I'm in this predicament in the first place, and Mia walking in, presence wanted or not, gives me a solution.

"Check Instagram!" I scream to her. Her eyes widen at my command.

"Sorry?"

"ARE MY TITS ON INSTAGRAM?" I hate the word *tits*. I hate it for so many reasons, but I just repeated what she said in the hopes it might make her move quicker. Despite this, she doesn't comply.

"You put your tits on Instagram?" she asks instead.

"JUST CHECK IT!" I cry, rushing over to her.

Slowly she takes out her oversize phone from her undersize jean pocket, unlocking it with face ID. She's so sloth-like in her actions I'm already beside her, towel clutched tight with tension, when she's reached my Instagram profile. I grab the phone off her, scanning through my stories, but no. I check again; the bath filling up, the gin, the bubble bath, and then my toes wriggling in the water. After that, nothing. I click on my profile to make sure nothing else was permanently saved.

"I'm surprised," Mia says while I work. She leaves me with her phone by my door as she wanders farther into my flat. I ignore her, reloading the page in case her phone was just slow to pick up any new story. "I'm all for breasts on Instagram, but I'd have never guessed you would have wanted yours out there. Not that there's anything wrong with your girls. They're just like mine I always think, only a little smaller."

I look up at her as my heartbeat starts to slow, my face giving away my feelings to that particular statement.

"Oh, I like your size better," she says, clearly misunderstanding me. "Much more manageable."

"I didn't mean to. I dropped my phone and I thought . . . it doesn't matter."

I take a deep breath, trying to calm my galloping chest. It's alright; my personal preference for the internet's view of my body parts remains intact. That's what matters here, I think.

I feel a slap of cotton against my face taking me out of my daydream. I have to blink a fair few times to work out where it even came from. As I look to the floor by my feet, the offending articles become apparent.

"Did you just throw a pair of knickers at my face?"

"It was a good shot, wasn't it?" Mia smiles cheekily from the far side of the room, by the sofa. She carelessly lifts a few of the jumpers from the pile, holding them up to her for size. "Wear them, don't wear them, I don't mind."

I would be angry with her, I would, only that her being here has just saved me hours' worth of worry. I click her side button of her phone to blacken the screen, noticing, before it goes away, her lock screen photo: a man, very similar-looking to all the others she's dated, kissing her cheek affectionately. I try not to audibly sigh when I place it on the edge of my kitchen counter. As I change into the pants she's thrown, I watch as Mia examines the mess I've left these past few days. I'd hoped this was something she'd never see, but there's nothing I can do about it now.

"Bit of redecorating?" she asks comically, her hands running over piles of unsorted clothes. "Oh, this is nice. . . ."

"How did you get in?" I ask.

Mia waves the keys, still in her palm, while she leafs carelessly through a mound of skirts.

"You gave me your spares, remember?" she says.

Of course I did. It was the last time I saw her, only that was seven weeks ago and so much has happened since that I completely forgot. Still, I didn't expect her to just use it like this. I lean on the kitchen counter, watching her, wondering how I feel.

I know we haven't spoken properly in well over a month, but in a weird way, Mia being here feels normal. And it's much harder to be angry with someone when they're right in front of you, being reasonable. From far away, my anger toward her grows exponentially, and yet when she's walking through the debris of clothes spread out across my flat, some of those feelings have settled back to far more manageable levels of irritation.

"I've just been . . ." I try to think of the best way to explain this. "Busy."

"You're always busy. That's your thing."

"Being busy isn't my thing."

"Oh please," Mia tuts, "you've been busy since you were like . . . sixteen."

"I've been *working* since I was sixteen."

"Still, your place has never looked quite this . . . *interesting* . . . before."

Her tongue toys with the word interesting, making her true meaning abundantly clear.

"Yeah, well," I say, not wanting to justify the disaster zone. "I've been extra busy recently."

Mia never comes to my flat. Never. Unless of course . . .

Ah, that'll be it. It'll be the only reason she does come to me.

I almost didn't realize it, because every time she's been broken up with, she's usually looking her "least" Mia. Her bold colors are usually subdued in one way or another. She's not usually this quick to crack jokes. But I guess this makes sense given the last thing I screamed at her over the phone.

"I'll see you when your next boyfriend has broken up with you and you ask for even more money."

I didn't realize she'd take me quite so literally.

I should be more angry or upset, but strangely I'm genuinely grateful that she chose me. I'm still pissy with her of course, but if she's here because she needs her big sister again, then I can't help it. It feels good to be that big sister that she needs. Especially after my little display just now. So, I take a deep breath, and after reaching for an oversize pink jumper close by to go over my bra, I head toward the kettle.

"So, who broke up with who this time?" I ask her.

"If that's your way of asking 'How's Kit?' then the answer is 'He's great actually, we're better than ever. Thanks for asking'," she replies, clearly annoyed. Not annoyed enough to say something but annoyed enough to pull a face at me.

So, she's not here because of a breakup?

"You quit your job then?" Mia asks, moving on the subject before I have a chance to linger.

"What makes you say that?" I say, a little too quickly.

"Because it's 3 p.m. on a Wednesday and I just caught you sharing your nip nops with the internet. I'm going to hazard a guess that that's not for data collection purposes."

At first, I'm about to lie. I don't want to get into this with her, and lying seems like the quickest way around it, but then I remember there's not many other reasons why someone would be at home, doing nothing at this time.

Still, I don't want to talk about it. Not with anyone, but certainly not with her.

"I happened to be in the area when you first posted, so I thought I'd see if it was real time and it turns out, I was right."

"I needed something new," I summarize.

"Is this what you were actually mad at when you blew up at me on the phone?"

"No, Mia," I confirm. "Believe it or not, I was actually angry *with you*. I still am."

I place her tea on the edge of the counter, not wanting to get too close.

She meets me in the middle, picking up her tea without thanks and reaching back for her phone before wandering back over to the arm of the sofa to lean against.

"It doesn't matter, I came here for you to forgive me."

"You did?" I ask skeptically.

"I did. Because I know exactly what it is that will make all this better and I wanted to see the look on your face when it happens," she says proudly, turning to her phone.

Oh really, Mia? Well, I for one, can't wait to find out what she's thinking.

A little whoosh sound echoes out around us.

"Check your phone," she tells me, grinning conspiratorially.

I point to my phone in the rice, no words needed.

"Oh, sort of ruins the effect there," she says in a minor huff, but then perks up again quickly. "Oh well, it's all gone through anyway," and then, to clarify it all, "I'm paying you back," Mia says proudly. Her eyes are all lit up in an early victory, but mine don't match her enthusiasm. I set my tea down on the side slowly, in case any emotion causes my hand's grip to loosen.

"Sorry?"

"I get it, you really care about your money," she tells me, "so I'm giving it all back to you."

I open my mouth to speak, but words don't find a place there. So, I close it again.

"I give it back. You stop being pissed with me. We can move on and forget all about this," she says, like it's the catchy jingle of some product on the shopping channel.

I blink a few times. This is what she thinks is going to solve our problems, is it? This is the grand one-size-fits-all-solution? To pay me back money she owes me and then insult me for it?

"Are you kidding?" I say, my voice rapidly picking up volume and tempo.

"I am not," Mia laughs it off, turning her phone to face me. "It's done now! The money's back in your account! It's over!"

She shows me the bank transfer receipt, as if proving a point. I'm about to make mine, only something distracts me.

"Three hundred twenty pounds?" I read. "That's us all settled up, is it?"

Mia looks at her screen, as if she might have shown me the wrong thing, but then pockets her device.

"What, did I send too much?"

"I've given you at least a hundred pounds every time you've broken up with a boyfriend. I've paid your rent countless times, your electricity bills, I've even cleared your debt with that nail salon that was giving you a hard time, and you think all of those handouts add up to a grand total of three hundred and twenty-three pounds fifty?" I stutter, completely flabbergasted. This girl has no idea what things cost. She doesn't seem in the least perturbed. Instead, she just shakes her head.

"Well, tell me how much then and we can put all this behind us and move on?"

"What, so you've always been broke, but now suddenly you have all the money in the world?"

"Tell me how much!" she tries.

"I'm not having your latest boyfriend bail you out here! That's not how it works!" I plant my hands on the kitchen counter behind me. I need something to center me right now.

"My *boyfriend* isn't bailing me out."

"Well, that's worse!" I tell her. "Don't you dare take out a loan for this! You know how that worked out for Helen."

"This isn't even close to Mum's situation!" she argues back.

"If she hadn't taken out that loan—" Our voices are both rising, in volume and tempo.

"She took out that loan because she loved us!"

"Oh really?" How did we fall back into this argument again? "Crappy way of showing love: running away from her family."

"You have no idea what she went through!" she cries at me.

"And you do?" I fight back. And that shuts her up. I can see her mind whirring, her mouth opening and closing.

"Well, it's not a loan," she says, a little quieter this time, and I realize I hardly have the energy to fight with her about the thing this argument is about, let alone bring in more grievances.

"This isn't about Helen," I tell her, rubbing out the pain in my face. "It's also not about the money."

"It isn't?"

"It isn't."

"Then what is?" she asks.

I sigh, looking down to my feet.

"You really can't think of any reason?" I ask, yearning for her to come up with the answer. I can't tell from the look on her face whether she's purposefully trying to hide something, or if she genuinely can't think. Either way, she leaves me completely unanswered.

After a few minutes of rolling her eyes, she stands, leaving her half-finished mug on the counter and heading for the door.

"Fine, whatever. I can see you're too pissed to talk about it still. Why don't you call me when you're done being a gigantic arse?" she says, and I know—I just know—she's trying to get a rise out of me. But I don't take the present she's leaving. Instead, I bite back my words, watching her stroll to my door.

"Oh, you'll text me back this time, will you?" I snap.

She looks over her shoulder, obviously confused, then shakes off the feeling.

"I'm taking this with me," she says, picking up a dress that was lying on the love seat-wardrobe and taking it with her.

Don't rise to it, Daisy, I tell myself. Say nothing. She just wants you to react. When she reaches the door she turns back, clearly checking if I actually mean what I say. I do. So, I say nothing. Getting the hint, she shrugs, like it's no difference to her.

"Love you," she says, more out of habit.

"Love you too, obviously," I reply back.

And with a little twist that causes her luscious waves to flick around like a whip, she leaves.

I had such a sour taste in my mouth once Mia left that I just didn't want to do anything. I always get it, every time I mention Helen, my mother.

So much so, that as I brushed my teeth that night and saw the bath was still full of my leftover bathwater, I couldn't even stomach leaning over to pull out the plug. Knowing how these past few weeks have been, I probably would have sat on the love seat moping for another pointless day in the life of useless Daisy Peterson if it wasn't for one thing: I had a date with Archie.

Not a date date. A work date. Or not a work date, but a friend helping another friend (even though we barely know each other so

I don't know if you count it as friends) date. I mean, he literally has a girlfriend, one that I met, and who was completely beautiful so I'm only going over to help because I . . . well, I don't know, but for good reasons . . . date. Maybe I shouldn't try and define it.

So, the next day I rumble through my jumble of outfits still spread around my flat and I find a dress I haven't worn in forever. Pastel blue, white spots, skater dress style like nearly all of the others. It reads semiprofessional, with her life together, which is the kind of vibe I'm striving for even if it's not the kind of vibe I actually have. It's also, and this is important, the garment I own that smells the least like smoke.

Then I walk the fifteen or so minutes from my door to his.

It's a glorious day outside, cool but not freezing. Mid-April means that spring has officially sprung in London. Sunny but not blinding. It's the kind of soft light that Instagrammers will be running outside for in multiple outfits, stocking up their content for rainy days.

As I wander through the afternoon shoppers of Clapham High Street, I try and remember what Archie actually looks like. I think, with over a week since I last saw him, that I've rose-tinted my view a little. His eyes, as I picture them in my mind, are large and green and hypnotizing. His face is near perfect, his stubble rough but not out of control. Those things aren't actually the case, I think to myself as I turn to one of the side roads as a shortcut. That's just what I want to remember. That's the filtered version of the real thing.

Except, when he opens the door to greet me just a few minutes later, I realize how wrong I was. If anything, that beautiful image in my mind falls short of the real thing.

His jeans are rolled up at the bottom, his bare feet wriggling against the hardwood floor. His white T-shirt is tight, a loose gray hoodie pulled up at the sleeves. Glasses? They're new. Thick tortoiseshell frames, rounded around those startling emerald irises. I like them. I like them very, very much.

"Daisy," he says, and it has that subtle Scottish tone to it. It sounds so good coming from his lips. And with that, my latest fight with Mia disappears from my mind.

17

Archie's studio is in the basement of his house, although in a way, the whole house is his studio. Even as we descend the stairs— back down the jungle corridor and through a door in the gallery kitchen—the explosion of light makes you feel like you're entering a sky lit loft space, not a basement at all. The ceiling is painted an indescribable shade of blue, the walls a brilliant white. It's a larger room than I was expecting, running the full length of the house, and filled to the brim with paintings and empty canvases propped up against the walls. A few pieces are hung, but done in a way that makes them look more temporary. The two trestle tables are stocked up with paints and pencils scattered around, and two easels, both holding works-in-progress, stand side by side next to them.

"That smell!" I say, unable to help myself as it hits the back of my sinuses. It's strong, the whole room lingering with the thick scent of acrylics.

"The ventilation isn't great down here," he says, almost like an apology. He heads for the thin, long window close to the ceiling, running around the back wall.

"No, it's . . ." I almost can't put my finger on it. "It weirdly reminds me of my primary school. . . ."

He laughs, abandoning the window quest. He stands, central to the room before me, pushing his thick glasses back up the bridge of his nose.

"Makes sense. Painting is something we do as children all the time. It's a way we're taught to express ourselves. Before we can write, we can draw. We're visual creatures. It's a vital part of communication, which means it's a vital part of our education, drawing." He looks around the room, as if taking in his own work for the first time. My eyes follow his. "And then we grow up. And we find our own preferred means of connection, and a lot of people never pick up a paintbrush again."

I mean, it's true. I can't recall a single time past infancy when I thought to draw anything.

"You liked art as a kid?" he asks.

I shake my head, then shrug, trying to even remember.

"I'm not sure. But it certainly wasn't something my grandparents would have approved of, so I'm not surprised I stopped it."

"They didn't approve of art?" he asks, perplexed.

"They didn't approve of anything that wouldn't offer a healthy paycheck," I reply, before I realize what company I'm in and how that might have come across. "I'm not saying you can't earn anything from art. I'm just saying it's harder to earn from that than, say . . . accountancy."

He doesn't comment on that. Instead, he adds: "I'm sorry they disapproved."

"Oh, I don't blame them," I reply quickly, suddenly thinking I've painted my grandparents as terrible people when in fact they were my stability. "It was my mother's fault. I think they learned from their mistakes by the time they started looking after us." I shrug, not sure how I got into something this deep so quickly. "I guess I'm glad of it. It always gave me a strong work ethic."

In the small silence that follows, I panic that I've offended him somehow.

I should probably reel it back.

"Speaking of kids, where are your girls? Where're Cara and Bailey?"

"School," he replies, and suddenly I feel like an idiot.

"Obviously," I say, rubbing the back of my neck. "Sorry, that was—"

"Another thing you didn't need to apologize for," he says.

Maybe to avoid apologizing again, I start walking around the room, taking the paintings in one by one. Despite all the ones I've seen having very similar qualities, there's a huge variation down here. Landscapes, portraits, buildings, fields. There's a lot of realism in his work, that's for sure.

But more specifically, there is one creature that stands out quite considerably.

"I take it you like dogs?" I ask.

"It seems on that front we're aligned. My daughter tells me you're a dog person."

"She told you that?" I say, impressed they even remembered.

"Oh, Cara tells me *almost* everything. She's at that age." He sits on the bottom step, walking around the room. "Bailey on the other hand. Well, she used to. And one day she just stopped. . . ."

My automatic response is to tell him she will, but then again, who am I to say? I don't have kids. And it wasn't like I always told all of my feelings to my grandparents. So, I fill the silence a different way.

"She's eleven, right?"

"Eleven turning sixteen, more like," he sighs, leaning his head back against the wall. "Talking back at me. Fighting everything. She takes life so seriously for such a young'un."

That makes me smile. Then I realize that he's not saying it in a cute way, and me smiling at it, well. It looks wrong. This is clearly something he's struggling with.

"I'm not . . . That's what people used to say about me when I was a kid," I justify. "I think it's an older sister thing maybe. I had Mia to look after, and she never acted her age, so I had to compensate. She's still a child to this day."

He cocks his head, listening.

"Mia's my sister," I add quickly to context, "I have a sister."

He nods. "I knew that too."

"Cara?"

"*You* mentioned it, actually."

"Ah," I laugh. "Great memory there."

"But Cara did too. I promise you there's not a detail spared."

My mind takes me back to the interview, and suddenly I feel a little seasick at the thought. I lick my lips, pursing them between my teeth, bracing for impact.

"I'm guessing she told you all about my ex-boyfriend too then," I say. Archie looks down at his feet, less embarrassed and more . . . I can't quite tell. Respectful perhaps.

"She mentioned he never deserved you," he says, looking back up. Those tortoiseshell frames really magnify his eyes. They catch me, and I feel myself pulled into their orbit.

"I don't think she got the full picture there."

"I think you don't give her enough credit. Kids can be the harshest critics, but also the truest insights. They say things as they are, a lot of the time. None of this fuss and bother of worrying about feelings."

"She only heard my side."

"Sometimes that's enough," he replies.

I try to remember what Cara told me.

Disrespectful. That's what she called him.

Well, in truth, he did end a year's worth of relationship over one message. And then nothing, not an explanation, not a phone call. And when I think about some of the things he did . . . no, I'm just saying this because I'm in front of a lovely, kind man with beautiful magnified eyes.

I was the one who was lucky to have Jackson. I was the one who disrespected him by blowing up in front of his clients. Didn't I?

I need to get out of my own head and remember where I am. I blink a few times.

"So, Instagram," I say, pointing to the room around me. "Shall we make a start?"

The painting of a Yorkie stands before me, sitting neatly in a beautiful lush green field, her wide, brown eyes up and slightly to the right, as if looking at something off the canvas. The kind of eyes that you'd never say no to. Just looking at it, I can feel the softness of her fur.

"I think this might be my favorite picture in the whole world," I say, as I hear footsteps coming down the stairs behind me. They stop as they hit the bottom.

"Oh?"

I keep staring at it, every second taking in something new. Something I missed the first time. It's raining in the picture but raining the most colorful droplets. Not droplets at all, actually. Letters. Hundreds of them. A's ricocheting off D's, running next to L's and falling beside T's. Some big, some small, some bold, some slim. Arial to Times New Roman. Fonts that span the length of Microsoft Word's repertoire.

It's truly mesmerizing.

"I hope you don't mind; I've moved a few pictures around. I just wanted to see if there were any themes, and group them together. But then I found this under a few of the others and it's just amazing! I think this should be your profile picture for sure!" I tell him, turning around to face him. "A zoomed-in version, that is. I've gone ahead and taken a few videos already. I know the magic is in the detail here but I'm not sure you'd see it in the little profile. I didn't even notice the letters the little dog was wearing until I'd been staring at it for a full five minutes."

On her collar shines the letters A–Z.

Only then do I take in his expression. He's standing there, with both cups of tea he went up to fetch, but his warm face has fallen ever so slightly. His eyes are blinking back thoughts. Thoughts I so wish I could hear aloud.

"Oh sorry," I say, reading the room. "Is this—"

"No, it's alright. I just . . ." He looks around at all the other art around him, as if that's easier to look at somehow. "Can we leave that one out?"

"You don't like it?"

"I just don't . . . want it out there."

I look back at the picture, and then I realize. It's probably his old dog. I've never actually owned a dog before, but I remember my teacher bursting into tears the day her old Labrador passed away. She was inconsolable. He was part of her family, and then suddenly he was gone.

I think about my grandparents. How it felt when my Nan slipped away from us. How empty I felt.

As I turn to see him, I see that same guttural feeling. That same emptiness.

"Sure," I say, turning away from it.

"I'm sorry to be difficult," he says, placing one of the mugs on the bottom stair and looking at just about everything except for that painting. "It's only because—"

"You don't have to justify it. It's cool. I won't touch it. In fact, you'll be the one to hit post on all of them, so you'll never post something you don't want to. How does that sound?"

He looks instantly relieved. A hot man stepping under a cool wash.

"Sounds good." He smiles gently.

"Sounds great."

He walks over closer and hands me my tea. Then walking past me, he heads over to the picture of the Yorkie. Finally he looks at it, and I see something in his eyes.

Yes, definitely an old dog. Damn, I wish I hadn't loved it so much.

"Right." I put on a smile, as he shuffles the painting back to the hidden depths of the studio. Carefully he covers it back up with the blanket. I wait for him to be finished, before I say, as cheerily as I can, "Shall we get started?"

"So, you want to be a full-time painter? A little to the left, I think."

"God, no!" He laughs, moving the whole easel a little more directly under the light. As he sets it down, I suddenly see my mistake. I don't know why I thought this was a good idea. Half the painting's cast in shadow from this angle. Turns out, it's not quite as easy as point and click, this whole picture taking thing. I'm not sure why I thought it would be. I walk around, um-ing and ahh-ing, and patiently he looks up at me like I'm the expert.

"How come? This is clearly your passion."

"Exactly," he says, like the conclusion to a riddle. "Never turn your passion into a full-time job."

"Isn't that exactly the opposite of what people say?" I question. "'If you love where you work, you'll never work a day in your life' and all that?"

"If I painted every day, it would become a chore. I don't want my escape to become a burden." Strange. I guess I would never have thought of it that way. "Plus, painting's a lonely old sport. Parenting can be too, at times. I think I'd go mad if I couldn't work with people," he adds.

"How is parenting lonely?" I ask, almost by accident. I don't know many people with kids. Tiring, I've heard. But not lonely.

"It's a different kind of loneliness," he says. "It comes in those moments when they do something you're proud of. Like the first time they correctly say a word they've never been able to say before. Or when you catch them reading, alone, by themselves, engrossed. These little moments that you want to capture in your mind, that you think—I'd love to share that with someone. I'd love to watch that with someone who feels the way I feel too. Only, sometimes you have no one to share it with."

I swallow, not wanting to ask the question that lingers in the air unspoken.

"Shall we try another angle maybe?" he says, moving on. It's probably a blessing. Now I don't have to think of what I'd ask. I nod as he starts to move things around again.

"So, what, you just want to earn a little more on the side?"

"I don't know," he says, stepping back so I can take the picture. "Maybe. More I want to clear out this room. At least some of it. Truthfully, I probably would haven't done anything if you hadn't asked."

"But you work on commissions I'm guessing?"

"Not yet."

"Oh. Well, how did your work end up in the bakery?" I ask.

"Sallie's a mum at the girls' school. She's done a few pickups for me when I've been delayed somewhere, so I did it as a thank-you really. She always said she liked the one in the living room and when I first saw the bakery she'd created—well, I got inspired."

"So, no one's paid you for any of this?" I say, pointing all around me.

He follows my gaze.

"Not yet."

"But it's good."

"Thank you," he says, nervously.

"No, it's like . . . really good. But I thought . . ." What did I think? I think I thought the obvious. I think I thought what every thirty-something thinks when they're in a really, really lovely house in Zone 2 London.

"This is a two-bed?" I ask.

"A three-bed actually."

"With a basement. In Clapham." I mean, I'm paying top dollar for a small one-bed in a much less desirable street in the same area. Without even thinking I say: "I imagine rent's a bomb."

"Ah," he says, nodding awkwardly. "Yes. I see where you're going here. It probably would be. But I'm one of those painfully annoying people who actually own their house outright."

"Outright?" I gasp, then cover my hand over my mouth.

Note to self: don't talk finances with people. It makes them feel uncomfortable. Only, I'm fascinated. Because when I thought he was renting, I thought, "How on earth does he afford this on an odd-job salary?" And now I know he doesn't, I'm thinking, "How on EARTH did he afford the deposit?"

I shouldn't ask how.

I definitely shouldn't ask how.

"How?" my mouth asks for me.

"I sold my soul a long time ago," he says in a world-weary way, looking around him. "But even then, I wouldn't have been able to get this without . . . help."

He sighs, looking around the room like it's an old friend. His parents must be rich. Although, as if to answer that question he corrects my thought process: "Inheritance mostly. This here," he says, looking up and around him, "is the product of two only-children losing their family members in quick succession. My family. Then her family. Then her of course."

All the color drains from my face. He says it so calmly. So thoughtfully.

She died then.

His wife died.

I don't know what to say. What are you supposed to say under these circumstances? I feel suddenly raw, like someone peeled back my top layer, and I'm flustered, not knowing how to cover up.

"Please don't think . . ." I whisper quickly. "Obviously—I didn't mean . . . I didn't know—"

"Why would you know?" he asks softly.

I swallow. Not even knowing what to say, and yet somehow completely understanding that I will never be able to understand. That the roof over his head is held up by shadows.

For some time we just stand there, looking at one another, uncertain. Or at least I'm uncertain. The shock of it rocked me, deep. I can feel a swell of emotion inside me, that isn't equaled in him. This isn't the first time he's told someone. But I can see the razors digging into his soul on the retelling. An old wound, leaking at the edges.

"You can ask," he says, clearly seeing me shuffle in my shoes. I'm not sure when I stopped taking photos, but the phone is just resting in my hand, firmly by my side, forgotten.

"You don't need to—" I say, feeling horribly inappropriate.

I can't ask him how his wife died. You can't ask someone that.

"People never ask," he says, taking a breath deep enough to rock his body forward to the tips of his toes before resting back on his bare heels. "I find it weird that people don't ask. I know they're wondering. And it's an elephant in the room. I know Zoe," he says, with a forgotten smile. "She wanted to be a great, great many things in her life. But never an elephant."

I accidentally let out a laugh, then catch myself. I can't believe I just did that. Who laughs at someone who's been through such unbelievable misfortune? I go to apologize but then stop myself. Because I realize he's smiling with me.

Still, unsure, I bite my lip. But I do exactly what he asked.

"How did she pass?" I ask.

He takes a deep breath, as if even though he knew it was coming, even though it was his choice, he still needs to ready himself for the words. That last intake, before he submerges himself into the ice-cold water.

"A car accident," he says simply. "She swerved off the road on black ice."

"I'm sorry," I say, instinctively. As there isn't much else you can say. The words linger. Floating around us in a haze.

Only whatever tension he might have had before the words were spoken leaves him.

He opens his mouth, then shuts it.

"Another thing you don't need to apologize for," he says finally, his voice so soft it tickles the air.

And, as if the universe knew the conversation was coming to an end, his phone starts ringing.

He looks down at it, as if about to dismiss it when his face curves into a frown.

"You need to take it?" I question.

"I won't be a minute," he says seriously. "Please, work your magic down here. I'm not sure how long this will be."

"All alright?" I ask him as he joins me once again. I couldn't hear his call, per se. But whatever I did hear didn't sound like an easy conversation.

"Sorry, it's an old friend. He's going through a pretty awful divorce. Just needed my help."

"Crikey."

"How's it looking then?"

How is it looking?

Great question. Well, I've got maybe two "fine" pictures but this Reel idea definitely isn't working how it should. I show him what I've got anyway.

"Look. I'm giving it a go here, but turns out, I'm not a natural," I admit. I think he might be more mad, given that's why I've come over and all. Only he just shrugs, as if he saw this coming. He probably did to be fair. I asked him to move the easel at the beginning about thirty times.

"What's with the clicking?" he asks.

I flip to my trusty Google Sheets.

Username	Reel	Shots Needed	Views	Likes
@MrArtAttack	(Insta link)	1. Hand in front of picture 1, clicking 2. Hand in front of picture 2, clicking 3. Hand in front of picture 3, clicking Repeat	2.4M	134k
@PaintByNumbersNeil	(Insta link)	1. Blank canvas 2. All tools needed, shot one by one 3. Finished canvas	2.0M	308k
@FlowersToFrames	(Insta link)	Artist drawing sped up to 30-second Reel	1.8M	125k
. . .	. . .	. . .	. . .	. . .

"Last night I checked out the most current trending reels on Instagram for paint themes and saved the ones I thought were possible here. I was trying to re-create this one. See? I thought it looked simple enough. . . ."

We watch one together. The camera points at a canvas, out comes a hand. Click, the canvas has changed. Click, the canvas has changed again. Click, on and on it goes until the time and the song come to a close. I found these four paintings that showed similar-looking dogs in different seasons and thought I'd be able to copy it somehow. But my hand's apparently not steady enough when it's facing the images, and not quick enough at clicking.

I hand my phone over to him to get a better look.

"You made me a spreadsheet?" he asks, confused.

"My whole life would be run on Excel if I could. This was quite a manual one of course—we don't have access to the accounts data here to play around with and I don't like dodgy third-party tools— but even manually pulling them together in a file like this means I can do just a little manipulation like . . ." I hit the filter on the top and organize it instead by most likes. "So, the one at the top has the most interactions now. Those with the most views may also have the most likes by proxy, so you can just see who has the highest watch-to-like ratio or something, all in a few clicks. Makes picking between them a little easier."

He scrolls down.

"I mean, I saved all the reels too, so you can just look at the saved folder in Instagram itself . . ." I murmur, realizing that the spreadsheet isn't exactly the most visual tool. "And I added an array at the end of hashtags people used—that was just copy paste—so I could pull out the most impactful ones."

"This is great," he murmurs, looping through a few of them.

"I used to tell clients all the time; it's all great coming up with a new concept, but re-creating trending videos is an easy win. Oftentimes the template is already there, and the audience always is."

"You know, I have friends who would love to have this kind of expertise . . ." he says thoughtfully. That really makes me laugh. Expertise?

"I mean, literally anyone can do this," I say bashfully, "you just scroll on Instagram and make note of the reels you like. That doesn't require any skills."

He shakes his head, his tortoiseshell glasses falling down his nose until he pushes them back up.

"I meant the data bit."

"Oh," I laugh, "this is hardly data! I mean, everything's data I guess, but this isn't like . . . insights or anything. I need access to sales data for things like that."

He continues to flick through them, pausing on one in particular. It's an artist, drawing at super-speed. Three hours in thirty seconds, and suddenly the canvas is complete.

"I've noticed that a lot of them are just as much about the artist as they are about the art itself . . ." I say, noticing how much the Reel focuses on the painter. "How do you feel about being in one?"

He wasn't expecting that. He pushes his glasses up again, then looks down at his bare toes as they wriggle against the paint-stained floor.

"Should I . . . change?" he asks.

I planned to stay for an hour, maybe an hour and a half max, but before I know it, three hours have passed and I'm still here. He was up for painting something live, so I set his phone pointing at a canvas on a time-lapse while he got to work. As he painted, I continued to move around him, taking photos of different works from all angles and taking a few of him. Portrait mode. Although he doesn't even need portrait mode to look good. If my photos are anything to go by, he looks good from every angle.

There's not a moment of silence between us either. Every time I think the conversation must be coming to an end, we find a whole new topic to cover. I genuinely don't recall having this much to say to anyone before, apart from Mia—who doesn't count—or Betzy—who also doesn't count—but with Archie it just flows.

At every point I've worried I've overshared, he shares something right back and suddenly I don't worry about it.

His parents were both from Glasgow, not the city, but the outskirts. It was a pretty idyllic childhood, but his family moved over to London with his mother's job back when he was a teenager, and he barely remembers his life there now.

"I hear my accent slipping away with every passing year. My mother would be horrified."

Even in saying it, I can hear his accent getting stronger. Like he's trying to prove something.

"You still sound very Scottish," I tell him, meaning it to be a compliment.

"And in Scotland they'll tell me I sound English. It's like I don't quite fit anywhere."

They spent some summers traveling back to visit relatives, but most of them have passed away now, and he's somehow let the years slip by without crossing Hadrian's Wall.

"So, your parents never moved back?"

"They stayed, probably to be closer to me when I chose to study in the city, but they were a lot older than most when they had me. They passed, just before Bailey was born actually."

"I'm so . . ." I'm about to say sorry, but one little look up at me in anticipation and I hold the thought. "It's sad they never met."

"You'd never know," he laughs, like it's water over a steady bridge. "I swear that girl is just like my mam half the time. There's this look she gets when she's mad, this little knot on her forehead, and I swear to god, that's a Bonnie Brown trait, through and through."

It's so refreshing to hear someone talk in such an unabridged manner. Addictive almost.

"You mentioned your grandparents earlier," he prompts. "Were you close?"

"Good memory," I tell him, and because he's shared with me, I feel myself naturally opening up in a way I just haven't with anyone else. Like around these dog-framed pictures is a safe space for just about anything. "Well, my grandparents practically were my parents. My dad left when my sister was a baby. And Helen was always away for months on end. In fact, she'd only come back when she needed another handout from my grandparents. If it wasn't for that, I don't think Mia or I would have ever even seen her growing up."

"You call your mum Helen?" he asks.

"She was happier traveling the world and sending us postcards than she was actually being with us," I justify. "People who don't want children shouldn't have them. She clearly never wanted to be a mum, so I don't call her one."

"No," he says to clarify, "I mean, you just called your dad your dad. But you called your mum Helen."

"Oh," I say, and it's interesting because I never realized I did that. But in fact, I've always referred to my dad as my dad. Not that I've referred to him often. "I guess my dad didn't really hurt me. He just wasn't there. But Helen . . . well, she knew what she was doing. She used to come back for a week, sometimes more, and every time Mia would treat her like royalty returning. I would too at first. And then . . . just like that, she'd leave again. Telling us she'd be back soon. That next time she'd take us with her and we'd all live together in . . ." the memory makes me shiver, "in some mansion or whatever. She was always one big promotion away from cashing out and being with us forever, that's what she used to say. I don't know, we were young, I believed her for a long while. Only then she'd disappear for months on end, and I'd be the one picking up the pieces with Mia, and the cycle would start all over again."

"What did she do?"

"Oh well, it was this skincare company she bought into. Literally, actually. Because it turned out to be this huge pyramid scheme. The top dogs all got put in jail, I think—but we didn't know that at the time. All I knew is that she'd leave us to 'work' and still come back months later begging my grandparents for money. I used to hear the arguments in the kitchen. It was awful."

"I can imagine," he replies, his voice so gentle and understanding.

Turns out, he's an excellent listener too. Even when he's drawing, I can see the words being taken in and digested. It somehow makes talking so much easier.

But I'm not here to talk, which I have to keep reminding myself, only as it turns out, the work is fun with him too. In fact, by the time that 3:55 p.m. comes around, I've finally pulled together the Reel we've spent the afternoon making.

"You like it?" I ask, showing him the thirty-second clip of the time-lapse I took of him drawing. The pencil whizzes around the paper until seconds later the blank page is a sketch of a beautiful tricolored Cavalier King Charles spaniel, sitting on a large stack of books. It might just be a rough etching, but it's unbelievable to see the picture take on life like that.

"If only it was that quick and easy, eh?" I ask him, smiling proudly.

"If it were quick and easy, it wouldn't be as fun," he replies, before he watches his own hands create life. Again and again. "You're amazing," he adds, and I can literally feel my whole heart soar at the compliment. I feel like I can breathe again. Like I have a purpose.

And then I realize, he didn't say it's amazing. He said, "You're amazing." Me. He was complimenting me.

I look up and he smiles at me, the most perfect genuine smile, with those perfect green eyes. Oh, if only this moment could last forever. If only this feeling, this all-encompassing warming feeling, could never leave.

"You made it easy for me." I shrug, but I can't help but feel a rush of blood pounding every tip of my fingers and burning at my cheeks.

He has a girlfriend, I tell myself quickly. *This is not a date.*

"You should show all this to Tasha," I say. I suddenly realize my mistake; now it's obvious what I was thinking. Bringing up his girlfriend, completely out of the blue? Oh gosh, that's embarrassing. "You know," I add quickly, as if it might help. "She can help repost. She has a bit of a following."

He laughs, looking at his hand as it taps against the kitchen table beside me. Finally he looks back up.

"Tasha and I broke up," he says.

I gulp. Hopefully not visibly.

So . . . he doesn't have a girlfriend? *This is still not a date,* I tell myself.

"My girls have to come first," he says, taking a deep breath. I don't say anything. I didn't ask for an explanation, and he doesn't owe me anything, but my god, I wanted to hear it. "She didn't understand that."

He leans in, probably to look back at the post I was sharing with him but I catch a whiff of his aftershave as his jawline levels with mine and the proximity between us is suddenly intoxicating.

This is not a date, I think, desperately losing conviction. He has kids! I don't want kids. And his kids have to come first. He just said that.

Almost as if he can hear my thoughts, his eyes peel up to me. He takes a few steps back.

"Look, I don't want you getting the wrong impression here. I only just broke up with someone and I'm not looking to jump into anything—"

Oh thank god. Now I don't have to justify the whole kids thing.

"It's cool," I interrupt quickly, relieving him of any tension. "I just got dumped, remember. I'm not exactly looking for anything here. I just came because you asked for help."

"And I called because you offered it," he concludes, "but look, you said on the phone you were lonely. Well, I am too. I thought, sometimes it's nice to have someone around to be lonely *with*."

And he has summed up something that fits perfectly in my life, even if he—having two kids—doesn't in any other context.

"That sounds like the start of a beautiful friendship," I tell him, trying to remember what film I'm quoting when something breaks my meandering thoughts. Because it just hit 4 o'clock, and as if on cue, chaos rolls through the door.

18

"Daddy!" I hear, followed by the swift steps of an excitable six-year-old as Cara sprints down the corridor to the open door of the kitchen.

Archie stands quickly, taking a few steps back and toward the kitchen door. He times it well, for just as he reaches the doorway he is all but rugby tackled into a giant hug from his youngest daughter.

The sight of it makes me laugh, which in turn makes Cara's head follow the sound right back to me.

"It's the headless lady!" she cries, but she doesn't let go of her dad in a viselike grip.

"Oh, please tell me that name won't stick." I wince.

Bailey walks in the door a little more calmly behind her sister.

"Hi," she says, her face perfectly neutral.

Cara looks up at her father, her chin against his chest. "Penelope wants to talk to you. She's by the door."

"Alright, alright," Archie says to her. He turns to me. "I'll only be a minute."

As he goes, I don't know why, but I lean back in my chair, just enough to see right through the corridor.

There's a woman standing there. By my guess, the same woman

who dropped the girls off. She's in her late thirties, and rather striking. A beige, printed maxi dress with a big knit jumper, her long curly hair braided to one side like Elsa from *Frozen*.

I shouldn't snoop. I move my chair back as Cara comes and takes a seat next to me, pulling both her feet up instantly. Bailey's hovering by the door, more unsure.

"I've come to help your dad with some Instagram content," I explain, knowing Bailey wants to know even if she doesn't ask.

"Can I see?" Cara asks.

"Of course."

I hand over the phone, peering over her shoulder to watch again. Every time I do I love it more.

"What's this music?" she asks.

"'Gonna Buy Me a Dog' by the Monkees."

She looks at it again, frowning.

"No," she says finally, decided.

"No?" I ask, confused. "It definitely is—"

"No, it's all wrong. It won't do at all."

My cheeks blush bright red. I feel like I've just been corrected in class by a teacher. Oh my. I mean, I thought it was . . . well, quite good actually.

"You need to use something I've actually heard of," she says, and I can already see her hit the edit button.

I open my mouth to correct her, naturally reaching for the phone, when I pause. Because what she has just said is actually . . . well, it's correct. It's something I told my clients all the time. If an audio clip is already trending, your post will naturally do better.

Only, I wasn't really thinking about that when I was doing this post. I just typed in "dog" and picked one I liked. Like an absolute rookie. So, I put my hand back down on the table, watching her hit the little audio button.

While Cara cycles through a few song clips I've never heard before, I notice Bailey hasn't moved from where she's standing in the kitchen doorway. She's keeping an eye on what's happening with Archie by the door. She looks a bit nervous. Is she in trouble maybe?

"Hey, Bailey," Cara asks, looking up at her sister. Bailey turns, like she's just been caught out. "What's that song that goes 'Foooooorget, marry, kill her, no! Just choooooooose love—'"

"'FMK' by Minotaur," Bailey replies, which is incredibly impressive given how little Cara gave her. I don't recognize the song one bit. But I do recognize the name:

"Minotaur?" I ask quickly.

Bailey's eyes grow curiously wide, at my quick response time. "You know Minotaur?" she asks.

"No, I . . . yes . . ."

Because the memory flashes back quickly.

The client meeting. That was the headline:

FMK—THE CHOICE IS YOURS!
YOUR CHANCE TO DECIDE WHERE MINOTAUR'S
GIRLFRIENDS SIT ON THE FMK SCALE.

So . . . they're popular? I mean, I guessed they were a bit popular based on the fact they were all over the *Finder's Keepers* website. But popular enough for these two girls to have heard of them?

I don't know why that shocks me.

I'm also hoping both of them don't realize that the term "Forget you" is the censored version, probably. I move on before the thought lingers.

"You know I followed your advice," I tell Cara instead. "I tried to show the world my authentic self."

"Oh yes?" Cara asks, wide-eyed.

"Well, it turns out my authentic self almost set my flat on fire. I don't think I like my authentic self much."

Cara raises an eyebrow as she looks up from my phone: "Are you sure you were doing it right?" The sass is another level.

". . . Doing . . . being me right?" I question. "Burning pizza is definitely authentic me."

"Burning a pizza?" Bailey asks. I'm glad she's joined us, even if it is at my expense. I've been watching her eyes drift back toward the door where her dad is still talking to Penelope.

"I was cooking . . . not a pizza, actually. And burnt a pizza in the process."

"Impressive," Bailey replies sarcastically. And I think to reply to her somehow, only Cara interrupts, "Here." She shoves the phone under my nose. "I fixed it for you."

There it is, the same thirty-second super-fast version of Archie drawing, only this time with a new tune. And I hate to say it, but the song is super catchy. Like next-level catchy. And weirdly, it does work. I mean, the lyrics aren't even slightly relevant to the drawing of a dog in a library, but it works.

"You need to change the grid picture too, before you post. Here, give it to me," Bailey adds.

I do as I'm told. She toys with the grid post, then hands it back.

"You can post it now," she says, satisfied.

I didn't think to do that. How are two preteens better at Instagram then I am?

"You need to go big, or go home," Cara tells me.

I look up. Is she . . . telling me to leave? Those big green eyes blink at me, like they've just instilled the greatest wisdom there is.

"Sorry?"

"Cooking is too small. You want a big change in your life? Think bigger. Emmy Pea says you need to go big, or go home."

"That's what Emmy Pea says, is it?" I ask.

"It is."

I completely forgot about Emmy Pea.

"I do quite like home," I murmur to myself.

"No!" Cara corrects, laughing. "You need to go big."

"Bigger than burning a margherita pizza?"

"Bigger!"

"I'm just worried that . . . if I go any bigger, I might set fire to half the city . . ." I begin, but then I hear the front door close.

Archie's footsteps start walking back my way.

I look over to Bailey, who is now biting down on her lip again hard, trying to squash the nerves. Oh, I see. So, she really is in trouble.

When Archie comes back into view, he's looking exhausted, as if the trip he just made to the doorway and back was a hundred miles long and this last stretch into the kitchen is the same distance all over again. He looks straight at Bailey, tilting his head in a "you want to speak first?" way, but she clearly does not. Pretending so hard not to be fazed by anything, she walks purposefully to the other side of the kitchen table that I'm still sitting at. Within seconds she reaches into her dropped backpack and picks out a sketchpad and some pencils, spreading it out across the table.

I can see the parts at play here, and I don't want to make this any harder for them.

"I think I'm going to head out," I say quickly, standing and grabbing my backpack from the corner of the kitchen.

"Are you sure?" Archie says, trying to perk himself up. He flicks his eyes over at Bailey, who has taken out some headphones. I smile at him, in as understanding a way as I possibly can.

"I should head home. I have to think what I can do to . . . think big." I smile knowingly at Cara, who laughs. She might well have clocked what's going on between her sister and dad, but she's playing ignorant, and I don't blame her.

"Let me walk you to the door," Archie says sweetly.

"You going to be alright?" I ask him this time, nodding my head toward the kitchen.

He grits his teeth, lowering his voice in case of eavesdroppers.

"It's nothing. Another day, another teacher's note. She's been doodling in class. Not listening to teachers. It's always the same story."

Something about the way he's saying it reminds me of our conversation earlier.

"Well, if you need someone to talk to, you can always reach out," I say. "I'm not a parent. I'm not going to pretend I know anything or can help." I add quickly to justify it, "But you told me earlier that being a parent is lonely during the good bits. I'd imagine it's probably lonely during the hard bits too. So, if you really want to give this 'lonely together' thing a go, you can always call."

I don't know what's wrong with me.

I'm cringing. I can't believe that that came out of my mouth.

"Anyway," I say quickly before my cheeks glow in shame, "today's been fun. Thank you."

"Thank you?" he laughs. "I'm the one who needs to thank you. Will you send me an invoice?"

"An invoice?" I laugh. "No, absolutely not. I just spent half a day here and produced—at best—one Reel that *your* daughters just fixed, apparently."

"You gave me a Google Sheet of logically ordered ideas."

"One Google Sheet for saving my life?" I look up to the sky in feigned thought. "I reckon I'm still getting the better end of that deal."

"I meant it when I said I have a few friends who could really use your expertise," he says. "I know a lot of people in small businesses. A little bit of Excel could go a long way. Even if you don't want *my* money, let me at least introduce you to them? They might not be able to pay much, but it would be something."

I nod. It wouldn't be a bad way to make a little income while I wait for my next role.

"That would be great," I say.

"Good luck" are my last parting words, and with a small "I'm going to need it," he disappears back inside.

And as I'm walking away from them for the second time, I feel genuinely sad in a way I wasn't expecting. Maybe it's the aftermath of a pretty perfect afternoon after three weeks of misery. Or maybe, just maybe, it's because I know the conversation that's about to happen in there isn't going to be easy, but I'd take a difficult conversation in that house any day over the silence of the empty flat I'm walking back to.

Suddenly I'm glad I have someone to be lonely with.

19

Maybe it's because of that loneliness that barely an hour after I arrive back home, I find myself once again on Instagram, staring at Jackson's profile.

I started off trying to find Emmy Pea.

@EmmyPea—nope.

@Emmie_Pea—some American girl with 132 followers and a private page. I'm guessing still nope.

After assuming I must have misremembered the name, I search for who I do know: @Jax_O.

I'm not even sure why I'm on it. I just spent an entire afternoon definitely not thinking about Jackson. In fact, I've been thinking about Archie. And those beautiful green eyes. And the way his bare toes wriggle against the floorboards. And about that soft smile that just opened me up.

But I have to be realistic here.

I just had a lovely, lovely afternoon.

But Archie clearly friend-zoned me. Which I'm happy with of course, because he wouldn't fit in with my life: I don't want kids.

Helen didn't want kids, that much was evident, and I suffered because of it. Now unlike Helen, I actually have a viable career path, one that I fully enjoy and doesn't leave me in debt to my eyeballs. I don't want anything to slow that down.

Even though it is, right now, however temporarily, very . . . slowed . . . down.

But the point is, I shouldn't have to change for a man.

So, even if Archie is wonderful. Even if his eyes melt me and his words warm me. I don't know how we would ever work. He said it before: his girls will always come first. He needs someone who will understand that.

And I'm not that woman, because my work will always come first. Which leads me back to Jackson.

On I scroll, through picture after picture. All of them I've seen before. Him at football. Him outside a restaurant. Him on a run.

And it isn't just Jackson either. Because he's not the only one looking at my stories here—Layla follows me too. Rich has been watching them.

People who I may one day work with again. I need them to think I have my shit together. How else will I ever get hired again? Because it's been a month and a half, and the best I have in my inbox is a few "we'll be in touch if something comes up"s.

So, I have to keep going. I need people to think I'm doing great. Because no one wants to hire you if you're a big mess.

Having already gone through all of his pictures, I head back to my Jackson Interests spreadsheet, thinking what else I could try. . . .

Category	Accounts Count
Client	160
Public Figure	72
Sports	59
Travel	27

Go big or go home.

I go to bed with just the smallest idea in my head, that grows and grows, until, after the most spontaneous twenty-four hours I've ever had of last-minute flights and packing, I step out into the crisp May air of France's glorious capital.

"Bonjour, Paris!" I cry out loud, because this is the kind of impulsive thing I've seen in movies as the romantic music blasts in the background. I have "La Vie en Rose" playing through my headphones so I have everything going for me for the perfect cinematic moment.

I wander through the streets, weaving my way through groups of strangers. Every single person that passes me, I want to stop and tell them, "I can't believe I'm in Paris!" But I don't, because that really would be strange. It just still feels so unreal to be here. I'm a planner, someone who prepares for everything, and yet here I am with a small suitcase that I packed this morning, one hour after I booked the airplane and four hours before my flight.

I look over to the Arc de Triomphe, trying to take it all in, then I weave through some of the smaller side roads all the way to the water. I cross the river by the Musée D'Art Moderne, and before I know it the Eiffel Tower is before me in all its splendor.

It's about 3 p.m., but I bought a sandwich on route and I missed lunch, so I take a seat on the grass by the tower's feet, looking up at it as I enjoy my *jambon-buerre*. Paris in April, on a particularly lovely day. There are a few shy little clouds circling the sky, but otherwise the lush green below my feet cuts right into a perfect sea blue above. It feels completely magical.

Baguette finished, I take out my phone, trying to work out how embarrassed I should be taking a selfie here. By the look of it, I shouldn't be embarrassed at all, given there are hundreds of people around me doing just that. So, I line up my shot, trying to find a good angle and take a few practice shots. There are two men annoyingly just a little in the way when—wait, is that . . . ?

I turn around quickly on the spot.

I saw it in the background of my selfie, but there it is in real life.

One of the two men in my background is suddenly on one knee, a ring in his hand. His partner has tears in his eyes as he accepts, and I watch on with tears in my own eyes as the two embrace.

A proposal! In Paris!

It's the most romantic thing I've ever witnessed!

I watch as they drop the box in their happiness, bending down together and laughing as the one proposing places the ring on his partner's finger.

The beginning of the rest of their life, I think to myself. And then I catch myself.

Why does that suddenly make me feel a bit . . . sad? I didn't think I was a "marriage" kind of person. And yet, I find myself wondering how long they've been together.

Is it over a year?

And how long before they asked each other the big questions? The life questions?

Because in our one year Jackson and I only had one conversation on the subject, and it wasn't exactly Nicholas Sparks–worthy. . . .

❧

I lie back against the arm of his sofa, sipping my drink while Jackson finishes a work call he had to take.

Of course, like any good millennial waiting in any capacity, I'm scrolling through Instagram.

Georgia's engaged.

There she is, holding up her left hand to the camera where a beautiful little ruby shimmers against the filter's glow. Behind her, her boyfriend kisses her on the cheek in happiness.

I smile instantly, sitting up a little straighter as if to tell someone, only no one's there. Jackson's still on the call in the other room.

Georgia is one of my favorite colleagues. She's friendly, sweet, but more than that she's hardworking and determined. She's the kind of colleague who you know will get the job done, so it's always a pleasure to work with her. And she looks so happy here. It's a cute picture, and a life-changing event. Of course she's happy.

After a few minutes, I lean back against the seat.

I mean, my reaction was instant; it's the same reaction I get every time a rom-com ends with a perfect kiss or a marriage proposal. It's the beautiful warm tingles of satisfaction that romance exists in the world.

And yet, is it as life-changing as those films make out?

"Sorry about that," Jackson says, sitting down beside me. *Immediately his hands roll around my legs, lifting them over him. It won't be long before my jeans are discarded for the night.*

Only, my mind is a little elsewhere right now. Almost accidentally, and totally without thought, I ask him, "Do you want to get married?"

Jackson almost chokes on his drink.

"I'm not asking you," *I laugh awkwardly, only just hearing what it must have sounded like out of context. I go red just thinking about what a strange position I've just put him in. I don't want him thinking I'm pushing him into saying something or . . . Quickly I try and justify it.* "I don't know if I do."

"You don't?" *he asks, surprised.*

"I mean, I don't know. But . . . I guess the main example you have of these things is your parents, right? And my dad split before I can really remember so I can't say I have anything positive to go off. They were married, and it didn't stop him from leaving. I don't understand what the wedding, what the rings, what the marriage really does, if it doesn't hold a family together."

He doesn't say anything, but his body twists toward me.

I don't think I've ever told anyone this before.

"I don't want kids either," *I say, and suddenly I'm so nervous I'm not seeing straight. Because this could be a game changer: a relationship ender. If he wants kids, I know that might change things for him.*

Oh gosh, I didn't mean for this to be "the talk." *Or even* "a talk." *I just had a reaction to an engagement photo.*

He looks out to the Thames below his feet, as if in thought. I feel so raw. Self-consciously I pull my legs off his and tuck them into my chest for support.

Well, I've started the conversation now, I might as well see it through.

"Do you? Want it all? Two kids, a wife, a dog?" *I ask.*

He takes a deep breath, as if not sure he should dare speak it.

"I'm not a dog person," *he says finally. And, by the way he moves around, leaning in to kiss me, I can see that in his mind, this conversation has now concluded.*

As his lips make contact with mine, I'm glad I can't say anything.

I should feel happy. The kids thing hasn't drawn an immediate line under this. Although, I weirdly feel a little foolish.

Because I did just open up there. And in return, he's just tugging at the button of my black jeans. But then again, maybe this is too early on in the relationship to have any kind of serious chat, I wouldn't know. I've never really had a relationship this long, because work has always taken priority, and no one has ever understood that. Any fling I began would end after the fourth or fifth night of me working late.

But Jackson understood that. Instantly. It's why we work so well together.

Only it means I don't know what the etiquette is. Apparently, nine months is still too early.

"You alright?" he asks, and I realize in all my thinking I've forgotten to kiss him back. So, I shake it all off.

"Yeah," I lie, because it's easier, wondering how long it will take before you can just be yourself in a relationship.

❧

It's so strange, in hindsight, to think how little Jackson actually knows me. I might have thought it was odd before, but now, having spent time with Archie, I find it increasingly bizarre. I mean, Archie—who I've met only a handful of times—knows all about my grandparents. While Jackson . . . well . . . he didn't ask.

And worse, actually. He clearly wasn't interested.

I look at the beautiful couple now, sitting back down on the lawn hand in hand. Oh, how perfectly happy they are.

Were we ever that happy?

I thought we were. But then again, I *thought* we were ready to take the next step.

❧

"My sister's coming around with her boyfriend next Friday," I say, trying to make it sound light as Jackson plates us up some of the Greek food he ordered.

"That your way of telling me you're busy?" he replies. He's humming away to the sound of Maisie Peters and I let her voice lull me toward more confidence.

"I wondered if you might want to meet her," I say quickly.

"I'm in Greece."

"Don't you leave on Saturday?"

"And you're talking about when?"

"Friday. The day before."

There's a very small pause.

"Meet your sister?" he repeats.

"She's the only family I have."

"So, you're asking me to meet your family?" Jackson says, sliding the Greek salad and chicken souvlaki over my way. He grabs a large chunk of chicken, ripping it apart with his teeth.

"Well, yes. But, it's just Mia." I wait for a minute so he can chew and swallow, but the silence while I wait for his digestion to work feels unending. So, my mouth opens and there I go again, speaking out every thought that passes: "She's cool. She's dating this musician guy at the moment. Unbrushed hair, always talking about a record deal he's never going to get—you must know the type. It's like her kryptonite. I swear they're a dying breed, and yet she seems to have a never-ending supply of them."

Because I've been talking, Jackson's taken another bite of his food. Which means when I stop talking, I still have to wait for him to finish. So, I keep going.

"She says this one is really the one this time though, so you never know," I conclude, laughing at myself, because Jackson's still eating and can't laugh with me.

After what seems like an age, he finally replies, "Sure."

I try to hide the smile that brings out in me. The relief running through me. He's going to meet my sister. Our relationship is officially moving out of this flat and into the big wide world.

"Now," he says. "Let's eat."

❧

I hear another little round of applause and my head turns to the other side of the lawn. Another proposal? That's a bit awkward. Surely, they saw the one on this side of the lawn first.

Still, it's cute. The couple embrace and I can't help but smile all over again. Like a little dagger to my rib cage, I remember that Jackson never used to kiss me in public. He never even went outside of his flat with me.

But that was because of me, wasn't it? I didn't want to run the risk of other people seeing us. I didn't want rumors to begin that I was sleeping my way up when that simply wasn't true. If I wasn't as bothered, would he have wanted to take me out? I have literally no idea.

Because meeting Mia was the first time we were going to break that barrier, only it didn't exactly pan out as I'd hoped.

❧

Jax_O
Something came up at work
Think I'm going to be late tonight
Me
np
I won't start cooking until about 8 anyway
Jax_O
I'll try and make it after dinner

After dinner?
I'm walking home on Friday night, the night of the dinner party, an expensive bottle of wine in hand. I bought it especially for the occasion. I can't have Jackson think I'm a cheapskate now it's finally my time to host.

Me
Can you not just postpone whatever it is until tomorrow?

I can see he reads it, but no response comes through.

I stand there for a full two minutes, which is a long time to just be standing very still on the streets of London, wondering if those three little dots will appear to say he's typing. But they don't.

I feel it in my gut. The annoyance. The anger. I'd put so much on this night; the first time I'd ever introduced a boyfriend to my sister. The first time Jackson and I wouldn't just drink and sleep together. But sit at a table, in company, talking.

And last minute, he's just sent a text?

I'm so horribly, gnawingly upset.

But after two minutes of his silence, I feel something else too.

For although this kills me, although I'm so annoyed I could literally cry, I should have seen this coming. This is not just any man; this is Jackson Oakley. We fit so well together because I understand: work will always be his number-one priority. As it is mine, sort of. It's why we only make one time block a week. Why I never push him for more. Because making him feel bad about working is like making someone feel bad about breathing.

I don't know though, I just thought . . . what did I think? That I would be the exception to that rule.

But I don't want to make him feel like crap. Then he might not come at all, and I definitely don't want that. So, cursing myself for my last text, I text again:

Me
It's cool
Just drop me a text when you're on your way x

And to that, there's an instant response:

Jax_O
X

❦

Ten minutes later I hear another round of applause.

Three proposals. Three proposals in (I look at the clock) twenty minutes?

It's gone from being adorable to feeling like some sort of personal attack. I smile, because I don't want to be rude, but suddenly I also don't want to be here. So, I get up and go, the rest of Paris still left to explore.

Except love seems to follow me like a lingering blue cheese. Outside the Louvre, another one. Outside Notre Dame, another.

I know Paris is the city of love, but why does the love need to follow me specifically? It feels like it's taunting me. What a fool I was, forever thinking Jackson and I were the perfect pair.

I can't risk running into another proposal, so despite being in the heart of Paris, my "authentic self" is in bed, watching *Emily in Paris* with room service instead.

This sucks.

Still, the world doesn't need to know I'm miserable and I can't have Paris be for nothing. So, I post the picture of me from earlier, with the Eiffel Tower in the background.

"Je t'aime" I caption, with a red, white, and blue heart.

And then I sit back, on my lonely bed at heartbreak hotel, and hit play.

Go big or go home.

Go big or go home.

That's what I think about all night. I can't stay in this city any longer, I just can't. But is that my problem? Am I not thinking big enough?

A wild thought crosses my mind. I dismiss it, and yet somehow rethink it moments later. After a dozen or so cycles of that, I check my bank balance.

The thing is, given the fact that I've worked nearly every day since I was sixteen without a holiday, break, or even a side hobby, I actually have quite a lot of savings.

Go big or go home.

So, that's settled then, I'm going to do it. I'm going to go big.

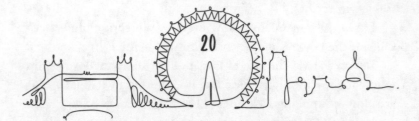

20

Ted Stevens sounds like the name of a '70s folk artist, but apparently, it's an airport. As my second leg of the journey weaves me over the most epic mountain landscape, I'm starting to come around to this Ted fella more and more. The peaks I fly past look right out of *Lord of the Rings*. I take picture after picture from 35,000 feet high, and not one does it justice.

The plane comes to land almost over the sea, before the runway appears from nowhere and just like that, I've landed in Anchorage, Alaska. Home to 288,000 people, between two to three hundred black bears, and most importantly of all, Betzy.

"I'm by a moose!" I tell her excitedly through the receiver.

"Like a picture of a moose?"

"No, like . . ." I turn, my head centimeters away from a full-on, life-size moose. "Like a real, fake, probably-once-living taxidermy moose."

"Ah! The moose! Hold up!"

I hear a shuffle on the other line, and I wait patiently with my little suitcase. My phone beeps and I assume it's Betzy again but it's not.

Mia
You're in Alaska?!?!?!

You didn't tell me you were leaving the country!

She must have seen the Instagram story I posted while I was waiting in line for customs.

Me

It's not nice when that happens, is it

I reply bitterly, ignoring the "?!?!?" she texts back.

Instead, I people-watch, beside my new moose friend. Until there, walking toward me, in the actual flesh, is my old flatmate.

"Betzy!" I squeal, going against the advice on the loudspeaker and abandoning my luggage (only for a few seconds) as I rush over to greet her.

Her jet-black hair is longer than I've ever seen it, almost down to her waist, but her bangs still remain, cut sharply and precisely. Trademark Betzy. She used to forever be wearing these tight jeans; only she's wearing black leggings and a big old college sports hoodie right now, one of Patrick's by the size of it. She literally looks like she's one of "them" now.

And she looks healthy too. London always drained her of color, but here it's like she's somehow in high definition. Her color's a little brighter, her smile a little wider. She looks good. She looks great even.

And I just came off a flight, after a terrible trip to Paris, so I look horrible. But I don't care.

"Welcome to Alaska, friend," Betzy says, and my, oh my, that Cumbrian accent feels like home.

"I'm so sorry this was all a bit spontaneous," I say. "I would have thought when traveling over four thousand miles I would have planned a little more," I tell her as we drive. She doesn't live far from the airport, which is a real blessing because I have seriously done my fair share of traveling at this point. I can't wait to have a shower.

"Fuck planning," she tells me. "I just care that you're here!"

"So, what's new?" I ask.

"My friend's just travelled nearly twenty-four hours to come see me. What's new with you?" she immediately swings it around. "Where has this career break taken you then?"

"Well, so far, to France, and to here. And France sucked."

She laughs at that, indicating as she pulls into a house.

I'll repeat. A house.

"Is this Patrick's mum's house?" I ask, because I know they all live close.

"It is not."

"His sister's?" I try again.

"It is my house."

"It's your house?" I ask again.

"My house," she repeats.

"You have a house?"

"I have a house."

Because that's what it is. A whole house.

It's got a pointy roof and a beautiful cabin feel to complement the forest it apparently sits beside. The wilderness seems right at the door, like at any moment a bear could just casually wander in for tea.

An actual house.

I'm still in shock as she leads me through the hallway. The inside of the house looks pretty dated, but when she leads me through to an open-plan kitchen space it looks like she's begun some renovation. There's an actual kitchen island. Like all those home renovation accounts I've seen. Like Archie's too, I find myself thinking. It's fresh, clean, and the window overlooks even more trees. This whole place just feels completely unreal.

"It was Pat's grandmother's house originally," Betzy tells me as she pours me some iced tea from the fridge.

"This is the reason you moved here?"

"Well, that and my family are all a twenty-minute radius away," comes a low, gruff, deep American accent. My eyes light up as I see him. Naturally I throw my arms around him.

"Patrick!"

I should hate this man. I should hate all 5 foot 9 of him because this is the man who stole my friend away to the other side of the world. Only I can't hate Patrick, because it's physically impossible. You meet Patrick and you love Patrick. He's a happy-go-lucky guy and it's beyond infectious.

He's a yoga instructor, and he wears that title with the same pride he wears his sweats daily. He is the ultimate sunshine to Betzy's blunt exterior. She's not grumpy, she knows how to have a laugh alright, but she is to the point. And Patrick, more often than not, doesn't have a point to anything. He's just doing things because he enjoys them.

And I'm standing in his *house*.

"But it's huge!"

"It's four bedrooms," Betzy says proudly.

"Four? What are you going to do with all those bedrooms?" I gasp.

"Well, in four months one of them will have a new little soul come to join us," Patrick says. "New little soul." Patrick actually says things like that genuinely. It always astounds me.

"Like a tenant?" I ask absentmindedly.

And then I see Patrick and Betzy turn to one another, unsure. I say "unsure." Betzy looks furious. Patrick looks Patrick, and by that, I mean he very rarely looks anything other than happy. But unspoken words are being spoken before me, and I suddenly realize. I look at Betzy. Her fresh face. Her glow. And I look at her stomach, hidden under one of Patrick's large hoodies. Then I look at them again.

"You're pregnant?" I ask, my heartbeat rising.

"I thought you would have told her," Patrick says directly to Betzy, very apologetically. You can't be mad at Patrick. It's physically impossible.

"We're pregnant," Betzy repeats. Only she's not smiling. She's saying it like it's a factually accurate statement.

"You're . . ." I do the math, which only takes a long time because I completely forgot the number that he said. "Five months' pregnant?"

"It felt strange to tell you over the phone," Betzy tries to justify, but she's lying. And I've just worked out why.

She didn't not tell me because of the phone. She didn't tell me because I was in a bad place. And because of one other, vital thing.

So, I clarify, "Betzy, just because I don't want kids doesn't mean I'm not unbelievably happy for you to be having them."

She looks at me uncertain.

"I know you think women can't have babies and careers, but I think I can and I don't want to hear you tell me I can't," Betzy tells me, with the air of a rehearsed speech. Maybe it was, prepared in advance, knowing I might make a comment. "I know it will be harder, sure, and I know I'll have a few months out for sure, but I'm not ready to give up teaching. And I want a family. So, please don't tell me I can't do both."

Have I really pushed this point so hard she needs to justify her own life planning? The thought that she didn't tell me because of it makes me feel so completely gutted.

So, I walk right up to her, trying to show how genuinely happy I am through every muscle of my body.

"You're having a baby," I say, tears prickling at my eyes. I launch into the most careful, longest, warmest hug.

"And you stink," Betzy replies bluntly. "Now how about having that shower?"

I'm jet-lagged. So jet-lagged. So while everyone else in this house (did I mention it's a house?) sleeps happily (or as happy as you can sleep with a five-month baby swirling around in your womb), I am wide awake.

I got tired embarrassingly early time their time, so it annoys me I wasn't tired enough just to sleep through.

What do you do when you wake up at 2 a.m.?

Me
You up?

I can't help myself. I've been thinking about him. Maybe it's because this whole thing was Cara's idea? Yes. That's probably why.

And he's my friend now, right? Sort of. And you can text friends.

At least that's the lie I tell myself.

> **Archie**
> It's 11 a.m. here and I have kids. Yes, I'm up.

> **Me**
> Oh good. Me too.

I realize I need an excuse to text him. I didn't have one handy. Only his last text did give me a little inspiration.

> **Me**
> I feel like you have more expertise than I do.
> What's a good present for someone who's about to have a baby?

> **Archie**
> Great question
> How close are you?

> **Me**
> I spontaneously just traveled half the world and spent a fair chunk of my savings just to come see her

> **Archie**
> So, not that close then?

> **Me**
> Exactly. Casual acquaintance.

Suddenly an Amazon link comes through.
Travel Mug.

> **Me**
> . . . I feel like you saw me say my friend was "having a baby" and you interpreted it as "camping"

> **Archie**
> This was the best present we ever received when Cara was born

> **Me**
> I think you need better friends if this was the best one . . .

> **Archie**
> You can laugh, but the first mantra of parenthood is "get ready for cold tea."

Me
Catchy
Archie
Discarded cups of half sipped tea were everywhere
that first month with Bailey
It was always just when the tea brewed that she'd
need feeding or changing. The cup would end up on
the side of the sofa, on the corner of the floor, back on
the kitchen counter.
By the time whatever you were doing was over, it was
freezing. Or worse, lukewarm
Me
That is worse
Archie
So, this keeps your tea hot
Plus, it doesn't spill, so a kicking screaming child won't
result in accidental burns or stains
Me
You've made a travel mug sound like an essential item
You should add Marketing to your never-ending list of
jobs

That's actually a pretty decent present. Certainly, an original one, one that no one else would have got for her. Sadly though, with that finished, I've run out of reasons to continue the conversation.

I bite my lip, trying to work out if there's anything else I can ask him that might keep him for longer.

Wondering *why* I want to keep him for longer.

Before I can even start typing, I get a text.

Archie
So, where is "halfway around the world"?

Looks like he wants to keep the conversation going too. Suddenly I'm glad I woke up at 2 a.m.

*   *   *

The next week floats by like something in a dream. Betzy works half days, or at least she's managed to wrangle it down to half days for me, so in the morning I laze around the house or go on short walks and in the afternoons, we explore all the sights Anchorage has to offer.

Turns out, Alaska is beautiful. Thank god that Betzy has the same shoe size as me, as hiking boots turn out to be a must, and believe it or not, I didn't pack hiking boots in my solo-traveling-romantic-getaway case to Paris. My pastel colors are, for the time being, exchanged for Patrick's never-ending supply of college hoodies and Betzy's leggings. When the three of us go out together, we all match. It's actually adorable.

We walk up mountains, have picnics by the water and go on daily bear hunts. That's what Betzy calls forest walks. I think she's joking. I hope she's joking.

We have home-cooked dinners (Betzy cooks, I watch) and at night, the texts keep coming:

Archie

You know Alaskan salmon is the best salmon there is

It barely needs any seasoning

Slice of lemon and you're good to go

Me

Quick reminder of the pizza incident . . .

Archie

You make a great point

Remember it's 911 over there, not 999 for the fire department

Me

I love the trust you have in me

The next night:

Archie

Bailey got an A in art today

Me

That's amazing!

Archie

That is amazing

What's not amazing is that I only found out when

I unraveled the screwed-up piece of paper she just

threw at her sister's head

Me

Did you talk to her about it?

Archie

She put her headphones on

Like it was no big deal

Cara was pretending like the paper ball wounded her

whole body so I had to focus on that for a while

"Wounded her whole body." That makes me giggle. That's exactly the sort of thing Mia would do all the time. If I nudged her, she'd cry out like I'd just pushed her off a mountain.

Me

This probably doesn't help

But my sister threw some knickers in my face last time

I saw her

And she's 28

So, that bit's pretty normal

Archie

Noted

By the middle of week two, I start to fill up my mornings too. With Betzy still at work, I think of all the other things I can do while I'm here.

Patrick offers to take me to his morning yoga class, but I genuinely couldn't think of anything worse. "Exercise is food for the soul," he tells me. Which is very Patrick of him, but if my soul does in fact have an appetite, I think it's probably more inclined to go for the pizza and Ben and Jerry's option.

However, it must sink in a little bit, for on the Tuesday of the second week, I decide to go for a jog.

The thing is, I'm still technically in a funk. I still lost my job in an incredibly embarrassing way. I still got dumped by the most beautiful man I've ever met. I'm still in a fight with my sister. I just keep forgetting about that stuff when I'm with Patrick and Betzy, because I'm enjoying myself too much to remember. Only when the house is empty, it starts to creep back up on me.

I may not want to "nourish my soul," but I did read somewhere that jogging is excellent for your mental health. So, when my memory starts to come back, I decide to try it out. Within seconds I realize why people think it's so good for you. It's because running sucks.

It like really, properly sucks and I'm thinking so much about how much it sucks, that I'm not really thinking about anything else. All my other thoughts that I usually overthink, they're out of my mind because I'm exhausted and tired and my legs hurt and that all has to take precedence.

But then I reach a point where I can't go on anymore. So, I stop, trying to catch my breath, and for the first time in this whole jog attempt, I look up. Before me is a huge body of water. I knew it was here somewhere—they live close to the coastline—but it's completely breathtaking, even if the breath hadn't already been taken from me because of that whole running thing.

It's the kind of view I immediately want to capture. And I can, I realize, taking out my phone. I spend a while, trying to get the right angle. Except no matter what I do, it never quite shows the full picture. I take a few anyway.

"You want me to take one with you in it?" a man's voice asks from behind me.

A man? Out here while I'm on a jog?

I almost laugh out loud as I turn around to see. My conversation with Betzy comes immediately back to me:

There I am, on a jog by the Alaskan sea when I stumble into the arms of a handsome but rugged Alaskan fisherman. He'll have a beard. And a tattoo of a fish.

Is this really my rom-com come true?

I mean, it can't be, because I'm pretty sure this man is actually just a boy. He doesn't have a beard, but I'm pretty sure it's because he can't grow beards yet. Plus, even if he *was* my handsome Alaskan fisherman, I'm not sure I'd be interested.

Because why is Archie's face filling my dreams? Why is his smile flickering into the corner of my mind?

Because I like him.

But I can't, I keep reminding myself.

He has kids. And I don't want kids. Plus, he friend-zoned me.

Still, this sweet boy is standing there in his dark hoodie, his hand out waiting in case I want to take him up on his offer.

So, I hand my phone over to the nice stranger, who takes a few steps back to line up the shot. I suddenly feel a bit awkward. I hadn't thought about which pose to try. Maybe one where I'm looking out to the view?

Only I don't have that much time to pose. Because it turns out, the boy wasn't trying to take my picture. He was trying to steal my phone.

Without missing a beat, he starts to sprint away from me, my phone clutched in his claws.

"WHAT?" I scream after him uselessly, before I start to sprint after him. He's quick. Very quick. But then I think about my texts with Archie and . . . no, I can't not text Archie later just because some arsehole has stolen my phone.

So, I sprint harder, my feet hitting the ground with such a force I feel I'm flying. I don't take in my surroundings, I just sprint.

And surprisingly, I catch up with him. Just as we hit a more pedestrianized road, my hand makes contact, grabbing his arm and spinning him around. I hold on, pulling him to a stop.

"Drop the phone!" I splutter, glad to have a few other people out and about witnessing this. There's only a handful of them, but I can see in the corner of my eye one of them has taken out their own phone. To call the police? No, probably not, given it looks like they're just filming.

Trying to get away from me, his left hand grabs my right wrist, and I would be scared, I would.

Only my whole body knows what to do.

Using the flow, I step to my right instantly, his hand still gripping on to me twisting him round. Then using my left I push at the join of his forearm swiftly and strongly, launching him to the ground smoothly where I can use my knee to hold him down. He's on the ground and pinned in less than ten seconds.

Karate. Black belt.

I didn't lie to the girls when I told them that in my interview. I may not have ever done any in real life before, but I studied it for so long the moves are ingrained within me.

The boy is stunned. A little winded perhaps, but more just confused as he lies on the ground, pinned. I use the opportunity to reach out to his hand and grab my phone. Then I stand up and move away.

The boy gets up instantly, sees the phone being pointed at him from the other side of the street, and realizes it's not in his best interest to stay. Turns out filming isn't quite so useless after all. Off he sprints, far, far away, hopefully never to be seen again.

And strangely I don't feel bad about any of this. In fact, I feel like Scarlett Johansson in *The Avengers*. I feel absolutely kickass. And as for the jogging—I think I've nourished my soul enough with it for today. So, I ask the next passerby for directions, and walk, far more casually, back to Patrick and Betzy's.

"I mean, it's just a normal city at the end of the day. There are little shits everywhere on this earth," Betzy tells me as I recount the tale over a delicious salmon roast. Archie was right of course. A bit of lemon and this fish is unreal.

Patrick picks up his phone, toying with it as we speak.

"I couldn't have been more of an idiot. I literally gave him my phone."

"You are a buffoon," says Betzy, showing her usual levels of sympathy. "But I've seen tourists do a lot more stupid things than that."

"Looks like you're internet famous already," Patrick laughs, twisting his phone around.

"Wait, what?" Betzy gasps, watching the video with me. There I am, grabbing his arm and he twists around. And then, down he goes. A few seconds later I wave the phone in my hand in victory— and off he runs out of shot.

It looks a little less epic than it felt, but it still looks awesome.

"How did you find this?" I ask.

"I just Googled 'girl robbed Anchorage' and this popped up." He's smiling on, like he usually is, looking suitably impressed, but Betzy doesn't look like that at all.

"Oh, so they could film you, but not help you?" she questions, but my mind's turned down a different route.

"Do you think I'll get in trouble?" I ask worriedly. The thought just springs into mind. Is taking down a robber safely and without harm a criminal offense?

"I think you're good." Patrick shrugs. "How come you know how to do that anyway?"

It's a bit of a long answer. One I know Betzy's heard before. But I guess Patrick hasn't, so I summarize as quickly as I can.

"Some boy at school pushed Mia when we were kids. I'm pretty sure he was trying to flirt with her. She was beautiful even as a kid, so he pushed her and I just saw red. I ended up punching him. My grandparents realized that I probably needed to . . . not punch people, even when they were being mean to Mia, so they signed me up for these karate classes instead. And I loved it."

"Protecting your sister? That seems like a pretty great reason to learn self-defense," Patrick notes wisely.

"Seems like a pretty great reason to punch someone," Betzy adds.

"I don't know if it has something to do with Dad not being there and Mum not being around, but I've always felt that I've needed to be the one to defend her I guess."

"Talking of," Betzy interrupts my thoughts, "are you two speaking again?"

I sigh.

"I shut her down last time she tried. I wasn't ready," I say sadly.

"So, what actually happened?" she asks gently. "What was the fight about *this* time?"

And I instantly sigh again. Because the fight wasn't *really* about her at all.

❧

I get a text from Jackson just as I'm heading up the stairs back to my flat.

@Jax_O
I'll text when I know timings x

I know he's already told me this, I do. Only, when I read that text, it seems to sting all over again. I can't help it—I'm embarrassed. I've told Mia he's going to be here for dinner, and instead he'll be here for late-night drinks at best.

Mia's due in about twenty minutes anyway so I need to put on my happy face. It's enough time for me to put the oven on and—

Nope. Looks like Mia's due right now, given she's slumped outside my door.

I'm about to say something—shock at her arriving early to mine for once—when my eyes stop me. She's wearing monochrome, head to foot. Black jeans, black oversize hoodie under a black coat. Dark gray bralette underneath, that I suppose is supposed to be a top.

Her face is ghostly, mascara runs thick down each eye. Both of them are so puffy and small beneath the makeup it's hard to even see them. My heart stops.

"Mia?" I run toward her. She looks up at me, brushing more tears from her eyes as she accepts my hug. I'm down on all fours, bringing her head to my shoulder and I can feel the vibration of her cry against me. "Did someone hurt you?" I feel anger. So much anger and confusion. Why is she dressed like this? Why does she look like this?

"He said I wasn't on brand!" she cries out. Her voice is muffled by my shoulder, so I lean back, taking her in. She doesn't look hurt, physically, but it's hard to tell under so many layers.

"*Who said what?*" *I ask again, before moving to stand. "Here, let me help you. Let's get you inside.*"

I help pull her up, which is difficult as she's wearing thick, black, heeled boots that make her a good six inches taller than me.

"*Len. He said I wasn't 'good for the image.' So he broke up with me.*"

"*What?*" *My door opens and I usher her inside.*

"*He broke up with me!*" *Mia cries forlornly. I misheard her. I must have misheard her.*

But now she's clarified, something instant snaps inside of me. Really? She's not hurt. She's not harmed. And we're back here again.

This would be the . . . seventh time this has happened?

I drop my bag on the floor and walk over to the kitchen, suddenly a lot more relaxed. I open the cupboard by the sink to get some glasses out, ready for my expensive wine.

I take a long, hard look at her. This thick-mascara-wearing, chrome-character portrayal before me.

"*This wasn't his image?*" *I ask, pointing to the outfit as I pass her the glass of red.*

"*No, this* is *his image,*" *Mia says, taking a seat at the small round table. I grab the bag of tortilla chips and rip them open, placing them on the table between us. "I saw he was moving away from me so I thought I'd do a Sandy from* Grease. *You know, the big ending? The cigarette foot stamp and . . . well, I turn up at the gig, looking all . . .*" *She points to herself, like it's something to be proud of, "and I thought he'd take it all back. But he didn't. He said it 'didn't suit me.' That it didn't suit me!*"

I sit down, leaning back into my chair, and already grabbing a handful of the crisps.

"*It doesn't suit you,*" *I agree, because that's 100 percent accurate. She looks like a caricature.*

"*Gee, thanks, Daisy. Just what I need.*" *Mia scowls.*

"*All I mean,*" *I correct, "is that you shouldn't have to pretend to be someone else to be liked, Mia. You should be enough as you are.*"

"*But obviously I wasn't enough as I was! That's the point!*" *Mia cries, right into her wine. I bet she can't even tell it's not the cheap stuff.*

"Well, then he wasn't the right one," I say, a little more sympathetically now, because I am. A bit. I hate it when she cries. Especially if she cries because of someone like what's-his-name (I literally can't remember).

"But he was!" Mia insists, before describing in intimate detail exactly why and how. I sip my wine and eat my crisps and, when the origin story commences, I decide it's time to put our food on.

There's something I admire in the way Mia falls in love. It's so completely and immediately, as if she's forgotten all her previous heartbreak and baggage and she still lets herself free-fall into emotions at the first chance. By the time we've finished the bottle, the dinner, and the story, I check my phone. It's 11 p.m.

Still no word from Jackson. This was supposed to be a dinner party with him. And instead, it's once again a Mia breakup story.

"Well," I say to Mia finally as the dinner plates get roughly fitted into the small dishwasher. "You can obviously stay here. Until you can find somewhere."

"You don't mind?" Mia asks gratefully.

I hand over my spare key to her before I forget, and she accepts it, slotting it into her back pocket.

"No, not at all," I say, and I don't.

Secretly, and I mean this secretly as Mia must never know, but I like it when she stays with me. It brings back all the feelings of looking after her all through our childhood. Of all those nights in our grandparents' spare room together. I don't miss those days, I don't. But I do miss her. Sometimes.

"Oh, thanks, Dais." She jumps up from her seat, toppling over her (thankfully already finished) glass, and launches into a huge hug that traps both my arms in.

"I actually had another favor to ask you, while we're on the subject," she continues.

"Oh yeah?"

Suddenly the little tweet of a text pops through to my phone. My heart stops. Jackson. Jackson's finally on his way.

Ignoring Mia a little, I grab my phone, but I already know what it's *going to say. He said he was going to text before he came over and here it is: at 11:18 p.m. Better late than never. Mia's a night owl anyway— she'll stay up. I just hope he's still got some energy left in him when he—*

> **@Jax_O**
> Sorry. Can't make it x

Oh.
Right.
Mia's still talking in the background, but I can literally feel my heart drop down into my stomach.
He's not coming.
I can't cry in front of Mia. I'm her older sister. I'm the one that has her shit together.
"So?"
Mia breaks my thoughts. She looks nervous. My head feels like it's ringing. It's the first thing I've ever asked him for, ever. And he's let me down.
"Sorry?" *I ask.*
"Just a hundred or so. It would just really help to—"
"Money? You're asking me for money?"
And so our fight begins.

"You're turning into Helen!" *I scream.*
And we both go silent, feeling the weight of those words heavy in the air.
"This is nothing like Mum," *she says, determination in her voice.*
"Running to family to pay off her own mistakes? Sounds a lot like her to me."
"That's not even slightly—"
"It is! Here you are asking me for more rather than getting it back off Liam!"
"Liam? Who's Liam?"
God, I don't remember. Wasn't that his name? I pause, stuttering, because I can't think of any other boys' names beginning with L.

"Luke?" I try. I shouldn't have tried. My point is valid, my argument solid, but my upper hand is waning given the unbelievably angry look that has now shot across Mia's face.

"Lenny?" Mia screams back, and suddenly I'm worried about my neighbors.

"That's what I meant!" I spit whisper back, but it's too late. Mia's gone.

"You didn't even remember Lenny's name? We've been together for, like, three months and you don't even respect me enough to remember his name? I'm your sister! Or did you forget that too?"

"Don't be ridiculous."

"Ridiculous? Just because we don't all have these high-powered relationships like yours and Jackson's—yes, I know his name despite never meeting him. In fact, wasn't he supposed to be here tonight? Where is he?"

I feel the blood leave my cheeks.

"Oh, so now you realize," I try, clutching at straws to turn this conversation around. "You've been so wrapped up in your own life that it only took you until near midnight before you even realized—"

"Did he dump you? Is that why you're being such a little bitch about this?"

If there was going to be something that set me off tonight, that would be it. The embers were churning, but like a gas stove twisting right to high heat, I feel my mouth suddenly explode.

"I'm being a 'little bitch' because my SISTER is asking me for money AGAIN! I'm not your bank account, Mia. You can't just come groveling to me every time some man lets you down!"

"Don't take it out on me if your 'businessman professional' has fucked you over."

"GET OUT," I scream. And I mean it. I really, really mean it.

"Alright, calm down," she says, her voice instantly cooler, but I can't. I've lost it. My mind is racing, I'm burning with rage, and the last thing I need is Mia around me to make me feel worse about everything I already feel like crap about tonight. "GET OUT, MIA," I scream. I push the chair out of the way so hard it flies back to the floor, and I stomp straight to my front door. I throw it open, and it hits the back wall with a thud that echoes out. "GET OUT NOW."

"Daisy, I don't have—"

"I don't care! I don't want to listen to it!" I scream. "Call me when you've got my money back from your thieving ex and you've finally learned its value. Now get out."

And without another word, Mia leaves.

❧

"I took it all out on her when it was Jackson who had completely let me down," I sigh, shaking my head. It makes me cringe even thinking about it. If I could only rewind time and tell Mia that.

"I know you liked him," Betzy says, "but the thing is," and I think for a second, she's going to impart true wisdom on me. I prepare myself. Only she follows it up with: "Jackson sounds like a complete wankhead."

"He isn't a . . ." I stutter, pulling a face as I copy that word: "*wankhead.*" Did she seriously just use that term? I move on: "He was just . . . busy with work and . . ."

"Classic wankhead behavior. Make you think the wankhead-edness is because of something you did and not just because of general wankhead-ery."

"Probably best to stop using terms like 'wankheadery.' I'd prefer our kid to stick to the more conventional insults and swear words," Patrick chimes in, before excusing himself. He probably senses this is a conversation more between Betzy and I, but he doesn't go far. His yoga mat is set up in the next room, and instinctively he wanders over to it, stretching. Post-meal yoga?

"Fair," she answers him, then leans in closer to me. "Tell me, you were with him for over a year. Did you actually love him?"

That's a big word.

"Well, maybe, I don't know," I say, trying to work it out. That suddenly feels like a long amount of time, when it didn't feel that long together. Not with Jackson. Not with one evening's time block a week, max.

"You would know if you do."

I stop, unsure how to answer. For how could I love him, when I was never actually myself around him?

I might not have had to dim down my clothing choices or quit Instagram, but I guess . . . I do talk a lot. Naturally. I can't help myself, I fill silences, even when I really, really shouldn't. But I had to bite back words nearly every time I was with Jackson. Because he likes people to be direct, and to the point, and so to make him like me, I bottled myself up.

But maybe that's just what you do, at the beginning, I think to myself. You always have to dull down some parts of your personality, you can't give them 100 percent Daisy from the get-go!

But then I think about Archie.

I mean, he got 100 percent Daisy from the start of the Frankenduck saga. And he's still texting me back. He didn't dump me by text after a full year of being together on the day he knew I was getting fired.

"Oh my," I whisper, only now seeing what I should have seen all along.

Patrick moves from sun salutation to a warrior. Betzy leans in, her face showing a level of sympathy her words don't quite reach.

"Did the shiny suit and terrible marketing chat glamour you the same way black mascara and spiked boots does for Mia?"

Oh gosh. I think . . . I think she's right. I rub down my face with this horrible realization.

"Why didn't I see this?"

"Because pricks with pretty dicks are a dime a dozen. And we women are taught in numerous conscious and subconscious ways throughout our whole life, that we're the lucky ones who get to ride them if we play by their rules."

"Betzy . . ." Patrick murmurs from the corner.

"I don't mean you. You're great, babe," she tells him, acknowledging the prompt. "Do you know that statistically, most women wait until they are fully qualified for a job before they apply for it, while a man will apply even if he has as little as fifty percent of the criteria necessary? Well, it's the same with dating. More men try their luck with women who are—and I hate this term—'out of their league'—than women go for men who they consider to be above them. It's like we all have a built-in repression system, telling us we're not worthy when we're with someone we think is amazing, when we are. Because no one is out of the league of anyone else. We all bring something different to the table."

It is true. I never once thought I was worthy of Jackson Oakley. I mean: I said his whole name, nearly every time: Jackson Oakley. Like he was some mythical creature I'd somehow stumbled upon.

In my head, I hear Cara's voice, screaming from the inside of the shopping cart.

"I AM WORTHY!"

If I only had an ounce of Cara's spirit maybe I'd never have found myself in this position in the first place.

Patrick moves back to warrior. I watch him, processing it all, while Betzy concludes, "Well, if who you really are didn't fit with Jackson, then he was the one not worthy of you. You shouldn't ever have to be someone you're not for a man."

"You can't say that." I shake my head, turning back to her. "Everyone changes who they are a bit in a relationship. Even you've changed. You have Patrick-isms."

"I do," Betzy agrees, looking over to him. He's sitting with his legs crossed in front of him, finishing off his meditation with his eyes shut. He peeks one open at the mention and smiles as he catches Betzy's eyes. It's adorable. "But I'm not being someone I'm not. I've just changed who I am. And the difference is, he's changed too. That's what happens when you meet your match. You change together. Because love isn't one-sided. It isn't."

She leans in, and I don't think I can handle any more hard truths. But she doesn't burst any other bubbles. Instead, she takes my hand.

"You are beyond worthy of love. And I know, because I love the real you," she tells me.

And it's everything I needed to hear and more.

"I love the real you too," I reply.

"And I love the real both of yous," says Patrick from the other room.

"There's a lot of love to share," Betzy agrees. "Now, I'm beyond hormonal and very loved up. So, let's switch on a rom-com so I can swoon a little more."

21

It takes me two hours and the remaining half bottle of the red wine to calm down. By then I'm in my bed, watching my phone clock as it turns to 1:30 a.m. I try to put my phone down and sleep, but that's not happening.

I click on my messages to Mia, half expecting to get some angry text from her that will help me feel in the right again. Except nothing comes through.

She's probably asleep already, I think. That would just be so typical her; fresh out of a major argument and she's probably sleeping soundly like a little baby. Except . . . where? If she's broken up with her boyfriend, then not there. She was between houses which is why she was staying here. I just sent a girl out on the streets of London at 11:30 at night with nowhere to go.

Oh god.

But I'm still angry. So I text.

Me:

Just text me to tell me you're safe.

All of our texts are always littered in little x's. It's second nature to me to finish off a text to her with one. But not this one.

Proud of myself, I stare at the screen for a while waiting for her reply.

Another hour I spend on Instagram or the news apps I have. Just scrolling. Aimlessly scrolling. The dog videos help, sort of. It helps in the way something hugely unhelpful helps, in that I'm not distracted, but I'm doing something and that's better than doing nothing.

I go back to my messages when the clock hits 2:30 a.m.

Me:

Text me please x

There we are. I added a kiss. Maybe the reason she didn't text me back was because she was worried I'd just shout at her again when really, I just want to know she's not dead in some ditch.

Oh gosh. Might she? Be dead in some ditch?

Me:

Mia?

In a panic I go straight to BBC News. Nope, no immediate news articles of a body found are circling. That somehow makes me feel no better.

The whole night I toss and I turn. I switch off my phone, tell myself I'm worrying for nothing and try to sleep. And then ten minutes later I sit back up, switch my phone back on, and wonder what else I can do to stop the worrying.

I go on her Instagram, and then remember. She doesn't have it anymore. She deleted it a few boyfriends ago.

How else am I to know she's safe?

And then suddenly there is something. At 6:09 a.m. I see it. Hours I've spent not sleeping and panicking and fretting and sweating and at 6:09 a.m. when I turn back to my messages I see the little read receipt.

For a minute I think the sleep deprivation might have kicked in, so I look again. She's read it at least. But is she really that immature that she's not getting back to me?

Well, if she can read it, then she must be alive. And have access to her phone, which she would be able to ring the police on if she was in a bad situation, so just like that, my worry subsides. Instead, it turns to another emotion. A strong one. I'm now furious all over again.

I don't know why I was thinking about that moment, but when the rom-com we're watching pauses, I realize that I wasn't concentrating enough to hazard a guess at what might come next.

Luckily, Betzy goes first.

"I think the snowboard instructor is going to turn out to be the French pen pal she wrote to as a kid. I think her fiancée will get caught cheating on her with that blonde girl and she's going to do something dangerous and climb a mountain and then they're going to get stuck there overnight and he's going to have all these sexy survival skills and he's going to keep her alive till morning and then they'll marry and have ski babies."

I mean, apart from the fact it was set in a ski resort, all of that feels a little wild to me.

"What do you think?" she asks.

Except, my mind is a little elsewhere.

"You know that CV thing," I ask her instead. "Do you think men have it right? Should I be applying to more roles that I'm not qualified for?"

"If you want," Betzy says, putting the controller down on her growing bump. She rubs it thoughtlessly, twisting her head around. "Have you had no bites?"

"I think maybe what happened in that boardroom . . . I think I'm blacklisted somehow."

"Blacklisted for telling a company quite accurately that they shouldn't degrade women?"

"Blacklisted for calling their CEO a tool."

"Ah, yes." Betzy nods. "Well . . . maybe. In reality of course, you're asking people to make a new role for you in a company. It takes a lot of people to sign off on a new role, and lots of people usually means a long time. It could just be a matter of patience needed here. I'm guessing you haven't seen any open vacancies you'd fit?"

"Not at companies I know," I say.

I feel like it hasn't just been two weeks since I arrived here. Things fell into place so naturally for the both of us. I feel like we're back on our old green love seat, in our old flat, like normal.

"What did you like about your job anyway?"

"Everything." I shrug. "I liked doing the analytics. I liked decorating the decks."

"Did you like the social media aspect?"

"I don't really know. That's just . . . what happened really. Actually, I guess I liked it better when I was working with client sales data. That was a lot more fun to find insights from."

"Well then, have you ever thought about branching out from marketing then? A different kind of analytics?"

No is the answer to that. I haven't thought about that. And actually, maybe that's what I really need. A much bigger change than just a new company. Using my skills in new ways.

I turn back to the screen, feeling some energy returning to me.

"OK, I think she's going to fall over on the slopes, get amnesia and this snowboard instructor is going to help her recover. She's going to forget all about her fiancé—and I agree, I think he's going to cheat with the blonde girl. Then when she remembers it will be too late, she'll be in love with this snowboarder instead which means despite cheating on her, the fiancé will just get off scot-free."

"Right, so there we have it. A survival story or the unusually common in rom-coms case of amnesia both leading to badly behaved men never getting their comeuppance. Let's see what we have in store for us today."

And then, happily, she hits play.

As we pull up to the airport, I almost can't speak.

I've just had two magical weeks and the fact it's ending is heartbreaking.

I don't even think it's the location either. Sure, having a nature reserve a short drive away totally helps, but for me it has nothing to do with the setting. It's all about the company. Being with Betzy and Patrick is almost like being with no one at all, but the best kind of no one. When you feel you can just be you, without anyone watching, but you're doing it with company.

Only that company lives in Alaska, and I don't.

The car pulls up to the drop-off, and we sit together, both of us not moving, both of us not sure how to freeze time and make this last forever.

Finally, because silence really isn't my thing even in moments like this, I break it.

"So, are you going to wait five months to tell me your little Betz-rick has entered this world?"

"Betz-rick?" Up raises that little eyebrow of hers as she takes her hands off the very stationary vehicle.

"Or Pat-zy. Oh!" I gasp excitedly. "That one actually works! Little baby Patsy."

"Veto," she replies with her deadpan face. Then she looks down at her stomach, and a small, hidden little smile flickers on the corner of her lips. She looks so radiant. And happy.

Now I think about it, what a difference this makes to the over-worked, tired, frustrated Betzy I lived with. I mean she was great, the greatest flatmate I could have asked for, only she never used to *love* her job. It was just "OK."

And beyond that, London wasn't her chosen city either. It was just where the university was, so that's why she lived there.

She used to watch rom-coms in the evening to escape. She used to spend her evenings cooking because it was something that got her out of her own head. She missed having the peak district on her doorstep.

It isn't like she hated life before. Only she didn't love it.

And then she fell in love with Patrick.

Happy Patrick. Patrick who didn't take life seriously, who wasn't set in any ways. Patrick who sold her this beautiful country with beautiful views and a different pace of life to city living.

And now she's here with him. Living the life he spoke of.

Sure, falling in love moved her away from everything she knew, but it wasn't a world she'd ever wanted. So, actually, it's worked out.

"You know, I'm planning on setting up a private Instagram," she says, looking up at me. "For my family back at home."

"Am I family?"

"You're family."

I smile at her, but I can feel the weight in her words generally. Patrick's family will be all around her out here. She'll have support. But she was always pretty close with her extended family. It must be hard, knowing you're raising a baby they'll never be able to "pop in" to see.

"The power of social media is that it can make miles and miles feel like a scroll away," I reassure her. "Although . . . you know, I've been out here for like . . . two weeks now, and I only posted one story when I'd only just landed."

"Does that make this a wasted trip?" she says, her voice sly and judgmental.

"It makes it a better trip," I tell her. Because I was genuinely loving life off-screen enough to not feel the need to put it out there. The only picture I even took was the one before my phone got stolen. Which makes me realize . . .

My thumbs move quickly, the picture not even needing a filter before I post it with a little jogging emoji and an American flag. It'll upload once I get reception.

"See! I've officially been here. It'll be on my grid post and everything."

"I know you know this, but it's totally possible . . . not to post too," Betzy says. I look over to the water, stretching out as far as the eye can see. "It's possible to just enjoy life without having to tell others about it."

"Ah, I'll have to correct you there, Betzy. See, I've been told I have to *show* my authentic self. At all times."

"That sounds like the kind of crap Mia would tell you," Betzy giggles.

I think about Cara instantly. In many ways she is a bit of a mini-Mia. She's far sassier than Mia ever was, but they both have those big eyes that get anything they want. They both want the world to watch them.

"Mind, even when you don't post I still need you to text me,"

Betzy replies. "I don't care if the rest of the world doesn't get to see you. I still want to."

The free airport Wi-Fi must have kicked in, as her warm words are rudely interrupted by a little buzz. I pull out my phone, wondering if it's flight updates.

It's not.

Archie

Safe flight x

I can't help but hide the little glimmer of joy that waves through me when I read that. Betzy must see it too as she says:

"I know losing your job sucked. I know Jackson ending it with you sucked. And I know this is a Patrick-ism," she rolls her eyes at the very thought, "but I genuinely think that maybe it was all for the best. Maybe you did need to take a pause before you find your feet again."

She looks over to me, and I can see she's about to cry. It's already too late for me. I'm saying goodbye to Betzy, with no fixed date to when I'll see her again.

"Because you will find your feet again," she says. "Better feet."

"Manicured feet?"

"Painted in a pastel rainbow," she concludes.

"I love you," I say quickly and quietly.

"I love you too," she replies, and it's a perfect, perfect goodbye. Until she adds: "Now I have a baby pushing on my bladder and I've wanted to wee through this whole conversation. So, however nice this is, let's get you gone."

22

Once I've checked in my luggage, I walk over to my gate nice and early.

I have a DM.

The only person who has ever really DM'd me is Jackson. Can it be? After we've just spoken about him, after I've just realized how little we had—is this him finally making his way back into my messages?

I hit the little paper plane symbol with bated breath and—

I instantly feel sick in a whole different way.

@Georgia_K

Georgia. The last time I saw her was the day of the client meeting. The way I just left her there . . . and then I got fired, so I couldn't even apologize to her in person. And then, well, a little selfishly I just forgot. I've been so wrapped up in the whole "being unemployed" thing, that despite having very little to do, I haven't done the one thing that I probably should have: apologized to her.

I have no idea of what kind of groveling she must have done when I left her. I have no idea how those clients must have treated her after I treated them so sourly. I dropped her in the middle of the ocean without a raft and didn't even give it a thought to see where she ended up.

Perhaps, if I'm really being honest with myself, I didn't want to. Because getting in touch with her meant recounting once again a day that I never want to speak of.

I gulp, wondering whether just before a twenty-four-hour flight is the right time to deal with this. The thing is, I'll be thinking about it for all twenty-four of those hours anyway; I might as well know what it says rather than worrying about the unknown.

I take a deep breath and open it.

> **@Georgia_K**
> Hi Daisy. I hope you don't mind me reaching out to you like this on Instagram. HR wouldn't pass along your personal email. I can see you're traveling right now. It looks like you're making the best of what must otherwise be a really terrible situation that you've been placed in, and I'm so glad to see it.

I pause then. That I've been placed in? She was there! She must know that I placed myself in this position.

> You might have heard this from someone else already, I'm not sure who else you're still in contact with as I know how loved you were in the company, but I just wanted to make sure you knew what happened in the days following your departure.

That makes me pause too, because it's made me realize something I hadn't actually noticed before.

I'm so loved in the company, am I?

So loved that no one else has reached out. At all actually. No texts from anyone saying how sorry they were to see me go. No one asking what happened. I'm not sure I would have wanted to talk about it, but . . . I don't know. It would have been nice to be offered the option, wouldn't it? They all cared when I was working all around the clock to progress their decks, their success, and their careers, and yet once the company dropped me, they were happy to drop me too. *So loved in the company?*

But something Archie said rings in my ears for some reason: am I the elephant in the room here?

Could it be that no one knows *what* to say, so no one is saying anything at all? And can I really blame them for that?

Even if I would prefer them just to reach out.

> Well, you might have guessed, but we lost them as
> clients.

Ah, there we are. So she's getting in touch to make me feel terrible. It's working of course: guilt literally floods me. I'm suddenly feeling hurt enough. Maybe I don't want to read the rest. I don't want to be made to feel more miserable than I already am.

> After you left, they expected me to disagree with the
> points you made, and I just didn't. Because I completely
> agreed with you.

What? I blink a few times, rereading it to be sure.

> Delivery aside . . .

That's a beautifully tactful way of saying "despite your absolute breakdown."

> . . . the points you made were valid: it was horribly
> degrading to all of the women involved. So I told them
> I agreed with that, and they cancelled our contract with
> us. Only soon after, this happened:

There's a link to an article. Wincing, unsure, I click it.

Minotaur's management has demanded *Finder's Keepers*, a boutique magazine under the multimillion-pound Elites Collection umbrella, issue a formal apology for using a "thoughtless and incorrect interpretation" of their latest song "FMK" as an excuse to "bully and degrade the women they love."

"The song is all about how to call out people who categorize women into such baseless categories, and *Finder's Keepers* seems to have done exactly that," says the band's front man, Kit Parker.

Finder's Keepers has already lost exclusive interview deals with a number of celebrities over the article . . .

I scan through, my eyes devouring it all. Then I head straight back to Georgia's DM.

Well, as you can imagine, the management team went from avoiding my eye contact to suddenly singing our praises. Dropping them in advance of that article meant our brand wasn't pulled into the mud with them, and other magazines got in touch asking us to represent them because of it. We gained multiple clients overnight thanks to you.

I don't know why this makes my heart soar, but it does. I can't help it. They deserved to go down. I just can't believe I never saw that article before!

I'm saying all this partly because I think you should know, but also because there's a huge case here to get your role back, if you want it. I know you said some things that weren't ideal, but given the subject matter and what's happened since, I actually think Matthew would take you back in a heartbeat. I know I would vouch for you. Nearly all of us would. I can't tell you how many times I've overheard your old team saying how your leaving has left a black hole in the whole department.

Really?
It's such a shame no one told me. Not one person.

But you were, and probably will be, one of my favorite colleagues of all time. Your hard work was inspiring.
Plus, off the record, I completely agreed with you. Their CEO was a tool.
Anyway, if you want your job back, please let me know. Because I will fight for it personally, tooth and nail if I have to.
I'm always around if you ever fancy meeting up, no worries if you're busy living the high life!

Thanks for everything,
Georgia

She signed it off like an email and everything. How perfectly professional she is.

And here I am, buzzing in an airport preflight, full of positive emotion which is just something I wasn't even slightly expecting to feel right now.

I could get my job back?
After all of this, I could be back at Branded?
I mean, not for sure, but it's worth a shot?
I begin my reply instantly: telling her how happy I am to hear from her. How appreciative I am for her words. How sorry I am for what I did, no matter what the outcome. I'm only about halfway through when I get a text message come through.

As if I couldn't be smiling more, I find myself forcing my lips even wider when I see who it is:

Archie

You're probably on the flight already—but for when
you land . . .

I mentioned to you last time we met that I had some
friends who might be interested in working with you?

Well, one in particular has been desperate to get
some of her admin in line and was hoping you might
have some free time?

At first, I feel just a little twinge of disappointment. He's only
texting me for work.

But then another feeling takes its place; because that's just fine
by me. Because we're friends, I remind myself. Only friends. We both
said that.

Plus, I've just felt a whole new wave of excitement after Georgia's
message. It's time I get myself back in the game. So, I reply instantly.

Me

I'd love to!

Archie

Ah, brilliant.

Looking forward to it x

Me too, Archie, I think, as my flight is finally called. I pocket
my phone, feeling a new pep in my step.

Me too.

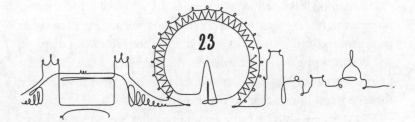

23

Archie opens the door with a wide smile across his face, and—almost like an instinctual reflex—I feel my lips turn just the same way. Strange, I knew I was looking forward to seeing him (for work, I remind myself), but I didn't realize how much until I saw his door and felt an unfamiliar flutter whirling around.

"I'm so glad you came," he says, his voice as smooth as honey. And—although I can't say this aloud—I realize how glad I am that he's glad. Because I am too. I really, really am. Except, before I have a chance to tell him that—or in fact anything—he cuts through by saying: "Pen's in the kitchen already. I can't wait to introduce you."

Ah. Right. Straight to business then.

But that's fine too, I tell myself, now purposefully maintaining that smile across my lips and pretending it's actually fine in a totally professional manner.

"Lead the way," I say.

It turns out, the woman who Archie brought me around to help is the same beautiful woman who dropped the girls around the other day. From far away, she looked lovely, but from close up Penelope is simply beautiful. Auburn curls right down to her waist, and a makeup-less smile that outshines Maybelline adverts.

And she's got a really cute business too. She runs a craft shop that began on Etsy, selling wool made from local farmers to her hometown, but as it gained popularity, she tried adding a few other platforms too. Only now she's struggling to keep an eye on them all.

"Really, I just want one centralized place where I can get all the figures I need for Mr. Taxman and see how much stock I have left for each item. I don't even know if that's possible."

"Oh, it's possible." I smile and, taking her laptop away, I start adding data connectors to Google Sheets to pull in all four shops into one big sheet. I make a series of pivot tables for tax purposes, and another more specifically for stock.

"It will color red as soon as you're down to your last ten across the platforms and drop you an email too, and when you add more stock in this cell," I say, pointing it out, "it will update across all of the platforms. Plus, it will shine orange if there's a 'surge.'"

"A surge?"

"If suddenly the product becomes particularly popular. We used to realize that if something is featured on a TV show, or an influencer adds it to their must-haves, that suddenly there would be an influx of people toward a certain product, even if the product itself is old. Like chess boards suddenly became increasingly popular after *The Queen's Gambit*. If the rate of purchase doubles in a small space of time, this will flag it in case you then want to market it more. You never know when these trends happen, but they happen fast and they're usually over in no time at all so if you're not on it, you'll miss it."

Combining the data together also means I can do all kinds of fun things like finding the right platform for each product ("It looks like the colorful wool does better on social media platforms like Facebook Marketplace, while it's actually the more natural colors that do better on Etsy, so maybe it's worth changing your store images to match those audiences?") and finding correlations between the goods ("I can see across all the platforms that nearly seventy-six percent of those that buy your 'white chunky wool,' also buy the knitting needles to go with it. So, have you ever thought of pairing them as a set?").

"Selling them both together?"

"Well, why not? With a small discount of course to both of them separately, but I'd imagine you'll see a huge uplift in the sales of knitting needles without too much of decrease in the purchase of wool. . . ."

"Well, it's never a bad thing to have a spare set of knitting needles around . . ." she says wisely, taking notes.

And it doesn't take me nearly as long as I took making reels for Archie, because this kind of thing comes second nature to me. I adore it. And given I've never worked with small businesses, nor have I worked with arts and crafts stores, all the insights are new to me.

So it's fun.

It's really, really fun.

Only there is one thing missing: Archie.

When Archie introduced us over an hour ago, I expected that he'd hang around. I'd come to *his* house, so I assumed he'd be present. Except he made us some teas, gave us very top-level introductions, and then left us to it.

I find out how wonderful Penelope is though. She's a mum of another girl in Bailey's school.

"But really, I only met Archie when I was going through my terrible divorce. I used to live not far from here, but my house never looked anything like this of course. Archie just needs to touch a wall for magic to appear. He's helped me design my flat."

I agree with her completely. There has so far not been a single room in this house I haven't thought was extraordinary. Although I can't help but note that that's the second time he's been associated with a divorce. Are his friends just particularly unlucky in love?

She told me that Archie and she hit it off immediately when they met, always leaning on each other for pickups and last-minute childcare needs.

"Really, he's one in a million, that man. You don't find them like him anymore," Penelope says dreamily, and I find myself sighing at the fact.

"I hear you," I say accidentally, and then realize that's probably inappropriate, so I justify it quickly: "I feel like any other man would have court-martialed me out of their house the way I came into it. But he's been great—"

"Are you kidding?" Penelope interrupts, completely surprised. "He said you found his girls wandering around Sainsbury's alone and, with absolutely no obligation, stayed with them until that terrible ex of his went to collect them."

"Oh," I reply, probably just as surprised. I blush instantly. So, he's talked about me? "That's not actually . . . well, it is but I didn't meet him then. I came for an interview, and I ended up—"

"Shielding his girls from the argument he had with Tasha. Yes, he mentioned that too."

"Did he mention that I ended up in tears on his couch? Hardly a fantastic first meeting."

Penelope laughs at that, a sweet laugh. One not filled in the least bit with judgment. Because she's kind like that.

"Was it Cara?" she whispers conspiratorially. "Oh, she has that effect on people. She once made me cry for an hour because I told her I needed to go to bed early to get my beauty sleep and she said, 'You're already beautiful. Inside and out.'"

It makes me giggle, but something about the whole thing gives me a pang of jealousy. Because the more we talk, the more I'm sure: my assumption was true. There's something there between her and Archie. And given she's beautiful, talented, great with his kids and so kind, I can't fault her; I can't help but see how perfect she is for him.

But that's alright, I say to myself. I'm here for work. And it's good work! I love playing around with new datasets. I love finding quick improvements that will make her life easier. I love being the expert here, and she's made the afternoon fly by, even if it wasn't quite what I'd hoped for.

After the whole afternoon of pulling everything together, we emerge out of the sitting room and into the light of the kitchen at about 4 p.m.

"He'll be out fetching the girls at this time. I expect he'll be back any minute. Fancy a tea?" Pen says, as if it's normal that we're in Archie's house alone together. I didn't even hear him leave. She can't have . . . moved in already, could she? It feels strange to be in someone's house when the host isn't home. Before I get to overthink it too much, Pen's voice cuts right back: "This has been vital for me, you know. I didn't even know where to begin. . . ."

"Oh, I'm glad you thought it," I say, genuinely happy to have been of service: "If you get stuck at all you can always drop me a line."

"You know, I know so many people who could do with a day like this. Would you be open to more work if I pass your name on?"

More work? My cheeks glow at the thought of it. More things to take me out of my perpetual boredom of unemployment. I nod, a bit scared that if I agree out loud my voice will crack.

"Which reminds me of course, I know we haven't talked money yet, but how does three hundred pounds sound for this afternoon?" she asks. £300? If I'm honest, it's the first time I've even thought about it but I just gave her a very basic rundown of something I could do in my sleep. Hardly worth £300. She misreads my surprise entirely: "I was only basing that on how much I'd previously paid my web developer, so if I'm completely out of line, please just let me know! Of course if you'd rather take an ongoing commission for work on those platforms then I'm sure I can—"

"I'll tell you what, I'll send you an email with all the details and if you have any issues, you can just let me know," I say quickly, which is the fluffy response I used to always give at work when I had no idea of how to answer. But £300 for simply doing what I already love doing? That doesn't sound bad to me.

In some perfect twist of timing, we both turn our heads to the sound of the lock being turned.

"That's my cue," Penelope says, smiling and satisfied. "It's been wonderful meeting you. You really are brilliant—but I knew that before. If there's one thing that Archie never does, it's exaggerate, and he couldn't stop singing your praises."

I don't even know how to begin replying to that, because I'm so completely shocked by it. I'm so lost that I just stand there like a grade A fool as Penelope greets Archie by the door. I'm still looking completely foolish as Archie shuts the door behind her, turning back to me.

I look down at my waist, laughing. When did Cara start hugging me? I was so in my own head I didn't even see her sprint toward me.

"Hello, Cara," I say, the contact of another human warming my whole body. She looks up at me with those big eyes blinking furiously. I notice Bailey has wandered straight upstairs to her room wordlessly. Archie's eyes follow her, not sure of what to say, and I feel for him, utterly and completely in that moment.

"Were you able to show cross-product correlations to help Pen with her marketing?" Cara asks, sweet as sugar.

Wow. I don't think I ever said the word "correlation" until I was well into my twenties.

"How on earth did you know that phrase?" I ask.

"It's what you told us you did in your interview to be our nanny," she says smartly.

Ah, yes. I did.

"Well, in hindsight, those skills probably weren't vital to look after you. But yes, I helped Pen."

"How did it go?" Archie asks, a little nervously, I think. Maybe more because of Bailey's frosty reception than anything. But given what Penelope's said to me, I can't stop smiling.

"It's been incredible. Thank you," I tell him, and if I'm honest, I'm not even sure what bit of it I'm thanking him for. Shaking off the feeling as Cara peels off me, I start my own journey to the front door.

He laughs as I pass him.

"Daisy, where on earth do you think you're going?"

I've just reached the yellow door when I stop, turning back. He has that familiar cheeky grin spread across his stubbled cheeks.

"Well, I don't want to interrupt your evening."

"But you're staying for dinner," Cara says pointedly.

I chuckle at that, looking up at Archie as if that's a funny thing. Only he's got the same expression as his daughter right now. Two peas in a pod.

"Am I?" I ask.

"If you want to," Archie adds.

"You want to," Cara concludes.

They make quite the pairing those two. Archie flicks his hair back into place, not that it has a place.

"I really don't want to impose—" I begin, but really, I want to impose. I very much want to impose.

"I don't know what *impose* means, and I don't care. Because you can't go to Disneyland, and not tell me about it. It's illegal."

"Oh," I grimace, catching Archie snigger. "I didn't actually go to Disneyland. . . ."

Her jaw drops.

"You went to Paris, and you didn't go to Disneyland?"

"No, I went to Paris to go to . . ." I grimace. "Paris."

She looks between the two adults in the room, horrified.

"Adults are so weird," she concludes. "Well, you'd better tell me about that then anyway," she says, like it's a poor substitute but one she's willing to let slide. With that, she wanders back into the kitchen, expecting us both to follow.

And our eyes lock. Those beautiful green eyes.

Is it strange to say I missed them when I was away? Because seeing them now, I know that to be true.

"So, it's settled," Archie concludes. "What can we get you to drink?"

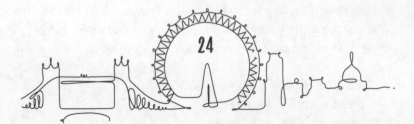

24

When Archie told me "fish and chips," I was imagining a takeout from a local chippy. It seems however, that those cooking implements on the shelves are, unlike mine, not just for show. The fresh cod is hand-breaded and seasoned. The chips are cut thick and par-boiled before being put in the oven, filling the kitchen with the beautiful smell of rosemary. As I watch Archie working away with his sous-chef Cara at his side, I suddenly see the appeal of culinary-based activities.

Bailey only joins after the third time her father calls her down to eat, and I can see she's not ecstatic about there being someone else joining them.

She sits silently, playing around with the food on her plate while Cara asks me question after question about my trip.

Before I know it, I'm recounting rather dramatically my entire encounter with the boy at the beach.

"Wait, you actually *do* know karate?" Bailey pipes up.

It's the first thing she's said since joining us, and the rest of us—who were all laughing away (I might have embellished a bit) all pause at the interruption.

"I told you that I did. In my interview."

"I thought you were lying."

"Oh, I wouldn't lie in an interview. That kind of thing will always come round to bite you. You want proof?"

I look over at Archie for permission, but I can see he's clearly just happy his daughter's taking an active interest. So, I pop out my phone, finding the video online. It doesn't take long.

"That's you?" Bailey asks, clearly looking between the video and the woman before her to spot the differences.

"As I live and breathe," I tell her. Cara runs around the table just as Bailey starts the video again.

"I didn't see that skill on your CV?" Archie dares to comment, his eyes more fixed on his eldest than on me. She's interested, and he doesn't want to break the spell.

"Martial arts aren't usually a prerequisite for nannies or data analysts," I reason.

"Will you show me how?" Bailey asks, looking only at me.

I rub the back of my neck at the thought.

"Well, I wouldn't be able to show you everything. I did it so long ago I'm sure most of it's gone by now." I wince, as her face—which was looking at me with some interest—falls. I need to bring her back, so I add: "But some of it's pure muscle memory."

I look over to Archie, who is watching on, a little unsure.

"In fact, let me demonstrate here. Archie, why don't you help me?"

"Yes!" squeals Cara beside him, pushing him up as Archie looks like he's just been chosen against his will by a stage magician. He's laughing, a bit nervously. We clear some space around.

"Is this going to hurt?" he laughs.

"If it does, I'm doing it wrong," I reply, widening my eyes.

On request, he reaches out for my wrist and, not even pausing for thought, within seconds I have him pinned to the floor. The girls both gasp, Cara turning hers into whoops of joy while Bailey pulls up her legs under her to get a better shot. Even Archie looks stunned.

"How did you do that?" Bailey asks curiously, fully invested.

I show her by walking forward into the empty space beside Archie, and using my free hand, I carefully chop down on his inner elbow until his balance is overthrown and he collapses backward. Of course, he is more than happy to be floored several times over as I demonstrate again and again. He's keeping his eyes on me, but I can see how they flicker to Bailey. I wonder how long it's been since they've both been involved in the same thing like this.

"Now you try," I say, and with very little prompting, Bailey takes my place. "Gentle, now," I say as Archie has a mini sweat of panic. "You need to get your movements fluid. This is defensive, not an attack."

But Bailey doesn't go for the jugular. Instead, she's measured, slow. Determined not to hurt, but to get it right. She is literally the perfect student, unlike Cara of course, who when it's her turn, gets it all wrong by rushing it all—although Archie dramatically falls despite it all being for effect.

Even I'm a little surprised when Archie finally looks at the clock. "Ah! We're already past bedtime! Come on, girls, let's head on up."

Eight p.m.? How did it ever reach 8 p.m.? There's a little protesting of course, but both the girls eventually submit to the idea. I'm not surprised—as I slide back into my chair, I realize quite how exhausted I am. Traveling and jet lag are also catching up with me.

For the second time today I feel Cara's arms around me before I see them.

"I still think you're a fool for not going to Disney," she says happily.

"Cara!" her father reprimands.

"Noted," I reply as she runs upstairs.

Even Bailey shares a "thanks," daring the smallest smile before heading on her own way up the stairs.

"I'll be right up," Archie says to the girls, then turns to me. "I won't be long. Can I give you a top-up?"

He opened up a bottle of sauvignon blanc for us to go with the fish. Suddenly I worry I've overstayed my welcome. The girls are heading to bed, which means one thing: "I should go."

"If you really want to, sure," Archie says, biting his bottom lip.

"But if not, stay, I promise this won't be long. Otherwise we'll waste the bottle."

It seems like a bad excuse, but I can't help it. I'm tired, and I'm probably going to start aching soon, but I also really don't want to leave. It's been one of my favorite evenings in . . . well, forever. At least in this country.

"Sure," I say, and I see Archie's face grin like a Cheshire cat, before he disappears upstairs to his girls.

25

I can hear the footsteps above me of Cara, I assume, brushing her teeth and sprinting by the sound of it. How she has any energy left is beyond me, but I hear her squeals from where I sit on the burnt-orange sofa in the beautiful sitting room, staring at that hilarious painting of two puppies eating cake.

It's such a brilliant painting. One puppy just about ready to blow out the candles while the other, naughtier pup is already mouth around the icing.

I take a sip of my wine, feeling a strange sadness hit me.

Because all it makes me think of is Mia.

Mia and me.

And everything that happened between us.

❧

A week after she left my flat I still haven't heard anything from her.

Given she's not on Instagram, I can't even stalk her from afar. I get why she's angry. Now I've had time to think it all through, I'm a bit angry with myself. Sure, she's careless, but I was projecting on her and . . . I had a right to be annoyed, but I shouldn't have chucked her out like that.

I get a few texts from Jackson, not quite apologizing but certainly giving excuses; a call ran over . . . a client was in trouble . . . I couldn't say no. . . . All things I expected, I just put so much on this one night that I feel annoyed by it all. Plus, if Jackson had just been there, I wouldn't have fought with Mia.

Jackson left on the Saturday for a boys' holiday and arrived back the following Sunday, but with work taking precedence, my next scheduled time block didn't fall until the Thursday a week later. By then it's been almost two weeks of radio silence on the Mia front.

"I know she was alright the night she left, otherwise she wouldn't have triggered the read receipts," I tell Jackson, as I sit on his sofa, my legs tucked up tight underneath me, "but I just wish she'd text me. Or call me. Or something. I don't even know where she's staying."

"Sounds tough," Jackson replies. He's spread himself out, his legs splayed, his arms wide as they wrap around his sofa. The week in Greece has given him a tanned glow. He's in his usual white shirt and chino combo, his top button undone.

"Like, at what point do you call the police?" I ask.

"The police?"

"To file a missing persons?"

Jackson laughs, before he realizes I'm being 100 percent serious.

"Daisy, she's not a kid. So she's pissed at you, she doesn't want to speak, big deal. Give her another week or so and she'll just reply again and probably act like nothing happened."

"But I don't even know where she is!"

"Probably living back with that ex of hers."

That's not something I'd thought before.

"But he ended it with her?"

"She'd have found a way. Probably another reason why she's not getting in touch. She's probably embarrassed to tell you that she's back with him."

I take a deep breath. Gosh, I want to believe him. He speaks with such confidence that it's hard to disagree. A warmth that instantly comforts me. I unpeel from where I am, and—carefully with the drink still balanced in my hands—I crawl over to where he is and tuck myself into the nook of his arm. He pulls me close, kissing me lightly on the forehead.

"You really think so?" I ask.

"I know so," he says, putting down his drink. "Now, I have something more important to tell you."

More important than my sister's health and well-being? I try to keep my face neutral as he continues.

"I've just secured us a pitch with Finder's Keepers. They're a magazine under the Elites Collection—a multimillion-pound company with hundreds of magazines under their belt. If we secure this work with them, we could be opening up to endless opportunities. We're talking big money here."

"Oh," I say, not hearing anything that's more important than my sister.

"Well, I want us to deliver something our competitors don't have. You." I go red at that, mostly because I didn't see it coming. "I want to show them that we have the edge. Maybe if you send me over some of the more generic insights, we can send to them in advance. Can you do that?"

I shrug.

"Of course."

Then he takes my drink out of my hands. Slowly he uncurls from me, twisting himself on top, ready for the night's activities to begin.

And I want it. I do.

But I can't help but think as his light kisses trail down my neck: how can he "know" Mia's alright, when he's never met her before?

"You know, I might go home," I say, feeling something click inside me. I'm not really with Jackson tonight. I'm elsewhere. And if I can't be in the moment with him, then it's not the right moment to be with him.

"Really?" he asks, and I can't pinpoint the tone.

"I just need a few days I think," I say warily. "It's not you."

"Are you sure?"

"Yes, I'm sure, it's not you. I'm just . . . I'm . . . I think I need to go home."

A whole month after I kicked Mia out of my flat, I'm walking with a completely artificial pep in my step toward the Finder's Keepers offices with Georgia by my side. I'm wearing my usual client attire: the smarter side of smart casual. Blue jeans, heeled boots, and my pastel yellow jumper. Georgia's close behind me, wearing a black pencil skirt with a white shirt like she wears most days. She's a very formal woman, which I really admire. I also admire just about everything else about her; she works hard, she has a positive attitude, she has brilliant ideas. I notice that engagement ring sparkling on her left hand.

Their offices are not too far—the other side of Piccadilly—and the streets are packed as always. I've already Googled what the door to the WeWork they use as their office space looks like so I can see it ahead of us clearly. A man overtakes me and I get a huge whiff of something deeply unpleasant as he goes. It makes me notice him, in a crowd of anonymous faces.

I know that face. I may not have been able to stalk Mia on social media, but I have been following this man so I recognize the hair—all matted and rock star circa 1970. It's him. It's "Lenny." The man who just overtook me is Mia's ex.

Jackson's words ring in my ears: "I'd put good money that she's living back with that ex of hers."

Maybe he's right. It's literally the only lead I have. I don't hear what Georgia says to me, because my eyes are on him as he walks into the Pret right next door to the offices. I'm sure it's him. 100 percent.

"Ready?" Georgia asks, mentally preparing. This was a meeting given to us by Jackson, the VP of Marketing. It's a big deal to Georgia too. This could be promotion-worthy if it goes well.

I blink a few times before the reality sets in. The meeting. Jackson's clients.

But, I think, already decided, I still have a few minutes.

* * *

"Mia?"

"Yes, Mia. Mia your ex. Or maybe not your ex. Maybe your girlfriend?"

"Mia's not my girlfriend," he says.

I'm really having a hard job trying to hold my breath and speak at the same time. Sadly it's a bit hit and miss, as I feel the stale tobacco mixed with the body odor of someone only not washing because it might "alter his perfected appearance." Honestly, this man is intolerable. I have no idea why Mia liked him.

More importantly, I have no idea where Mia is. And Lenny's words are not helping to soothe my soul.

"So, she's not been living with you?" I ask, feeling more and more desperate.

"No."

"Then where is she staying?"

"Fuck knows."

I came in here hoping for the pit in my stomach to be filled with knowledge and now all I'm doing is panicking more. While I feel my heart start to crumble, my hands shake, I can see this man has not read the room. Instead, he leans back on his bar stool, his green juice in his hand.

"That girl is fake as shit," the fake rock star tells me. "She can burn in hell as far as I care."

And something inside me twigs. Because when someone is mean about Mia, I just see red. My trigger has been pulled. I wouldn't be able to stop myself if I tried.

"That girl," I hear myself saying, my voice thick and fast, "is fucking amazing. So, what? She loved you enough to try to be the woman you wanted her to be? She's a ten, and not just a ten on good days, a solid ten while you need to douse yourself in water, soap, and about twenty gallons of aftershave or something because you absolutely stink." I can feel the heat of my cheeks exploding out of my skin. My voice gets louder and louder, my whole body almost tearing out of my clothes like a scene from

The Hulk. *"So don't tell me she's 'fake.' You know what's fake? Being privileged enough to literally own a shower, and then putting on this 'too rock to wash' persona. I swear to god—if she really is 'burning in hell' right now as you say, you will be joining her. Enjoy your shitty life."*

I'm angry. I'm angry and I'm scared, and this man's face looks incredibly like someone in desperate need of a reality check.

I look at my watch, then panic all over again. I need to go. The meeting is in five minutes now, and Georgia's just outside. I don't have time for this. I'll have to postpone my anxiety attack until after this meeting. Not even bothering to give him a second look, I turn and flee, heading straight back toward the WeWork door.

"Ready?" I ask Georgia as I rush to her side.

She looks confused, looking at my hands and probably questioning why I just went in when I didn't even come out with anything.

Plus, I went in half normal, and came out breathless, unsteady, rocked to the core. I feel weak. But I can't be weak right now, I'm at work. So, instead I move us swiftly forward. But all I can think about, all that's really circling my head, is where the hell is Mia? Where is my sister? Because as far as I'm aware, no one has seen or heard from her now in one whole month. Four whole weeks. Thirty whole days.

And why the hell did I let Jackson Oakley convince me not to ring the police?

26

I've been so in my own head, that I don't notice Archie until suddenly he's there at the door, watching me as I'm standing still utterly transfixed at the painting of those puppies. He must have taken his contacts out upstairs, as on go the rounded tortoiseshell frames.

"Sorry," I say quickly, coming out of my daze.

"Sorry for what?" he laughs sadly, "for making Bailey smile tonight? That's tough, I'm telling you. Believe me, you have nothing to apologize for in this household."

A smile plants itself on my lips absentmindedly as I pull myself out of the panic I was just reliving. This house suddenly feels so safe. So warm. What a wonderful way to be raised.

"So, it went well with Pen today, did it?" he asks.

"It did!" I say back happily. "It just felt great to be working on something really, although I got a little bit of good news on the way back home."

"You did?"

"I think there's a shot I may be able to get my old job back," I say excitedly. He just looks on, curious. "Well, I've written to my old manager and the head of HR, giving a business reason why they should take me back. One of my old colleagues, Georgia, has backed it already. It's really touching actually, to see someone fight that hard for you."

"And how would you feel about returning there," Archie asks, "after the way they treated you?"

I guess I hadn't really thought about that part. I was so excited about the role I didn't think about how it might feel to return.

"Gosh," I sigh thoughtfully, "well, I guess it will be a little bit like meeting up with an ex after a bad breakup."

He laughs at that, gently, sweetly. And maybe because it's been playing on my mind, but I suddenly turn it around to ask:

"Talking of breakups, and this is going to sound bizarre, but are you some sort of divorce guru?" I say, fueled potentially by the small amount of wine within a very jet-lagged individual. "Only Pen mentioned she met you through hers, and there was that man on the phone . . ."

"I'm not sure a law degree gives me guru status."

"Ha!" I guffaw. Then I pause. Because he's sort of not laughing. Which means . . . "Wait, are you serious? You're a lawyer?"

"Guilty 'as charged' as the terrible joke goes."

"You're a *divorce* lawyer?"

"I only dabble these days. And I'm also a barman if you remember. And 'just a handyman,' and a life coach—your words—and a great many other titles too."

I'm very confused right now.

"But being a lawyer is like . . . a career!"

"Being a dad is a better one, for me at least, I assure you."

I'm stunned. I have to physically remember to shut my mouth. Because becoming a lawyer is hard. It's highly skilled. It's incredibly well paid. And I highly doubt the other jobs he's done—it doesn't look like they'd be even close to the same payslip.

"I have been robbed of a great many things, but through it, I have been gifted time with my girls. I'm not going to waste it sitting through tribunals." He takes a long sip, looking around the house. I wonder what aches he still feels, knowing how he got it. "I worked out a long time ago exactly what I needed to feed them, clothe them and make them happy. And the other odd jobs I pick up are for company or for headspace. I need both to survive."

I'm in awe.

"I'm pretty sure even if my mum had the money, she would never have done something like that. She was too busy living her exciting life to give that up for us."

It just comes out of me. I wasn't expecting to divulge it, but there's something about his presence that opens me up. I also feel like I just interrupted his life with mine, only instead of turning the tables again, Archie leans in.

"You really think so?" he asks, so gently it really does make me think. So, I tell him.

"She used to come back with all these photos on these disposable cameras she bought. We'd all go with her to get them developed, and then she'd spend an hour or two every visit just adding them to her photo albums and going through them with Mia and me. She had so many of these thick bulky photo albums, one a year at least, sometimes more, completely filled with her travels.

"And the first few times she went through them with us, I remember looking at all the locations and thinking about how wonderful it must have been. But the older I got, the less I cared about where she was. What I saw instead was her face. Smiling. Ear to ear in every picture. And she'd cycle through them, telling us the stories behind every one, stories that didn't include us at all. All the happiest moments of her life, so far away from Mia and me, and she let us know it."

Archie nods thoughtfully, sipping his wine, his hand loosely running the length of the sofa's arm. He bites down on his lip, before asking:

"Are you sure they were the happiest moments of her life?"

"She had about a bazillion pictures to prove it," I tell him. "And not once in any of her trips did she take a picture with Mia and me. We didn't fit into her photo albums. We barely fit into her life."

"And you know that, because you saw pictures of her smiling

elsewhere . . ." he summarizes, and then gently—oh so gently, he adds: "Well. It must be true then."

I pause, at that. He's not exactly being sarcastic, but with the tone of his voice, it could go either way. I think about telling him it definitely, definitely is true, but actually . . . well, he's got a point. Doesn't he?

I mean, isn't that slightly similar to what I've been doing? Showing people I'm having the time of my life when really, I've been miserable?

I lean back against the sofa's edge, sipping my wine, wondering.

The silence settles between us, and unlike every other moment of my whole life, I don't immediately seek to fill it. In fact, a few minutes pass, while my thoughts are still galloping away.

Because I can't be wrong about this.

Helen was happy in every single one of those shots. She'd barely stay a week before she'd be back out on the road somewhere. She was never there. Never.

"You know I studied a case on those multilevel marketing schemes," Archie says finally, grabbing the bottle to top up both our glasses. His tone has shifted. Far more practical now. "Horrible things. You have to remember that those who entered in were sold a promise. Easy money. It wasn't well known how they really worked. So many people fell for the trap. It left so many in so much debt that they just couldn't keep their heads above water."

I know Helen was in debt. That's why she was forever asking my grandparents for money. But I can't say I ever looked into it that much. I didn't want to. Because it was the job my mother chose over me.

"I don't know why anyone does them," I say, my face naturally soured, because she still chose that career. She could have chosen anything else, and chose that.

"Well, I'm guessing your father didn't leave much to you or Mia," he says softly.

"Ha!" I gasp involuntarily, "God, no. Nothing as far as I'm aware."

He nods slowly, swirling around his glass.

"Quite a daunting task, looking after two young girls with no money. I'd imagine you'd probably turn to whatever you think would offer the most amount of cash in the smallest amount of time possible. . . ."

That's not even slightly . . . no, that can't be. . . . More than that, she was having fun. She loved spending time traveling the country. I know.

Because I've seen it.

Why does this conversation suddenly feel like it's reopening something I closed shut many years ago?

"I don't mean to pry," he says quickly.

"It's alright . . ." I murmur, still wild in thought.

"I don't mean to . . . I don't know. I don't know Helen. I don't know why she did what she did, or how you felt. You would know best, of course you would," he says. "But I also know I never intended on being a single parent. Not many people do. You do what you think is best, with no one to tell you what kind of job you're doing."

"Oh, my grandparents told her. I heard the arguments," I say quickly to justify it. "She knew what she was doing."

"I'm sure you're right," he says, genuinely on my side.

Although, I guess the problem my grandparents had was the money. She always needed money. Money to get her out of the debt she would so often find herself in and they didn't have any to give her . . . no. I can't think about this now.

So, I think about him instead.

Which is easy, because he's the kind of man who makes thinking about him easy. I still can't believe I couldn't even ask Jackson what his favorite color is, and yet with my feet up on his giant orange sofa I find myself saying:

"I still can't believe you raised two kids alone. I mean, I thought about getting a dog a year or so ago, back when my flatmate moved out. I thought maybe they'd be great company in the evenings. Only then I remembered I kill plants and I figure that doesn't bode well for keeping a pet alive."

"Ah yes," Archie says, his eyes rolling up to the ceiling, "the classic kids are like pets are like plants comparison."

"No!" I cry, accidentally loudly while he chuckles away. I put a hand to my mouth, remembering the girls asleep upstairs. "I didn't mean I was likely to kill your kids."

"Oh, I knew that. You very kindly mentioned to me in your nanny interview that you were 'not a murderer.'" I cringe at the memory. "It filled me with an abundance of confidence, I can tell you." He smirks.

"My point is," I say, trying to get back on track, "I couldn't keep two plants alive, and your kids are thriving."

Archie thinks for a minute, his eyes looking to the picture of the puppies before him.

"I don't know about thriving. Recently, Bailey's just completely closed off. You know she's always wanted to be an artist. She draws on everything. She used to come home desperate to show me what she'd drawn, only then she stopped showing me her work. Like she doesn't need me."

He takes a deep breath, his chest rising and falling into the orange cushions. "Cara on the other hand," he says, smiling faintly, "well, she wants the whole world watching her at all times."

Now where have I met someone like that before?

"I think that's how sisters are made," I tell him, thinking only of Mia. "They learn to balance each other out, whether that's a good thing or not."

He stretches out his neck, quickly turning to the second picture of the room. The one of the dog and the exceedingly long shadow. Then he looks back at me.

"You know, Zoe didn't want just two children. When she had Bailey, she held her in her arms and told me right there and then. She wanted all of them."

"All of them? You make them sound like Pokémon you need to collect!" I find myself laughing with him into my wineglass as I was about to take a sip. Archie runs a hand through his untamed hair. He runs a hand over his five-o'clock shadow. Nodding at the memory fondly.

"I thought she was mad. My parents weren't around, and hers— they were for a bit actually but they lived up by Cauldren Falls so too far to help out. But she was determined. She was the one who picked their names, but I saw the theme emerging. I'm Archie, so A. She was Zoe, Z. It was her choice entirely to name our children Bailey. Then Cara."

"Like . . . A, B, C?" I giggle.

"Exactly."

"And she wanted . . . twenty-two more babies to fill out the rest of the alphabet?"

Archie's laughing properly with me now, I can feel the sofa cushions vibrating under us.

"I wouldn't have put it past her, you know?"

"Twenty-four babies. That's a lot of babies."

"It's a lot."

"You might have needed another house."

"Oh, I don't know," he says, looking around the space. "Babies are very small. Only about," he holds his hands out a little way before him, "yay wide or so. . . ."

"Daddy?" a small voice whimpers.

Both our heads turn instantly, our laughter cooled.

Cara's standing by the door, a giant stegosaurus toy tucked into her chest.

"You can't sleep?" Archie says instantly, jumping to his feet and rushing to her side.

I should leave now, I think, but this little corner of the sofa is so comfortable I forget to say it out loud before it's too late. Archie's already walking up the stairs, with a quick "I'll be back in a minute."

It would be rude to leave while he's upstairs, I think, but I can feel the weight in my eyes and my blinks become just a little longer. Putting my glass on a coaster on the coffee table, I shut them. Just for a minute. Just until Archie gets back. Just until . . .

27

I wake up to the sight of two large green eyes blinking at me.

It's very disorientating. I blink, several times over.

"I made you a coffee," Cara says, before I can convince myself that this is all some sort of mirage. "You said you were a coffee fiend."

Oh gosh, I lift myself up, turning the blankets down. When did I get blankets?

I'm still lying across the orange sofa, warm and snuggly with an extra pillow under my head. Cara's standing beside me, holding a mug which—surprisingly this time—isn't part of her toy tea set. This is a real mug. With real coffee.

"Thank you for remembering." I blink, sitting up properly.

I stayed the night? That jet lag must have really caught up with me. I genuinely can't even remember falling asleep.

I take a sip of the tepid brew she hands over and—oh. It's atrocious. For one, I think it's comprised of one quarter instant granules, three quarters cold milk, making it lukewarm at best. It would be better if it *was* cold. It's also the Willy Wonka of all supposedly "hot" drinks: so sugary I feel my eyeballs want to explode.

"You said you liked your coffee milky."

"You are right, I did say that." I realize, not correcting her that it was "hot milk" I was referring to.

"And I went for six sugars, but it still tasted really sour," Cara says quickly, looking nervously for my response.

I take another sip, dramatically slurping and finishing with a theatrical "Mmmmm."

"Just how I like it," I reply, trying to keep my face from giving me away. I am honestly going to be doing cartwheels all day if I finish this off. I look up and can see that Bailey's joined us too. She's sitting on the armchair, crunching down on a bowl of cereal and looking at me strangely. I'm not surprised. I wasn't supposed to be an overnight guest. I wasn't even supposed to be a guest.

"We're going to the zoo," Cara tells me. I turn back to her, combing my hair with one hand, feeling the knots all clumped together.

"That sounds fun," I say.

"You have to come with us," she says.

"Cara, that's not how you ask someone," Archie says. I can't help but smile as our eyes meet. He's standing by the door with two mugs in his hand, fully dressed for the day already. What time is it? I haven't even checked.

"The zoo needs you," Cara tries again. "Don't let the baby animals down by not attending."

"Cara!" Archie laughs. "I brought you another coffee, just in case," he says, placing it down before me. I don't make an immediate grab for it, keeping Cara's locked in my hands but far away from my lips for now.

"Morning," I whisper, feeling the blush to my cheeks.

"Will you please come to the zoo with us?" Cara asks again. "I won't take no for an answer."

I look up to Archie. He looks at me too, and I wonder which of the two of them had this idea. I look over to Bailey, swinging her legs off the armchair as she slurps up the remaining milk in her bowl. I'm going to guess this wasn't her idea.

"Do you mind if I join?" I ask, looking only at her.

She purses her lips and a little frown appears on her forehead.

I think she's confused that I'm even asking her. Like her opinion doesn't matter. But it does. It really does.

Finally she shrugs.

"Yeah, whatever," she says quickly.

So, I turn to Cara.

"Then I'd love to," I reply.

I didn't think I was a "zoo" kind of person. If I've ever been to one before, then I certainly can't remember it. And yet, as Cara excitedly pulls me from one animal to the next, reading off facts from the noticeboards like she knew it all already, I find myself having the best day. We watch the lemurs as they squabble with one another, then curl into each other's fluffy tails to make up. We stay for a while in the giraffe viewpoint, seeing how elegantly they nibble away at the leaves of the trees. The penguins are Bailey's favorite. She's brought a pad and pencil with her, and as we sit there having a midmorning snack that Archie's cleverly brought with him, she stays on the edge of the wall looking into their enclosure, sketching away.

"I used to do just that," Archie whispers to me.

He joins her, not long after, and while Cara tries to count out the remaining grapes, I watch as Archie admires Bailey's drawing, giving her some pointers that she doesn't immediately reject.

I suppress a smile, but keep Cara entertained until I can see that Bailey's done for now, then we head over to the giant climbing frame in the center of the park for the girls to play.

"Did you ever hear from that man of yours?" he asks as we sit on a park bench not too far away.

"Who, Jackson?" I say. He wants to talk exes? "Nope."

"Is that . . . sad?" he asks.

It's an interesting question, because it should be. This whole Instagram quest I was trying was mostly to get him to reach back out. Only after everything Betzy's helped me realize, I'm not sure I need him, or even want him, to get back in touch.

Because Jackson never wanted this side of things. He never wanted to walk around a zoo with me, or have home-cooked dinners with me. Sure, I don't want kids. Maybe I don't even want wedding bells. But I want *more* than just wild sex in the same flat, once a week at best. I want love.

In just a few meetings, I've told Archie more than I've ever told Jackson in our time together. All Jackson wanted was someone to drink with after work, on his terms.

"Not really," I reply earnestly. "Not at all," I correct, which gets me immediately thinking of course. "How are things with Penelope going?" It feels far more charged a question than I intend it to be.

"Pen?" he laughs. "We've been friends for forever."

"You're not together?"

"God, no!"

Suddenly I feel embarrassed, my cheeks lighting up.

"I just thought . . . she was at your house."

"No, no. We sometimes babysit for each other. She helps drop the girls off and vice versa. She's just been a good pal, that's all. She'd say the same for me."

"Well, she was singing your praises," I say, not really sure.

"Then she's a very good friend. Next time I'll keep my mouth shut about who it is I like to her if she's going to give the game away that obviously."

Oh my. Oh my oh my oh my.

"So, you're not seeing anyone?" he says, as if clarifying the point.

"I'm not," I say, feeling the little buzz in my stomach. I might be getting the wrong read of this, but it feels loaded.

But why is it loaded? He is the one who friend-zoned me and I, someone who knows they don't want kids, accepted the zone with open arms. It was my appropriate zone, even if every cell of my body says otherwise.

I'm scared now. Because if I'm reading this right, if he does say something, then our friendship is as good as over. His texts have been the highlight of every day since we've been apart. And I'm not ready for this to be over. So, when he opens his mouth, I hold my breath, so unsure.

"It seems my assumption was correct then."

"Oh?"

"It is much better being lonely with you than without."

Why does that make me feel giddy?

"Look, I know I said that—"

"So, we've talked about it, and we've come to the conclusion that you're a sheepdog."

As Cara joins us, Archie closes his mouth. Bailey's trailing behind her. A part of me is relieved at the interruption, because that means words haven't been said. Words that once said can't be unsaid. Only another part of me seems to be aching to hear him finish that sentence.

Still, I have a small child before me who has apparently come to a vital conclusion, and that has to take precedent.

"In what way am I a sheepdog?" I ask.

Cara looks at Bailey for support, and with one nod she has all the confidence she needs to continue.

"You like to work, you're loyal—you said so yourself in your interview—"

"Well, I am that . . ." I agree.

"And you're fluffy."

"I don't know if that's a compliment," I say, looking at Archie for guidance.

"I'm sure it is." He shrugs.

"So, I'm a sheepdog?" I conclude.

"Yes," Cara replies.

"Good to know," I reply, wondering if there'll be another opportunity for Archie to finish that sentence. And wondering, if he does, how I feel.

We don't find ourselves able to speak alone again until the tropical house. The building is filled with the most beautiful trees and plants, spread out in a temperature-controlled room turned up to a sweat-glands-inducing high. Cara seems immediately at home, rushing all around the heated walkways as she spots the butterflies flying freely all around her. Bailey wanders separately, a little farther back, slower. She stops, taking out her pen and her pad. She places her headphones around her head, then focuses in, ready to draw.

Leaving just Archie and me. Again.

"You know I'm just like Bailey there. I have to have music in the background when I work, always."

I watch as her head bobs up and down to the beat, her pencil gliding smoothly over the paper.

"I think I'm probably the opposite. Silence is golden."

"Silence is probably my least favorite thing," I reply truthfully. "I'm big on filling silences."

"I've noticed," he replies, and I wonder if I should be embarrassed by that. The word "sorry" seems to be pinching at my tongue, only before I can fill the silence he does:

"I'm very envious you have the confidence to fill it."

"Confidence?" I choke, "it's not confidence! It's more like . . . anxiety!"

"You'd never know," he says, before adding, "I hope you're not anxious around me."

Cara squeals just a little way away, unsuccessfully trying to convince a glorious orange butterfly to land on her hand. She sprints around a woman in a green coat, helping her own toddler reach up to feel a beautiful flower growing close. We watch her together, as the silence settles. So, clearly, I fill it.

"Do you know what she's even listening to?" I ask.

Archie smiles, probably for the same reason I'm smiling.

"I bet it's that band they're obsessed with right now. I should remember the name . . . something mythological. Oh—Minotaur."

I stop walking.

"Minotaur?" I repeat absentmindedly.

But it's not just the band that's ringing in my ears. It's something else. Something I've seen that catches my eye and stops me.

Because I was wondering why that woman in the green coat looks so familiar, and now it's just clicked into place.

A cold current runs through me, as my mind takes me back to that meeting room.

❧

As we go through the shared space of the WeWork, following a woman wearing a bold red '80s-looking pantsuit, I try so hard not to think about Mia.

We wander down past wooden communal desk spaces and into a glass meeting room at the end of a corridor, while I try not to think of her helpless, lost, sleeping out on the streets alone.

The other two women stand and greet us, and I shake their hands and smile my widest pitch-perfect smile as I let Georgia introduce me as her colleague, because I don't have words right now. I'm elsewhere. Worrying. Panicking. My eyes glance over the tablet they've given me but I can't really concentrate on anything so instead I just focus on blinking. Blinking and breathing.

"Now, before you start, we just wanted to share with you the direction Paula Mead, our new CEO, wants Finder's Keepers *to go."*

"Is this the next issue?" Georgia asks, eyes on her own tablet.

"It's already released. We're all very happy with how it's turned out."

"I can see it has a completely different feel to it," Georgia says. I can hear she's using her tactical voice here. I can see from the look in her face that she's a little thrown. She looks at me for backup.

One of them, a woman with a blue neckerchief, points a remote toward the large screen at the back of the room. "Paula brings a wealth of experience from the world of celebrity with her. You can see that she's . . ."

But somehow despite my internal monologue, Georgia's eyes pierce through. She looks lost, a little unsure. She leans in close to me.

"This is . . . interesting . . ." she whispers, so quietly the others don't even hear.

But I don't find anything interesting right now, because I'm in the middle of a client meeting in a blind panic that my sister is dead. But these are Jackson's clients. So, I need to hold my shit together. Just for the next hour. Quickly I shake off all emotions, relaying the smile on my lips and desperately ignoring the ringing in my ears.

"Yes, sorry," I say, "I just . . . please, go on."

Given I'm not quite sure who was speaking, I'm not sure who to address it to. But the last Finder's Keepers employee, a woman with a high ponytail in a big gold scrunchie, starts to talk so I guess it was probably her. The screen lights up and it takes a minute for my eyes to adjust to the picture before me.

Except all I see as I look at that screen is Mia. Mia holding hands with a brand-new wannabe rock star.

Wait.

No, that's real. It's very, very real.

I blink, leaning in closer to see if my eyes are deceiving me.

My heart suddenly does a backflip, a front flip, a side flip. It keeps flipping over and over because that's her. That's actually her. It's Mia.

She's safe.

She's alive.

I finally look down at the iPad they handed over to me and Georgia, and I see it all over again—I see the image clear as day. How did I miss it? How was I so in my own head that I couldn't see what was right in front of me?

She looks good. She's back to wearing her big bold colors, a bright orange jumpsuit and green thick sneakers, and she's hand in hand with a . . . well, cleaner version of the man I just threatened in Pret. She's safe. She's alive. She's completely fine, better than fine! She's on the cover of a new magazine. It's such a relief to see her, let alone to see her like this. She's smiling, the kind of smile that seems so perfectly genuine. Thank goodness. My sister is safe and fine and alive and—

Which is when it occurs to me: she's actually better than fine. She's having a great time.

I've been sick to my stomach with worry for the last four weeks, hating myself, hating life, hating everything. And she's been living her best life. One text and I would have been alright.

And just like that, I'm more furious than ever.

I scan the photo for every detail, trying to get some clue to what *kind of life she's living without me, and just like that, the final trigger fires.*

FMK—the choice is yours!
Your chance to decide where Minotaur's
girlfriends sit on the FMK scale.

"What the actual . . . ?" I whisper. To myself.
Only I'm in a very, very small room. So, everyone can hear me.
"Is something bothering you?" the woman in the red suit asks.
Yes. This team of women is asking strangers whether my sister is worthy of fucking, marrying, or killing. And they're laughing about it.
About. My. Sister.
My trigger is pulled, and just like that, I blow.

෴

There's a reason that memory comes back. A very big reason.

Because it was that afternoon that that calendar invite appeared on my phone:

Calendar Invite from Stephanie Chu:
6:30 a.m.—Room 9.10—Daisy Peterson Catch-up

"Stephanie," I whisper to myself.

I didn't realize that Archie was still speaking beside me. Because that woman in the green coat, holding up her toddler, is the Head of HR's assistant. Jackson's old assistant. It's Stephanie Chu.

As if her ears were burning, she turns. We're too close to her to pretend not to notice. I know I have to say something. By the way her face has fallen, she knows the same.

"Do you mind?" I ask Archie, "it's . . ." But it's too complicated to say. So, I summarize, "an old colleague."

"Of course," he replies, and then—as if to give me some space, he wanders over to where Cara has run—still on her quest to be a butterfly's landing post.

"Hi, Daisy," Stephanie says softly as I approach. "Bertie, why don't you go to Daddy for a few minutes?"

She puts the boy on the ground and happily he sprints toward a gentleman a little farther off, looking at the aquarium with a much older child. Satisfied he's safe, Stephanie turns back around.

"How have you been?"

"I've been better," I reply, only realizing after it's been said how accidentally honest it was. Maybe it's being around Archie that's had an effect on me. But then I turn, seeing Bailey with her headphones on, drawing away. And with a smile I add, "I've been worse too. How are you?"

She bites her lip, looking up. I can see already the awkwardness in her face. Her dark eyes are scanning her surroundings, probably to find a quick exit route.

But I won't be the elephant in the room, I think to myself.

"It's alright. I know it must be weird seeing me, given everything."

If I'm acting normal here, then maybe that will allow her to be the same. This doesn't have to be weird.

"No, it's not that," she says. "You know I've been wanting to reach out to you about a hundred times. More. I just . . . wasn't sure if I should say anything."

"About the job?" I ask. She must know I'm trying to get my job back.

"About Jackson," she corrects.

That's unexpected. Although, as the bullet lands, I feel a whole new level of awkwardness I never thought I could feel.

"Ah, so you did know," I say sadly.

She nods.

"I worked it out a long time ago. So, yes, I knew," she says, taking a deep breath for bravery. "Just like I knew that RL stood for Rebecca Leech. And ED stood for Emma Dalton."

I don't know what that means.

"Emma Dalton the intern?"

"Emma Dalton the intern."

I start to feel a bit sick in my stomach.

"So, he's moved on from me?" I say, almost like a whisper. Because it's not like I want Jackson back in my life. I'm pretty sure I don't. But it still stings. It hasn't been long, and he's already exchanged my time block for someone else in the office?

"Maybe, I don't know. But I do know ED wasn't put in *after* you . . . she was there when I was still working for him . . ." Stephanie says again, more slowly.

It takes a while for me to even work out what that means.

"Jackson was cheating on me?"

"Maybe it's not my place to say. I'm so sorry if I've overstepped. It's just . . . I only realized what those initials meant after months of working for him back when Olive Freshman made a comment to me. OF. She was furious because I hadn't scheduled her in. Jackson asked me to remove it from his diary. He apparently didn't even tell her. He just ended it, removed her, and left her completely in the lurch. And only then did I work out the rest of you."

She looks to check on her family before she even continues.

"I asked to be moved immediately once I found out. I wanted to tell you. I wanted to tell all of you, but . . . I just didn't know what to do. So, I moved jobs instead."

To Gemma's assistant. I assumed it had been a promotion. Turns out, it was a requested move.

"Technically, he's not doing anything wrong, so my complaint was dismissed. None of you is under his direct line management. You're all consenting adults. But I think he's a pig and I couldn't be a party to it anymore. I just couldn't."

She's telling me that he cheated on me? Worse. That he cheated on me multiple times, with multiple people in the office.

I guess I only ever saw him once a week, tops. I never really asked him where he was all the other nights or weekends. I thought he was working late like me. Or out with clients. I never in my wildest dreams thought he was . . . with women I sat beside? I mean, Rebecca only sat three desks away from me. We sometimes got coffee together. . . .

I feel so stupid.

"I'm sorry, maybe I shouldn't have told you."

"No," I say, my lips quivering. "I'm glad I know."

"For what it's worth, I think you're great. I've seen that email you sent to Gemma. They're really considering rehiring you and I think they'd be fools if they didn't. I just . . . I hate knowing something that you should have known."

Her toddler rushes back over to her, grabbing her leg, and she smiles apologetically. Probably for many reasons. But she has nothing to apologize for. Nothing at all.

And with that, she says her farewells and within seconds she's left the tropical house completely. I don't blame her for her speed.

Archie wanders back over to me, bringing me back to the present.

I'm in a zoo, with Archie. Who isn't Jackson. But it's hot in here. So hot.

I can't breathe properly, and Bailey—she's still drawing, deep in thought. And Cara's still looking at the butterflies; I can't move them. But I need air. So, I turn to Archie, speaking faster than I mean to when I say:

"I think I need to go home."

He doesn't bother hiding his concern at that.

"Are you alright?"

I think about lying, but weirdly, I don't.

"I just heard some bad news and I need . . . I think I need to be by myself for a bit."

He nods, in complete understanding, and without asking me for an explanation or holding me back, he simply says:

"I'll tell the girls."

"Thank you," I tell him.

"I'm always here if you want to call," he concludes.

And the best part about it is, I know he is.

I'm on autopilot all the way home. I'm glad my legs know where they're going, because it isn't until I reach my own front door that I realize I'm even home. When the door shuts behind me, the numb, achy feeling that shadowed me since that meeting with Stephanie rears its ugly head.

So, he was cheating on me.

What actually counts for cheating these days?

I guess we never had "the chat." For whatever reason, I thought adults didn't need to have it. I thought there was a mutual respect, because he was a respectful kind of guy.

Only he wasn't. Clearly.

I go through a lot of emotions in very quick succession. Anger. So much anger. In my fury and frustration, I kick a path through my clothes all over the floor, picking up a bra close to me and lobbing it cathartically across the room. Not that it goes across the room. It only makes it about half a yard before the shocking aerodynamics of underwear sets in and it limply falls to the floor.

Then sadness. I shake for a little on the brink of tears, but never quite going over the hill. Because every time I'm about to go over the edge, I wonder why it is I'm about to cry.

Is it because he was the man of my dreams?

Well, to that point, he wasn't really. Betzy was right. He did just send me one breakup text and then ghost me. He knew that he didn't send me a calendar invite that day, and yet when I thanked him for something, he didn't question what. He could have had the respect to listen to me. He could have at least listened.

So, no. He was not the man of my dreams.

Am I going to cry because of the other women?

Well, sure. I think Olive is beautiful. Maybe if I thought about it I'd wonder why on earth he liked Freckles McFrecklesface over here when he had the stunning part-time model Olive Freshman. Maybe I should be self-conscious that I'm not good enough. Only I'm not, because it clearly wasn't personal. It wasn't just one girl he's done this to, it's several.

And the reason that I do keep almost crying but not actually crying is because I'm humiliated.

I feel like an idiot. I can't believe I never questioned it. I can't believe I thought the reason we never did anything outside of his flat was because I was the one worried about being caught. In case it ruined *my* reputation.

And then a weird, heavenly kind of clarity. Because I'm not going to cry for my own humiliation. No one else knows. Apart from Stephanie, but no one else knows and no one else cares.

And it's just made one thing abundantly clear: fuck him and his cheating ways. Screw that. Why on earth did I put so much effort in to get a like from him on Instagram?

So, I don't cry. I sigh. I breathe. I rinse my face off in my sink and I feel like a whole new woman. A fuck-you-Jackson-Oakley woman.

Because life is too short to linger in anger.

Which makes me think of Mia. Obviously.

I'm holding on to something for no reason. Why am I so furious with Mia? I saw her face in that magazine and lost my shit, but that wasn't her fault. It was the fault of a misogynistic headline.

All she did was fall in love.

That gives me even more reason to do something I should have done ages before.

I call Mia.

"Daisy?" Mia's voice speaks from the other end.

I'm a bit surprised if I'm honest—I really didn't expect her to pick up. It's very rare for anyone to actually pick up a spontaneous call, let alone one from someone who shouted at you the last time you spoke.

"Please tell me this isn't a butt dial," my sister continues.

That makes me laugh. Then sigh. Because she's genuinely happy to hear from me. I can hear it in her voice. So much history between us and she's ready and willing to sweep it all away, the second I call.

"Hi, Mia," I say, and then realizing how terribly impersonal this all is, I change tack completely. "Do you want to meet up?"

28

The door backstage is entirely unglamorous compared to what I was imagining. What with a long line of excited audience members in jaw-dropping outfits by the entrance, I was expecting a literal red carpet for where the talent enters. Except, instead, we get a little door which leads to a completely low-key foyer.

"Erm, hi," I say to the woman behind the desk. She's wearing one of those pilot headsets and looks up at me without even breaking a smile. I overcompensate with the widest most awkward smile I can deliver. "I'm here to see Kit?"

"The entrance to the show is just around the back there," the woman says, pointing back the way we came.

"Oh no, I mean. We're with Mia?" I try again.

"Mia?" she asks. It occurs to me that this is probably what a lot of fans use to get in backstage. Pick a random name, hope they are in the mix somewhere. No wonder she looks so skeptical.

But before I have to worry about confirming it, I hear footsteps jumping down the staircase and there, before me, is my sister.

And she looks incredible.

She's wearing a popping red dress that shimmers out like a 1920s flapper. She even has a matching headpiece too, although no exotic feather from the top. Her hair is braided in an incredibly complex array of knots, and something floods me inside. Happiness for seeing her? Sadness that it has taken this long for me to feel this way again?

"Daisy!" she squeals excitedly. "Oh my WORD, I've never seen you look so wonderful!"

It's like the way I treated her has faded entirely into the background with her. Like what matters most is the here and now, and maybe that's exactly right. Maybe that is what matters.

And I do look alright. Not Mia alright, because no one can compete with that, but I've made more than a little effort. I used my living room wardrobe to its full capability and laid out all the outfits that looked acceptable in a row. Then, with some Calvin Harris classics as my baseline, I tried each and every one on until I found the winning number. It was a pale green dress with a high neck and short sleeves I bought about six years ago, and still somehow fits perfectly. If I hadn't done this, I'm sure I'd never have found it again to wear, but with some black boots and a jean jacket, I somehow don't feel completely outdressed by my sister. Which is a feat. I feel underdressed next to her when she's wearing PJs and I'm in day clothes.

"Thanks for inviting us backstage," I say, pointing back to where Archie, Bailey, and Cara still linger. Bailey and Cara both have their lips sealed shut, their eyes wide.

"Are you kidding? I'm so happy you wanted to come! Come, come—can you get these guys passes please, Nina?"

The girl with the headphones, satisfied we genuinely do know the band, hands over some lanyards.

"And you must be Archie." Mia launches right in for a hug immediately. "You're just as dreamy as Daisy said, obviously."

"Oh yeah?" Archie laughs, looking over to me. I don't get enough time to say a word before Mia's moved on. Typical Mia, making sure I never get a chance to defend myself. Still, I shrug over to Archie, who laughs my way.

It's been two weeks since that day at the zoo, and I've somehow seen them every day since. When Archie texted the next day wondering if I wanted company, I thought, well, I do actually. Because feeling crap alone is crap. Feeling crap with someone else around, someone you don't mind seeing you that way, is just that little bit better. So, I came round for dinner, and Archie respectfully didn't ask but I told him anyway.

And the next night was fajita night, and I love fajitas. And the evening after Cara wanted to play a board game that required four people and it would have been rude of me to say no to that, and on it went.

And it's not just Archie of course, the girls have been brilliant company. They didn't seem to mind me being around, which I was worried about at first. In fact, I got to teach Bailey a few more karate moves, and she even showed me a little of her WIP drawings. A lot of the time it was Cara and Archie cooking, and I'd sometimes pass them something (usually the wrong something) but more oftentimes I just sat and watched. Lord knows I'm better at sitting still than I am at cooking.

But actually, I've been surprisingly busy. Pen put me in touch with Jade, who put me in touch with Sita who referred me to Mo and on and on until each day I seemed to have someone new to introduce to the wonders that an excellently formatted spreadsheet can bring. They didn't pay much, but something is better than nothing, and I still had time to research other companies I might want to apply for. Companies I would never have thought my skills could help.

This here, seeing Minotaur at the O2 in Brixton, is just the end to a pretty brilliant fortnight that somehow emerged like a phoenix from a horrible set of circumstances. It was entirely and wonderfully unexpected. So, this here, is a thank-you. A big one. Orchestrated entirely by a sister I thought would hang up on me, and yet somehow didn't.

"And you must be Bailey and Cara," Mia says, leaning down to their height to talk to them. Bailey's keeping her mouth sealed shut, but I expected that from her. What I didn't expect was for Cara to do that too. She looks like she's seen a ghost.

"Well, it's just wonderful to meet you guys," Mia says happily. "I hear you like Minotaur?"

Bailey nods, Cara just looks up at her sister for guidance. That's strange.

"Well, let me take you up to meet Kit. He's heard all about you," Mia says, and I can see both of their eyes bulge at the use of this man's name.

We rise up the stone steps and on through a very light corridor filled with framed photos from past gigs. There seems to be a hundred doors, but Mia walks confidently and purposefully in her incredible six-inch heels as she sweeps through the halls like her own personal catwalk.

"You know, it means the world to me that you're here," Mia whispers to me as we walk a little ahead of the others. "I've been so desperate for you to meet Kit."

"I can't wait to meet him," I say, surprising myself with how genuine I am.

And when I meet him, I realize how different he is. He's rugged and grungy and striking, like all the others, but he's also a complete gentleman.

He kisses me on both cheeks, hugs both of the girls, and asks them questions about which songs they like and says how grateful he is that they listen to his music. He tells me how much he's been looking forward to meeting me, and how much he loves my sister.

None of the others said that. If they did, and I'd like to think they did, they didn't think it was important for me to know. But this man understands, it's vital. He's looking after my baby sister.

"Let me make something clear," he tells me, "I thought singing was my whole world, before your sister came along. Now I know it's bigger than just one passion."

So beautifully articulate.

And when they kiss, I don't feel horrified or grossed out. I get those little tingles I get in every rom-com ending. Because what I'm looking at, before my eyes, is love.

As the curtain call summons them to the side of the stage, Mia shows all of us a sneaky way into the front to watch. It's perfect; a little away from the main crowds but with the best view.

"Did you see Cara?" Archie whispers to me as we wait for the band to take to the stage.

"She was lost for words!" I reply, stunned.

"I think that's the first time that's ever happened."

I laugh, watching as Cara and Bailey whisper to each other excitedly in front of us. The band enters and a roar of applause echoes through the audience. I feel Mia tug at the sleeve of my jacket.

"He's really good," Mia says nervously, as they strum their first chord. The audience goes wild.

"I'm glad, but that's not what's important to me," I tell her, although at this point I need to shout, because their first song has begun and although it's fast, fun, and catchy, given we're next to the speakers at the front, it's very loud. "I care that he's good to you. That he's good *for* you."

"He's that too," she shouts back, already twisting on the spot.

"I can see how happy you are," I reply, twisting with her.

And somehow, for the first time in about fifteen years, I find myself dancing with my sister.

We used to do this all the time as kids. We used to slam on some Britney Spears and flounce all over my grandparents' living room. We used to be all five members of the Spice Girls and sing our hearts out to A1's "Like a Rose." But then time moves on, and those moments, without realizing it, fall away into adulthood.

Until moments like this. When I'm standing, dancing with my sister in the middle of the O2, feeling so free and happy I could literally fly.

And Archie's dancing too. He's not too bad either, although he's very much keeping to the easy sidestep, twirling his daughters around him one at a time.

Slowly as the set goes on, Cara's white cheeks fill.

Before I know it, all of us are dancing together, and I'm singing away to songs I definitely don't know the lyrics to. I hate to admit it (do I even hate it?) but they're really good. Kit in particular. He's got the voice of Lewis Capaldi, Freddie Mercury, and Johnny Cash all rolled up in one. It's unbelievable what raw talent he has, and I see the sparkle in my sister's eye as he turns to her, in front of everyone there, and dedicates his next song her way. The pride in his voice as he does so is heartwarming. He's proud of her. And for once, she looks exactly like Mia always looks to me: herself.

When the break begins and the lights go up, Mia whisks off backstage. She offers to take us again, but I know we'll just slow her down with the girls. The second she disappears from view, my phone pings.

"Oh my," I gasp.

"All alright?"

"Yeah, it's just . . ." I turn my phone so all three of them can see. "Mia must have been taking pictures of all of us—I didn't even see her do it!"

"Oh, I LOVE this!" Cara exclaims, specifically looking at one of her and me, hands in the air together under the blue light.

"These are cool," Bailey murmurs as we keep flicking through them. There are suddenly several in a row of just me, lit purple, blue, pink and yellow as the lights above me must have changed. I look . . . well, I think I look good. They're so natural. So thoughtless. I'm just having the time of my life. Genuinely.

"Can we turn those pictures into a Reel?" Bailey asks when I've reached the final one.

It's one of Archie and me. He must have been whispering something into my ear, and I have my head back laughing away. His lips are only centimeters away from my ears, his eyes only on me.

It weirdly takes my breath away.

I look to Archie, who's looking at me. Why does it look like we're both thinking the same thoughts? The same dangerous thoughts for two people who are friends. Just. Friends.

"Can we?" Bailey repeats, and it shakes us both out of our trance. "Just the ones of you dancing maybe?"

She adds, flicking back to them, "I have an idea I think would look cool."

I turn back to Archie, but this time for him to weigh in. They are his girls after all, but he just shrugs approval.

"Go for it," I tell them, hoping my voice doesn't sound so dreamy as I think it does.

Both the girls crowd over the phone together instantly.

"How do you even know how to do this kind of thing?" I ask them.

"Sarah's brother has a phone."

"And Kitty's sister," Cara adds.

"And Fred's sister too," Bailey concludes.

"You stop them from having access and they get it anyway." Archie shakes his head, but I can see he too is interested. He's looking at them proudly as they work together, whispering ideas. Cara seems to be quite the taskmaster, but Bailey's just appeasing her for the most part. It's clear she's still the one in charge, even without being the loudest.

I wonder if that's how Mia saw it, when we were little.

"Can we post it?" Bailey asks, twisting the phone around.

It's actually . . . well, it's incredible. The photos that Mia took have a hypnotic feel to them. The whole thing is filled with such unfiltered joy. And the way the girls have compiled them together, one after the other, the beat of the song dancing with me; it's about a hundred times better than any Reel I could make.

I read the caption: "xoxo." I love it. Very simple. Very *Gossip Girl*–esque. Perfect.

"Absolutely," I reply, watching them both smile as they hit post.

Before she hands the phone back to me though, Bailey opens my photos again.

"What is this?" she asks.

She must have seen it while pulling the Reel together. I quickly panic at the thought—as I can't remember what photos are on there. Did I take any in that FKME bodysuit? Please god, I hope not.

"Isn't this your studio, Dad?" Bailey asks, twisting the phone around again.

I sigh in relief as I see a dog portrait—one of many stored on there.

"Oh, it's just a shared album I made when I was helping your dad. Maybe you could help us pull some of these together into reels at one point," I add, holding my hand out for my phone back. But she doesn't give it to me. Not right away.

She's transfixed, and it takes me a while to see which one she's lingering on. It's the one of the Yorkie. With all the multicolored letters raining down around her. I smile instantly, but Bailey seems to be frowning.

"This is in the basement?" she asks quickly.

Archie looks over, feigning slight disinterest.

"It's there if you want to see it."

"This isn't on your Instagram," she says, and she looks up at her dad for an explanation. A serious one.

"I'm not going to," he replies plainly. Calmly. An end to the conversation.

"Why not?" Bailey demands, her voice getting louder.

"We can talk about this later," he says gently.

"Why not?" Bailey says again, a little stronger, more determined.

"We don't need to—" Archie begins, but the lights suddenly lower. The break is over and with it, this conversation.

I flick my eyes over to Bailey, who just silently hands my phone back over to me.

Archie keeps his eyes on the stage, clearly done with the subject. And before I can ask him, even if I wanted to, Mia pops back beside me.

"Ready to fall in love with the man who I'm in love with?" she asks me.

"Ready," I reply.

By the end of the set, Cara comes close to me.

"This is the greatest day of my entire whole life," she whispers, and it almost makes me well up.

Because I'm trying to work out what my best day is. Is it the day I got a promotion at Branded? That was a good day, but probably not the "greatest" one. Or the day I first hooked up with Jackson? Fat chance there.

I mean, when I really, really think about it, this is pretty great. I went from being in a bad place, to a pretty good one. I have my sister to one side of me, and we're not screaming at one another, and I have Archie to my other.

Archie my friend.

Archie who has been there for me, when I needed someone.

Archie whose eyes I'm starting to see when I close my eyes to sleep at night.

Maybe, just maybe, it's not far from being the greatest day of my entire whole life either.

29

When the gig is over, I walk Archie out and stay with them until the Uber arrives. Cara is already sleeping in his arms, and although she looks far too old to be there, Archie has her curled up against his chest as he stands beside me.

Bailey too seems to have her eyes closed, leaning against me for support as I see the silver sedan pull right up. Bailey gets in first, then Archie carefully places in Cara, leaving the door open ready.

As he turns to look at me, I feel myself grow literally weak at the knees. Why? Why does that happen?

Archie's my friend. My *friend,* I remind myself. He has to be. Because he has two someones in his life that makes more than friendship impossible. It just feels a bit like my body hasn't caught up with my mind's logic. I can't help but feel a smile fire through my cheeks, which doesn't even begin to show how happy I am about this night.

"The girls are going to be speaking about this for weeks," he whispers, as if trying to elongate the time we have. He looks inside the car, his two girls almost out for the count. "You sure you don't want to jump in here? We can take you home?"

"No," I say sadly, "I should speak with Mia while I have the chance."

Archie nods.

With one hand still on the car door, he leans over. Slowly, thoughtfully, he lands a kiss on my cheek. That's a friendly thing to do, right? I wish I didn't feel this perfect buzz whisper through me. I feel like we're quickly getting into dangerous territory.

"Text me when you're home," he whispers.

"It was never about the money," I say.

The two of us have found a bench, under a small streetlight overlooking the Thames. The night is so still, so peaceful. It feels like the perfect night for resolution. She twists her face toward mine, for once, actually listening before talking.

"I reacted terribly that night. I was out of order. I was so mad with Jackson that I took it all out on you. So, I'm sorry about that, I'm really sorry."

I blink up at her, and to my surprise, she's nodding at me sympathetically, but staying quiet, as if sensing I'm not done. I lick my lips, looking out to the cool Thames water for comfort.

"But then I didn't hear from you for a *month*, Mia. A whole month." I try very hard not to make my voice seem whiny or pained. She's listening. I don't need to go on about it. "For the first few days I thought, maybe she's found somewhere safe but her battery has died or . . . I don't know what I thought. But a month? I was about to call the police. I kept having visions of you, terrible visions. And I was so full of regret already but to not even have the chance to apologize? You blocked me on everything. I thought I'd lost you."

"That's why you got mad at me?" Mia asks, her voice soft.

"Of course!" I reply, "and when I saw your face in that magazine, gosh. The relief I felt was like nothing I've ever experienced before. I could have cried; in the middle of the meeting I literally could have cried because I knew you were safe. I was fine with you being pissed with me, but as long as you were pissed with me and safe."

"You cried in a meeting?"

"Actually no, I blew my lid in a meeting and got fired."

"You got *fired*?" she gasps. "I thought you quit!"

"I called the CEO of a multimillion-pound business a tool, so I got let go."

Mia opens and shuts her mouth, multiple times over.

"Was she being a tool?"

"She was. But sadly, calling people names across a boardroom isn't exactly a 'professional' response. In fact, your boyfriend said the same thing far more elegantly not long after. He got her to apologize and everything."

"*Finder's Keepers*," Mia whispers in understanding. "Is that the magazine?"

I nod, shrugging my shoulders like it was water under a bridge.

"They were being tools," she agrees, shivering at the thought.

"No one speaks like that about my sister."

"You got fired for me?" she marvels.

"No, I got fired because I lost control. You're not to blame here. Not really."

She shakes her head softly.

"But you love that job. . . ."

"I loved. Past tense," I say, only this time, putting Branded in the past tense hasn't hurt me. Not even slightly. "But I was there for thirteen years. I didn't even look at other jobs. I never questioned what else might make me happy and now I have. In fact, I have an interview next week."

"For a competitor?" she asks, like I'm doing something naughty.

"Not even. It's a dog food company."

"Oh! You love dogs!"

"I do. And they need data analysts galore to help with their personalization department. Honestly, it sounds amazing. They use data to work out taste preferences for certain breeds and ages to help cater toward different dietary needs and then they have a whole second department to analyze the transportation logistics . . ." I look at her face, her eyes have glazed over. "And you don't care."

"No!" she agrees. "But I care that you care!"

I chew down on my lip.

"I had no idea you were worrying about me," she says truthfully.

"How could I not be?"

"I don't know. It didn't even occur to me," she says, before adding, "but I didn't stay silent because I was pissed at you."

Now it's my time to be thrown.

"You weren't?"

"Oh, I was pissed with you," Mia laughs, "that's true. But I also knew you were right. I was following the exact same pattern that I always was and was letting a man stomp all over me. That night, the night I left yours, I went straight back to him with your words burning in my mind. And I unleashed Bitch Slap Mia."

"Oh?"

"Unfiltered, bitch slap Barbie me," she says, making me chuckle. "And I screamed at him and I told him that he owed me my money back and that his reasons for keeping it were bullshit and that I'd sue him for all he was worth. And then he just gave it back. All of it."

"He did?"

"He did. And I stayed the night in a hotel room that I bought with my own . . ." she begins, looking at my eyebrow raising, "well, *your* money, that *I* got back from Lenny and I felt so elated. So empowered. Because I'd taken up my space and I'd got back what I was owed. You would have been so proud of me."

Warm intoxicating pride was filling me up like a Froyo dispenser.

"I mean, I probably wouldn't have recommended you go screaming his house down," I say, "but I agree with the sentiment, sure."

"Well, it also got me thinking. You gave me some harsh truths, and I just knew that I needed to act on them. I needed to sort my life out. Start my own line of work. Not bend to what a man wants me to be. And so I did just that. I started my own business, I embraced who I was—and I earn money for it!"

"From what?" I say.

"From Instagram!"

"But . . ." I take out my phone as if to prove the point. "You deleted your Instagram?"

"No, I started afresh." She types in a new handle and hands it over to me. "The last one I had was full of tales of who I wasn't, so I wanted something that was wholly and completely me."

I swipe through some of the images—videos of her makeup-less, makeup-full, dressed up to the nines, and in her comfy joggers. Intermixed with it all are pictures of words that all sound so inspirational:

"Don't let someone else define you."

"Just keep swimming—Dory, a very wise fish."

"These are good pieces of advice," I muse, wondering why they sound familiar.

"Go big or go home."

"Sadness is never silly."

And then I notice.

@MEP.

M. E. P.

Mia Emily Peterson.

"You're Emmy Pea?" I gasp.

"My old handle was taken weirdly." She shrugs uncaringly, like the name was neither here nor there.

"No!" I correct. "You're the mystery woman Cara won't stop banging on about!" I'm completely shocked. Floored. I feel like a thousand lightning bolts have just sprung to action in my mind all at once, blinding me. "Oh, no wonder Cara was so quiet when she met you! She adores you!"

"Isn't she too young for Instagram?"

"Well, yes. Definitely, but that's another thing entirely," I say, completely stunned. "So, you're an actual influencer . . . ?" I say again.

It was Mia? So, it was her advice I've been following all this time. The advice that led me here in fact, back to her side.

Once the shock calms down, I hand Mia back her phone.

"I am proud of you, so, so proud," I say earnestly, still blinking in absolute shock before I remember to add, "but I'm your family. I don't just need to be there for you when you're living your best life. I want to be there for the lows too. I would have helped you. If I'd known where you were, I could have been there for you."

Instantly she looks nervous. She looks like she would rather say just about anything other than say what she's thinking.

"Well, I couldn't exactly afford to live in a hotel room forever, and I don't like staying on people's sofas . . . it messes up my hair . . ." she begins.

And in the pause that follows, I feel my stomach drop. Because something dawns on me that never did before. She doesn't want to tell me, and there's only one reason for that.

"You stayed with Helen, didn't you?" I say, so she doesn't have to.

Mia nods, biting down so hard on her lip it looks painful.

And the smallest shot of anger courses through me, before I realize something strange: this isn't anger at Mia.

It's not even for Helen.

It's at myself.

I think I have a hard truth to learn here: Betzy, not telling me about her pregnancy. Mia not telling me about her living situation.

I think perhaps when I don't want something, I make it impossible for others to share their own opinions. I literally *make* an elephant in the room. One they then don't want to talk about with me. So much so, they'd rather hide it from me completely.

"I didn't even know you were still in touch with Helen," I say softly.

Mia twists back, facing the river, but is quickly unsatisfied. She jumps to her feet quickly, pacing.

"You know, I'm just going to say it," she says finally, like she has an agenda. "She's our mum."

"I know," I agree, but she's not listening to me. Because she thinks I'm about to blow and she's trying to stop it.

". . . And I know you think she's this truly horrible person, and I get that. She wasn't there and that sucked. But like . . . have you ever actually asked her about that time she was away? Because I have. And I'm telling you now. She hated it. She said she went all across the country, almost completely alone, desperately trying to sell stock of something she never believed in. She thought it would be an easy win. A way to make money quickly so she could afford to move out of Nan and Grandad's once and for all. She didn't have a head for business like you. She didn't know what she was signing on for."

"I know," I say again.

"No, you *have* to listen to me," Mia continues, not listening to me. "She bought into that stupid scheme and once she was in she didn't know how to get out of it! She tried for years to find an exit route but kept falling into debt at the end of every month and being forced to stay on to try and make up for it the next month. Trying to leave it is the only reason she ever asked Nan and Grandad for help! She knew they didn't have much! She would never have done it if she had any other choice!"

"I know." I nod.

"The only reason she was doing it was because of us. Because she loved us. She wanted to build a world for us which meant we didn't have to sit in hotel rooms half the country away from our children one day."

"I know," I say again.

"And you'd know all this if you just unblocked her on any medium. She's sent you emails and texts. But you never gave her the opportunity to explain herself. Not once."

"I guess I didn't," I agree.

"You didn't?" she says, and it looks like I've finally broken through.

"I know," I repeat. I shake my head sadly. "You know, I was so convinced she loved being on the road that I never, not once, thought to Google the company she worked for. I knew it was a pyramid scheme, because Nan and Grandad used that term so much growing up, but I didn't know how it actually worked. But that's the point. Most people who joined up didn't know. They just did it and got stuck in the system."

I shake my head, hanging it low in my arms.

"I'm not saying I suddenly forgive her. Because of her, I thought the real me wasn't worthy of love. Because my own mum chose this amazing life over me."

"But she didn't!" Mia begins.

"But that's what I *thought*. Because that's what I *saw*. And if she'd just been truthful with us back then, if she hadn't shown us pictures of her incredible adventures or if she'd somehow added us to the mix, then maybe I would have understood. But she kept insisting that her life was great, and that she was having so much fun."

Mia bites her cheek as she takes a seat, not really knowing what to say.

"I'm glad you're still in touch," I say finally. "I'm glad you were safe with her."

"You know, she asks about you all the time. I show her pictures. She says you look just like Nan."

"That's . . ." I begin, about to contradict her, but I stop. Trying to remember. "I guess I do a bit."

"It's the freckles."

"It's definitely the freckles," I giggle, touching my own cheeks as I think of Nan. And then, just for a second, remembering the good times. The times she was home. The times we were altogether as a family. "You know, I think I want to see her."

"You do?" Mia says, her eyes sparkly like a Disney princess.

"I think so."

"Well, I know she'd love that," Mia says happily.

This just feels so good to have it all in the open. It makes me so unbelievably sad that the reason she hid anything from me was all because I was so regimented on my views of Helen. I somehow made her scared to tell me she didn't feel the same way.

"You know Betzy didn't tell me she was pregnant because I made such a big deal about never wanting kids. And you didn't tell me you were safe because you were with Mum. I'd rather people tell me things, even things that might hurt me, rather than hiding them away."

"Betzy's pregnant?"

"She's going to have a child with an American accent." I smile. "How weird is that?"

"I guess that's what your fella must think. Scottish and his daughters speaking the Queen's English. It's hilarious."

Archie. Even just Mia referencing him makes me feel a little bit warmer inside. And then I remember to add:

"He's not my 'fella.' He's just my friend."

She looks at me skeptically. I try to avoid her eye contact.

"Sure," she says. So, I change topics quickly.

"So, tell me about this rock star of yours. The one who wrote a song called 'FMK.'"

"It's ironic. That's the whole point of—"

"I know, I read the article," I say. "You know, he's very articulate. He sounds smart. He can sing like nothing else. But that's all incidental. What really matters here is: are you happy?"

Her eyes sparkle like a cartoon rabbit's.

"Oh, I am, Daisy. I am. He's the one. I know it."

"You do?" I laugh. "I mean, you've been with him for a couple of months."

"And I knew within five minutes."

"That's statistically improbable."

"Love's statistically improbable," she replies to me. "But it still happens. Every day. So, don't be a statistic. Be an exception to the rule."

"Are you going to post that?" I smirk.

"Absolutely."

We both take a breather, and then, out of nowhere, I feel her warm arms around me. She pulls me in close, squeezing me tight, holding me together. And suddenly we're not twenty-eight and thirty-one. We're seven and ten. And it's us against the world.

"I think I finally worked out that work doesn't come first for me."

"It doesn't?" Mia questions.

"You do," I say, and then because that's beyond corny I cringe and add: "But work comes a very close second."

She giggles at that.

"For what it's worth, you're more than worthy of love. Because there's no one in the whole world I love more than you." She whispers into my ear. "The authentic you."

"I love you too, Mia," I say.

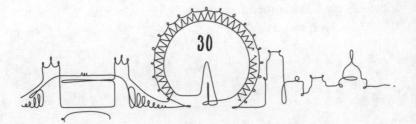

Archie

I'm starting to get the hang of this whole Instagram thing

Me

You realize that phrasing makes you sound ancient right?

It's like something my Nan would have said

Archie

Did your Nan have 478 followers?

Me

Good point.

That's a lot of influence.

You'd better use it wisely

Archie

I'll show them another dog painting probably

Me

Good choice

The texts keep coming. All through the next week. Two days I spend focusing in on my interview with The Kibble Crew, researching the history of the brand, the conference talks they've given online, looking at their LinkedIn profiles. The more I look, the more I like it.

And I'm actually enjoying myself too. I have such a drive; a real purpose that I feel I've been missing since I lost my job. Sure, I am currently living in a complete shit hole, but one that I feel will get cleaned. Just as soon as I've finished this interview. Because I'm feeling good about this.

I can get back into the working world. A world I've really missed. Looking back at the last couple months, I have surprised myself with how much I have had fun in unemployment.

But that doesn't mean I'm not yearning to get back into a workplace. I'm desperate to give presentations on my findings, to unearth things others have missed. I can't wait to get right back into it.

But I'm only human of course, which means that I can't help but be distracted once or twice across the space of the day. I go through my Instagram reels as if on autopilot.

A dog Reel.

Another dog Reel.

Brian went to a gig last night.

A third dog Reel.

And then I click on my dancing Reel that Bailey made me.

I actually love it. I'm sure some of the two-hundred-odd views are just me watching it over and over, and I know that may sound vain, but it's really because behind all those photographs I'm thinking of Bailey. And Cara. And Mia. And Archie.

It fills me with such joy, that I want to relive it.

Only when I have relived it, for the fifth time that hour, I notice I have a notification.

Maybe Mia, I think, tagging me in a Reel about another baby animal. She has more variation than me on species and now we're talking again, it's like we never stopped.

Except, when I see who it is I feel a bit sick.

Jax_O liked your reel

He liked it. I've been on Instagram for the last twenty minutes, and this notification is brand new. It's in real time.

It leaves such a sour taste in my mouth. That sickness becomes a strange nausea I can't settle. I stand up, walking carefully (around the piles of clothes and grains of spilled rice), trying to outpace my own discomfort.

Jackson Oakley watched me, just a few minutes ago.

Well, fuck him. He doesn't get to watch me anymore. He lost that privilege. He was my main reason for getting back into Instagram in the first place, and now just seeing him like something makes me want to delete it all forever. It makes me want to open my crappy window and throw it out to the street.

And then, while I'm pacing, while my heart's hammering, while I'm fretting, I see another notification.

A message.

No, it can't be. He can't have . . . slipped into my DMs?

I put my phone down, physically walking away from it. I don't even want to read it. I don't want to hear what that man has to say. To think I ever yearned after his time block. A time block! As if that was all I was worth.

I won't read it.

Only it might not be from him.

But obviously it's from him.

But what if it's not?

So, I do it. I bring up all the courage I have and I open my messages page.

Jax_O
Check your emails . . .

I click off the second I see his name, but it's already too late. I forgot that it shows you the first part of the text automatically.

Check my emails?

Why would I need to . . . ?

No. Don't do it. He doesn't deserve your time.

Only, that's such a weird way of slipping into my DMs, isn't it? Why my emails?

So, I open them. Hating myself but too curious to stop.

I doubt Jackson is referring to the three marketing emails I've received from clothes brands, but there is one that has just landed in my inbox.

One that stops me breathing.

Gemma Taylor <Gemma@Everest.co.uk>

Daisy,
Thank you for your email.

Management have been in discussions all this week, and I am delighted to inform you that we would love you to come in for an interview.

I have CC'd in my assistant Stephanie, who will help find a time that suits all.

Many thanks,
Gemma
Head of HR
Everest

I can't breathe.

My flat stills. The creaks of the floorboards silence beneath my feet and the old pipes find their peace.

My old job.

I could have it back, I could have it all back! The life that I've missed; sitting at my desk on the second floor with my fellow analysts. Gossiping by the coffee machines.

But when I think about it, when I really think about it, I realize I don't want to interview.

Not at all.

Because I already know I can't work there.

Jackson aside, I can't work for a company that won't allow for, as Betzy put it, one fuckup in thirteen years. One that no one, not Jackson, but also not even my manager, talked to me about or found out my side for. They just fired me.

Maybe I deserved to be fired.

But I also deserved to be listened to.

Within seconds I'm decided. Absolutely and completely: It's time to move on.

So, feeling like some weight is lifting instinctively, I reply back.

Hi Gemma,
Many thanks for your email.
    I'm grateful for the opportunity, but I'd like to formally rescind my application.
    I appreciate everything Branded has taught me through the years, and I will always be proud to have worked there. But I think now is actually a good time for me to explore new opportunities.

Best wishes to all of you,
Daisy

I feel so fucking good. Sure, I'm saying goodbye to Branded, but this feels like I'm saying goodbye to them on *my* terms.

I feel elated. Sky high. Walking on an actual dream.

And then I remember why I looked at my emails.

So, I go back on Instagram to see the whole message.

Jax_O
Check your emails
I think you're going to like what you see x

What. A. Prick.

Acting like nothing just happened then?

Acting like he hasn't just ghosted me these past weeks?

That angers me. That full-on red-hot steam angers me. What a complete arsehole. To take credit for this. As if he was the one who orchestrated it. As if it was all his choice when I'm guessing it has nothing to do with him at all.

Screw him.

Have the upper hand here, Daisy, I whisper to myself. Be the better person.

Only I can't help it.

So, I reply back, before regret could possibly set in.

Me
Wankhead

I write, thinking only of Betzy, and I don't care if it's immature, it feels so fucking good.

And then, before he can say anything, or before I can even know if he's seen it, I block him.

Because he doesn't deserve any more of *my* precious time.

I give my phone a few hours break after all that, but when I look back at the screen at lunchtime, I see a text arrive that makes me smile.

Archie
You hungry?
Me
Very. I have eaten nothing but cereal all day
I hope Cheerios are as nutritious as they claim

It's lunchtime, two days before my interview. I'm ignoring the pile of T-shirts and panties on the floor at my feet as I curl myself on the green love seat, researching away on GitHub best practices.

My doorbell rings.

Confused, I reread Archie's text.

Me
My doorbell just rang

> Is this another salmon teriyaki come to keep me
> company?

I laugh as I hit send, wondering what it genuinely is as I start the journey out my front door and down the stairs to the main front door.

Archie
Nando's today
You like chicken, right?

My heart beats quickly. He got me food again?

I feel a huge swell of something fill me, opening the door wide to greet the delivery driver.

Only it isn't a delivery driver at all.

It's Archie.

In the flesh. Standing before me with a big, wrapped canvas at his feet and a brown paper bag with a beautiful chicken logo facing out to me.

He's wearing an open blue shirt, rolled up in the heat, over a white T-shirt. He looks all shades of unbelievable. His feet are—unsurprisingly—not bare given he had to walk here. No glasses today. Only beautiful emerald eyes.

"I've come to interview for the nanny position?" he asks.

It takes me a while to clock what he said. The edges of his eyes have already crinkled over before I can even smile with him.

"I came to deliver this," he says, handing over the Nando's. "And it came with this."

He holds out the canvas between us, wrapped up to protect it from the London dust. My jaw drops in awe.

"You painted something for me?"

"Incorrect. Bailey painted you something. As a thank-you."

It's quite a big canvas in his hands. And wrapped up under brown paper.

No one has ever painted me something before. I feel a bit stunned, unsure. But Archie just hands it over to me.

I look up the stairs behind me, then back to the painting.

"I was just . . . preparing," I tell him.

"I won't disturb you. I know how important this is."

His hands go up in innocence as he takes a few steps back, like it was no big deal. But I don't actually want him to leave, because I just did something awesome, and I want to tell someone, and that someone was always going to be Archie.

So, I blurt out: "I got an interview for my old job at Branded!"

"Daisy!" Archie says proudly, stopped in his exit. "That's incredible!"

"I told them I don't want it . . ." I say, and when it leaves my lips it just feels right.

"You didn't?" he asks.

"I rescinded my application. I think it's finally time I've worked out that there are more companies out there than just Branded."

"And you feel good about this?" he says, scanning my smile for any hesitation. The smell of glorious chicken rises from the paper bag in my hand, and if I wasn't happy before, I am now.

"I feel really amazing," I say truthfully.

"Yes!" Archie fist pumps the air in excitement for me. "That's incredible! You have to celebrate life's little victories, and knowing what you want is a victory!"

He lunges forward and grabs me, pulling me out of the doorway and spinning me in the air. I squeal in delight as Clapham Road cars must see me being whisked around in his arms.

As he puts me down, I feel how close his face is away from mine. He lingers, out of breath. We both are. But we stay there, locked in the moment.

And so of course, I have to ruin the moment.

"You can't come up."

Immediately he takes a step away respectfully, as if he never meant to overstep. But he hasn't. That's not why I just said it.

I said it because I was about to ask him to come on up. Only then I remembered the way I live, and I realize I can't have him see that.

"I wasn't suggesting . . ." he says quickly.

"No, I mean . . ." There's no way of backing out of this without actually telling him the truth: "Upstairs is a mess."

He blinks a few times, entirely amused.

"I'm fine to not come up here, Daisy, I was just delivering the painting, but I also hope you know that I don't care about mess."

I remember the basmati all over the floor.

"I think you'd care about this one."

"I have two young girls. I'm used to mess."

I remember the bras on the kitchen table.

"Not in this proportion. And I've seen your house. It's spotless."

"You've not seen Cara's room."

He's laughing, but he'll stop when he sees it. He'll stop wanting to be my friend when he sees who I really am.

I can't believe I've let it slip to ruin the way I have. I think I've maybe been punishing myself for everything I lost by living in such a state. I wanted to *see* the pain, and in letting my flat fall to ruin, I saw it alright.

"I'll leave you to it. We'll find a time to meet up. With or . . ." He looks a bit daring. "Without the girls."

Is that . . . a date? Is he asking me for a date?

And when I catch his eye I realize . . . Well, I know actually. I don't want to be his friend. I haven't wanted that in a very long time.

Instead of words, he leans in, and I feel my heart double in pace, unsure. And then his cheek touches mine, a kiss, the formal kind, the kind where lips don't make contact. And yet he's made contact. And he's so close I can smell his aftershave. It smells incredible.

But he has kids.

How many times do I have to remind myself of that fact? How many times do I have to tell myself that he has kids, and I don't want them? And I shouldn't have to change for a man.

"Text me?" he asks. "When your interview is over?"

And I think about how I'm sure it will be the first thing I'll do. And with that thought, a pragmatic little devil whispers into my ear.

I don't want this to end. I can't end it.

But I also don't want kids.

Maybe this is the easy way out, I think to myself sadly. Because once he's seen upstairs, he's going to be the one to turn and run. Exposing it all, putting it all out in front of him, I couldn't blame him for not wanting anything else from me after that.

And all this talk of meeting up without the girls, all the ambiguity of it all, will suddenly be made clear and it won't be my fault. Or at least, it won't be my *choice*.

And I can't have it be my choice. These feelings I have for this man are so much stronger than I've had for anyone. They're more vulnerable.

"Come up," I say before he can leave again.

Archie looks from left to right, unsure.

"I don't need to, I came here to give you this. I'd never assume—"

"Come up," I say again, surer this time. "If you want."

Because he's going to go upstairs and realize I can't possibly be someone he ever wants to see. He's going to take one look and leave.

And it will hurt.

But I don't know how else to break away from him. I know I don't want to.

He takes a breath.

"I don't want to be that guy here," he says slowly, "but you're giving me very mixed messages."

"I'm not saying come up for . . . anything in particular. Tea maybe. But . . . my place is a state."

"You mentioned."

"And if you think you can handle that and still, well . . . I think you should come up."

He rubs the back of his neck.

"I can handle it," he tells me. "Lead the way."

I take a few steps forward before I dare to turn to face him. I can't believe I just agreed to this.

I wince as he blinks into the light. I feel so vulnerable right now.

My junk is piled up all around him. I feel more naked than if I was literally naked as his eyes scan it all, his expression so neutral.

Oh gosh, I can't watch this.

"This isn't how I live. Not normally," I say quickly, my cheeks filling. "I've just let it get out of control recently. Honestly, if you'd seen this place before I met you, you would have seen a completely different flat. One that's not so . . . this."

His eyes stop scanning and find mine.

"You made out that it was terrible," he says, his soft Scottish lilt bouncing off my walls.

"Well, it is," I say, my arms out as if showing him what he can clearly already see. He fiddles with the edge of his glasses, as if changing the perspective.

"Sure, I wouldn't have picked that shade of tiling myself for a kitchen but it's very passable, I promise you."

"The tiles?" I say, confused. "No, I didn't mean—I meant the clothes. My crap. Everywhere."

"Oh, the clothes?" he says, looking at them as if surprised I'm even mentioning them. "I barely noticed the clothes."

He's joking of course, and it really makes me smile. Laugh even, looking around them and biting my lip.

"I haven't had the chance to clean," I giggle, suddenly seeing the funny side of it all.

Where did my embarrassment go?

He walks over to me, very delicately treading his own path as not to tread on any of my garments spread over the floor.

"Just to be clear," he says as he draws close. "You almost didn't invite me up because of a few stray clothes?"

"Well, yes . . . no . . . And the green tiles . . ." I add.

"We all have our crap, Daisy," he says seriously. "You don't need to hide it."

And suddenly the atmosphere has changed, because I've just put myself out there, and instead of running like I thought he would—like I thought anyone would—he has stayed.

I knew I liked him. I knew I *more* than "liked" him. But I didn't realize that anyone had the power to make me feel like this. *Like I'm worthy.*

And I think by the look in his eye, that he feels exactly how I feel. That friendship isn't enough. That this has evolved, and denying it isn't possible anymore.

He looks at me with eyes asking an open question, and I don't object. If anything, I'm willing him on. Pulling him closer.

His hand slides around my waist. If it was open for interpretation before, it isn't anymore. It's very clear. We both know it, and we both feel it. With a little tug he pulls me in close and I feel his chest make contact. I look up and right into his eyes, which are looking at me like I'm everything he wants to see, and more.

His fingers naturally weave themselves through my hair before he moves his hand back and around to my face. My cheeks. His thumb strokes around the star constellations across my nose and I feel my whole body melt.

And then his eyes change. And I know what he's about to do. He smiles, before his eyes close and he leans in closer toward me, closing the gap.

As he's about to make contact, I can feel my heart doing cartwheels already. I can feel the bubbling of butterflies in the pit of my stomach.

I must not ruin this moment, no matter what, by saying something stupid like:

"Stop."

Only.

That's exactly what I say.

"Stop," I whisper.

And I hate myself for saying it. I hate my lips for speaking it. I hate my mind for thinking it. But I do, think it, speak it, say it.

He pulls back instantly, unsure. He heard me say stop, and he's stopped. It's exactly what I asked for, but in this instant, exactly the opposite of what I want.

"Is something wrong?" he whispers.

Oh god. Am I going to do this?

Yes, of course I am. I have to. Because I know if he kisses me it's game over. I'm not sure I'll ever be able to say what needs to be said. So, I take a deep breath. And bravely, so bravely, I say:

"We can't," fighting every urge in my body. "We can't be together."

"Oh right," he says, taking a full step back. He looks a little awkward, as if to apologize for completely misreading the situation.

"No, it's not . . . it's not you. I want this. I can't tell you how much I want this. Only . . ." And here it is. The moment where reality ruins the romance: "We don't fit."

He twists his head around, completely confused. His hand still rests on my back, but I can feel his arms fall slightly. His grip loosens.

"Why not?"

"Because . . . because you have kids. And your kids have to come first."

"My kids *will* always come first," he says, a soft frown appearing between those beautiful green eyes. He's clearly not following. "But that doesn't mean I can't be with anyone. It just means I need that person to understand that."

"No, you don't . . ." I stutter, getting flustered. "You have kids. And I *can't* have kids."

"OK . . ." he says. And again, I feel his grip loosen. He looks down, as if to my stomach. Then his eyes come back up to mine: "That's not a problem. . . ."

But I've just realized what he thinks.

"Not medically. I mean I can't have kids *in my life*. Full stop."

That's the moment that it kicks in. The moment his hand comes off my back and goes back to his side. The moment he steps away.

"It's not *your* kids," I say, not wanting him to misunderstand me, "I love your kids. I've never met kids like your kids. Cara, well, she's basically a compliment PEZ dispenser. The level of sass she has is the level of sass I've always wanted. And Bailey, she's so talented and creative. The way she looks after Cara is exactly who I wanted to be with Mia. I love your kids."

I can see that he wants to smile. I can see the edge of his lips, the quiver of his dimple. But then, as if remembering why I'm saying this, he keeps his face neutral.

"So, what's the problem?"

I sit down on my closest kitchen chair, probably on a stray T-shirt, my head in my hands as a wave of tears hits me.

"I can't be that woman who meets a man, falls in love and cancels everything that's important to her just to be with him. I can't be that girl."

He sits down next to me, a distance apart and yet turned only in my direction.

"I would never want you to cancel anything for me," he says gently.

"Well, just being with you would cancel it. I can't have kids in my life."

He leans back, and I feel the distance sting. Oh, what I would do to be back in his arms. But I have to stay strong. His life isn't compatible with mine. I've known that from the start.

"Tell me why?" he asks simply.

I take one long, deep breath.

"You defined me once as a working woman. Well, that's exactly what I want to be. It's what I've always wanted to be. I can't be with someone who stops that."

"Why on earth would you need to stop your career?" I can see he's just not getting it.

"Because that's what happens! Kids kill careers! They don't mean to, but they do."

"Why do you think that?"

"Because I've seen it! It happened to my mum. You know, she wanted to be a midwife before she had me? She told me once. She grew up desperate to be a midwife, started the training a few months after she married my dad and hey, presto—she's pregnant with me. I ruined her life, just by being born. I ruined her hopes and dreams and her grand plans. Instead, she got lumped with two kids who she didn't want to begin with, quit her dream job, and ruined her whole life by picking a career that would work for us.

That didn't even work for us in the end. That didn't work for her either. She just ended up just asking her own parents for handouts. And I don't have my parents to fall back on when I fail. I have no option to fail. So, I can't. I can't risk it, I can't do it."

He nods, sympathetically.

This would be so much easier if he was angry.

"Your mum has her own unique story here," he says gently. "This doesn't mean you have to quit your career to have kids."

"It's not just my mum. Just look at you. You had to quit your career because of your kids!"

He blinks a few times, as if this is new information to him.

"You think I quit being a lawyer because I had kids?" His tone has changed. It's hardened.

"Well, you did! You said if yourself. You quit—"

"I didn't quit being a lawyer because I had kids. Law and family aren't mutually exclusive. I know many lawyers who have kids."

"That's not . . ." I begin, not sure how to phrase it. "But being a single parent—"

"It has nothing to do with being a single parent either," he says. "I know single mothers who are partners in law firms. I know single fathers who are working their way up. I didn't quit my job because of Bailey and Cara."

I stop, blinking back the tears.

"Then why did you quit?" I ask, confused.

"I quit because my wife died." I feel the air still around me. Those butterflies have turned to lead in the pit of my stomach. "Zoe didn't leave me. She didn't divorce me. She died. And next thing I know, I'm sitting in a room listening to the reasons person X should get the beach house. Or hearing them shouting because person Y wants a glass vase and I'm thinking, they don't know how lucky they are. They were fighting over 'stuff.' Just trivial fucking stuff. And do you know what I would give to fight with my wife over stuff that doesn't matter, just one more time? Do you know what I'd give to spend just one more day in the same world that she lives in? All I wanted to do was to shake them and tell them how lucky they were that they even 'got' to divorce one another. How lucky they are that the mother of their children was alive."

He takes a deep breath, the words clearly weighing heavy on him. He didn't think he'd have to say any of this today, that is clear.

"Now, people go through divorce for all kinds of reasons. Some of those reasons are terrible. I respect that. I understand that it's a horrible thing to go through for everyone. But I wasn't seeing that back then. So, I wasn't the right man for the job. I couldn't listen to it anymore. So, I quit. And when I thought about what other law practice I could go into next, I realized I never even wanted to be a lawyer in the first place. So, why would I get back into it again when the only thing I wanted to do was something that let me hang out with my kids? Life is short. And if I only have so long left, I want to make sure I'm spending it with the people I love."

He shakes his head. I don't even know what to say to that. I feel like someone's ripped something out from my chest. Like I'm breaking for him.

"So, it wasn't kids that stopped me practicing law. It wasn't love either. It was *life* that changed me. You want me to blame something for my career change? Try blaming the black ice on the road that night. Or the tree her car crashed into. That's what's to blame."

I don't know what to say.

My lip is quivering. I feel so stupid. So, completely stupid.

Why didn't I see any of that before? Because it went against my narrative. Because I have no idea what it's like to have two kids and no partner. Because I saw my mother.

"If you must know, falling in love is why I became a lawyer in the first place," he says. I'm glad he's spoken again, because I clearly don't know what to say to him. "Being a lawyer . . . It was what my parents wanted for me. They were sensible people. A lot like your grandparents I'd imagine, and being an only child, I always thought I should follow their chosen path. Only one week into studying for my LPC and all I wanted was to quit. I hated it. I was going to be . . . I didn't even know. An artist maybe and . . . then the girl next to me asked if she could borrow my green highlighter.

"I'd barely taken a single note, but she had almost written the lecture out verbatim. She was driven. Ambitious. So, so focused. Just like Bailey. She didn't just want to be a lawyer, she wanted to be the greatest lawyer there was. She didn't just want to pass the exams, she wanted to get the best marks anyone had ever got before.

"We couldn't have been more different. The only reason I had a highlighter was to doodle, while she specifically wanted the green one so she could color code her notes correctly. She had yellow, and blue and pink and she wanted to add a fourth category to her strangely specific categorizations that I could never get my head around. I mean she was the kind of woman who even categorized her font when the color categorization ran out—important in block capitals, good to knows in cursive. So, I let her borrow my high-lighter. And the next day I returned because I wanted to see her again.

"And I didn't quit, because quitting meant I wouldn't sit next to her. And I took that exam, because she was taking that exam and I didn't want her to go through it alone. And five years later this woman, this lawyer, becomes my wife.

"So, yes, I guess I was that man who fell in love and cancelled everything important to me just to be with her. I became a lawyer for her. I became a good one, because she inspired me to be great. And when she told me one day she wanted kids, I became a father for her too.

"And thank god I did. Because not a day goes by when I think that that woman didn't change my life for the better. Zoe wanted to be a great many things in this world, and I wanted to be the man by her side while she did it. It would have killed me to think that loving me stopped her from doing any of them."

He shakes his head, slowly, sadly. I feel glass shattering through my very bones.

"I was never asking you to give up your career for me, or my girls. I wouldn't ask you to. Loving someone isn't sacrificing every-thing else you love. It's making two beings who might not fit per-fectly, fit imperfectly instead. It's about supporting one another.

And sure, it's often about compromise too, but you work out those compromises together. That's what I hoped we'd be able to do. Because you're the kind of girl I'd want to make compromises for."

He looks back down at his feet, and I suddenly want to move closer, to lift his chin up, to look him in the eye and tell him how I have this all wrong. But he continues speaking to his feet.

"I have been so, incredibly lonely, and in this vast pit of loneliness that is life, I find myself a lot less lonely with you."

I gasp, involuntarily.

Because he has said everything I feel. Everything I would never have been able to articulate. And I should jump right in, and tell him: that he's exactly who I want to make compromises with too. That none of the rest matters.

Only he speaks again.

"But you are right. My kids will always come first. And if you don't want kids, then I don't want my kids to have someone in their lives that doesn't want them."

And with that, he stands, as if he is suddenly sure. And he picks up the painting he came over with that he left by the door, and with it, he goes.

And I feel my whole heart rip.

31

I want to run after him, but I don't.

I want to say how sorry I am, how stupid I am. I want to tell him how much I want him. Because I want him so much it hurts.

Only I don't do any of those things.

Because despite everything he said, I can't be wrong about this. Helen showed me that. And I've only known Archie and his girls for the last few months. I can't ruin a decade-long career for three humans I met weeks ago. I'm not going to be that girl.

So, I don't text him. Instead, I just cry. Small tears, running down my face as I try and remember why I've done this. As I try and justify it.

But no. I need to just stop thinking of him. I'll do just about anything to stop the ringing in my ears. Which is when the text comes through:

Mia

Mum's free tomorrow morning? xxxxxx

Well, that's a distraction. So, fuck it, sure. Let's just get all the hard stuff out of the way. Maybe seeing her will validate everything I've just said. I can't tell if I need that or not.

But I'll do it.

So, I text back.

Me

Sure. Set it up x

Then I look at the Nando's bag he left. I need a short-term fix here to get out of my head before I overthink all of it and crumble. So, I dive into the bag, hoping to find a lemon. My best alternative is lemon and herb sauce . . . I mean, it's a poor substitute but it's something. So, I rip off the packaging and down it like a shot.

Urgh! No. Definitely not shot-worthy. I gag instantly. For something delicious on chicken, it's absolutely disgusting when drank.

I try and pretend that's the reason I feel slightly nauseous all night.

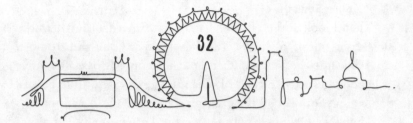

32

Helen looks older than I remember, but I guess that's what happens when you don't see someone for over a decade. The decade happens, whether they are in your sights or not. She looks, well, a lot like me actually. Just older. The freckles on her cheeks are still there in full force. Her blonde hair has whitened a little, just at the edges. She's wearing jeans and a loose summery shirt. Paler than Mia, bolder than me. Somewhere in between.

The café was Mia's choice and you can tell. Everything is a sickly pink in here, but I don't think either of us is looking at the décor right now. Only at each other.

She looks a little different from how I imagined. Over the years I vilified her. I'd distorted her features, and yet, she just looks normal now. She looks human.

She smiles when she sees me, a little awkwardly, unsure. I couldn't even tell you what my face looks like. It's just so hard to control your face when you feel overwhelmed, and that's exactly what I feel as I walk across the coffee shop and sit down beside her.

"Mia said you like coffee," she says, pushing over a latte. "Or rather, she says you still like hot milk, just like you did when you were little. Only you need the coffee in it to justify it now you've grown up."

When I was little? I think sourly. She was barely there for my childhood.

And then I remember it's probably best not to make snap judgments. Not right now. I'm here to listen to her. Actually listen, and really, all she's done so far is get me a coffee I actually like. That was nice of her. And talking about me with Mia? That's a good sign, I guess. Shows interest at least.

It's funny. I usually have so much to say. But right now, I don't really know what to say at all. So, I simply thank her, looking down at my latte, thinking.

"You look so well," she says, not sure where to begin either.

I can see she too doesn't like silences.

She squirms in her seat. I must have got that from her then.

Only just as she's about to fill it, I realize there's a lot I don't want to talk about. So, I cut in before she can ask me questions about myself that I'm not sure I want to answer.

"Mia tells me you're a midwife now?" I ask.

She looks relieved that I've taken an interest. She smiles.

"Yes, I am," she says. "I trained a few years ago. I should have done it a long time ago. Back when you were young instead of taking that stupid job with Vale Skin Care."

I nod. And I almost don't say anything at all, only I can't let it rest.

"You should have," I agree. I can see my words sting. I can see her face contort. But she nods acceptance. "It's so strange hearing you call it stupid. I used to think you loved that job."

"Oh, I was miserable. Every second. I hated it so much," she sighs, shaking her head at the thought.

"But all those photos you showed us . . ."

"I forced a smile for every single one of them," she says.

"Why take them then? Why show them at all?"

"Part of me took them because I didn't want you worrying about me. But mostly," she looks disappointed already, "mostly it was because I didn't want to admit that I made a mistake. I wanted to prove to my parents, to you, to everyone, that I'd chosen the right path after all."

I let her continue because she wants to say more. And I think I'm finally ready to hear it.

"I know I never should have joined that bloody company. I just panicked. Your father left and I had two small children, and I was forced to live back with my parents again. I felt humiliated. On so many levels." She swirls the cup of coffee that sits in front of her. "And a friend of mine had just bought in and she was telling me how much money she earned, and how quickly. Minimum work, huge profits. She'd just bought herself a car, and I was struggling at the time to buy us all lunch. I should have known even then that it sounded too good to be true but she was living the lifestyle I wanted."

She pushes the coffee away from her, as if she hates the taste. Maybe she's feeling as sick as I am, being here.

"But I wanted to prove I could do it and do it all. I wanted the best life for you. And I reasoned to myself that timing wise, back then *was* the best time to do it. While you were still little and wouldn't miss me as much. If I just made enough money in a year, maybe two, then I could sell out of that business and spend more time just being your mum without the financial woes. Only I took out a loan to buy the initial stock, which meant I was horribly in debt before I even began."

I think if I'd heard this at any other point in my life, I might have just thought these were all excuses. I wouldn't have listened. But things have changed. So, I nod. But when she finally braves looking up from the table to catch my eye, I can see the embarrassment in her face.

"I'm sorry—you probably don't want to hear all of this. I told myself I wouldn't go on about it and here I go, going on."

She really is like me, I think. Filling the silence.

So, I let her off the hook because I know that feeling.

"I understand why you did it."

"You do?" she asks, looking up at me hopefully.

"You were in a bad place and didn't want people to know. You wanted to show people you were living your best life." I almost cringe as I speak, thinking about what I was trying to do on Instagram.

She looks so grateful, just to have me speak. And then she shakes her head, like her whole mind aches.

"I'm glad you understand, because here, years later, I still don't," she says. "I gave up everything I really wanted in life for a career that turned out not to be a career at all."

"No one knew." I shrug.

"Even still. I could have made money a hundred different ways. But I can never make up for the time I wasn't with you."

I take a sip of my latte, mostly to be polite. My stomach almost can't handle it right now, only I need to do something with my hands. With my face. Nervous energy burns through me as hot as lava.

"Well, are you happier now? As a midwife?" I ask, trying to move on.

She takes a deep breath.

"The job is better. Much better. That's for sure. But I wish I knew back then that my happiness was never about what job I did. That's not what matters in the end. It's about spending time with the people that I love."

Suddenly she leans across the table, taking my hand with an urgency I wasn't expecting. I let her, unsure.

"I know I have a lot to make up for there. Daisy, I understand why you're angry with me. I'm angry with myself. But I am so, so sorry for not being there. For not being the mum I always hoped to be for you. The mum you deserve. But I am here now. You might not want me, but I'm here. And I'll always be here for you, whether you ever need me or not."

Those words, words I've wanted to hear all my life. Words that make me feel seen. Feel understood. Feel . . . loved. I mean, it doesn't make me forgive her. One coffee doesn't make up for a lifetime that we've lost. But the more we talk, the more I realize I don't think it is too late to try again. It's harder, sure. But it's never too late.

She takes a deep breath, as if that is a weight off her shoulders. Like a mirror image of each other, we dab at our watery eyelids.

We talk for another hour or so after that, mostly about Mia. She's common ground for both of us, and the more Helen asks, the more I remember. Baking with her in Nan's kitchen. The time she got suspended in school for wearing a skirt that was too short and telling teachers to "Fuck off and let her express herself."

The only time she comes close to speaking again about her role is when I tell her all about the dance parties I used to have with Mia.

"I remember them," she laughs.

And, perhaps a little thoughtlessly, I say:

"I used to put music on every time I heard shouting in the kitchen, so Mia wouldn't hear."

She looks ashamed then, shivering with the memory.

"Every time I came back home they made me feel like a failure. I'm sure they were trying to do the right thing by me at the end of the day, but I think there was just a lot of hurt there. I hated feeling like a failure. So, I shouted my way through it, telling them they were wrong, telling them that this was all going to work out in the end." She looks up to the sky, as if in thought. "If I could just go back and shake myself and tell myself to hang my bloody pride up at the door. If I'd just accepted what they said, I could have had a very different life." She leans her neck a little lower and I actually feel sorry for her. That was something I never expected to feel. She looks back up at me, determination in her voice as she says: "I'm so sorry you had to hear all that. And I'm sorry you had to protect Mia from it too. That's such a big responsibility for such a young girl."

And even hearing it gives me validation somehow.

When we have both worked out that neither of us is going to actually drink our coffees, we call it a day. But actually, this hasn't been what I thought it was. It wasn't a horrible encounter. It was a human conversation between two people with a lot of history. So, when she says, just before we part: "I'd like to see you again. When you have time. If you have time." I find myself nodding, slowly.

"I'd like that too," I say.

The first thing I want to do when I leave the coffee shop is text Archie.

I want to tell him everything that was said and that it wasn't anything like I'd imagined. That I realized that Helen was just a human, who made a series of bad choices and thought it was more important for us to not worry, than it was to tell us the truth.

But I can't text Archie.

I think about the fight, and it instantly makes me feel sick.

I try and remember everything I said. Do I still think it?

Yes, I have to still think it. That fight has to have been worth it. Because sure, Helen fed me that line that a job was just a job but spending time with the people you love is more important, but like . . . that was because she didn't love her job! She hated it. And I love mine. Loved mine. OK, fine, well, I love *having* a job.

So, I don't text Archie.

Instead, I text Mia.

> **Me**
> Thank you for setting that up
> I really needed that
> **Mia**
> Did it go alright?

I think of her beautiful bold face saying that aloud. I bet she's been thinking about this all afternoon. So, let me relieve her.

> **Me**
> I think its step one
> But for what it's worth, I'm ready to keep stepping
> forward
> **Mia**
> I love you

She texts back in reply, instantly.

Me
I love you too

When I open the door to my flat, I groan.

When you make a big mess, it remains there haunting you until you sort it. And I know I have an interview to prepare for tomorrow, but I think what I've discovered is that I will use any excuse to put off this mess in front of me. Maybe the trick is to just do it, regardless of what else there is.

So, I get to work.

I don't just shovel the clothes back into the bedroom, I begin sorting them first. Most of them need a wash to get the smoke smell out, so all of those go straight in the machine which slows me down but doesn't stop me.

Weirdly, having all the clothes laid out across my kitchen has let me see what I actually have. I have kept clothes in my cupboard unworn for years now, and it feels so good that within the first two hours of folding and organizing it all, I have almost two big bags ready for a charity shop drop-off.

I start a second load of washing, for my sheets this time, and all the cutlery and crockery that ended up on my bedside table ends up back on the kitchen counters.

I work slowly, but methodically, and most importantly, to music.

My bedroom is complete to the sound of Bastille. My bathroom shimmers to the glorious tones of Sigrid. My kitchen requires four whole playlists to finish off, and even then, I switch it to the *Hamilton* soundtrack for a boost in the final push.

It works. For before the evening is complete, my flat has been restored.

It's back to being my flat again. Tidy, clean, and acceptable to visit by everyone.

And I think about texting Archie.

But I have an interview tomorrow, and instead of preparing for it all day, I have been tidying. So, I open my laptop, and start that instead.

* * *

The only way I can describe the Kibble Crew's offices is by imagining if someone had personally designed a Willy Wonka chocolate factory, but specifically for me.

Firstly, their color palette. Their logo is pink and green pastel on a light blue background—all accidentally in keeping with my clothing choices of the day: a pale pink blazer over jeans and boots. The walls are all coated in the same spread, making me seem like some sort of chameleon within these walls. Like I instantly belong.

Secondly, and more importantly, there are dogs. Everywhere. And I think perhaps they might be a huge distraction, only a lot of them are just chilling: by their owner's feet, curled up in their beds, a few on laps.

And on the walls, there are more dogs. Photo frames. Drawings. Dogs everywhere.

And if all that wasn't good enough, all around the dogs are big screens, cycling through a series of monitoring dashboards which are absolutely fascinating. We're talking all kinds of metrics on show: base sales, linear correlations, ROI curves.

I could stare at them for hours.

Only I don't have hours, because Colin from the data analytics team met me in reception bang on time for my meeting, and led me straight up to a meeting room with a large screen.

"So, I'm afraid you're going to have a hybrid interview," he tells me, plugging in the HDMI. "Marie's tuning in from home as her little one Betty isn't feeling so well today."

"No problem," I tell him, looking out the glass windows of the room to where three dogs are all playing tug-of-war. That sausage dog is never going to win, but it's adorable that he thinks he can take on a Labrador and a husky like that.

One little ping shows the two of us have officially dialed in. The woman, who would inevitably be my boss should I get this role, is a woman in her late thirties.

She's not disguising the fact she's wearing sweats. Her hair is messily on her head, and I don't think she's wearing makeup. And yet, she definitely means business. That's amazingly refreshing.

As we do our introductions, I get a shot of nerves whisper through me. Because everything about this company I love so far. I want this. I really, really want this.

Then my interview begins.

It isn't until about fifteen minutes in when it happens. I'm halfway through telling them about a previous piece of analysis I ran back at Branded when I hear a small voice.

"I'm sorry, Betty is teething so she's a little needy right now," Marie says over video call. And little Betty, who has until now been just off-screen, suddenly comes into view.

I don't know why I thought maybe Betty was a dog. Maybe because of all the dogs in the office around me. Only Betty's not a dog, she's a little girl. Just over a year I'm guessing.

"Hello, Betty!" Colin cries gleefully when she comes to view, like this is totally normal. He waves, giving the little angel a big, gooey-eyed smile.

And I can't help but stare.

Because in front of me is a woman working from home with a small child, and making it look like it's that simple. She hasn't given up her career for kids, I think to myself.

And she's not completely distracted, either. She's balancing a beautiful cherub-like face on one arm as she's asking me to describe a time I used an AB test.

She is balancing it all. She's making it work.

And Colin isn't sitting there judging her for it. He's making faces at her daughter to amuse her in between talking to me about my previous experience.

And then I remember that I'm in an interview, and it's incredibly rude to stare.

"So, tell me why you left Branded," Marie asks.

Oh god. The shame. So, what do I do, lie to them? Fabricate a different version of the truth?

Why, when I prepared so much for this interview, did I not prepare the answer to that one, very obvious question?

So, I do the unthinkable. I tell the truth:

"A magazine I was working for posted an image of my sister with the headline 'FMK: the choice is yours.' It asked their whole audience to rate the girlfriends of this band into these three categories: The M stands for Marriage. The K stands for Kill; you might be able to work out what the F stands for. Anyway, I was furious with them. They treated my sister appallingly, and I couldn't stand it. So, I acted incredibly unprofessionally and said some pretty juvenile things to their marketing department." I bite my lip, not sure if that means I've just ruined this whole interview. "I might add of course that they did end up issuing a formal apology for the article they ran. Still, I shouldn't have acted the way I did."

"FMK?" Marie repeats, looking over to Colin. They give each other a look I can't decipher and I really, really think I've blown it.

Only then Colin turns to me, and the look in his eye isn't disappointment. It's excitement.

"Your sister is dating someone from Minotaur?" Colin asks. "Oh my god, which one? Is it the one with curtains?"

As the interview concludes, I know two things for sure.

The second, less important one, is that I want this job. I loved the offices and the dogs. I loved the work they had to offer me. And mostly I loved the people. Colin was hilarious. He made me laugh multiple times in the interview and Marie was so warm and friendly. She made balancing life and home look easy. Or at the very least, possible.

The most important thing I know though, as I leave that office, is that clearly my assumptions were wrong. Very wrong. And the only person I want to speak to as I exit those offices is Archie.

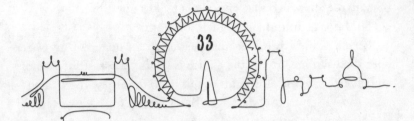

33

When the tube doors shut, I know I have one whole journey to prepare. Kings Cross to Clapham North. That's twenty-five minutes on the Northern Line; twenty-five minutes to work out how to fix everything with Archie.

As I've learnt, doing anything spontaneously isn't my thing. I like feeling prepared.

So, I start to run through the words in my mind, over and over, rehearsing. And then I realize I can do better than that. So, I take out my phone, and open Google Sheets. I write things I know I want to say in one column, and in another I order them how I think they should be said.

Meeting your girls in Sainsbury's might have been the best thing that ever happened to me	6
I'm sorry if I made you feel in any way that I didn't want Bailey and Cara in my life	5
I'm sorry I seem to forever say sorry to you	8
I'm sorry I made such an assumption about your life	1
I'm sorry I made such an assumption about your career	2
I'm so sorry about your wife	7
I want to fit imperfectly into your life.	10

I think your kids are beyond brilliant	3
I think you are beyond brilliant	4
I think you're perfect	11
Archie, I want to make compromises with you.	9

Satisfied, I hit the filter button and change the order:

I'm sorry I made such an assumption about your life	1
I'm sorry I made such an assumption about your career	2
I think your kids are beyond brilliant	3
I think you are beyond brilliant	4
I'm sorry if I made you feel in any way that I didn't want Bailey and Cara in my life	5
Meeting your girls in Sainsbury's might have been the best thing that ever happened to me	6
I'm so sorry about your wife	7
I'm sorry I seem to forever say sorry to you	8
Archie, I want to make compromises with you.	9
I want to fit imperfectly into your life.	10
I think you're perfect	11

I have to change platforms at Kennington, so my nose is in my phone as I get off one train and walk across to the other platform to wait. I read and reread what I have.

The internet on the underground is super patchy, but I can see I have some bars. Enough for a notification to come through: one I almost dismiss automatically to keep reading through my notes.

But I pause.

@ArchieBrownArt has posted.

I signed up for all notifications on his account, so I'm not surprised it's telling me. But I'm a little surprised he's posted.

I hit it, curiously.

Strange. I didn't think he ever wanted to post that one.

Looking back at me are the beautiful wide brown eyes of the Yorkie. I zoom in. I wonder why he wanted to post it now. It is stunning. The reflection in the Yorkie's eyes, the raindrops of letters in the background. All colors, all fonts.

Her cute little necklace with the inscription A-Z.

I try to shake off the feeling.

Only looking at it now . . . it's funny, it looks just a little bit similar to the two dogs in the living room. What did Cara call them again?

Squirtles? Skorkies?

I look up. The next tube is still two minutes away. So, I Google Skorkies.

Did you mean Scorkies? Google asks me after a painful Wi-Fi buffer.

I guess so?

I hit it, and the page takes another second to render. I hate tube internet.

"Scottish Terrier and Yorkshire Terrier mixes."

That's funny. The girls are part Scottish. And that's when it hits me.

Where did he say Zoe was from again? It has something to do with witches, or magic, or . . . Cauldron Falls! Yes, that was it!

I look it up.

Cauldron Falls is a waterfall close to West Burton, *Yorkshire Dales*.

Oh god, it all falls into place.

The girls are half Scottish, *and half Yorkshire*. They are, literally, Scorkies. Scorkies who have lived in London all their lives, and so don't have accents even close to their mother tongues.

The puzzle pieces keep falling.

Because the Yorkie in Archie's studio, it's not an old dog of his. Not at all. Why did I not think of this before?

It was supposed to represent his wife.

What did he tell me about her?

She was the kind of woman who even categorized her font when the color categorization ran out.

The letters in the air, the different fonts, the different colors.

"A to Z, Archie to Zoe," I whisper aloud.

I go back to Instagram and zoom in to that necklace again.

He's posted a picture of his wife.

Once again, I feel a stone-cold punch to the back of my throat block off my airways. I feel my stomach drop down to the bottom of my sneakers. And just like last time this happened to me, in the boardroom, just before getting fired, I feel like the life that I always wanted was before me, and I'm ripping it away.

I know what posting this must mean then: that he doesn't want me.

The tube pulls up and I sit there, waiting for the final two stops.

I guess it means that I messed up too much.

I head over to my notes and hit the little x to remove them from my screen. I've already done the damage here; I shouldn't hurt anyone any more by trying to get him back.

I look at the caption:

"xoxo"

Wait, that sounds strangely familiar.

That doesn't sound like him though.

Oh. I think I know what's happened here. I think—

The tube doors open, and without another's second hesitation, I begin to run.

Archie pulls open the door, his paint-stained hands gripping hold of the beautiful yellow door of 32 Dalton Avenue.

His hair looks all kinds of tousled, his five-o'clock shadow building on his cheeks. He's in a plain T-shirt and jeans, rolled up on the bottom with his bare toes wriggling beneath him. When he sees me, he takes a breath, like he's completely unsure.

"I'm here to speak to Bailey," I say, before he can speak.

"To Bailey?"

"Yes. Is she in?"

Archie looks confused, then worried, then all kinds of emotions between those things.

"I'm not sure that . . ." he begins, uncertain.

"It's important," I tell him. "I wouldn't ask otherwise."

He still looks unsure, so before he can shut this down completely, I continue: "This isn't about us, I promise. This isn't some elaborate scheme to win you back. I mean, I was planning one of those. I had a planned speech and . . . it doesn't matter. It's not that. I promise. But I need to speak to her."

He looks at the seriousness in my face. I think he might say no. It's totally within his rights to. Speaking to his ten-year-old, without him there. It's a really big ask.

But then he looks at me, really looks at me, and with complete trust, he calls out: "Bailey!"

There's a shuffle from upstairs.

"Has she done something?" Archie asks me.

"I'll . . ." I begin, and I realize I am in completely new territory here. I don't know what the etiquette is. "I'll tell you after?"

He nods.

"Bailey!" he calls again.

From the top of the stairs, his ten-year-old appears. Her hair, cut short and sharp, whips around as she turns the corner. She's already dragging her heels. She only posted it ten minutes ago and I can see she's wary about the repercussions. But she's standing strong. Defiant.

She knows I know. Well, that's a start at least.

Her room is just as incredible as the rest of the house. It's moody and bright all at the same time. Geometric wallpaper skims around the room highlighted with lines of white and metallic silver. Her furniture is all shades of pink, but not that pink usually associated with young girls. Grown-up pinks. Fuchsia pink. Strong pinks and light pinks, all blended. Fairy lights hang in festoon strings across the ceiling, making the main lights seem redundant. The last wall behind the bed is painted entirely with chalkboard paint, making the room seem darker somehow. It's filled to the brim with chalk drawings. Some in thick pinks and blues, some in finer whites with crisper edges. Animals, all kinds of animals, just like the jungle below. Only Archie hasn't drawn these.

"You did all this?" I ask her, mesmerized.

She looks at them with me, her guard up. She nods curtly.

"They're absolutely incredible. You have a real talent," I say earnestly, still taking it all in. I can see her cheeks flush at the compliment, but she keeps her whole head turned down now.

Gosh, I would have loved this room growing up.

Bailey sits on her bed, her knees tucked up to her chest. She looks so much like her dad already. It's not as simple as saying "her eyes" or "her cheekbones." It's more tangible. It's the way she bites her lip. The way she tilts her head.

I keep the door of the bedroom open wide, but I know Archie's stayed downstairs with Cara. I can hear them both, moving around. Cooking dinner perhaps, although his mind will be up here with us. I can guarantee that.

So, I'll be as quick as I can. Because it can't be nice for him down there, not knowing.

Only I didn't get the time to plan this. I didn't get to write notes or rearrange a spreadsheet. So, I just have to come out with it.

"You know my mum used to go away a lot when I was a kid," I begin, and even though Bailey's looking only at her feet, I know she's listening. "She traveled all across the country, working for these . . . well, horrible people really, selling these little cosmetics."

I don't want Bailey to think I'm somehow comparing our situations, so I move quickly, before she has time to interrupt.

"And while she was away, she'd always take pictures of her on this crappy camera she owned, all around the country. There would be pictures of her outside Manchester's football stadium, Stonehenge, and Windsor Castle. There would be pictures of her on the beach, in fields, in cities. And when she showed them to us, I used to think she was having more fun on these adventures than she was ever having when she was at home with us. That she liked life better without us."

I can see a little twitch in the corner of Bailey's cheek. She's still not looking at me, toying with the frayed edges of her jeans, but by that little twitch alone I know she's listening.

"It was actually your dad who first made me question it, and he was right to. Because she wasn't taking those pictures because she was happy. She was taking them because she was miserable and stressed and lonely and . . ." I hate to admit this. "Missing us, I guess. In reality, she didn't want to be in Liverpool or Cornwall. She wanted to be with us."

Bailey fidgets, pulling at the hem until a loose piece of thread begins to appear.

"But she couldn't admit that. Least of all to us. Because that would be admitting that she made a mistake, so instead she just took smiling pictures in every place she went, knowing she'd be able to show Mia and me what a fun time she was having, and we believed her. Because we'd seen the photo."

Bailey looks over to her blackboard wall, following her lines. She thinks she's being told off, and is bracing herself not to care. I hate that. So, slowly, I take a seat on the edge of her bed.

"I guess what I'm trying to get to here, is that what we see in photos isn't always the whole truth. And I hated that my mum did that. Only, I've just tried to do the exact same thing. In fact . . ." I take out my phone, and trying to run through my head a little sense check, I open Instagram. Then I hand it over.

"Look here."

She scrolls through my pictures, starting at the Reel she made, before scrolling on through the others.

"So?" She shrugs, handing it back to me.

"Well, this one was taken in Alaska," I say, starting with the latest. "What does this say?"

She rolls her eyes at me, like this is going nowhere.

"It says you had a great time in Alaska. . . ."

"And it looks really pretty right? It looks great. Only about one minute after this was taken, I had my phone stolen."

She knows this of course. Bailey shakes her head, dismissing it immediately.

"OK, what about this one?" I say, moving on to the next. It's the cooking Reel. She watches it, me shaking basmati like an absolute pro before delivering up a perfect dish.

"Didn't you say you burnt pizza?"

"Yeah, I did. This was a takeaway. My cooking was a disaster. Only I didn't want people to see that. I wanted people to see this."

She watches it again, now knowing. A sly smile bends at her lips. It goes away when she spots me looking at her.

"In fact, not one of these show the whole picture. Not a single one." At this point I've already scrolled back to the old ones; the ones Mia took of me back in my flat. The ones I took to lure Jackson in.

What a waste of life.

Would I ever have owned up that they were fake? That I did it just to get him to notice me? Probably not.

"Fine, people can lie on social media. I get it," Bailey huffs, like she's been told this all before. She probably has. She hands the phone back to me.

"My point is that it isn't just about what I showed. It's about what *I didn't* post too." I move up a little closer to her so she can see what I'm doing. I scroll back to the first picture, looking at that perfect view of the sea.

"I loved Alaska. It was one of the best things I've ever done, because I was with my friend Betzy. Who I haven't seen in over a year. Who's just about to have a baby. Who I miss more than anything. But you won't find a picture of her on my account."

Bailey peeks over the phone.

"Why not?" she asks, and I can see just a little sliver of curiosity begin to bubble.

"Because I never even thought to take the pictures. We were having too much fun. And all these ones of me getting ready to go to things I never went to?" I reshow her the ones of me in Mia's clothes. "Well, I may not have gone out, but I had the best night with my sister that night. We laughed for hours—changing into different outfits, talking nonstop. Except you won't find her in any of them."

"Why not?" Bailey says again.

"Because that would have ruined the story we were trying to tell with the photos," I say, laughing at the thought. "But I didn't need to either. Because that was a personal moment between me and my sister, and I didn't need the world to see it to feel happy. I just was happy. And this cooking Reel," I conclude, sliding back to it. "You know I didn't go to bed crying that night. I didn't even go to bed hungry. And I have your dad to thank for both of those things. He made me see the funny side, when I really, really didn't think there was a funny side. He saved me," I say, and I mean that in far more ways than one.

He didn't just help me to show my authentic self. He helped me become this authentic self.

"Dad?" Bailey questions.

And I nod. Still, she bites her lip, unsure.

"The thing about Instagram," I say, taking my phone back, "is that it puts pressure on us to expose the realities that we would rather other people don't know about, but those realities aren't *just* the really bad stuff. It's the good stuff too. Sometimes, just sometimes, things mean more to us kept close than they do shown to everyone."

Which I guess leads me to my point.

"You know your dad didn't want to post that painting of the Yorkie, didn't you?" I ask, but I already know the answer. I was there when he told her, after all. She nods, her eyes glancing up at me, if only for a second.

"Do you know *why* he didn't want to share it?" I ask.

"Because he doesn't care about her anymore," she says quickly. Like that's a fact. Like that's the only option.

Oh gosh. If only she knew.

"I think you might find it's the very opposite," I tell her.

"It's not the same as your stuff," she tells me pointedly, her guard that looked almost to be dropping going right back up. "It's just a painting. He showed all his other paintings. It was just this one he didn't want to show."

"It's because it's not *just* a painting to him," I say, knowing I will never know how much that painting means to him. What he must feel every time he looks at it. A memory he can never recapture, gone. "And it's not just a painting to you either, is it?" Bailey thinks for a moment, then shakes her head. "It means something."

She takes a deep breath, nodding, almost reluctantly at first until, having thought about it, she loosens up her shoulders. Her legs uncurl from under her.

"I think what I've worked out here, is that contrary to what MEP says, you don't always need to *show the world* your authentic self. You just need to be it," I conclude. "But you know what, I'm not the person who should say, one way or another. The best way to know, is to ask. So, shall we go down and ask him?"

She looks nervous.

"He's going to be mad," she says.

"Not if you explain it."

"Cara's going to be there," Bailey says nervously.

"Well, I can take Cara out of the room."

She looks skeptical.

"How?" she asks.

I think about it. For one long minute I think about it. Then it comes to me.

"Maybe I need another interview," I say.

Cara, as it turns out, doesn't need much convincing to go into the other room. She needs a photographer, and my three-second interview of "Do you know how to switch to portrait mode?" "Yes," seems to qualify me.

Bailey and Archie emerge after some time, but they don't appear empty-handed. With a small toolbox in Bailey's hands, and a large canvas in Archie's, the two head straight for the living room and, curious, Cara and I follow them. Both the girls climb up onto the orange sofa, watching their dad at work as he removes the painting of the dog with the long shadow on the far wall. What with the Skorkies being there, I barely even looked at that one. It didn't look quite right there anyway, and with a quick flex of his biceps, it's off the wall.

Up goes the painting of the Yorkie in its place. It fits perfectly. From my angle, where I'm hovering by the door, both the images work in tandem. In fact, better than that. Because the Yorkie, in her beautiful field of rain, has eyes directly on that image of both her girls.

"I'm not going to hide it," Archie tells the two of them, falling back into the sofa after the picture has been exchanged. Cara jumps on him instantly, and although she clearly thinks she's a little grown-up to do the same thing, Bailey joins in.

And they're smiling. All three of them are smiling under the watchful eye of the dogs that surround them.

A beautiful, happy family.

My phone is still out from having taken picture after picture of Cara, so as subtly as I can, I switch it back on camera. Then I take the photo.

All three of them none the wiser. Not posed. A very real moment filled with love.

I look at my phone, seeing their genuine delight, and something sad triggers in me. Because this might have been mended, but I feel like I threw this all away. For nothing.

And I'm intruding. I should go, leave them to this moment together. I turn around, looking for wherever it was I left my backpack, when I hear from behind me:

"And where do you think you're going?"

I turn back. All six dazzling green eyes are on me.

"Well, my work as a photographer has concluded," I say, not wanting to impose.

"It has not," Cara tells me, as if that's obvious. "This is merely the interval."

"You should stay for tea," Archie says, looking at me with eyes that say there's so much left unspoken. "In fact, you definitely can't go until you've opened up your present."

"My present?" I ask.

He jumps up, walking quickly out of the room, but he's back before I've even had a chance to say anything to his girls. He's holding another canvas in his hands, this time one that's wrapped, and one I've seen before. It's the painting that Bailey painted for me. I look over to her now, and she smiles at me nervously.

When he passes it over I feel his hands graze mine. It sends warm sparks through me. And then he disappears, falling back onto the sofa between his two girls to watch.

So, I walk to the middle of the room where there's enough space and where they can all get a good view, and nervously start peeling back the wrapping.

"You haven't seen it yet?" Cara gasps, and then looks over at Bailey, who looks exceptionally nervous.

And I almost start crying.

It's not too dissimilar to the dogs Archie draws of course. The sheepdog has big eyes, and although it's not quite the realistic sketches her dad is capable of, it's really quite impressive. The highlights on the eyelashes, the long tongue pointing happily out of her mouth.

"It was my idea," Cara says, in case she gets none of the praise.

It takes me a minute to realize what's even in the background. A large graph. A big x and y axis labeled, and between them, a line rising up to the sky diagonally from left to right.

The whole picture is framed too, but with a border drawn in to make it look like a giant Instagram post. Underneath it, it reads "Liked by @Bailey and @Cara."

"What does the graph show?" I say, although it takes a while for me to be able to say anything at all.

"How much better your life has become since knowing me," Cara says. I laugh out loud to that one. "Us," she adds, looking over at Bailey.

"I just found a graph on the internet and copied it." Bailey shrugs quickly, correcting her.

So, this is me, is it? Well, I think they've captured it beautifully.

I turn to Archie, opening my mouth, then shutting it. My bottom lip is quivering.

These girls are incredible. This family is incredible. And to think I almost just threw all this away because I was worried it would interfere with my career! That's absurd. It's completely absurd.

Because I'm looking now at six eyes that I want in my life permanently. No matter what role I'm in.

"I love it!" I summarize because there aren't real words to describe the impact this is having on me. Just a feeling of complete elation. Of belonging. "I know just where I'm going to hang it up in my flat!"

"In *your* flat?" Cara asks, elongating the vowels. "Why would it go there?"

I'm not sure if I've got the wrong end of the stick here.

"Because it's a present . . . for me?" I ask, looking over at Bailey.

"But then *we* can't see it," Cara says, like a true little diva. "And that just won't do."

I laugh, because it's incredibly hard not to laugh at Cara, but I look over at Bailey, trying to work out what her face means.

"Do you want to keep it?" I ask her because she does look like she's taking those words seriously. This is something she's created after all. She might want it, even if it was meant for me.

"Is there a way we can all see it?" Bailey asks finally, looking over at me. "And I don't mean Instagram," she adds, looking over to her dad. He just shrugs.

"Well, there is one place . . ." Archie says, looking over to the final wall in the room. The one I'm standing by.

Given a window takes up the majority of one beautiful deep blue wall, followed by the Yorkie opposite me, and then the Skorkies on the wall to my left, there's only this one wall remaining.

Cara gets his meaning immediately.

"Oh yes! It would go brilliantly there! Put it up now!"

"No," I say quickly, looking at the other pictures in the room. A picture of me can't go in this room. This room has the pictures of Cara and Bailey. Of Zoe. I couldn't possibly be hung up next to all those. "This is your . . . I don't need it to be here next to . . ."

"Are you saying a painting done by my daughter isn't worthy of my sitting room?" Archie says quickly, a cheeky grin across his cheeks. He knows exactly what position he's just put me in.

"I'd never say that!" I gasp, smiling back at him.

"Then it's decided," Cara concludes for us. "The painting stays here. And so do you, so you can see it some more. Now it's time for us to continue the photography session, and I'm thinking outside, because my skin really glows in this light."

When the kids are finally settled in bed, Archie opens up another bottle of wine. I'm in the sitting room when he finds me, looking so proudly at Bailey's painting.

"You really like it?" he asks, handing me over a glass. I notice his glasses are back on again. I guess it's more comfortable to wear the glasses at the end of a day than contacts. They really suit him.

"Like it?" I laugh, "that's an understatement! It's the best painting I've ever seen!" My eyes turn to look at him. In doing so, my eyes casually pass by the pictures of the Skorkies and the Yorkie. "I mean, yours are great and all. But have you seen this?"

We both look at it together, side by side, our wineglasses out before us like a viewing at a gallery. In my peripheral vision, I can see the absolute pride in his eyes.

"I'm inclined to agree with you," he says. I can feel his arm as it grazes mine and it send goose bumps through me. But that has to wait, just a few more minutes.

"Did you work it out with her earlier?" I ask, nodding toward the kitchen. I don't mean to pry, I just can't help but be curious.

"I made a mistake," he says, shaking his head in shame. He turns around, looking at the Yorkie in its new pride of place in the whole room.

"You know," he tells me, "that picture used to always hang there. And then when Tasha came over the first time, she told me how much she loved it. She asked me to make one for her, and I . . . I don't know. I didn't feel like I could say no."

I realize I've seen it online. The little black schnauzer with the heel in her mouth. It must have felt so strange for him to paint a portrait because someone asked him to, especially in the same style as one that means so much to him.

"Well, I don't know. I felt weird about it. So, I took it down and hung something else there and brought it down to the studio so that Tasha couldn't see it anymore. Probably my first warning sign things weren't meant to be for us. And after I made one for Tash I somehow had to justify that it was *just* a painting. I made a few others just like it. . . ."

"Like the one in Sallie's?" I ask.

"Well, yes, that. But others too. I stopped eventually because it didn't feel right. But hiding it down in my studio? It didn't even occur to me that the girls would mind."

He shakes out his head, his hair loosening up.

"It's stupid. Of course, they did. And when I really think about it, that's when Bailey started to close up from me. She thought I was trying to replace her mother. That's why the Instagram mattered to her. That's why she did it."

"That's not a mistake," I tell him, "that's just a lesson. Now you both know how you feel."

"That's a lovely way of thinking about it," he murmurs.

After a long while, he takes a few steps back, sitting up on the edge of his burnt orange sofa, looking at the picture in front of him from a new angle: Bailey's creation in the background, and me before him, looking only at him.

"So, I'm ready," he says, waiting. He places his wineglass on the table beside him so I have his full attention. I swallow, hard.

"Ready?" I question, but I already know what he's asking.

"You said you had a speech asking me to take you back

apparently? Or was that just a ruse to let you in, just like the nanny position that never was?" He's smiling, teasing me.

I shake my head, feeling nervous. I've had such a perfect afternoon with them all, such a lovely dinner, one where we all talked and laughed and ate and everything just felt so right. Like I fitted in. Imperfectly, sure, but I still felt at home.

I've never been more certain that I was wrong in my life. Tonight has given me more clarity than any insight I have ever delivered.

So, I take out my phone, heading to my Google notes.

Then I look up, ready to deliver them, and find myself caught in his beautiful emerald eyes. He's moved closer to me already. A stray bit of hair has kiss-curled on the top of his head and it makes me forget everything I've just read.

"I'm just so sorry," I say.

"Apologizing again?" he says, moving just a little closer.

"This time I need to," I tell him seriously. "Because I was so delusional. I thought . . . I didn't know what I thought."

He licks his lips thoughtfully, nodding.

"I think you thought that thirty-odd years of believing something made it true," he says, taking one more step closer. "It takes a lot to change a belief that's grown up with you. But this afternoon, I just watched you put Bailey ahead of your own wants. I saw you put my girls first. So, have you? Changed that belief?"

"Yes," I tell him, without a pause. Because I have, truly. Life is a balancing act, but one worth balancing.

"That's all I needed to know," he says, like he's totally and completely relieved.

And I don't know at what point it happened, but he's somehow closed the gap between us. His hand gently curves around my waist and pulls me in to his chest all over again.

Oh my.

I can feel my heartbeat rising. I can feel my knees weaken. I look up and I see those beautiful green eyes looking back at me and I think the nerves are just going to pour out of me, but I must stay strong. I must not do something stupid and say something like:

"I love you."

Except I do. I say exactly that.

"I love you," I say, before his lips can touch mine.

I'm instantly annoyed I said anything. Why, why did I have to ruin the moment? Why couldn't I just have said nothing like a normal person and kissed the handsome man that was leaning in to me?

Well, it's because I'm not a normal person in front of him. I'm me. And me is not normal. She's excitable, and she speaks too much, and she's a lot. So, I say something. Because when I'm with Archie, I'm just myself.

He pulls away slightly, his head slightly cocked, listening.

"I know it's a bit mad, but I do. I think I love you. I know it's quick and I know you might not feel the same—that's fine if you don't. I used to laugh at Mia for falling in love so quickly. I thought she must be delusional, but I sort of get it now. I don't remember anyone letting me be so much myself before. And I love myself when I'm with you, which is so strange, because I'm basically . . . well, I'm a real Franken-duck. And I don't mind that in your company. So, I love you for it," I say truthfully.

Because I wasn't sure I could love myself. I wasn't sure I was worthy of it.

But he makes me feel worthy.

He takes a deep breath to take it in, which I'm not surprised about. I know it was a lot.

"You know the thing about dating when you have daughters," he tells me, almost apologetically, "is that you have to take things slow. You have to be sure before you say anything like that. It's not just about you and me here, it's about them too. And I can't introduce someone to them again who might hurt them by leaving."

I nod, completely understanding. Because my dad just left, with no care for who he left hurting behind. And I know what it feels like.

It wasn't like I was expecting Archie to say it back. I wasn't.

"The thing is though," Archie continues, "you've already gone ahead and introduced yourself to them. Without me being there."

"Ah," I reply, awkwardly.

"Yes, 'ah' indeed."

"We can take things slow, still," I tell him. "I don't mind—"

But before I can answer, I feel the wineglass swoosh out of my hand and into his. Then, with his other, he sweeps me off my feet back into a drop with his arms holding me off the ground, our faces inches apart.

Before I know it, his lips are on mine. That shadow tickles my face as he holds me close and kisses me, the kind of swoon-worthy kiss that you only really see in films. I'm swooning alright. I'm the one being kissed and I'm swooning.

Then he stops, holding me where he has me floating in the air almost, completely held in his arms.

"You're going to make it very hard to be slow." He smiles.

And then he pulls back, lifting me back to my feet. He hands me back my wineglass that he miraculously didn't spill a drop of during that whole sequence of events. Then he smiles, like that was a perfectly normal interlude to a conversation.

I feel dizzy with it all, from the drop, from him, from everything. My head is spinning in all the best ways.

And then he takes my hand, and gently wanders around the sofa where he sits making room beside him for me to shuffle in. He feels so warm, and weirdly, in the nook of his arm, I just seem to fit.

"I may not be able to say those words right now, but I will tell you this," he says, looking over to the painting that Bailey painted on the wall. Then he turns back to me, lifting my chin up ready to kiss all over again. "You're no Franken-duck, Daisy Peterson. In fact, there's a high probability you might be my da Vinci."

And it's the most romantic thing I've ever heard.

34

"You know," I say, looking down at the most beautiful little new-born that I've ever seen, "I think he has my eyes."

He's glorious. His snuggly little arms, his soft cheeks. I'm emotional in all kinds of ways I never thought I'd be emotional before.

So, this is why people have kids, I think. Because I'm looking at this new little soul who's only just entered the world, and I know beyond a shadow of a doubt that my life is exponentially better for him being in it.

"You do?" Archie asks softly, his soft accent purring at my ear proudly. His arms are wrapped around me, his neck finely balanced on my shoulder to see. "You've got bloody strong genes then, clearly."

"Can I see him?" Cara asks, her voice unnaturally quiet. I nod over to her, and carefully she walks over to her dad's side, shuffling up beside him to get the best view. She looks down with us at that perfect newborn face. Bailey follows, just a few steps behind, a little unsure and wordlessly, all four of us looking down lovingly at the beautiful, perfect angelic little newborn.

On my phone.

"I'm pretty sure godparents can pass down genes. I mean, I haven't looked into the science of it or anything, but I'm like ninety percent sure that's how it works," I tell them.

"Well, you are a data analyst. If you give me a stat like that, I'm going to have to take your word on it," Archie agrees.

"It also means she has a ten percent chance of talking total bull."

"Bailey!" reprimands her father. "How do you even know that term?"

His eldest doesn't even flinch.

"Megan's brother uses it all the time," she says proudly.

Christ, they get a lot of influence from older siblings.

"Why is a bull bad?" Cara asks sweetly. "Bulls are great. They're like cows but more epic."

I'm not sure I know how to answer that one, so I leave it to Archie as I keep looking, only Bailey walks to my other side, looking down at the baby, wrapped in a blanket like a little burrito.

"What have they called him?" she asks me.

"Oliver," I say, bubbling with pride. "It's after Patrick's dad, but it was always on Betzy's list so it's worked out perfectly."

Cara reaches her hand over and flicks through the carousel of images herself. The first one is just Oliver, but the ones that follow include Betzy too. She looks unbelievable. I can't believe the woman just gave birth. It makes me wonder if it's something I'd ever consider.

I've always said I wouldn't.

And even looking at this small child, I still don't. Not really. Not my own. But that doesn't mean there isn't room in my life for a little compromise, I think, looking over at Bailey and Cara together.

Only in the last picture on the carousel, the little newborn is already screaming. That makes all of us laugh. Including Bailey.

"I'm glad she's showing the full 360 of newborn life," Archie says, and for a second, we all sit there together. Watching. And then the little clock on the corner of my phone hits 8 a.m., and despite not wanting this moment to end, Archie stretches himself out. "Right, girls you have five minutes exactly before you're out the door. Cara, are you even ready yet?"

"Almost!" she squeals, running off.

The chaos that follows is the daily chaos that I've come to love.

I never realized that when I just woke up, dressed and headed to work, some of my colleagues were having whole mornings. They were having fights and makeups and chats around the kitchen table.

I didn't think I'd have time for anything different. Not back then. But it's taken me a while to realize not everything has to be a time block. Sometimes, when things are important, you can just make time.

Like this for example. Four months after that first kiss, I still find time to walk over from my flat to theirs before school.

This is not how I imagined dating to be. What no one tells you about dating though, is that when someone is right, it doesn't feel like dating at all; it feels like hanging out with an old friend.

With Jackson, I was over and in his bed before we'd even finish our drinks. With Archie, things have to be a little slower. The girls know I exist, of course they do, but I'm happy to go as slow as they need to be comfortable, because for them, I have all the time in the world.

And a lot can change in four months. Mia, for example. No longer am I only seeing her when she's broken up with her latest boyfriend, instead she's coming over on weekends to do shoots. And by that, I mean she's teaching Bailey how to point the camera, and Cara how to pose. Her boyfriend Kit keeps a pretty busy schedule, but he's on FaceTime all the time. Even when he's traveling the country on tour, he makes time for Mia. Always. And I love that about him.

Plus, working at The Kibble Crew is everything I thought it would be and more. I genuinely didn't think that analytics could get better than Branded, and then they gave me a whole new world of analytics to explore, and topped it by placing a real-life puppy on my lap. A dog-friendly office is my kind of office.

It's better. Believe me it's better.

And I'm happy. So, unbelievably happy.

A scramble later and all four of us are out the door.

Turns out the girls' school is en route to the station, so all four of us march the same way down the side streets of Clapham, away from that beautiful bright yellow door.

"BOP," Cara says as we reach the school gates. "It sounds fun when you say it all together like that."

"What is that? A dance move?" Archie asks.

"'A dance move'? Honestly, how old are you?" I tease.

"It's all their initials together," Bailey says, working it out for herself. I don't think I would have ever got there.

I wave goodbye to the three of them as I peel off a few roads early to the tube, but even then, I notice the little burrow in Archie's forehead. The little frown that's just appeared out of nowhere. He looks thoughtful, distracted.

I'll text him later, I think, crossing the road as the light shines out with a green man to the familiar signpost of "Clapham North Underground." It isn't until I'm at the turnstiles that I even realize I left my phone on the sofa where we were all looking at it.

Only that doesn't anger me. I don't panic about being late. No one will notice if I'm late—it doesn't matter what time I get there, only that I do the work, and given I love the work, I'm pretty sure everyone knows I'm going to do it.

Plus, Archie will be back home before me. So, I turn back around, walking with a little spring in my step back to my favorite yellow door.

"I'm here about the—" I begin, our favorite running joke.

But I can't even complete that sentence, because his right hand immediately comes out, wrapping around the back of my waist and pulling me in. Lifting my chin with his left forefinger, our lips lock on the doorstep.

And every bone in my body turns to putty in his arms.

"I left my phone on the couch," I sigh happily as he lets go, looking up at those sparkling green eyes.

"I know. I just saw it," he says, nodding me through the jungle hallway.

You'd have thought that it would have lessened in my mind

with time, only every time I walk through it I see something new. A new bird. A new detail on the largest frog, its tongue shot out of its mouth to catch a fly.

Despite the warm greeting, there's something a little off in him as he walks through to the sitting room. My phone's still on the orange sofa, which I travel to quickly, but by the time I get it and turn around, I can see he's a little distracted.

I could leave him to it, only I hate it when I know something's wrong. So I ask: "Are you alright?"

"I'm just having a . . . moment," he says thoughtfully, leaning against the arm of the sofa. "It's something that Cara said."

I can see where his eyes have drifted to. The photo right above me, of the Yorkie, her beautiful eyes looking at her girls. The colorful letters around her. I look at it with him, taking it in.

"Are you thinking about Zoe?" I ask.

And I wonder if I should feel awkward about asking, only I don't. *Because Zoe wanted to be a great many things, but never an elephant.*

"Life has a funny way of showing things, that's all," he says, his tone so quiet and soft I feel the need to instantly comfort him.

I think of Betzy too. By the look in Archie's eyes though, this isn't *funny* to him too. In fact he looks quite pensive. Sad, almost.

"Looking at your friends' baby, it just reminded me," he says, his eyes clearly following the paths of the thousands of colorful raindrops pouring down over the little pup. "From A to Z," he whispers, almost to himself.

I swallow, because I think I'm following, only it's not a path I was hoping to ever go down.

"You want more kids?" I ask, biting my lip. *Be brave,* I think to myself. *I have to be brave.* "Because . . . I just have to tell you now then. I don't think I do."

He looks up at me, confused.

Oh gosh. Please don't let this be it. I would never in a million years want to stop someone who wanted more children from having them, but I feel like it's not in my cards. It's tempting not to say anything at all, just in case this ruins everything. Because this man before me, this man of a thousand talents and even more jobs, this man is the man I love.

This is the home I love.

He has the family I love.

But if he wants more kids, I don't think I can provide that.

"Your kids are the greatest kids in the universe. I didn't realize how much I wanted them in my life until they exploded into it. And I love them, I do," I say, smiling up at that picture of the Skorkies. Bailey so serious, patient, waiting to blow out the candles. Cara ignoring the rules and launching into it. I love it, even more than I used to, because I love them.

That's what four months in the best company can lead to. The summer holidays began, and although I was working through the week, I sometimes found myself working from here. My evenings were spent in their company. My weekends were spent joining them on their adventures.

We traveled the country, from beaches to peaks, and we had the best time doing it. And in the pictures I took I was smiling, genuinely and completely, with all three of them by my side. Bailey painted nearly every landscape, and Archie every dog. Cara would lead the pack of us, demanding we have fun at every possible opportunity.

Four months. One long summer. And a whole lot of love.

But the smile fades as I know how I need to conclude this: "But for me, your girls are everything I want. I just don't see myself with any others. I never have."

Archie nods, listening. He's always so good at listening. And only after I finish, does he speak.

"That's fine," Archie says, and I feel a breath release. "I wasn't thinking of more kids. I'm not sure I'd want any more either, even if you did."

I can't help but be relieved.

But I've clearly misunderstood. So, I need him to clarify.

"We were A to Z. And we started filling our lives the way she wanted it: starting with B. Then on to C. And then she left," he says, and I can see his whole chest rise and fall in that pain. "And I had a hole in me that spanned so much more than the twenty-two letters we had remaining." He taps his chest at the thought. Small droplets of water prick at his eyes.

I sit beside him, looking up at that painting.

"No one will ever fill that hole," I say, knowing it to be true.

And then his eyes spin to the final wall of the room.

The sheepdog, sitting behind the slightly wobbly linear graph, surrounded by an Instagram box.

The only reason I get on Instagram now is to like Mia's pictures and see Betzy's.

"I was A, she was Z," he continues, looking at that Yorkie. And his eyes peel over the picture of the puppies before it lands back on the one of me. "I just feel like some things are meant to be."

His hand reaches out to my waist as he pulls me into a hug.

And I gasp because I've just worked out what he means. He takes a stray piece of hair and places it back behind my ear as his hands gently cup my face. And he looks at me. Actually looks at me. And I know, beyond a shadow of a doubt, that's he's seeing the real, authentic me.

"I love you," he says. So gently. So carefully. So beautifully. So considered. "I love you," he repeats.

And when I look into his eyes, I believe him. I feel utterly, and completely loved.

Then that burrow of concern crosses his face.

"You look a bit white."

"I do?"

"Are you sure you're not sick?" he asks.

I literally feel great. Not a sick bone in my body. In fact, I'm smiling ear to ear. I can't help it. He loves me. I love him, and he loves me.

"I'm not sick," I laugh in delight.

"Oh, I think you are. I think you may need to take the day off work."

He takes a step toward me, mischief in his eyes. Ah, I see where this is going.

"I don't take sick days," I tell him.

"Well, what about a sick *hour*?" he says, and I gasp as with a little tug he lifts me off the floor. I wrap my legs around him tight, squealing as his 5 o'clock shadow tickles against my neck. Because I know I need to go to work. I have things I need to do, sheets I need to manipulate, code I need to crack.

But I also have a man between my thighs, who I'd like to analyze a little more first. And I'll make up the hours. I know that.

The old Daisy would never have done such a thing.

But this is the new, improved Daisy Peterson.

The one who's about to accept the handsome man's offer and head upstairs. The one who's going to take advantage of a completely empty house. The one whose ear is being nibbled, causing a ripple of static to flood through my body.

"Maybe the tube's being slow?" I whisper.

"It is notoriously unreliable," he replies, and I feel the heat of his breath already on my lips as he leans in.

When our lips collide it's like a star explosion far greater and more epic than the freckles on my face could ever depict.

I may never be able to fill the gap that Zoe left, but the way we fit together is entirely different. We have our own adventures to begin.

Only, it isn't just Archie and Daisy.

It's Archie, Bailey, and Cara.

It's A, B, C.

And me.

ACKNOWLEDGMENTS

I'd like to start with a huge thank-you to my incredible editors at St. Martin's Press. Alexandra Sehulster is a dream of an editor, and Sallie Lotz, who jumped in at the last minute, was such a wonderful addition to the team. Alongside Rebekah West and Anna Boatman in the UK, working with you all is an absolute delight from start to finish and I've loved every second!

Cassidy Graham too—your emails light up my inbox. In fact all the team at St. Martin's Press deserves an enormous shout-out, for every note I get from you makes me smile from ear to ear.

A huge thanks is always due to my lovely agent, Megan Carroll, and the team at Watson, Little. Given we first started talking at the beginning of 2020, it took a full year to meet in person for the first time, but even when Zoom was our only means of communication—you've always been a huge support.

To all my favorite people, you know who you are! Thank you for always being there for me, even when sometimes it took weeks to hit that reply button on a message. I'm bad at multitasking, and when I'm writing, working, or mum-ing (which is a huge portion of my time) I usually switch my phone to that entirely antisocial "Do Not Disturb" mode. Thank you for your endless patience, your friendship, and your unending support. I love you all.

My boy is the best thing that ever happened to me, but he also makes writing a book just that little bit harder. My vision of being able to write for hours while cradling a quiet little newborn baby in my arms was hilariously short-lived. Which is why I have to thank my team of backstage babysitters, which includes (but is not limited to) my mother, my in-laws, and on occasion my brothers and my sisters-in-law.

An extra special thank-you goes to Rich, of course. You held down the fort a lot during this writing process and somehow made me feel sane in an otherwise chaotic year. Marrying you was fun. We should do it again sometime, but like, only if I never have to plan it again ever in my whole life.

And finally to Bear; even if it is harder, I'd still always choose to write with you by my side.

ABOUT THE AUTHOR

Luci Adams (she/her) started out working in tax before moving into copywriting, creating social posts for Apple Music, and assisting with Amazon and BBC productions at Working Title Television. She now works as a senior analyst at *The Guardian* by day and writes uproariously funny and inventive rom-coms by night.